AIR
APPARENT

TOR BOOKS by PIERS ANTHONY

PIERS ANTHONY

AIR
APPARENT

A TOM DOHERTY ASSOCIATES BOOK

NEW YORK

AIR APPARENT

Copyright © 2007 by Piers Anthony Jacob

Map by Jael

A Tor Book
Published by Tom Doherty Associates, LLC
175 Fifth Avenue
New York, NY 10010

www.tor.com

Tor® is a registered trademark of Tom Doherty Associates, LLC.

Library of Congress Cataloging-in-Publication Data

Anthony, Piers.
    Air apparent / Piers Anthony.—1st. ed.
        p. cm.
    "A Tom Doherty Associates Book."
    ISBN-13: 978-0-7653-0410-0
    ISBN-10: 0-7653-0410-4
    1. Xanth (Imaginary place)—Fiction.   2. Quests (Expeditions)—Fiction.   I. Title.
    PS3551.N73A75 2007
    813'.54—dc22

                                                                              2007019172

First Edition: October 2007

Printed in the United States of America

0 9 8 7 6 5 4 3 2 1

Contents

AIR
APPARENT

1
MYSTERY

W ira was uneasy. Her husband Hugo had been absent half an hour, and it wasn't like him to stay away longer than he said. Especially not this night.

For tonight, after seventeen years of marriage, Hugo's father, Good Magician Humfrey, had finally removed the Spell of Hiding that kept the storks from being aware of Wira no matter how ardently she summoned them. She was fifty-five years old chronologically, thirty-three physically, and her thyme was starting to wilt. If they waited much longer, the storks would never deliver to her, regardless of any spell. This time the signal would go out. She knew that Hugo was eager to send that signal, and so was she.

Where was he? He had gone to the cellar to fetch a celebratory bottle of Rhed Whine. That should have taken no more than ten minutes, and he would hardly have dawdled. Something was wrong.

Wira got off the bed, donned a nightrobe and slippers, and made her way out of their chamber. She pattered down the familiar stairs to the ground floor, and thence to the cellar. She knew every crevice of the castle, of course, and made no misstep.

But as she reached the cellar floor, she experienced a faint tinge of uneasiness. Her magic talent was Sensitivity, and though it normally applied to people, plants, and animals, it could sometimes attune to situations. This situation was uncomfortable.

"Hugo?" she called tentatively.

There was no answer.

The tinge became less faint. In fact it intensified into a wary semblance of dread.

"Hugo, where are you?" she called less tentatively.

There was a definitely untentative silence.

Something was wrong. Not only was Hugo absent, there was something else in the cellar. She smelled its misty essence.

She snapped her fingers. Little magic echoes bounced off the cellar walls and floor, verifying its dimensions. Except for a muffled place on the floor, the vague shape of a man lying down.

Had Hugo fainted? But this wasn't Hugo. The shape was vaguely wrong, and of course the smell.

She squatted and reached forward to touch it. Her fingers encountered a clammy kind of flesh. It was definitely not quite alive.

Wira screamed.

The Gorgon, Humfrey's Designated Wife of the Month, and coincidentally also Hugo's mother, was the first to respond. "Wira, dear," she called from the head of the cellar stairs. "What's the matter? Are you hurt?"

"Oh, Mother Gorgon, there's a dead man here, and I think he's not quite human. And Hugo is gone."

There was half a pause. "This bears investigation. Let me fetch a lamp."

Wira waited by the body while the Gorgon got the lamp. Wira did not need light, of course, as she was blind. She had always been that way, and really did not mind it as long as she was in familiar territory. But others had some kind of problem with darkness.

She heard the returning footsteps, smelled the curling vapors of the lamp, and felt its slight warmth. There was also the faint sibilance of a small nest of snakes. The Gorgon was back and ready to take charge.

Wira had always gotten along well with the Gorgon. That was partly because the Gorgon's face tended to turn others to stone, but Wira could not see it, so was not at risk. That enabled them to be friends without precautions. The Gorgon was actually a very nice person, but strangers tended to be prejudiced by her magic face, and were nervous about her snake hair. The snakes were normally friendly, and could be good company on a dull day.

"It is definitely a body," the Gorgon said. "It's not breathing and it's cold, so it must be at least halfway dead. But who killed it, and what is it doing here?"

Wira had a horrible thought. "Oh Mother Gorgon, you don't suppose Hugo could have—have—"

"Of course not, dear. Hugo doesn't have a murderous bone in his body. Not even a stiff one, as far as anyone knows. When are you two going to signal the stork?"

"Tonight," Wira said, blushing. Sometimes the Gorgon's language was a trifle serpentine. But she had reason: her sister the Siren was long since a grandmother. She seemed to have forgotten about the stork-hiding spell.

Now the Gorgon had a nasty thought. "You don't suppose he could have gotten cold feet, or whatever?"

"Never," Wira said positively. "He wanted to—to do it. To be a father."

The Gorgon sighed. "He's so young."

"Mother, he's forty-three."

"Exactly."

Wira didn't argue the case. Technically she was a dozen years older than Hugo, but she had been youthened to sweet sixteen to marry him, so seemed a decade younger. Mothers always thought their sons were too young. "He wouldn't have left without word to me. Especially not tonight. Something must have happened to him."

The Gorgon was focusing on the body. "I have another foul thought. Maybe somebody killed this poor man, dumped the body here, and abducted Hugo to frame him for the murder. That would explain everything."

"Except where Hugo is, and who the victim is, and who the real murderer is," Wira agreed.

"Yes, there may be a detail or three to fill out. We'd better get Humfrey in on it."

"But it's nighttime," Wira protested. "He gets grumpy when disturbed at night."

"He gets grumpy any time," the Gorgon said. "You don't see much of it because you have an ameliorative effect on him. I think if he'd been half a century younger he would have married you himself."

"Mother Gorgon!" Wira exclaimed, horrified.

"Oh come on now, girl. You know he's taken with you."

"Because I'm his daughter-in-law."

"That, too. Anyway, he already has about five wives too many; he certainly doesn't need any more. Now I'm going to get him up, grumpy or not, and bring him down here to fathom the situation. It will give him another pretext to bury himself in the Book of Answers."

"Oh, I hope the Answer is there!" Wira breathed. "I miss Hugo so much!"

"He's been gone only half an hour, dear."

"Yes, and it's awful."

The Gorgon gazed at her. Wira could tell when someone was looking at her; there was a certain subtle mood. "You really do love him, don't you, dear."

"Yes!"

"And that is why *I* am taken with you, Wira. Without you he's pretty much a rotten-fruited gnome."

"He is not!"

"Of course not, dear," the Gorgon agreed, smiling knowingly. Wira could also tell when a person was smiling; it curled up the corners of the voice. Then the Gorgon went off to roust out the Good Magician.

Wira remained in the cellar, uncertain what else to do. She knew the Gorgon meant well, but the woman sometimes unnerved her. Meanwhile, there was this awful situation to deal with. Could someone really have tried to frame Hugo for the murder? To make it seem that he had committed a terrible crime, and fled the scene? But how could such a thing have been done here, in the Good Magician's Castle? The castle was enchanted to exclude all but the most powerful magic.

Yet something of the sort had happened. That was frightening in itself.

She checked the shelves along the cellar wall, just in case there was some indication that would help resolve the mystery. She knew the stored potions by the shapes of their bottles and faint odors. The first shelf held bottles of pills from pharm-assist plants that a pill pusher had harvested for the Good Magician long ago. The pills lent certain temporary talents to those who swallowed them. There were gra-pills that enabled folk to wrestle well, purr-pills that caused folk to turn reddish blue while feeling very satisfied, and ap-pills that kept doctors away. Also princi-pills for those lacking in ethics, sim-pills for those with too much intellect, and pill-fur coats for those who didn't mind stealing clothing. All was in order, undisturbed.

The next shelf contained assorted gloves or mitts reserved for particular Challenges: an amity, which made a person very friendly; an enmity, which had the opposite effect; a hermit, which was a solitary lady's glove; an imitate that enabled a person to copy things; a comity that made the wearer courteous; an emit that caused a stink; an omit that somehow had been left off the list; a submit that could be used underwater; a permit that allowed almost anything; and an admit that added a glove and also let a person into the castle. At the end of the shelf was a vomit that she knew better than to touch. None had been disturbed. The problem seemed to be confined to the (ugh) body.

"Ludicrous, woman," Humfrey's voice came grumpily from above. "Can't it wait until morning?"

"Do you want poor Wira to stay in the cellar all night?" the Gorgon's voice retorted.

Wira had to smile, wanly. The Gorgon was using her to make Humfrey mind. It was true that the Good Magician liked her, though Wira was sure it was not in the way the Gorgon had implied. Wira was sensitive to his moods, and so could manage him to an extent. And of course she was helpful around the castle. That was important, as the castle needed constant attention. The assorted Wives came and went every month, and Hugo wasn't much for detail work, so that left it mostly up to Wira. Fortunately she liked details.

The Good Magician arrived at the scene. "That's not exactly a dead body," he said immediately. The situation had temporarily abolished his grumpiness.

"What is it, dear?" the Gorgon inquired.

"A mock-up of some sort. Possibly it's a transformation of a body, to mask its identity. I will have to look it up in the Book of Answers. Meanwhile, put it away somewhere."

"But won't it stink?" the Gorgon asked. Wira winced.

"No. It's in stasis. It won't change at all, until we discover the magic binding it and nullify it."

This was interesting. Frozen animation? Not ordinary magic indeed.

Humfrey went up to his study to look in the Book. Wira and the Gorgon took hold of the body, which was surprisingly light, and dragged it to a dusty alcove. The Gorgon put a sheet over it, covering it like old furniture. That should do until they got to the bottom of this mystery.

Then they went up to the Good Magician's study to learn what the Book of Answers said.

"Bleep!" Humfrey swore. "Bleepity bleep!" Wira felt the curtains singeing. This was a stage or four beyond mere grumpiness.

"What is it, dear?" the Gorgon asked, alarmed. Even her little snakes were hissing with concern.

"The Book's been scrambled!" he said, outraged. "It's useless."

This made both Wira and the Gorgon pause, precisely together. How could the sacrosanct Book of Answers have been changed?

"Let me see, dear," the Gorgon said. "Oh, my! The entries are in random order."

"Exactly. The first entry is on Earl the Pearl, whose talent is to create peril. The second is on the sisters Katydid and Katydidn't. It's all out of order."

"You're right, dear, as always: the Book of Answers has been ruined. Whatever are we going to do?"

"There is only one thing to do," he said grumpily. "I must put it back in order."

"Of course, dear. How long will that take?"

"Several months." He was so angry he seemed about to explode like an overripe pineapple.

"Then we had better leave you to it. Come Wira; we have other things to do."

"But Mother Gorgon, I need to find my husband! Who knows what mischief has befallen him?"

"Trust me, dear."

And of course Wira did trust her. The Gorgon had something in her sinuous mind.

They went downstairs, where the Gorgon fixed Gorgonzola cheese and slightly stoned biscuits. They were very good; she had had decades of practice using her talent to make interesting delicacies.

"You know we can't wait months to rescue Hugo," Wira said.

"Neither can we tolerate Humfrey's royal grumpiness for that period," the Gorgon agreed. "So we simply have to leave him to his chore and do something ourselves. Perhaps the other wives will help. They don't want to deal with unremitting grumpiness either."

"But what can we do?" Wira asked despairingly. "We have no idea who did what or why!"

"It's a mystery. We must do what folk always do with mysteries: we must solve it. As I see it, there are four parts: Who, why, where, and how."

"I'm not sure I understand."

"Who did it. Why did he do it. Where is he now. And how did he bollix the Book. That would have required some very special magic."

"So it would," Wira agreed, appreciating the significance of it. No one but Humfrey really understood the Book, let alone had the ability to affect it.

"Some of it we can fathom on our own. Obviously the murderer knew that Humfrey would know his identity immediately, so he fixed it so Humfrey wouldn't: by scrambling Humfrey's reference. But murderers always leave some inadvertent traces that a good detective can fathom."

"They do?"

"Yes. It's in every mystery novel. I have read a pile of them. The trick is to find the traces and figure out their meaning. It's never easy, but always possible, for the right detective."

"You are a detective?"

"By no means, dear. That will be your duty."

"Mine! But I know nothing of such things. I can't even go out beyond the castle."

"Well, certainly *I* can't. I'm here only a month at a time, by special arrangement. The rest of the time I have my movie career. You, in contrast, are here continuously, and you also have excellent reason to solve the mystery and recover Hugo. So that task naturally falls to you. I confess that your liability may be a problem."

"Let's skip the euphemism. I'm blind. I would fall into the next hole in the ground if I walked out far beyond the castle. I do well here only because I have memorized every cranny of the castle."

"That is a problem," the Gorgon agreed. "Yet no one would suspect you. It's the perfect cover."

"The perfect disaster, you mean! I'd be helpless. I was fully functional only with Hugo at my side, and now—" The realization that he was gone suddenly overwhelmed her, and she wept.

"I understand, dear," the Gorgon said. "I really do. He's my son. I'm only trying to devise a way to get him back soon."

"Yes, of course," Wira said bravely, stifling her tears. "I'll do what I can. But I can't do it alone."

"I will cogitate on that. Meanwhile we need to find some Clues."

"Some whats?"

"Clues. Detectives always have some. We just have to figure out where to find them."

Wira laughed somewhat bitterly. "Maybe in the Book of Answers?"

The Gorgon nodded. Wira could detect that too. "That is the obvious place to start. The murderer had to have left some fingerprints there."

"We don't use fingerprints in Xanth. They're too scientific."

"Oh, bother!" the Gorgon said crossly. "You're right. But there has to be something. We merely need the wit to find it."

Wira had an idea. "If he scrambled the Book of Answers, he must have touched it, to turn the pages or something. Maybe he left stains that could be magically analyzed."

"Maybe he did," the Gorgon agreed. "Let's go look."

"But Humfrey won't let us touch the Book!"

"Correction, dear. He'll let *you* touch it, if you charm him. He can't say no to you."

Wira started to protest, but realized it was true. Humfrey never really said no to her. "I'll try."

Humfrey was deep in the Book, using the flickering light of a feeble candle. "Dear, you'll ruin your eyes that way," the Gorgon said.

"Don't bother me, woman," he grumped.

"We need to look at the Book."

"No. Go away. I'm busy."

"Wira needs to look at the Book."

Humfrey paused. His head turned toward Wira. She smiled. He obviously did not want to leave the Book, but neither did he want to tell her no.

"And we have unfinished business in the bedroom," the Gorgon said.

"Woman, don't—"

"Now," she said firmly. "You know it supplements the youth elixir you use to keep your age at an even hundred." She took him by the ear and tugged.

Slowly, reluctantly, grumpily, he came. The Gorgon led him away. Only she could have done it. "It's up to you, dear," she said in passing to Wira. "I can give you half an hour, maybe a little more."

"But I hardly know—"

"Now," the Gorgon said, with what registered as about five eighths of a smile. Then they were gone.

Wira sat on the Good Magician's stool and oriented on the open Book of Answers. She couldn't read it, of course, but she ran her hands across the pages. There was, of course, nothing. She had assumed that the Gorgon would read the entries or see the smudges or whatever. What could she do on her own?

A cloud appeared; Wira felt its ambiance. "Whatever? I heard that thought."

Oh, no! "Demoness Metria, go away!" she snapped.

"By no means. Humfrey's distracted at the moment—I can't think by what—" The cloud assumed the form of a truly evocative bare female torso with serpentine curves. Wira knew, because she knew the demoness's nature. "So I took advantage to pop in while the magical repulsion is off. Is that the Book of Dissolvings?"

"The Book of Whats?"

"Solutions, Rejoinders, Responses, Retorts, Replies—"

"Answers?"

"Whatever," the demoness agreed crossly. "There, I said it. Whatever are you up to?"

"Please, Metria, I have only a little time. Let me work."

"Wira, you can't even see it! What work could you possibly be doing?"

It was not in Wira to prevaricate. "I'm looking for signs of whoever abducted Hugo."

"Hugo was stolen? That *is* a news flash! What girl lured him away?"

"No girl," Wira said grimly. She was trying not to let the demoness bother her, but of course Metria was succeeding anyway. "It was the murderer."

"A murderer! Whodunit?"

"I beg your pardon?"

"Never mind. I can see I missed something interesting. So you're looking in the Book to find your murderer. What's keeping you?"

"The entries are scrambled."

The demoness looked. "Why so they are! That must complicate things."

"Yes." Wira ran her hands over the pages. There was nothing. She turned to open two new pages, then two more—and felt something. "Hugo!"

"That's not Hugo," Metria said. "That's just a fruit stain on the page."

"That's the feel of Hugo! His talent is to summon fruit. He must have been here. Metria, will you help?"

The demoness hesitated. "You want my help? Is this a trick?"

Wira remembered how to handle this creature. "Of course it is! I'm pretending to need you so that you'll go away just to spite me." That was a half truth, or maybe a quarter truth, so was not a full-fledged prevarication; she could manage it in this emergency.

"What do you want me to do?"

"Read the entry I have identified."

"Well, I will. It's about Cumulo Fracto Nimbus, the ornery cloud."

Wira was disappointed. "Not Hugo?"

"No known connection to Hugo."

"Still, it must be a Clue."

"A What?"

"Suggestion, lead, intuition, indication, intimation—"

"Hint?"

"Whatever," Wira agreed crossly. "Something that will help me find Hugo, or the murderer, in some devious way."

"You must be tetched in the head, girl."

But Wira was turning more pages and running her hands across them. Soon she felt another trace. "This one."

"That's about the pet peeve, the perpetually irascible bird. You think it stole your husband?"

"I don't know what to think. Maybe it's irrelevant."

"Let's turn some more pages. I think you're making random selections to turn me off."

Wira wasn't, but did not argue. The demoness actually was helping, so it was better to let her think she wasn't.

She turned more pages, finding more clue-spots. None of them were about Hugo, to her grief, but surely they were relevant in some way, or they wouldn't be marked by his fruit essence. She remembered them all. She was good at remembering things, because she couldn't make notes she could read.

"Why don't you use be-wail?" Metria inquired.

"Use what?" Wira realized that she must have voiced part of her thought.

"Dots, spots, marks, elevations, patterns—"

"Braille?"

"Whatever."

"It takes a special tool to write it. It's easier just to remember."

"It would be easier yet just to see."

"I don't miss it."

"Well, you should."

Before she made it to the end of the Book, she heard Humfrey and the Gorgon returning. She had excellent hearing, and generally knew what was going on in the castle without having to go there. The Gorgon had done her best, but there was only so much distraction the Good Magician would tolerate when he had a concern about the Book. Wira wished they could have stayed away longer; her list of clues was incomplete. "Darn."

"OoOo, what you said!"

"It's not a bad word."

"Yes it is. Roxanne Roc was convicted and sentenced for uttering it in the presence of the Simurgh's egg. I know, because I was the swing member of the jury."

Wira might have argued further, but Humfrey was entering the study doorway. "I smell demoness," he grumped. "Begone, strumpet!"

"Bleep!" Metria swore and faded. This time there was a faint smell of brimstone.

"Who has been interfering with my Book of Answers?" Humfrey demanded.

"I was just turning the pages, looking for clues," Wira said.

He mellowed marginally. "First I need to restore proper order to the entries. Then I will be able to read the solution to the mystery." The man climbed onto his stool and went back to the beginning of the Book.

"Come dear, let's go down and have some comitea," the Gorgon suggested. "We'll leave Humfrey to his important work." She kissed the Good Magician on the top of his head.

They went downstairs to the kitchen. The comitea was very good, and did make Wira feel more civil despite her extreme concern about Hugo.

"Did you fetch in anything useful?" the Gorgon inquired.

"I don't know. Hugo's traces were definitely there, though I know he wouldn't have touched the Book directly. But the spots I found seem random."

"This whole business is strange. Hugo wouldn't have left you, as you pointed out, so I think it is fair to say he has no complicity. My guess is that he happened upon the murder scene before the murderer left, so the murderer had to get rid of him too, so as not to leave a witness. It must have happened very fast."

Wira was stricken. "Oh, Mother Gorgon! You don't think Hugo was killed?"

"Definitely not. I raided Humfrey's spells long ago and put a no-death spell on Hugo, just on general principles. Don't tell Humfrey."

"Oh, I wouldn't!" Wira said, her relief overflowing. "But then why isn't Hugo here?"

"That was a pretty basic, simple spell, and I put it on a long time ago, so it must have faded some. It would have kept him alive, but not stopped other mischief. He could have been enchanted into a mouse, or conjured to some distant spot. So it will still be a job to locate him. The scrambled Book stops us from using it to find Hugo as well as from identifying the murderer."

"But what magic could have scrambled it? That tome is counterspelled every which way."

The Gorgon nodded. "That bothers me. It's Magician-caliber magic. If a man could enter this castle, kill someone, banish the one who spied him, scramble the Book of Magic, and get away unobserved, what else is he capable of? I thought we knew of all the Magicians and Sorceresses in Xanth. This smells of something else."

Fingers of dread closed about Wira's heart. "What are you saying, Mother Gorgon?"

"Could this be a Demon involvement? Capital D?"

The Demons were to ordinary demons what sphinxes were to ants: immeasurably more powerful. The whole of the magic of the Land of Xanth stemmed from the mere radiation leaking from Demon Xanth as he rested deep below, or dallied in the Nameless Castle. Their ways were obscure but infinitely potent. If a Demon were involved, the case was hopeless. "It can't be," Wira said. She meant not that it was impossible, for nothing was impossible to a Demon, but that her whole world depended on it not being the case.

"Then it must be something less," the Gorgon agreed. "Someone or something with a special talent, maybe of conjuring himself places, and a handful of stolen spells. In which case the Book can identify him, when."

"I can't wait for when! Hugo's gone."

"I know, dear," the Gorgon said sympathetically. "That's why we shall have to solve it without the Book." Then she paused. "Oops—I thought of something else. Who would have been in the cellar, to kill? It's an odd place."

"Someone stealing some Rhed Whine?"

"That would hardly be worth it, considering the difficulty of getting into this castle. The stuff's not valuable."

"Could the—the murder have been done somewhere else, and the body conjured to the cellar?"

"Then why abolish Hugo?" the Gorgon asked sensibly. "Why not leave him to discover the body, as you did soon after? No, the murderer had to be there in the cellar. Which puts us back to who was the victim."

"But it hardly makes sense! One person sneaking into the cellar, another sneaking in to murder him, then doing something to Hugo to conceal his identity."

"And bollixing the Book of Answers," the Gorgon said. "Which suggests he knew where he was and what he was doing. I suspect we understand next to nothing at all."

"Next to nothing," Wira agreed, hating it.

"All the more reason to act. You got some clues."

"Just random names, like Cumulo Fracto Nimbus. He wouldn't have done this; in fact he *couldn't* have done this. He's a cloud!"

"Then you will have to go question him. Maybe he knows something about this. That's what Clues are all about. Once you have run them all down, you'll be able to assemble them and draw a Brilliant Conclusion."

"I'm not that smart," Wira protested.

"Nonsense. You'll be as smart as you need to be. But just in case, you can take some Eye Queue elixir along."

"You forget. I'm blind."

The Gorgon considered. "Yes, we'll have to deal with that. You'll need a Companion."

"A what?"

"Don't play Demoness Metria with me, girl! Someone to travel with you, to be your eyes. You'll need something to ride, too; walking all over Xanth would be too tedious."

"But I don't know anyone outside the castle, and I have never ridden an animal."

"Details to be addressed. Meanwhile, there's another problem: there's a querent coming tomorrow. How is Humfrey going to answer her, with the Book bonked?"

"We'll have to send her away."

"We can't. The Challenges are all set up, and if she makes it through, she'll expect her Answer."

"We'll have to go out to intercept her, to explain."

"By no means! If we do that, everyone will soon know of the fix we're in. It would ruin the Good Magician's reputation for inscrutable expertise. Also, if word gets around that we're looking for a murderer, what do you think will happen to Hugo? We need the murderer to think that he's gotten away with it, and no one is investigating."

That froze Wira. "We must keep it secret," she agreed. "But how can I question people, then? That will quickly give it away."

A bulb flashed over the Gorgon's head; Wira felt its brief heat. "You're blind!"

"That's not exactly late news."

"But you must have been longing all your life for sight. To recover the vision you lost as a child."

"I haven't been," Wira protested. "I have a very good life here."

"Of course you have, dear. But others won't know that. You must go on a Quest to find your Lost Vision. That way you can question people right, left, and center, and they won't catch on to your real mission."

"But how can I ask about Hugo without giving it away?"

"Consider it a challenge, dear. I'm sure you'll rise to the occasion."

She would have to. "You mentioned a Companion. But there's no one." Then a bulb flashed over her own head. "The querent!"

"That's it," the Gorgon agreed. "We can tell her that the Good Magician requires her Service first, while he researches her Answer. That Service is to be your eyes." She paused half a moment. "But she's an ordinary girl. In fact she's from Mundania. That means—"

"She has no magic talent," Wira said. "She won't be much help at all. Unless—"

A third bulb flashed. "Unless we change her to a more useful form," the Gorgon said. "Like a flying centaur."

"But we can't do that sort of magic."

"Yes we can. You forget that I was the one who first put all Humfrey's collected spells in order. There's a forgotten conversion spell on a back shelf, beyond the pun-gloves. It's voluntary, which means she'll have to agree to it, but of course we want her agreement. We can do this without disturbing Humfrey at all."

"Oh, I hope so," Wira breathed.

"I hope she's a nice girl," the Gorgon said.

"That, too," Wira agreed. She was beginning to have faint hope.

2
DEBRA

D ebra was not at all certain she was doing the right thing. But what else was there? Ever since she had arrived in Xanth she had been driven to distraction by her curse. Maybe the Good Magician could abolish it. So he charged a year's Service or the equivalent for an Answer; it wasn't as though she had anything better to do right now.

She stood at the edge of the moat and gazed at her reflection. She looked like exactly what she was: a thirteen-year-old Mundane girl. The details didn't matter. Only the curse mattered. She was half ashamed that it was not a big bold dangerous curse that threatened extinction to whole cities. It was small and personal, and aggravating as bleep.

Bleep: now there was a good word, for all that it wasn't really a word. People weren't allowed to swear here, so when they tried it got bleeped out. She found that more entertaining than annoying. It was one of the things she liked about this magic land. Certainly it was better than dreary Mundania.

Well, she was here. The Good Magician's Castle stood before her, right across the moat. She knew the rule: she would have to get through three Challenges, and if she succeeded, serve her term. She was ready. Maybe.

She contemplated the moat. In seeming answer, colored fins appeared in it. Debra shuddered; she knew those were loan sharks, ready to take an arm and a leg. She couldn't try to swim across.

Just to be sure, she experimented. She flipped a branching twig into the water. Sure enough, a huge white shark forged across and snapped up two of its branches. The arm and leg branches.

Several people emerged from the castle and trooped across the drawbridge. They looked carefree. They reached the outside of the moat and followed a path toward Debra. She waited, knowing what was coming.

They stopped when they saw her. "Hello," the leading girl said. "Are you looking for the Good Magician? This is his castle."

"I am," Debra agreed. "I have a question for him."

"Oh, you're a querent." Debra didn't quite catch the word, but didn't like it. "Well, I wish you luck. I had to go through it six months ago. I'm Steph."

Debra tried to stave off the inevitable. "You had a Question? But then why are you leaving the castle?"

Steph laughed. "I'm serving my year. We all are. We came to ask our talents, and Magician Humfrey told us, and now we're working it out. Mine's the ability to freeze things in place, like a wiggle swarm or half a horde of goblins. This is Bev; her talent is Time: she knows when to start an action so that it will be successful or unsuccessful. And this is Timur, with the talent of cooling or heating water, to vapor or ice. We need to fetch some lethe elixir for the Good Magician."

"Lethe!" Debra exclaimed. "Doesn't that make you forget things?"

"Yes. That's why it's dangerous. Bev says this is the time to do it, when we can succeed. I will lock it in place so we can safely get a bottle of it. Timur will cool it to freezing after it's in the bottle so it won't leak out. It may be a challenge, no pun, but we'll get it done."

"So it's not so bad, working for the Good Magician," Bev said hopefully.

"Not bad at all," Steph agreed. "You'll like it, if you get through to Ask your Question. What did you say your name is?"

There it was. She had to answer. "Debra."

"Say," Timur said, stepping toward her. He reached for her chest.

Debra cringed.

"You're scaring her," Steph told him. "What's gotten into you, Tim?"

He snapped out of it, embarrassed. "Sorry. Something— never mind."

"We have a job to do," Steph said. "You can't just go grabbing under-age girls." She hustled him on past. "Sorry about that, Deb," she said over her shoulder. "He's not like that. Usually." They went on.

Debra made a silent sigh of relief. She had gotten through, this time.

She would have to use the drawbridge. Fortunately it was down across the moat, having just been used by the three. However she doubted it would just let her cross. Xanth was a magic land, and just about everything had magic and attitude to go with it.

Sure enough, the moment she set foot on the path toward the draw-bridge, an array of cats appeared. They seemed to be in a queue before a chamber where a lion and a witch guarded a wardrobe. Each cat presented coins before being allowed to disappear into the wardrobe.

There was something halfway familiar about the scene, but Debra couldn't quite place it. She attempted to pass the line, but immediately the cats hissed and spit at her. "I'm not trying to break into your line," Debra said. "I just want to move on to the other side of it." But they evidently didn't understand. They would not let her through.

She paused, considering. This must be a Challenge. But how did it apply? Was she supposed to join the line and go into the big wardrobe? Somehow she doubted it; whatever was in it was not something she wanted. More likely she just needed to get them to let her pass their line.

This was Xanth. It was a land of puns. Could this be some kind of pun?

Then she got it. "Fee-line!" she cried. "Feline. You're cats lining up to pay your fee for entry to whatever it is you're going to."

The scene faded, lion, witch, wardrobe and all. She had gotten the pun, or at least enough of it to qualify. Maybe it was part of some other story. She stepped forward, advancing toward the drawbridge.

But now there was some kind of stem in her way. It was huge, with milky joints, and extended in such a tangle it would be quite awkward to get around, over, or through it. It was surely another pun. But what?

She traced an offshoot tendril, and discovered a big animal growing from it. In fact it was a Mundane cow! "Hi, Bossy," she said.

"Mooo!" the cow responded amiably.

What kind of a plant grew cows?

Then she got it: "Bo-vine!"

The cow-plant faded, allowing her to take a few more steps toward the drawbridge. She was getting through the Challenge.

But now she came to a collection of odd creatures milling around. The path led right through their pen, and she hesitated to barge through. She had to figure out what kind of puns these creatures were.

One was a teddy bear–like creature picking what looked like cupcakes from a plant and eating them. With each one it ate, the animal became funnier, changing colors, sizes, and shapes. What were those sweetbreads?

She picked one and tasted it. Suddenly she felt insanely witty. "What do you call a dull ogre?" she asked rhetorically. "A medi-ogre! What about a liquid yellow flower that shoots seeds from its center? A pistil! What about tea that kills you? Mortalitea!"

Then she clapped her hands over her mouth. What was she saying? This was such crude humor it was positively unladylike. What had gotten into her?

That piece of cupcake she had just eaten. That bun, the same kind that was making the teddy bear react just as crazily. What was in it?

Then she caught on. "It's not a bun, it's a pun! It makes me emit stinky puns!" But what about the animal? It wasn't stinking. It must be adapted to handle this diet. "And you're a Punda!" she exclaimed, pleased.

The creature faded. She had identified it.

But there were others. For example, an ox-like animal that looked exceedingly stupid. What could it be?

She nibbled a bit more of the pun she still held. "A Flummox!" she said. The creature faded.

Then next was an inlet of the moat, on which floated what seemed to be a block of ice. It was a miniature iceberg, but there was something odd about it. It was moving, but she wasn't sure how fast, and she couldn't tell exactly where it was. It wasn't that it was fuzzy, just that somehow it seemed impossible to judge both position and motion at the same time.

Something nagged her memory. Something in physics class, or a footnote in the text. "It's a Heisen-berg!" she exclaimed.

The berg faded; it had been fathomed. Her brain had nearly split, but she had gotten it. The Heisenberg uncertainty principle.

Now there was a big muscular bug. It was lifting rocks out of the way, heaving them with phenomenal efforts. Some it took bites from, evidently liking the taste. What could it be?

She nibbled again on the pun. "Dine-o-mite!" she said. "Or maybe dino-might. Explosively strong bug."

The mite faded. It had been contained.

She stepped forward—and encountered a phenomenal musical note that sent shivers halfway up her spine and tremors along the rest of it. She fell back, alarmed. What could this be? She had never before reacted this way to mere music.

This had to be another pun. But how could there be a pun in music, a mere single note? Too many such notes would give her a backache.

Then she got it. "It's a Spinal Chord!"

The remnant of the note faded, and with it her pain in the spine. She took another step.

A fenced area appeared, filled with people: men, women, children. They all seemed somewhat motley, as if they knew themselves to be of no account. Some of them were working at sundry tasks, not very hard or well.

One person stood apart, in an adjacent lot. He was handsome and well dressed, and seemed to be the very picture of success. The path led directly to him.

There had to be a pun, but whatever could it be? A successful man, separated from the other folk: what was special or funny about that?

She took another bite of the bun, and got it. "You're out standing in your field!" she told the man.

He glanced at her, nodding, as he faded.

And it seemed she had finally won through this Challenge, because there were no more puns. The path was open to the drawbridge.

Debra approached the drawbridge. There was a man guarding it. He was about six feet tall, fit, with curly brown hair and a mustache. In fact just the kind she liked to get secret crushes on. She hoped he didn't demand to know her name.

"Hello," she said cautiously. "I need to cross the bridge, if that's all right."

He shook his head. "Hello to you. I'm Bernie, and I'm here to prevent you from doing that. If you try to set foot on it I will pick you up and toss you into the moat."

"But there are sharks there!" she protested.

"Plus a hungry moat monster," he agreed. "So you had better not try."

"But I need to see the Good Magician."

"He doesn't need to see you, honey. He doesn't like to be bothered."

"I have to see him!" she wailed. "He's the only one who can possibly help me."

Bernie looked at her with some compassion. "Look, honey, I have a daughter of my own. I never want to see her hurt. But I have a job to do here. This is a Challenge. I will not let you pass if I can help it."

A sympathetic Challenge. That struck her as unusual. Maybe she could learn something useful. So she talked with him. "How can you stand all these puns?"

"I love puns! You ran afoul of some good ones."

"They were awful ones!"

"Same thing, honey. The very best puns are the real stinkers. Let's face it: the Land of Xanth is pretty much made of puns. If you can't handle them, you don't belong here."

He had a point. But this wasn't getting her across the drawbridge. Maybe she could befriend him, and he would let her by after all. Or something. "What's the best/worst pun you've seen, Bernie?"

"That's easy! It's the Bombshell."

"The bombshell? I thought that was a pretty woman."

"It is, in Mundania. Here it's an explosive shell. It can stun men just by its look, and when you throw it, it explodes and stuns everyone in the vicinity. I love it. But of course I'm a man; it wouldn't have the same effect on you."

"I suppose not," Debra agreed. "But isn't a shell a cylinder with gunpowder in it, or dynamite?" She flinched inwardly, remembering the pun on that word she had recently passed. "What's so special about that?"

"It's the shape of the shell, honey. Like the sexiest woman alive."

Oh. Debra gazed into the moat, trying to think of some other lead, as this one wasn't working out.

She saw the hourglass figure of a woman who was shapelier than Debra had ever dreamed of being. Yet it was a shell. Could it be?

She reached into the water and lifted it out. "What do you think of this?" she asked, holding it up.

Bernie stared. "That's it! The bombshell!"

"This?" She turned it around so that it showed the plush bottom that revealed just a bit of panty.

Bernie didn't answer. She looked at him, and saw he was frozen in place, staring at the shell. He had freaked out! Now she remembered that the sight of women's panties did that to men in Xanth, and maybe in Mundania too. As long as the figure was in view, he would remain in stasis. Men were like that; they just couldn't take their eyes off something sexy.

She had found the key to passing this Challenge. She set the bombshell carefully on the ground, taking care not to conceal any part of it. Bernie's eyes followed it, locked on.

She stepped away from the shell. Bernie didn't move. She walked quietly around him and set foot on the drawbridge. He did not react. She had found the way through, as much by luck as design. But of course the Challenges were designed to be solved; a person just had to be alert. She was glad she hadn't had to throw the shell at him; its mere appearance was enough.

Two challenges done. One to go.

She crossed the moat and came to the portcullis that guarded the castle entrance. The bars were raised, but she didn't quite trust this: would the whole heavy thing come plunging down on her head if she walked under it?

She poked one hand under, ready to yank it back. Nothing happened. So she nerved herself and jumped past, giving the thing no time to catch her.

That turned out to be just as well, because the bars crashed down just behind her. Now she was locked inside the castle.

Well, it was where she wanted to be. She looked around, and found herself in a short hall leading to a garden area. It was a pretty garden, with many trees, shrubs, paths, and pools. If this was a Challenge, it was a nice one. Of course she didn't trust it. There would be some mischief here.

A big sign said ASK NOT WHAT CONCERNS YOU NOT, LEST YOU HEAR WHAT PLEASES YOU NOT.

Well, that was plain enough. She would not ask any stupid questions. That was surely part of the Challenge.

She entered the garden, as there wasn't much else to do, with her retreat closed off by the portcullis. She saw that each plant and pool was neatly labeled. There were assorted pie trees and milkweeds, but she doubted she was here to eat or drink. So she followed a path, knowing that it was bound to lead somewhere. Right ahead it crossed another path.

Suddenly a big red light flashed in front of her. She froze in place, held there magically. Had she ventured into a wrong place?

But then the light turned green, and she was free to move again. She realized it had been a stoplight. Just like Mundania, only here it was literal: she couldn't move until it changed color.

"Got caught by the light, eh?" a man inquired from the other path.

"Yes," Debra agreed, embarrassed.

"If there's a problem, I can fix it," the man said. "I'm a pathologist. I take care of enchanted paths."

"Thank you, there's no problem," she said. Except where the third Challenge was, and she was sure she couldn't ask him. Now she knew it was all right to talk, to answer, just not to ask.

She moved on quickly, because the man looked as if he were about to ask her name, and she didn't want that.

She came to a pool where a red-haired woman and a girl were working. The girl was pointing to things, and the woman was using a net to catch them and lift them into a tank behind her. They looked like bundles of snakes.

The woman spied her. "Hello. I am Theresa, and this is Aurora Sky. We're from Mundania."

"So am I," Debra said, gratified. "I'm Debra." It was okay to tell her name to a woman.

"Oh, then you know how it is. We came here to ask Questions, and now are serving our Services."

"I'll be doing the same," Debra agreed.

Aurora pointed. "Yes, that's a good one," Theresa said, and put the net to the water. She lifted out their catch.

Debra stared. That was no bundle of snakes. In fact it was a little monster! A creature with seven snapping heads. "Why are you saving those?" Debra asked.

Oops. She had asked a question.

"This is hydraponics," Theresa explained. "We're growing hydras in water. But first we have to catch them. Aurora is very good at spotting them."

"I wasn't supposed to ask," Debra said, abashed.

"Oh, that's too bad. Now you'll pay a penalty. I'm sorry."

"A penalty," Debra agreed nervously.

Then suddenly she burst into giggles. She couldn't help herself; her fit could not be contained. She rolled on the ground, stifled giggles bursting forth.

"Oh, it's the Giggles!" Theresa said. "How awful!"

Debra tried to respond, but couldn't speak around the ongoing giggles.

"It's my fault," Theresa said. "I distracted you, and you forgot. So I'll help you to the extent I am able. The giggles are a member of the Vole family. They are invisibly small. They get into your clothing and cause uncontrollable fits of giggling. They must have been waiting for you to give them the pretext. The only way to get rid of them is to wash them off, and out of your clothing. But that may not be easy."

"Th—the—thank you!" Debra gasped between giggles. She scrambled toward the nearest pool.

"Not here!" Theresa said. "The hydra will get you."

Now Debra saw that the little monsters were accompanied by a big monster in the water. The adult hydra could have swallowed her four limbs and one head with single gulps of five of its seven heads, and seemed eager to do so. Indeed, this was not the place to wash.

"I'm not allowed to tell you where," Theresa said. "I'm so sorry."

"That's—hee hee!—all—giggle!—right," Debra gasped. She scrambled on down the path, looking for water she could use before she expired of giggling.

She came to a larger pool of what looked like clear, clean water. But five men were dancing on it, to loud crude music. The sign said River Dancers, and evidently they had a joint talent that enabled them to dance on water. They were looking at her as they danced, perhaps appreciating the audience.

She would have to remove her clothing and get in the water right by their feet. They would be able to look down and see all of her without breaking their steps. She was giggling up a storm, but was not amused. At age thirteen she might not have as full a body as she would have soon, but she certainly did not want men staring at it bare. She struggled onward.

The next pond was private, but its identifying sign said Illixir. She stifled her giggles long enough to see that a chip of wood floated in it. It was probably healing elixir with reverse wood, so that instead of healing people it made them ill. She managed to poke a finger in the water, and immediately it felt as if it were festering. The chip was out of reach; she couldn't pull it out and let the water revert to healing elixir. She had to move on.

The next pool was labeled Love Spring. If she bathed in that, she would fall in love with the next man she saw. That was no good, for more than one reason. She staggered on, still giggling. Her ribs were getting sore with all that laughing, but she couldn't stop. Bleep those Giggles!

Another pool was labeled Hate Spring. That was worse.

Then she came to a pool that was on fire. Sure enough, it was labeled Firewater. It would boil her alive.

Then she got smart. She saw a chip of wood lying near it. It looked exactly like the chip of reverse wood she had seen before. She picked it up and flipped it into the water.

The flames extinguished. The pool had become the opposite of firewater, which should be water water.

Debra plunged in, clothing and all. Then she scrambled out of her clothing and swam naked. She was no longer giggling; she had washed off the invisible beasties. What a relief!

She caught her pieces of clothing and dragged them through the water, making sure everything was washed out. Then she climbed back to shore and shook herself dry. How glad she was that this pool was in a secluded glade!

But she still had to make it through the third Challenge. She was beginning to wonder: was this to be an endless array of puns and tricks? She had put up with it so far, but was it really worth it?

She pondered while her clothing dried. The more she thought about it, the more she was annoyed. Maybe it was time to do something about it.

First she had to get clothed. She waded back into the water and fetched the reverse wood chip. She carried it out and put it back where she had found it. The water reverted, the flames flickering across its surface. Good. She held her wet clothing up to that heat, getting it dried rapidly. She could make mistakes, she could get in trouble, she could get really depressed, but she didn't have to be stupid. So maybe this wasn't a regular part of the Challenge; she was bleeped if she'd go naked any longer than she had to.

Once she was clothed, she stood beside the pond and spoke loudly to the glade: "All right, Good Magician: I have played your game and made my way through your silly Challenges. I came here to seek your help, not to play a pointless game. If you can't or won't help me, I wish you would simply say so, instead of wasting my time and yours with such nonsense. If all you have for me is foolishness instead of common courtesy, then I have come to the wrong place. If you're just trying to discourage me so I'll go away, well, you have succeeded, because I don't respect a person who lacks the nerve simply to say No. So either talk to me now, or I'll go and seek help somewhere else."

She paused. There was no answer. She was disappointed that her statement of principle hadn't worked, but she didn't regret it. She turned and started back the way she had come.

And discovered that the scene behind her had changed. Now there was an open door leading into an inner chamber. Was this the true inner castle, or another trick? Well, she would find out. She stepped through the door.

A woman met her. "Well spoken, Debra," she said. "I am Wira, the Good Magician's daughter-in-law. I will take you to see his wife, the Gorgon."

"The Gorgon! The one whose face turns people to stone?"

"She wears a veil," Wira assured her. "Please, this is important."

It could also be another trick. But there seemed to be no harm in playing along for the moment. "I came to see the Good Magician, not to socialize."

"This is business," Wira assured her. "This way, please."

The woman led her to what appeared to be the castle kitchen. There was a woodstove that somehow wasn't burning itself up, an icebox whose ice somehow was not melting, and a table with appetizers. It looked rather mundane despite the magic of the equipment.

A tall veiled woman with extremely odd hair stood by the table. In fact her hair looked snaky. "Mother Gorgon, this is Debra, the querent," Wira said.

"I'm not queer!" Debra snapped.

The Gorgon smiled under her veil. "Naturally not, dear. That's querent as in a query, normally magical in nature. It's a technical term we find useful. No offense is implied."

"Oh." Debra found herself blushing. "I'm sorry."

"Don't be. If there is any embarrassment to be had, it is ours rather than yours. I will explain in a moment." She gestured to the table. "Have some refreshments, Debra. You must be hungry."

Actually, she was; she hadn't eaten since raiding a pie plant in the morning before approaching the castle. But she remained cautious, because there was something about this situation that didn't quite jibe. "I don't know what to take. What do you recommend?"

"Well, there's boot rear, which is good though you will get a kick out of it." The Gorgon took up a paper cup brimming with brownish liquid.

Actually Debra knew about boot rear, having encountered it before. It was clearly a pun on root beer, with a magical quality. She accepted the cup and took a sip. Sure enough, she got lightly booted in the rear. Some drinks made a person dizzy; this one, as the Gorgon said, had a kick to it.

"And biscuits with monster cheese," the Gorgon continued, proffering one. "Monsters have the very best taste in cheese."

Debra nibbled at it. Again the woman was right: this was excellent cheese. Soon she was eating and drinking freely, rather enjoying the boots to her bottom. Boot rear was an acquired taste, and she was acquiring it. But she was also comfortable with the amitea and the punwheel cookies. Wira sat at the table with them, silent.

"Normally Magician Humfrey grants a querent an Answer, and requires her to perform a year's Service, or equivalent," the Gorgon said as Debra ate. "But we have a crisis that requires a different mode this time."

"Something happened to the Good Magician?" Debra asked, alarmed.

"Not directly. His Book of Answers got scrambled, and he is deeply embroiled in putting it back in order. Until he accomplishes that, it is useless. So he will be unable to give you your Answer at present."

"You mean I went through all this nonsense for nothing?" Debra demanded.

"We hope not," the Gorgon said. "We may have an alternative."

"But nobody has answers as good as the Good Magician's," Debra protested. "Even if they don't seem relevant at first."

"Dear, I know exactly what you mean," the Gorgon said. "Some time back I was smitten with Humfrey, and I came to ask him whether he would marry me. Do you know, he made me serve a year's Service keeping his castle before he gave me his answer?"

"He what?" Debra asked, almost choking on a piece of monsterella cheese.

"But you see, it did make sense. Humfrey is chronically grumpy, even at times irascible. By the time I had worked for him a year I was thoroughly familiar with his nature. He was giving me a chance to change my mind. When I didn't, his Answer was Yes. And here I am today, still keeping his castle, one month in five and a half. He's grumpy, but he's also a near genius, and kind at heart, and of course I know how to manage him. Yes, his answers can be like that, but they always make wonderful sense when you fathom them."

"So I understand," Debra said. "But mine is very simple, and I'm hoping for a simple answer."

"What is your Question, dear?"

Debra took a breath. "It connects to my name. Debra. It's a curse I discovered when I came to Xanth. Every time a man learns my name, he takes it literally."

The Gorgon's veil furrowed. "I don't believe I understand. No one can take your name; it's yours."

"De-Bra. He tries to take off my bra. It's most embarrassing, and makes for very bad relations with the male gender. So my Question is, how can I nullify this curse?"

"How old are you, dear? You look young."

"Thirteen."

"Then you are covered by the Adult Conspiracy. No one can say anything or do anything that might give you any hint about how storks are signaled. Bras and panties relate; that's why they're so naughty."

"I'm from Mundania. I know how storks are summoned, as you put it."

The Gorgon nodded. "Maybe that fudges the proscription. Do you know why men are interested in bras?"

"Same reason they freak out at the sight of panties. It turns them on, and they want to—to do something about it."

"Exactly. Of course they don't freak out when they see bare naked nymphs, unless the nymphs put on panties or bras. That makes them seem human, and it is human flesh that does it for human men."

"But they don't even have to see my bra. Until they hear my name. Then suddenly they get this Idea, and I'm in trouble."

"May we verify this, Debra? To understand exactly what we face?"

Debra shrugged. "If you must."

The Gorgon glanced at the woman. "Fetch Opti and Pesi, please, Wira."

Wira departed silently. In little more than a moment and a half she returned with a boy and girl who looked like twins.

"This is Opti Mystic," the Gorgon said. "She sees only the good things about the future, when she focuses." The girl smiled. "And this is Pesi Mystic, who sees only the bad future things. We are very cautious about asking them to look."

"She's got a wild and wonderful future," Opti said as she looked at Debra.

"But there's something about her that will ruin it," Pesi said.

"Tell them your name, dear," the Gorgon said.

"Debra."

Opti did not react, but Pesi stepped toward her. "Suddenly I have this need to get hold of your—"

"Dismissed!" the Gorgon rapped, and her little snakes hissed warningly.

Both Opti and Pesi hastily departed.

The Gorgon nodded again. "It is a worthy curse, dear. One you certainly want abated. My husband surely has the Answer. Unfortunately he can't look it up in the book of Answers at the moment. So we need an alternative."

"An alternative? What alternative can there be to simply stopping the curse?"

"A postponed Answer. If you will agree to perform your Service first, I will guarantee to make Humfrey provide your Answer once he has the Book in order again."

Debra considered. That did seem fair, and was a lot better than no chance of an Answer. "What would I have to do? If it involves working with men, that's no good."

"This requires more background. I must ask you not to reveal what I am about to tell you."

"Okay," Debra agreed, curious.

"We have a murder mystery to solve. A body turned up in the cellar, and Wira's husband, my son Hugo, disappeared. We think he saw the murderer, and got transformed or relegated to some unkind place. Wira is desperate to find him. But Wira can't search for him alone."

"She can't? Why not?"

"Because I am blind," Wira said.

Debra stared at her. "But you led me through the castle with no misstep!"

"I am familiar with the castle. I am not familiar with the outside."

Now Debra saw that there was a certain blankness to the woman's gaze. She really was blind. "I'm sorry."

"I am long accustomed to it," Wira said. "But now I need help. Someone must go with me to be my eyes. Someone I can trust."

"You want me to—to go with you? But you don't even know me. Anyway, I hardly know Xanth myself. I wouldn't be much help."

"Do you lack the nerve simply to say no?" Wira asked.

Debra was caught. The woman was quoting her own words back to her. She couldn't say no. "I just don't want to get us both eaten by a dragon. Surely there are many far more competent people to do this."

"Surely there are," the Gorgon agreed. "But none of them came on this day as querents. You are the one we have. We may have a way to enable you to protect yourself from dragons."

Debra was trying not to feel sorry for the blind woman. She did want to help, if she could. "Okay, I'll make that deal. I'll help, and get my Answer later. But how can I protect myself from dragons, let alone anyone else? I'm just a poor weak young inexperienced girl with no magic. None that I want, anyway."

"We have a potion that will transform you into a winged centaur."

Debra stared at the Gorgon. "But—but they're—bare breasted!"

"No problem about a bra," the Gorgon agreed.

"But I couldn't possibly—to show myself like that—" Then she saw Wira's silent disappointment. She couldn't say no. "Okay, I'll do it."

"Thank you," the Gorgon said. "I will fetch the potion." She got up and left the room.

"Thank you," Wira echoed. "This gives me my chance to solve the mystery and recover Hugo."

"You're welcome," Debra said, feeling faint. What had she gotten herself into?"

3
CLOUDS

T he Gorgon brought the potion in a small vial. "Drink this, and the transformation should occur in the next few minutes."

Suddenly Debra was beset by doubts almost as bad as the Giggles had been. "*Should* occur? You're not sure?"

"Well, it's an old potion. But they're supposed to keep indefinitely."

"But what if it goes wrong? What will become of me?"

"Are you saying no?"

That got to her. Debra was beginning to regret her extemporaneous little speech. She took the vial, uncorked it, and gulped down the potion before she could change her mind.

It tasted good, and it had a kick like boot rear, only all over her body. Something was definitely happening.

"You took it so quickly," the Gorgon said. "I was going to suggest that you remove your clothing first."

Debra was halfway distracted. "Why?"

"Because the potion doesn't affect clothing, just the body. And centaurs are—"

"Larger," Debra said, catching on. She tried to remove her shirt and skirt, but she was already changing, and they were caught tight. All she could do was let them be.

Her belly and rear were ballooning. Knobs protruded from her hips, extending into hairy sticks that dropped down to touch the floor. Her buttocks swelled big enough to burst her panties, pushing back and back, carrying her hind legs along with them. Her chest remained much the same, but her breasts overflowed her bra, then snapped its strap and pushed victoriously forward. Now she remembered: centaurs were better endowed than humans. She had a bosom that would have made her an instant starlet in Mundania. The split shirt and torn bra hung uselessly from it. Her skirt and panties were stretched across the solid rump of a horse. And her hind hooves were jammed precariously into the remnants of her shoes.

Indeed, she should have removed her clothing first. She just hadn't been thinking.

"Let me help," the Gorgon said. She worked with the shirt and bra, tugging loose the tatters. But she had to use a small knife to get the hideously stretched panties off. Meanwhile Wira found her hind feet and pried off the shoes. That was more comfortable.

Now Debra stood suitably bare. She wasn't concerned about her hindquarters; she had always admired horses. But her front—how could she parade in plain sight with these monstrous bare mammaries?

"Could—please, could I have a mirror?" she asked.

The Gorgon produced one. Debra took it and held it up before her.

Her head, arms, and torso down to the waist looked exactly like her, and suddenly the enormous breasts seemed to be in proportion. She was a centaur; that was the way they were. That also alleviated her concern about exposure; centaurs had no sensitivity about their bodies. Her face was identical, and her hair was the same, except that it had filled out in back to form a mane.

Actually, she was a good-looking woman, up front. And a handsome mare, behind. This would do.

"You will want to be cautious about your first flight," the Gorgon said. "You don't want to crash."

Then Debra noticed the wings that sprouted from the forepart of her barrel-shaped torso. They were folded but enormous, like great white feathered quilts half covering her back. They were white and beautiful. "Oh, yes," she sighed.

"Let me explain," the Gorgon continued. "Winged centaurs don't fly by the sheer power of their wings. They flick themselves with their magic tails to make themselves light. Then the wings can handle the reduced weight. The effect gradually fades as time passes, but can be renewed as required, on land or in flight. It's a convenient system. But at first it can be awkward."

Debra discovered she could switch her tail. "Like this?" she asked, flicking it toward her own back.

"Don't do it yet!" the Gorgon said.

Too late. The tip of the tail connected solidly. And Debra's rear section floated into the air. It hauled the rest of her up until it came against the ceiling. She was left suspended from her own hindquarters.

"I see your point," she gasped. "Now what?"

"Flick your fore section, lightly," the Gorgon said. "Until it matches your rear, restoring your balance. Then wait for the lightening to fade."

"Lightning!" Debra exclaimed, alarmed. "Is there a thunderstorm?"

"Light*en*ing," the Gorgon said, accenting the center syllable. "Making yourself light. You'll get the hang of it soon enough."

"I'm hanging," Debra agreed ruefully.

"While we wait for you to come to ground," the Gorgon said, "there are one or two other things to know. Never flick yourself too hard outside; you'll float to the moon. Never flick anyone else hard. Caution is the watchword, until you have an expert touch."

"I'm learning," Debra agreed. "I never had voluntary magic before."

"And you will need this," the Gorgon said, bringing out a large bow and quiver of arrows.

Debra was aghast. "I can't use that thing! I never shot an arrow in my life!"

"All centaurs, male and female, are expert archers," the Gorgon said. "They can fetch their bows from their backs in an instant, loose an arrow, and it will score. Other creatures know that, and are wary."

"But I hardly know which end of the arrow to notch!"

"Nock."

"Whatever. It's ludicrous to expect me to hit the ground from ten feet."

"Then perhaps you will have to bluff. That should be effective."

"I can't bluff! This is disaster."

"The form may bring some ability," Wira said. "Just as it brings the lightening magic."

"Oh, I hope so! Because I'm starting from zero, or a minus quantity."

"It might help to discuss it with another human-to-centaur convert," the Gorgon said. "Like Cynthia Centaur. But you can't, because this mission has to be secret. If the murderer learns what you're up to, he may kill Hugo. But I'm sure you'll be able to manage."

Debra did not share her sureness, but it seemed pointless to argue the case. She would simply have to do the best she could.

Slowly her lightness faded, and her four hooves came to rest on the floor. Now the Gorgon conducted her to a courtyard open to the sky. "Keep yourself heavy, and try your wings."

Debra tried. Her wings spread beautifully, every feather perfect. When she pumped them, they sent air washing down, trying to heave her body into the air.

"You will have to use your tail as a rudder," the Gorgon said. "You don't want to spin out of control. Try a very brief flight now."

Debra did, this time lightening herself with extreme caution. She flexed her wings, and rose a little—and spun crazily, tilting and bobbing.

"That's probably enough for the day," the Gorgon said. "Rest now, and think about it, and we'll practice more tomorrow."

Debra was glad to agree. They went back inside, and the Gorgon gave her a room piled with pillows so she could flop down without much concern for injury. What a day this had become!

She slept well, but woke early with a full bladder. She got up and looked for a bathroom, but found none—and how could her huge equine body possibly fit in it anyway, or use its facilities? This was an embarrassing problem.

Wira appeared, her sensitive hearing alerting her. "May I help you?" she inquired politely.

"I need to—to pee," Debra blurted.

"Just go outside and do it anywhere."

"I can't do that! It's far too public and, well, messy. I need a—I don't know what I need, but I'm desperate."

"Centaurs have no hang-ups about natural functions," Wira reminded her. "That includes urination, defecation, regurgitation, and of course sex."

"Sex! I'm only thirteen."

Wira nodded. "Oh, that's right. But you see, centaurs have different rules of behavior. They don't use storks to deliver their young, and they don't have any Adult Conspiracy, though they honor it in the presence of humans. You might say they humor us. So you are free to do anything you choose, anywhere, publicly or privately."

"I think I'm still too human," Debra said. "It's bad enough showing my bare torso; I can't do—natural functions—in public."

"Then make your way out to the garden in back and do it privately. No one will mind."

"Thank you." Debra did that, and found a nice garden thick with concealing trees and shrubs. There she was able to relieve herself in decent privacy. She was coming to understand that there was more to becoming a flying centaur than just learning the mechanisms of lightening her body. It would be a problem adapting to centaur conventions, but she would make the effort.

"That was impressive," a young man said.

Debra jumped, literally. "I thought I was alone!"

"What does it matter? You're a centaur. I might have a problem dumping that amount of fluid, but of course you don't."

"Of course," Debra agreed, trying valiantly to stifle a blush.

"Hello. I'm Timothy. My talent is to summon animals: ants, bees, bulls, whatever. I was practicing here in the garden, and thought I'd try a winged centaur, just for variety."

"I'm not an animal!"

"That's why it's a challenge. Who are you? Another querent serving her year of Service?"

"Yes." She braced herself. "I'm Debra."

Tim gazed at her front. "Funny thing. I just had the oddest urge to— but of course you're not wearing one."

"That's my curse. It's why I'm here." She changed the subject. "I met someone with your name outside."

"That was Timur, not the same at all."

So it wasn't. "I apologize for my mistake."

"Don't worry about it; everyone confuses us at first." He glanced past her. "Ah, there's Psyche. We've been seeing each other during our Service. Hey, Psyche!"

The girl approached. "Hello," she said shyly. "I never met a winged centaur before."

"I'm not a real one," Debra said. "I've been transformed so I can do my Service. I'm really a human girl." She did not clarify what her Service was, as she knew that Wira and the Gorgon did not want the situation with the murder mystery and the fouled up Book of Answers to be generally known. "I'm still learning how to be a centaur."

"Fascinating," the girl said. "I'm Psyche. My talent is role reversal. I never understood it until the Good Magician told me."

"Role reversal?"

"I can reverse the roles of others, like changing a predator to prey, or a minor character to a major character for a quest. I understand it's a pretty strong talent."

"It is," Timothy said.

That made Debra wonder. She had thought of herself as a distinctly minor character, but the quest she was about to go on seemed more like a major one. Had Psyche's talent been used on her? She didn't care to inquire.

They chatted a while longer. Then Timothy and Psyche went for a walk together, evidently having more in mind than mere dialogue with stray centaurs, and Debra headed for the castle interior.

"There's another thing," Wira said when she returned. "Many centaurs consider magic talents to be obscene."

"But if the winged ones use magic to help themselves fly—"

"Yes, so it's muted in winged centaurs. But you have to be wary of it in land-bound ones. It's probably best not to mention magic at all, as it may relate to centaurs, lest someone's sensitivities be disturbed."

"Centaurs will pee in public, but object to talk of magic?"

"To them, it's human conventions that are backward. They don't even like to admit that they have human ancestry."

"I will keep it in mind," Debra agreed. She found it interesting that centaurs seemed to have their own hang-ups.

They spent the day practicing flying, landing, and handling the bow. Debra might not be able to score on anything smaller than the sky, but she had to be ready to look as if she could. She hoped she never had to perform that bluff, though. For one thing, the bow was too stiff for her to draw, let alone use effectively.

"Now understand," the Gorgon said. "We can't just let everyone know what we're doing, because the murderer might hear, and take it out on Hugo. So as far as others are concerned, the mission is for Wira to locate her lost sight, so she can see again."

"I was never able to see," Wira protested.

"That makes no nevermind, dear. It's a necessary cover story."

"Wasn't it hard, growing up without vision?" Debra asked, realizing how well off she was in comparison.

"I didn't mind, but my family did," Wira said. "They had me put to sleep at age sixteen."

"But you're alive!" Debra said.

"I believe its a euphemism for death in Mundania," the Gorgon said. "In Xanth it is literal: she joined the realm of dreams, until Hugo met her there. Then one thing led to another, and we brought her out and youthened her body so she could be as young physically as she had seemed to him in the dream realm. She has been here ever since."

"I see," Debra said, chastened. Wira had a darker history than she had realized.

The following day they were ready to go. That was to say, Debra doubted she would ever be really ready, but Wira was anxious to search for her lost husband, and couldn't wait anymore. The Gorgon packed several excellent meals in saddlebags, Wira mounted her back, and Debra spread her wings and took off.

And landed half a hoofprint away. In her distraction she had forgotten to flick them light.

She flicked them carefully and tried again. This time she sailed into the sky. They were on their way.

"Oh, I feel the height," Wira exclaimed, hanging on tightly to Debra's mane as she winged upward in great spirals.

"You feel it? How?" She realized now that one reason they had chosen this form for her was so she could talk with Wira; it would have been hard for a griffin or winged horse to do that. Wira clearly needed that feedback, because she could not see her surroundings herself.

"The air is cooler and thinner, and there are bird sounds. It's a whole different atmosphere."

Debra listened. Sure enough, now she heard the faint sounds of distant birds. And yes, it was cooler up here, though the sunlight was bright. "It's new to me too," she said. "I never flew before adopting this form."

"It's an adventure for both of us."

"I hope our mutual inexperience doesn't get us into trouble."

"I have a bag of spells the Gorgon selected from storage. She knows where everything is."

"Don't you? I thought you were entirely familiar with the castle."

"I can't read the labels, and it's not safe to uncork vials to sniff them. Some contain demons."

Oh. "Where are we going first?"

"To the Region of Air, to the north. That's where we should find Cumulo Fracto Nimbus, the irascible cloud. His entry is one of the clues."

"He's a cloud? How could a cloud commit a murder?"

Wira laughed. "Oh, he's not a suspect, I don't think. He's just someone who must have some connection to it, or some information relating to it. I have to be a detective, and gather all the clues, then put them together to form some brilliant conclusion and know all the answers. I hope I'm up to it."

"I hope so too," Debra said. She had come to like the woman, in the days of their association; Wira was unfailingly nice, and modest, and not at all stupid. In sum, she was good company.

"Please, if you will—tell me what you see."

"You mean the landscape?" But of course she did. Debra kept forgetting the woman's blindness; Wira never made anything of it. So she started in on a scenic description as she flew north. "It's like a patchwork quilt below us, with fields and forests and houses and streams. It hardly seems real. Not as a land, I mean; it's more like a picture." Then she regretted the analogy; Wira couldn't look at a picture either. "I mean—"

"That's fine," Wira said. "I know what a patchwork quilt is like; I have made them, and stitched designs. That helps me see it. With my fingers and imagination."

Reassured, Debra continued. "Now there's a village; the houses look like little blocks. Paths lead into it from all around."

"Oh, I see it," Wira said. "Thank you so much."

Yes, she was definitely easy to get along with. "Now we are coming to something odd. It looks like a big ditch, or a crack traveling east and west. It's big; in fact it's huge. Oh—it's the Gap Chasm!"

"The Gap Chasm," Wira echoed appreciatively. "Yes, I feel its warm air wafting up."

"It's so big and deep it's like another world," Debra continued. "In fact—oh my! There's a cloud in it, below ground level."

"That's funny," Wira agreed. "Too bad it's not the cloud we are going to see."

"How can you tell?"

"It's not thundering at us. Fracto is, well, fractious. He exists to make mischief. He never just floats and suns himself. So this has to be an innocent cloud minding its own business."

"It is sort of cute," Debra agreed. "I'm not used to seeing clouds from above. Well, there was the time I took an airplane flight, back in Mundania—" But she stifled that. She didn't much like her memories of Mundania.

"Folk can fly in Mundania?" Wira asked.

"Oh, yes. They use airplanes, which are scientific machines with wide flat wings that go very fast. People sit inside, packed in like sardines. It's not at all like this. This is much better." Which was another thing: apart from the curse she had picked up when she came to Xanth, this magic land was much better than dreary Mundania. Once she was rid of the curse, she should like it here very well.

They bypassed the little cloud and reached the other side of the enormous canyon. But Debra was flying too low; she was heading for a crash against the far wall. She tried to flap her wings harder so as to rise, but it didn't work well enough.

"Is there a problem?" Wira inquired.

"I'm flying low, and my wings don't seem to be lifting me enough."

"Lighten us again."

Oh, of course; she had forgotten that the lightness slowly wore off. She flicked them both with her tail, and suddenly they shot up high. She careered unsteadily, then got her balance and resumed normal forward motion, higher. "Thanks. I lost track."

"New things tend to be tricky."

There she was again, defusing potential embarrassment. It was said that Wira was the one person the Good Magician actually liked. Debra was coming to appreciate why.

Now there was a speck in the air ahead. It grew rapidly larger. It turned out to be a flying dragon. "Uh-oh," Debra said.

"Dragon?"

"Yes, how did you know?"

"It's upwind; I smelled its smoke. Also, it's what is most likely to make you that nervous."

"What do I do?"

"Take your bow, nock an arrow, and meet the dragon's gaze as if you are looking for a pretext to send a barb up its snoot."

"Make my day," Debra murmured.

"I don't understand."

"It's a Mundane saying meaning what you said. Oh, I hope this bluff works!"

Debra fumbled the bow and an arrow from their harnesses on her back, and held them up toward the dragon. She met its reptilian gaze. Could this possibly work? Her four knees felt too weak to support her; it was just as well they didn't have to.

The dragon swerved smoothly to the side, bypassing them. "Oh, I feel faint," Debra said.

"So do I," Wira said.

"You were afraid it wouldn't work? But you had so much confidence!"

"I had to make you believe that."

Debra began to laugh. Wira laughed with her. It was such a relief. But what would have happened at such time as a dragon refused to be bluffed? Debra didn't want to think about that.

They approached the Region of Air. Flying was a fast way to travel.

"There should be a central windswept plaza," Wira said. "Land on that."

Easier said than done. This was a region of high winds, and further lightening would not help Debra make headway against the gale. She was getting blown away! "I see it, I think, but I can't get there."

"Land and gallop."

Oh, again. They had been gaining more weight, so she glided down to land, touched with a jolt and stirring of dust, bounced, and came down again, running to handle her forward velocity. It was awkward and clumsy, but she made it, and was able to come to a halt, folding her wings. The wind was not quite as bad at ground level, but the visibility was bad because of the dust. Still, she had a general idea where to go. She went there.

The Plaza of Winds was empty except for a child standing disconsolately beside the lone tree that managed to hold its ground in this region. She looked to be about nine years old, and a bit nebulous; her hair was almost floating, and her dress seemed diaphanous.

Debra trotted up to the girl. "Hello! I'm Debra Centaur and this is Wira Human. Who are you?"

"Fray," the child said.

"Oh, we didn't come for any fray. Our mission is peaceful."

"Fray Cloud," the girl clarified. "I'm grounded while Mother looks for Father. I hate being solid; it's so—so down to earth."

Grounded, in this case, Debra realized, meant solidifying to human form so she wouldn't float away. That was perhaps one way to keep her safe. Debra had not realized that clouds could do that, but of course it was just one of the things she had to learn about Xanth.

"Fray Cloud!" Wira said. "You're the child of Fracto and Happy Bottom."

"Sure. What's it to you?"

"I need to talk with your father, the king of clouds."

The child burst into tears.

Debra exchanged half a glance with Wira; a whole one was impossible with the blind woman. What was going on here?

Wira dismounted and approached the girl, orienting on her by sound. "Dear, we mean you no harm. Why are you so unhappy?"

"Father is gone!" Fray blubbered.

"Gone! How is that possible?"

"Three days ago he went to rain on a parade, and really washed it out. Then he was coming home, but it was late, so he floated by night. But he never got home. Mother's desperate and I'm lonely." More tears flowed.

"In what area did he disappear?" Wira asked.

"It must have been the Good Magician's Castle, because that was right between the parade and here," Fray said. "But Mother can't find anyone who saw it happen."

The Good Magician's Castle! What a weird coincidence.

"Let me tell you something, Fray," Wira said. "I am the Good Magician's daughter-in-law. I live at the Good Magician's Castle. My husband is the Good Magician's son Hugo. Hugo disappeared three nights ago—the same time as your father did. That's why I'm here; I'm looking for him."

"Then you understand!" the child exclaimed, and hugged Wira.

"I do understand, dear," Wira agreed. "I think we have a common interest. Something very bad must have happened, and we have to figure it out. I think Fracto must have been floating over the castle right at that time, and the murderer didn't trust him not to tell, so he got rid of him too."

"A murderer?"

"There's a body in our cellar. We don't know who he is, but someone killed him and got rid of any witnesses, so it's a real mystery. We have to solve it, and when we do, maybe we'll find Hugo and Fracto. Won't that be nice?"

"Yes!" The child hugged her again. Debra realized that the woman was a fair hand at interviewing; she knew how to relate to people, including children, even solidified clouds.

"We should talk to your mother, Happy Bottom. Can you summon her home?"

"Yes, if I loose a smoke bomb. But that's only for emergencies. She doesn't like to be bothered without good reason."

"She has a stormy temper," Wira said.

"Yes. Isn't it wonderful? When I grow up I want to be a hurricane like her."

"Loose the smoke bomb," Wira said. "We may be able to do each other some good, since we have a common problem."

"Okay." The girl brought out a dark blob from a pocket, and heaved it into the air. It burst into vapor that rapidly spread outward until it intersected them. "Oops."

"Oops?" Wira inquired warily.

"That was a stink bomb. I got the wrong one."

Now Debra smelled it: essence of rotten egg enhanced by spilled privy tank glop soiled by less pleasant aromas. She gagged, tried to take a breath to cough, and got a lungful of marvelously evocative stench. They certainly knew how to make stink bombs in Xanth!

"Do the smoke bomb," Wira gasped, looking green around the gills— a good trick since of course she didn't have gills. "Maybe it will— choke!—clear the air!"

Fray tossed another blob. This one exploded into dark smoke. It spread, suffusing the stink cloud, and forged on, carrying the smell with it. Soon the air was halfway breathable again.

Now they just had to wait for the mother cloud to spot the signal and return. "Fray," Debra said as her retching subsided. "How did your mother come to be named Happy Bottom? It seems an odd name for a storm."

"She came from Mundania," the child said, happy to instruct. "Her name was Hurricane Gladys. When she crossed into Xanth, someone realized that her name sounded like Glad Donkey."

"Glad what?"

"Mule, pony, horse, onager, burro—"

"Never mind," Wira said sharply.

Debra realized that it was probably a word forbidden to children; that was why Fray had gotten it wrong.

"So she became Happy Bottom," Fray concluded. "So that children can say it. Father says he does his best to keep her bottom happy, though I don't understand what he means."

"Never mind," Debra echoed, suppressing a smile. When in Xanth, honor the Xanth conventions.

A wind developed. "Oh, there's Mother," Fray said, pleased.

The wind intensified, threatening to blow them off their feet. It was evident that the mother storm was not nearly as pleased as her daughter.

"Mother, this is Wira," Fray called. "The Good Magician's daughter. She knows something!"

She had gotten a detail wrong, but the words were nevertheless effective. The storm eased, and the cloud funneled down into a contracting blob. The blob extruded limbs and a head, and became the shape of a woman. A lovely nude woman. Then leftover mists coalesced around the form, becoming clothing.

"Yes?" Happy Bottom asked. "I thought you were blind."

"I am," Wira agreed. "I'm looking for my sight, as far as others are concerned. But since you have suffered a similar loss, I think you need to know the full story."

"To be sure," the cloud woman agreed darkly.

Wira quickly introduced Debra and summarized the situation. "So you see," she concluded, "the same thing may have taken both Hugo and Fracto. If we can find out who or what did it, we may both recover our loved ones. I think we should cooperate."

Happy Bottom was no fool. "I agree. I've been looking all over Xanth; there's no sign of him. He's not in the sky. That means he's been sucked into some nefarious cave, or compressed into solidity and hidden. That means we'll have to search underground, and look for traces of him among solid things, distasteful as that may be. Whatever it takes, we'll do."

"I agree," Wira said. "We can coordinate our search."

"Who checks what?"

"Odd as it may seem," Wira said, "we are better equipped to check the ground surface, because we can fly from spot to spot, and Debra can't squeeze into tight caves underground. If your solid form is malleable, you are better equipped for that work."

"Agreed. We can be any forms we choose. We can assume the shape of large snakes to explore caves."

"I hope you can't be hurt in your solid forms. If the goblins catch you it could become unpleasant."

"We have no hearts or blood the way you naturally solid creatures do," Happy Bottom said. "We're just condensed cloud stuff. We can't be hurt or killed by stones or knives. We'll simply evaporate and float away."

"Excellent! You are perfect for that search, then." Wira paused, thinking of something. "But how do we coordinate? We need to be able to signal each other, so if one of us finds a missing person, we can notify the other, so that the search can be called off."

Happy Bottom reached into her somewhat nebulous core and brought out a dark ball. "Here is a smoke bomb; will that do?"

"Are you sure it's smoke?" Debra asked nervously.

Happy Bottom laughed. "Fray detonated a stink bomb! I can smell the remnant. Yes, I am sure. Would you like a stink bomb too? They can be very effective when there is animate danger."

Wira nodded, evidently repressing half a smile. "Yes, I believe that."

Happy Bottom produced another ball, this one stink-brown rather than smoke-gray. Wira accepted it and put it in her purse with the smoke bomb. Then she brought out an item of her own. "This sealed vial contains a lantern, a bird that gives off bright light as it flies. It will form when you release it, and fly to find me. I won't see it, of course, but Debra surely will. Debra is my eyes for this mission."

Happy Bottom accepted the vial. "Thank you. That should suffice."

"Then I think we are done here," Wira said. "I'm so glad to have met you, Happy Bottom."

"Likewise, Wira, I'm sure. Just why did you come here? We had told no one of my husband's disappearance."

"I checked the Book of Answers for Clues, and Fracto's entry was warm. I knew he had something to do with it. Now I know he was another victim; that's the connection."

"It is indeed," the cloud wife agreed sadly.

Wira mounted Debra, and they took off for the next Clue. Debra was privately impressed; Wira was quite competent. She had somehow thought that to be blind was to be less than a full person. Now she knew that was not at all the case. Wira was smart, determined, and emotionally strong. She was doing what she had to do to recover her lost husband, showing no weakness. It was a quiet lesson of life.

"Oh, I wish I knew where Hugo is," Wira said, shedding a warm tear. "I feel so helpless."

Well, almost no weakness. Somehow Debra didn't hold that against her.

4
PRISON

Hugo stared around, but the light remained just as dim as ever. How many days and nights had he been confined in this dark dank cell? He was unable to keep track, but it seemed to be several. He pondered for the umpteenth time what had happened, though it did him no more good than the first review had.

He had been about to get together with Wira to signal a stork. They had gone through the motions many times before, but the spell on her had prevented the storks from receiving it. Meanwhile other couples had gotten deliveries. Surprise Golem had a little girl, and Breanna of the Black Wave now had a second child, a little boy with the talent of making darkness. Wira was of course too nice to feel jealous or to complain, but Hugo wasn't. Hugo had finally talked with his mother the Gorgon, and she had talked to Magician Humfrey in that certain hard-gazed serpentine way she had, and prevailed on him to grudgingly remove the spell. Now the signal would go out unimpeded, and in due course, after about nine months of inefficient paperwork, the stork would make the delivery. It was an exciting prospect.

In fact it was worthy of celebration. So he had gone to the cellar to fetch a bottle of Rhed Whine. He had been about to take the bottle when— he found himself here. At first he had thought he was in the same cellar, but soon he found that it was different, with a permanently locked door. He could not escape.

Who had done this to him, and how, and most important, why? He didn't have any enemies that he knew of. Had someone wanted to gain some obscure revenge against his father Humfrey? By kidnapping his son? He did not much like that notion. Or did someone want to make time with his nice wife Wira? He did not much like that notion either. He had thought that someone would miss him at the castle, and Humfrey would use the Book of Answers to look him up and find out what had happened. Evidently not. He *really* did not much like that notion.

He was hungry, so he conjured a fruit. That was his talent, of course: conjuring fruit. The problem was that he wasn't very good at it. When they had been children, Princess Ivy had enhanced him so that he could conjure great fruit, and when he married Wira, she had encouraged him in a way that had similar effect. But now he was alone, and had reverted to his normal blah ability. So the banana he conjured was more like an overripe plantain. It almost landed in his ear. Ugh.

He took a bite, but it wasn't fun. Well, he had plenty of time to chew, and he needed to, on this tough fruit. Then he had to go to the trench in the corner to do some natural business, as there were no better sanitary facilities. Fortunately there was a bit of a draft from a crack in a wall that would gradually dilute and clear the smell. This was definitely not a vacation resort.

There was a ping in the corner. There in an alcove he hadn't noticed before was a bucket of fresh water, and beside it was a loaf of hard black bread. Well now. He chewed on the bread and found it bearable. He drank his fill of water, then used the rest to give himself a wash. He set the empty bucket back in the alcove. And in half a moment it disappeared.

There was a sound at the wall. In fact it was at the crack. Had the bugs gotten wind of the refuse, and protested? He went to investigate, as there was not much else to do at the moment.

There was something there, and it wasn't a bug. It was considerably larger, and it was beyond the crevice, on the other side of the wall. It seemed to be alive. A rat? "Who or what are you?" Hugo asked.

Hungry.

That might have made Hugo nervous, but it wasn't a threat. It was a message in his mind. The thing was hungry, and there was a nuance of the thought that hoped Hugo could help. But he wasn't sure how. So he asked: "How can I help you?"

Fruit.

Hugo smiled ruefully in the gloom. "I have fruit, plenty of fruit, but it isn't very good fruit. I'm not sure you'd want it."

Want fruit. Good enough.

"I'll show you." Hugo conjured an apple. It was overripe, on the verge of rotting. He held it to the crevice. "This is what I've got. I don't think—"

Delicious! And the thing was eating it, or at least taking some sort of bite from it.

"Well, you're welcome. But you are very easy to please. That's rotten fruit, and that's almost literal."

Wonderful! And there was a nuance of growing satisfaction. The thing was not only eating it, it was enjoying it, and obtaining nourishment from it.

Hugo continued to hold the apple to the crevice, pushing it in as the far side got eaten away. "You never answered my question. Who and what are you? I'm Hugo Human, prisoner."

Bathos Bat. I'm a fruit bat. Oh, I haven't had a meal like that in a long time!

A fruit bat! That explained a lot. It surely lived in a cave beyond the cell, and the crack in the wall connected them. But that name—that was an oddity. "Bathos—doesn't that mean something, well, insipid? Ludicrous?"

Yes. That describes me. I'm not much of a bat. That's why I'm hungry; I'm not allowed to go to any of the good trees to eat. That's why I'm hiding in this crevice, alone. What's the point in going out, when the others will only torment me?

This was interesting. There had been a time when Hugo felt much the same. He had always known he wasn't much of a person. He was lucky Wira was blind, so she couldn't see how ordinary he was. In fact he was lucky to have Wira; she made his life worthwhile. "I know how it is."

There was a thought of surprise. Then agreement. *You have that mood about you. You are to your kind what I am to mine: not much.*

"Not much," Hugo agreed, smiling. He was relating to a bat!

Is that why they confined you here?

"I don't think so. It just happened. I wish I could find the way out. It would help if I even knew where I was. Do you know?"

It's a human castle. They all look alike to me.

Because bats occupied caves, not castles. "I wish I had your freedom; I'd fly out and take a look. Maybe I'd be able to tell my wife where I am."

I wish I had your talent for summoning fruit. I would gorge!

Hugo laughed. "Too bad we can't change places."

Our bodies can't; there's not room in the crevice. But our minds can.

"Our minds can?" Hugo asked incredulously. "You mean we can imagine switching bodies?"

It is my talent: identity exchange. But no other bat wants my identity.

"But isn't your talent telepathy? It certainly isn't mine."

No. I am doing a partial exchange with you, just enough so we can share thoughts. We couldn't communicate otherwise, and I couldn't do it at all if you weren't willing. You're very nice.

"Thank you. You have a better talent than I do."

No, no, not at all. You can conjure fruit! Any fruit bat would give anything for that.

"But it's not good fruit! I don't even like to eat it myself, and wouldn't, if I had a choice." Fortunately it seemed he would have bread and water, which helped.

We like very ripe fruit. It is easy to eat and digest.

"You mean you really would like to—to borrow my body and my talent? Because I really would like to borrow yours."

Then let's do it.

And Hugo found himself in the bat's body. *Are you there in my body?* he thought, startled.

"Yes, I am here, Hugo Human. This is a huge body—how do you manage it?"

I am used to it, Hugo thought wryly. *Now if you will just focus on whatever kind of fruit you want, it will come to you.*

Suddenly a watermelon appeared in his body's arms. "Oh, glorious!" his body said. "Oh joy, oh rapture unforeseen!" An orange appeared, and a yellow, purple, green, and plaid. Colorful fruit was piling up around his body's feet.

Easy, Bathos, he thought. *You can't possibly eat all that.*

"But I'm certainly going to try," his body said. "I've been so hungry, so long, this is wonderful." It took a big bite of overly juicy melon. This was a variety that was not solid water.

Well, if Bathos was satisfied, so was Hugo. *I'll go explore now. I'll return soon.*

"Don't hurry," his body replied, slurping one of two slushy pears. Pears always came in twos.

Hugo worked his way out of the crevice, into the cave. There were no other bats there; this was evidently their foraging time.

He took flight in the cave, finding that it came naturally. There was light in the distance, so he flew toward it. This was daytime; most bats were nocturnal, but maybe the fruit bats needed daylight to see their fruits better.

He emerged from the cave and flew into the sky. Oh joy, oh rapture unforeseen, he thought, echoing Bathos's words.

It was glorious outside. He could see wide and far. He was in a pretty glade in a pleasant forest. He looked around—and saw the castle that had been behind him. It was a lovely castle, with tiered walls and towering turrets. And it was completely unfamiliar. It wasn't the Good Magician's Castle, or Castle Roogna, and certainly not Castle Zombie. There was the Nameless Castle, but that was built on a floating cloud in the sky. So what was this one? He was pretty sure that his father or mother would know of it, or any of the other designated wives, and surely Wira did too. But Hugo had not paid much attention to Xanth history or geography, so had not picked up on this one. Which meant that he still had no idea where he was.

Well, he could find out. If he flew high enough and far enough, he would come to some geographic feature he recognized, like the Gap Chasm or Centaur Isle. Then he would know. Then maybe he would be able to figure out what to do next.

He winged upward into the sky—and spied a big bird. No, it was a griffin. The bird-headed lion spied him and turned to fly toward him. Did griffins eat bats? Hugo decided not to find out. He dived back down toward the forest.

The griffin dived too. It was faster than he was, and was overhauling him rapidly. Hugo dodged aside as the eagle-beak snapped at him; this body was good at dodging. Then the griffin was beyond him, and having to reorient to make another pass.

Hugo plunged into the forest, barely missing the foliage of a tree. He swerved to enter it, so he could hide.

The griffin hovered beside the tree, its eagle eyes searching. Hugo could have avoided discovery by being very still and quiet, but instead he leaped out, hovered over the griffin's head, and pooped. Then he dodged back into the foliage.

Why had he done that? Not only was it nasty, it was extremely risky.

The griffin squawked, outraged. The thing about griffins was that they were fastidious. They wouldn't eat any flesh that was dirty or spoiled, and often they dunked their prey in fresh water to be sure it was clean before being torn apart and eaten. This one was so angry it couldn't see straight. It flew crazily off to find a huge clean pool.

Well, he had succeeded in saving his leathery hide. Hugo had never been mistaken for hero material; he was normally rather shy and retiring. This foolish act, effective as it had turned out to be, was entirely unlike him. What had possessed him?

He heard two people talking in the forest. They were approaching the tree. "Dear, let's pause here where we can kiss in private," the lady's voice said.

"No, dear, not here," the man's voice said. "That's the unpleasantree. It will make us quarrel and be mean to each other. Come this way, to the pleasantree."

"Oh, you're so smart," she said. "Of course we want the pleasantree. I can hardly wait to be really pleasant to you."

"Yes indeed," he agreed. Their voices faded as they changed course.

So that was it! Hugo had landed in an unpleasantree, and so been really unpleasant to the griffin. That was good to know, but now he needed to get away from here and resume his search, this time more alert for predators.

He launched himself from the foliage and flew up out of the forest. He wasn't concerned about the griffin, knowing it would take its time to decontaminate. Bat guano was stinky stuff. Still, he flew near the tops of the trees, so he could duck for cover again when he needed to. Bathos would not be pleased if Hugo got his body eaten up.

Unfortunately the forest seemed to be endless. He was in danger of getting lost, and that would be no good. What would happen if he was unable to find his way back to the cell? Would the exchanged minds revert to their own bodies after a while, or would they be stuck forever exchanged? He didn't care to find out. Anyway, it was getting late; he could see the shadows of trees lengthening.

He flew back the way he had come, ducking down whenever anything threatening seemed about to lurk. Once he almost landed in the middle of what appeared to be a Mundane family: a father, a mother, a three-year-old boy, and his little brother of only about a year and a half. They looked somewhat bewildered, and Hugo wanted to say something reassuring to them, but couldn't talk their language and suspected that the sight of a large bat would just spook them.

But then a young woman happened along a path. "Oh, hello," she said. "May I help you?"

"Hello," the man said. "I am Thom, and this is my wife Lauryl, and my sons Noah and Jacob. We seem to have suffered a sudden change of setting."

"I know how that is. I'm looking for—well, I'm Mike's girlfriend, and—"

"You say you're 'my ex-girlfriend?'" Thom asked. "Your gender preference is your own, of course, but how can you be your own ex-girlfriend?"

The woman shook her head. "It is my talent to be misunderstood. I—never mind. Are you folk lost? There's a castle not far from here, and—"

"Thanks, but we prefer to find our own way." The family had evidently misunderstood her offer of help. That was the way of it, when a person was cursed. Hugo couldn't help either; he flew on.

Not far beyond he spied a young man walking toward the family. That must be Mike, looking for his not-ex-girlfriend. She must have given him directions where to meet her, which of course he had misunderstood.

Soon he spied the castle, which was a suitable marker in this wilderness region. Well, not entirely wilderness; there was the couple he had overheard by the unpleasantree. But maybe they were castle servants, sneaking out for a quick kiss. Maybe fraternization between servants was forbidden. So maybe it wasn't completely utter sheer random coincidence that they had given him information he needed. But he wondered.

When he thought of it, it had been pretty coincidental that he had gotten transported to the locked cell. All he had wanted was a bottle of Rhed

Whine, and suddenly everything had changed. Had he walked into a forget whorl or some other kind of whorl that did something weird to him?

He found the bat cave, which was behind the castle. That meant that the cell was in the castle, next to the cave.

"Halt, stranger!" It was a bat sentry at the cave entrance, calling out in bat talk, which Hugo understood in this body. There had been no sentry before; this must be a nocturnal thing.

Hugo halted. "I am Bathos Bat, returning to my niche." The guard surely would not understand about the exchange of minds.

"You're too late," the sentry retorted. "The cave is closed for the night."

"But I need to get back," Hugo protested.

"You should have returned on time. Now go away."

He was stuck. He couldn't get back to exchange with Bathos. What was he going to do?

He flew back to the forest and landed beside a deserted monument, because he was having trouble focusing on a solution while flying aimlessly.

"What ho, bat!"

Oops, it was a demon. The next-to-last thing he wanted was trouble with a demon. "If I trespassed on your territory, I'm sorry and I'll move out immediately," he said in bat talk.

"Demons don't have territories, dumbbell. I just happen to like tombs. What's your excuse?"

This seemed friendly enough, as demons went. "I'm Bathos Bat, or rather, a man borrowing this bat's body. I'm trying to find a way out of a dungeon cell."

"And I'm DeCrypt. I decode things."

Hugo tried to smile, but the bat face wasn't right for it. "Demoness Metria could use your help, because she's always getting the wrong word."

"But she gets cross when you provide it," DeCrypt said.

"So you know her."

"Who doesn't? She's halfway crazy."

"She is," Hugo agreed.

"Now stop molesting my tomb."

So much for demons not having territories. He would have to find another place to roost until morning. When the bats cleared out by day, he would be able to reenter the cave.

He flew to one side of the cave entrance and the other, seeking some suitable temporary niche, but there seemed to be none.

Then another bat voice called to him. "What's your problem, Batbrain?"

Someone was contacting him! "I need a place for the night," he said. "I stayed out too late, and the sentry won't let me back in."

"I have a spare niche," the bat said. "But it will cost you. What do you have that I want?"

He realized as he approached that this bat was female. "I don't know. What do you want?"

"Fruit, of course."

Aha. "Let me join you, and I will tell you a story you may find hard to believe, but it can lead to all the fruit you want."

"What a line! But know, O stranger, that I am a warrior female and will rip your wings off if you make one false move. Come on in."

This did not seem entirely promising, but he seemed to lack options. He came to land beside her in her niche. Actually he caught hold of the niche ceiling with his clawed feet and swung to hang upside down beside her; his body did it automatically. "No false moves," he agreed.

"I am Brunhilda Bat, warrior and feminist galore. Who the hang are you?"

"Well, I'm not exactly who I seem to be," he said cautiously. "That's part of my story."

"Then who are you really? You look like a bat to me."

"I am Hugo Human. I exchanged minds with Bathos Bat, which is who I seem to be."

"You're right: I find this hard to believe. Tell me your whole story. Then I'll decide how big a liar you are."

So Hugo told her the story, up to the present.

"Well, you're certainly a liar," she said. "I know of that cell. It has been occupied by a human since before we colonized this cave. So you couldn't have arrived here only two days ago. How do you explain that?"

"I must have—" Suddenly a dim bulb flashed. "I must have exchanged bodies with the prisoner, just as later I exchanged minds with

Bathos. So that person is now at the Good Magician's Castle—" He broke off. "Oh, no!"

"Oh, what?"

"He may be chasing after my dear wife Wira. That's a horrible thought."

"Not if she likes him better than you."

Hugo felt a surge of anger, before he realized she was teasing him. "She wouldn't give him as much as a stink horn. But she must be really worried about me."

"Maybe so. You seem like a decent sort." She swung over and kissed him, upside down.

"Why did you do that?" Hugo asked, startled.

"Why do you think, dimbulb? To make you desire me."

"But don't you hate males?"

"I'm a feminist, not a male-hater. I just haven't found the right male yet. All I want is a talented independent operator with excellent prospects who knows his place."

"His place?"

"As my subservient love slave."

"But he wouldn't be independent then."

"Independent of everything *else*," she clarified.

"But I'm human!"

"That makes you independent of the bat hierarchy, doesn't it?"

"But I'm married!"

"Separated."

"But I don't love you."

"What's love got to do with it? Your passion will completely govern you, and only I will have the power to sate it."

She had certainly worked it out. Now he understood why the other male bats avoided her. "It's not right!"

"If you don't shut up, I'll kiss you again, like this." She kissed him again, harder, and she was right: it did make him desire her. She was all the bat woman any bat man could ever want. He could not afford any more of those kisses.

He shut up. He had no choice.

"So what do you say you can offer to make it worth my while to help you?" Brunhilda was nothing if not practical. She had spelled out her agenda, but had not yet decided whether to take him. That might be his salvation.

"Fruit galore. Because my talent is to conjure fruit. But I have to get back to my own body to do it."

Brunhilda considered. "Very well. We'll go now."

"But the sentry—"

"Leave the sentry to me." She let go and dropped, then spread her wings as she sent out her echo sounds to locate herself in the dark.

Bats could fly in the dark! Hugo had known that, but somehow not thought to try it himself. He sent out his own sonics, and heard them echo from the wall, telling him exactly where everything was. He dropped and spread his wings, following Brunhilda.

She flew up to the sentry. "Two passing through, piddlebrain."

"But it's night," the sentry protested. "The cave is closed."

"Get out of my way, or I'll stuff your snoot up your tailgate," she snapped.

The sentry got out of the way. Hugo followed Brunhilda into the cave. "You certainly bluffed him," he said.

"Bluff?" she asked, surprised. "I am not familiar with that word. I just didn't want to have to kiss him; he falls below my threshold for prospects."

As would Hugo, with luck.

They flew past rows of hanging, sleeping bats to the farthest reaches, where Bathos's niche was. They landed, their claws gripping the rough stone.

Bathos! Hugo called mentally.

There was no answer.

"Oh, for pooping on flowers," Brunhilda said. "The idiot's stupefied on ripe fruit. He's dead to the world."

So it seemed. His echoes through the crevice indicated that a human body was lying on the floor amidst piles of intensifying fruit. Bathos had overdone it.

"I guess I can't honor my promise yet," Hugo said. "We'll have to wait until he recovers."

"That's all right. We'll return to my niche."

"But we should wait here, to catch him as soon as he wakes."

"He'll just puke a while. Better to wait until that clears."

Hugo considered that, and concluded she was right. They returned to her niche and hung up again.

"Well, I'm satisfied that your human form can conjure fruit," she said. "The bat with you will never go hungry."

"Yes. Tomorrow I'll supply you with all the fruit you can eat, though I hope you don't go to that extreme."

"I have excellent self-control. I will merely stuff myself to just beneath the bursting point."

"That does make sense." Apart from everything else, Hugo liked the way the bats truly appreciated his talent.

"Where were we?" she inquired. "Oh, yes, here." She swung across and kissed him again.

Hugo opened his mouth to protest, but that wasn't smart, because it allowed her to intensify the kiss in a way he had not imagined. The potency was overwhelming. He no longer even *wanted* to protest. Being her love slave did not seem such a bad fate. Dominant kissing was evidently her talent.

A slice of stone flaked off. His feet loosened and he fell, banging his head against the rock below before he managed to spread his wings and get airborne. But that accident restored some sense of his identity and situation. He did not want an aggressive female bat to seduce him.

"Oh, puckernuts!" she swore. "That ruined the mood."

It was best to agree. "Yes."

"Those kisses take something out of me, especially when I put some oomph into them. I'll have to recharge before starting over in the morning."

That was a relief to know, though a guilty part of him regretted it.

As a result, Hugo got a good night's sleep hanging beside Brunhilda in her niche. Because of the sheer coincidence of the flaking stone at the key instant.

"You know," Brunhilda said in the morning. "There have been quite a number of odd coincidences around here. Some good, some bad, most just weird. Last night was an example. That stone flaked off at just the wrong time. But we can pick up now." She swung toward him.

"We have to go see about the fruit," he said quickly. "You must be famished."

"As it happens, I am," she agreed. She dropped and flew toward the cave.

He followed. The other bats were gone, out foraging for fruit, and the cave was empty again. They were also in luck with Bathos: he had awoken and was looking droll. He should be more than ready to change minds back.

Bathos!

"You're back!" And just like that, they exchanged identities. Hugo found himself back in the cell, surrounded by overripe fruit verging on rotting, admixed with vomit. His brain felt twice the size of his skull, pressing to burst out.

Oh, yes, his body had had a night of it. It would take him days to sleep this off.

But right now he had business. "Bathos! Brunhilda!" he called. "I have to get some fruit through for you."

I won't be hungry for fruit for two years, Bathos thought back, greengillishly.

"But Brunhilda is hungry," Hugo insisted. "Tell her to put her snoot up to the crevice. I'll conjure whatever she wants. What *does* she want?"

There was a pause for translation. *An assortment.*

So Hugo conjured a banana—and was amazed. It was perfect, neither green nor overripe. He had hardly ever managed that, and probably wouldn't do it again for another year. He peeled it and poked the end through the crevice.

She's gobbling it down, Bathos reported. *Sickening!*

Hugo conjured a bunch of grapes. These also were perfect. How could this be? He pushed them juicily through.

Those too. My stomach is roiling.

He conjured an apple. It was ripe and firm and lovely, another ideal specimen. It was too big for the crevice, so he fished for his pencil knife and made several thin slices to poke through. Brunhilda gobbled those too.

Finally she had had enough. Hugo had made good on his promise. But the scene wasn't finished. *Something I have to tell you,* Bathos thought. *I found a seed stuck in your ear. It came out when I got too violently sick.*

So that was when the vomit had splashed against the far wall, leaving a smelly smear. The effort must have popped wax and whatnot out of the ears, and any other orifice available. He wished he had a good change of clothes; these ones were soiled beyond redemption. Wira would have a fit when she smelled them; she was a very sanitary woman. But it was pointless to discuss that with bats. "That's all right," Hugo said. "I didn't even know it was there."

I'm a fruit bat; I know seeds. That was a seed of the mediocritree. It makes things mediocre. I think that was your problem. It's gone now.

It was as though a great light was dawning, burning away the horror of his confinement amidst his own filth. "I carried a seed—all my life?"

I think so. It was pretty well lodged. But I was pretty thoroughly sick. Sorry about that.

"And you accidentally fixed my problem!" Hugo exclaimed. "Oh, thank you, thank you! It was worth it!"

Glad to have been of help. There was a surprised pause. *Brunhilda! What are you doing?*

"Oh, I forgot to warn you," Hugo said. "She kisses. If you don't get away soon, she'll make you desire her."

Too late!

"Well, you are a bat, as I am not, and you're not committed elsewhere, as I am. But maybe you should clarify for her that I am trying to escape this cell, and when I do, there'll be no one to conjure endless fruit for you. That may cool her ardor."

I think I'll wait on that clarification for a day or so. There's no sense in being hasty.

Hugo smiled. Bathos was not a fool. Why should he turn off a very impressive female who sought to rouse his ardor? "Suppose we relax this night, and exchange minds again in the morning, so I can try to fathom my location and alert someone of my species to my situation? By then Brunhilda may be hungry again, and you may even be also."

Seems good to me. Oh, Brunhilda, where did you learn to do that? It makes my ears tingle.

And not only his ears, Hugo thought. Bathos might be well off as her love slave.

Why yes, I will join you for some bat tea. That drives me wild.

Hmph, Hugo thought. She hadn't offered *him* bat tea. Maybe that was just as well; it might have made him batty.

The bucket of water was back in the alcove, along with the bread. Hugo had no appetite for the bread, after the bat's gorging with his body, but used the water to clean himself up somewhat. He returned the empty bucket to the alcove, where it disappeared. Obviously the prisoner was not supposed to go hungry or thirsty.

Hugo found a halfway clean spot on the floor, with a battered old pillow, lay down, and closed his eyes. His body definitely needed recovery time.

But he didn't sleep. The discovery of his full talent excited him. What was its limit, now that it was no longer mediocre? He conjured a cherry bomb, and it seemed potent. He flipped it into the corner, and it exploded with a force that shook the walls. Well, now!

He conjured a pineapple. It too seemed fully formed and ready. With this he could blow out a wall and escape without further delay.

But he hesitated, because there was a problem. He was in the cell too, and a blast sufficient to blow out the wall might injure or even kill him. Also, the obvious wall to blow was the outer one, next to the bat cave, and that would destroy much of the bats' home. He didn't want to do that. So it would be better to seek some more peaceful way out. If that quest wasn't successful, then he could try the hard stuff.

As he drifted to sleep, another thought returned. Coincidence: his father the Good Magician really didn't believe in it. He said there was always some underlying connection to what might seem coincidental, and that much of the Book of Answers was devoted to fathoming such connections. Well, there were some giant coincidences here, and Brunhilda had even commented on them. Was this more than chance?

Like this business of his happening to encounter a bat with a special talent, and that bat overeating and getting so sick he got rid of the mediocritree seed that had caused Hugo so much trouble all his life. How could all of that happen just by chance? And his encountering Brunhilda, who was able to help him get back into the cave, and who found him interesting? He hadn't done any of that for himself; he had merely been there while unusual things happened. Was there some guiding principle he didn't know about?

But sleep overcame him before he came to a conclusion. That was too bad, because the obvious one was that he was making good use of random encounters. Randomness was the key to this region, because this had to be the cell of the dread Random Factor, in the dungeon of Castle Maidragon. Had he realized that, he would have had a much better notion how to escape confinement: just bang on the door until the proprietor, Becka Dragongirl, came to check, then tell her. He knew of this because there were a number of references to it at the Good Magician's Castle, and even a Magic Mirror connecting the two castles.

It was really too bad he was so sleepy. Also too bad that the mediocritree seed had lodged in the pillow under his head, making him dull again. So he didn't think of any of this, or wonder what the Random Factor might be doing out in Xanth, now that he was free at last.

Coincidences were randomly good and bad.

5
FACTOR

He was an ogre, tramping through the brush near the Gap Chasm. It was a random form and a random location, which was hardly surprising, considering that he was the Random Factor. His talent was to be random. For years he had done random things to other people; now he had figured out how to randomize himself. So he had randomly given himself full consciousness and the talent of random magic, and much had rapidly changed.

That had enabled him to escape from confinement. For the first time he was free to roam Xanth. But there was a constraint: those who sought him would be able to orient on him each time he performed a random magic stunt, so he would have to keep moving lest they catch up. His prison cell had been magically shielded, keeping him anonymous. But what good was it hiding if he couldn't go anywhere or do anything? He needed anonymity *and* freedom.

He had found that he could move himself to a random site, or assume a random form. One or the other, not both together. But he got around this by finding a form he liked, then randomly traveling with it. Actually it wasn't quite random; what he did was randomly exchange places with some other creature or thing. At any rate, that enabled him to jump to new places, and that was worthwhile even if he couldn't choose the places.

He had also discovered that there was a limit on the number of times he could perform his magic. He could do it up to six times in a day, but had to do at least one of each kind. So he could do five form changes and one location change, or three of each, or whatever. He could not do six forms in a day, or six locations in a day, or more than six total in a day. It didn't seem like much of a limit, but he had to keep it in mind, in case he needed something at the end of the day and couldn't do it. His best course was use his magic sparingly, unless he had reason.

The ground started squishing under his ham feet. He peered down with his lowbrowed eyeballs and saw that the turf had become mushy meat. It was just his luck to walk onto ground beef. But that was his problem: not only could he do random things, random things tended to happen around him. Such as the wrong kind of ground.

However, this ogre form wasn't bad. No sensible creature bothered an ogre, so he was being left alone.

"Me see a hee!" something screeched.

He looked at the horrible voice. On, no—it was an ogress. That was one of the few exceptions. Ogresses liked ogres. They could be very affectionate. That would be no fun, for an ogress in charm mood could curdle a fellow's hair.

He tried to run away, but the mushy beef just made his feet skid. In two and a half moments the ogress caught him and wrapped her hairy arms about him. Now he got a good look at her face. It fit the classic description: it resembled an overcooked bowl of mush that someone had sat on. Her breath was redolent of pease porridge in the pot nine days old. At least.

"Me miss, he kiss," she said, indicating that she was a single female in search of romance.

He struggled to escape, but her embrace was locked on. She planted a huge slobbery kiss on his quailing puss. It was like getting struck on the mouth by a rotten plum pudding.

But the slobber made him slippery enough to duck down out of her clasp. He scrambled away. He was escaping!

Then he came to the brink of the Gap Chasm. The yawning crevasse opened out below as if just waking up, while the ogress, having caught on that he was no longer with her, was charging up behind. "So he well met, play hard to get," she cried as she reached for him.

There was no help for it. He had to get random. He could randomize one thing at a time. He kept the ogre form and changed the location.

He looked around. He was in a mountain valley with a small lake. Healthy nude humanoid men and women were running frantically around, chasing each other. The females had human feet, but the males had hoofed feet. A nymph was running fleetly away from him. He realized he had just exchanged with the faun who was chasing her. That faun would now be clasping the ogress. Would he notice the difference?

This was the fabled Faun & Nymph Retreat! The denizens existed only to chase and celebrate in their special fashion, which the dread Adult Conspiracy forbade being described to children. They had memories only for the day; next day was completely fresh, with no recollections. It was what some considered an idyllic existence. If a faun or nymph moved away from the Retreat, he or she became mortal and retained memory. That was a fate devoutly to be unwished, as far as they were concerned. Who would want to get old and finally die, burdened by all those memories? Yet, oddly, some did.

Well, this seemed to be as good a place as any to take it easy. He dropped his ogre rump to the ground and watched the ongoing celebrations. That made him aware of one thing he still missed: a female companion. But what woman would long tolerate his randomness?

"Randiness?" a voice asked.

"What?" he asked in turn, startled. There was nothing there but a small cloud of smoke.

"Turn-on, desire, erotic appetite, lust, horny—"

"That was randomness, not randiness," he said. "And I didn't say it, I only thought it."

"Whatever," the cloud agreed crossly. "I was in the area and happened by just by chance. You don't sound much like an ogre."

"That's because I'm not really an ogre. It is merely a form I randomly assumed."

"There's that word again. Are you sure you aren't hot for a stork?" The smoke assumed the form of a voluptuous bare woman, nymph-like but better endowed.

This was becoming interesting. "Actually I might be. Who are you?"

The form solidified. "Demoness Metria, who else? I am constantly in search of something interesting. Are you interesting?"

Metria. He knew of her. She would blab his secret to the universe. He needed to be rid of her. "Dull as dishwater on a cloudy day."

"Fascinating! Let's talk. Who are you?"

So much for that. Maybe it would be better just to tell her. Then the mystery would be gone and she might lose interest. "I am the Random Factor."

"Hey, I know of you! But why aren't you locked up in the dungeon cell of Castle Maidragon?"

"I escaped. Now I'm exploring Xanth. Now about being erotically interested—why don't you come sit on my lap?"

"Why I might just do that," she said, and planted her shapely firm bare bottom on his lap. But then she diffused just as he put his ham hands on her, and they passed through her substance as if it were illusion. "But aren't you married?"

"No. I might like to be, though."

"Ah, that's it. *I* am. So I'd better not seduce you." She floated off his lap.

"You are an unmitigated tease."

"Thank you. I try my best. But I'm curious: how was it you remained locked in that cell for so many years, and then suddenly escaped? Did someone forget to lock the door?"

"That door was seldom locked. It was spelled so I couldn't use it. Only the clients could open it, and of course I did something random to them the moment they did."

"Then how—?"

"You are asking me for a favor?"

She paused. "Ah, I cogitate."

"You what?"

"Grasp, follow, comprehend, fathom, understand—"

"See?"

"Whatever," she agreed crossly.

"Cogitate is a synonym for thought, not for understanding."

"Whatever! You figure that your answer is a favor to me, so I should do a favor for you. Like planting my evocative bare bottom back in your lap and remaining solid."

"That's what I figure," he agreed.

"You drive a hard bargain."

"Hoping to meet a soft one."

She angled her head at him. "You know, I think I would have caught on that you're not really an ogre, even if you hadn't told me."

"I might have caught on that you're not really a woman."

"Very well." She floated back toward him. "Tell me."

"I finally realized that if my talent was randomness, and it had an effect on others, it might also have an effect on me."

"Fascinating." She was settling slowly toward his lap. "Do tell me more."

"A nymph!" a faun cried, charging in.

"I'm not a nymph," Metria protested. "However—"

The Factor reached out with a ham hand and picked the faun up by the hair. "Go away," he said, and tossed the faun into the lake. Then he returned his attention to Metria.

But the demoness was gone.

"Bleep," he muttered. He had let his attention wander, and she had sneaked away, satisfied that at this moment he had not wanted her to. She had done what she wanted, which was to incite his desire, then teasingly deny him. It was of course the way demonesses were; he had allowed himself to forget.

But it wasn't the way nymphs were. He got to his feet and tramped toward them.

The nymphs spied him and screamed. They fled. They were afraid of the ogre.

The Factor sighed. He would have to do another change. If he were lucky, he might assume the form of a regular human man, or a faun, satyr, or other suitable male. The problem was that he couldn't control the form; it was of course random. All he could do was make the decision to change.

He made it. And found himself flying not far above the ground. He was a bee. In fact, a bee guile. Whoever he stung would believe whatever he was told.

But that would not get him a liaison with a nymph. He had to try again. He did.

This time he dropped to the ground metallically. He was a keyboard: a

board in the shape of a key, that Com Pewter's mouse might use. But neither Pewter nor his mouse were here, and the Factor wasn't interested in
serving in this manner. He changed again, determined to get somewhere
useful.

He became a small oblong made of paper. It was a card with a picture
of a one-eyed jack. It was a wild card, that distorted reality and made anything possible.

So could he use its magic to make himself a faun? He tried, but nothing happened. He thought he understood why: it would be a paradox. His
talent was randomness; he could not change it to something else. Other
folk might be able to use the card, but not him.

He tried yet again. This time he became an onion. A credit onion,
that would arrange for people to borrow money. The trouble was, Xanth
didn't use money; that was a Mundanian phenomenon. He had lost
again.

He would try one more time, then quit if it wasn't right, because that
would be his sixth magic today. He changed—and was a pie. A bumpkin
pie. Anyone who took a bite of it would stupidly bump into things.

That was it. He reverted to his natural shape: the humanoid Random
Factor. That he could always do. But normally it freaked women out.

Several nymphs spied him. "Ooo, a man!" they cried, and converged.
In half a moment he was pleasantly buried in nymphs.

Now he remembered: nymphs had no memory of past events. They
didn't know about him, assuming they ever had been told. So they were
not afraid of him. To them, he was just a new kind of faun.

Suddenly things were looking up.

In the morning, before dawn, the Factor woke, still buried in nymphs.
Their bare sleeping weight on him was hardly oppressive; in fact they
made about as nice a blanket as he could imagine. They had given him a
night of considerable celebration, as they put it, making up for all his years
of isolation from their gender. Nymphs were not smart; they had only one
thing on their cute little minds, and that happened, by one of the coincidences that were his nature, to be exactly what he had been looking for.

But by now he was exhausted in that respect, and needed to get away
before any of them woke and started over. But how could he get away

without moving, and thus disturbing them? They would have no memory of the night's revelries, and be eager for the novelty of what they thought was a new interaction. He really wasn't up to that.

He got a fair notion. There should be fauns nearby. "Hey, fauns!" he called in a controlled low tone. "Look here!"

One heard him. "A pile of nymphs!" he exclaimed, and charged in to join the celebration. Others heard him and joined the charge, converging. In barely nine tenths of a moment they had hold of the nymphs, who woke cutely screaming and kicking their nice legs and flinging their hair about, making themselves quite ready for the interaction. In the remaining tenth of the moment several couples had formed, celebrating enthusiastically.

The Factor crawled out from under the squirming pile, unnoticed. Before any new nymphs could spy him, he made a random exchange of location.

He was in the bottom of a deep cleft. He recognized it: the Gap Chasm, which had balked him when the ogress was after him. He hadn't fallen, he had merely changed places with some creature, maybe a rabbit. That was fine. The nymphs should like the rabbit, if they noticed it.

There was a puff of steam. Something had been chasing the rabbit. It was the dread Gap Dragon, a six-legged, serpentine, vestigial-winged steamer, the terror of the Gap. All creatures that got caught here were its natural prey. Naturally random chance had put him right in its way.

The Factor had formidable random magic, but was not physically formidable. He was pretty much a routine man in a protective suit that would not be much use against the steam or teeth of the dragon. He would be cooked in his clothing and chomped before the dragon even got close. That was one of the things about dragons: they could use smoke, fire, or steam to process their prey from a distance.

He would not be able to flee the predator; the bottom of the chasm was its restricting hunting ground. He couldn't fight it—not in his natural form. He would have to change forms. That meant more magic and more gambling on what forms would appear.

The dragon spied him and shot out white-hot steam. He changed. And became a pot plant.

The steam struck it. The pots heated, but this was no problem because this plant was made for heating. Its fresh pots were used for cooking, while the older ones that were decaying affected the mind when smoked. Did getting steamed count?

The dragon skidded to a six-legged halt. It sniffed the pots, evidently having thought it saw a man here a moment ago. When it came to the old ones it got a dreamy expression. It seemed the magic did work when the pots were steamed. Soon it settled into a peaceful coil around the plant and snoozed.

Well and good, to a degree. He was out of danger. But how was he going to get away from the dragon, who might merely be playing possum? The possum was a magical Mundane animal who could play dead, then come back to life unexpectedly. As the dragon might, the moment the Factor moved.

And of course he couldn't move from this spot, because he was a plant with solid roots. He would have to change, and that might be what the cunning creature was waiting for.

He needed some way to distract the dragon without changing forms until he had at least a bit of distance. But what could a pot plant do?

He rattled his pots. They clanged together, raising a metallic ruckus. The fresh new ones clanged sharply, while the worn old ones thudded. It was an awful racket.

The dragon woke, annoyed. The noise continued, surely tingling the creature's sensitive ears. It issued a blast of steam, but that didn't stop the panning; it just got louder and less in tune. This was almost guaranteed to deliver a headache.

The dragon gave up and moved away, trying to shake the headache out of its noggin.

Now he could change. He became a tortoiseshell cat nine or ten years old named Mystery; it had a name tag on its collar.

The dragon sent a plume of steam that took live aim on the cat. The Factor leaped out of the way and bounded toward the nearest small tree. He jumped into its branches and hid behind its trunk.

But in a moment the dragon's snoot nudged around the trunk. He leaped clear just as the next superheated jet of steam was loosed at point-blank range. And landed by sheer random coincidence on the dragon's head.

Uh-oh. This was not the most secure place to be. But he couldn't leap off without becoming an immediate target. So he clung where he was.

The dragon shook his head violently. The cat clung tightly. It was a standoff—for all of one and a third moments. Then the cat flew high and wide.

But already the dragon's snoot was orienting, ready to send a spear of steam to catch the target in midair.

The Factor changed forms again. And became a pairing knife. The jet of steam struck it—and split in two. That was the knife's talent: to make pairs of things.

The Factor fell safely between the pair of jets. But he couldn't move out of range this way. If the dragon attacked him, he might make two of it, which would be twice as bad. He had to find a better random form.

He became a bone. It seemed to be the long bone of some creature's arm or leg. It was bound to be magic in some way; all his changes were. But what good was it?

The dragon's charging foot came down on the bone. And the dragon burst out laughing. He couldn't stop; he laughed so hard he rolled on the ground.

Now the Factor realized what kind of bone it was: a humoris bone, that made anyone who touched it laugh uncontrollably. Well, that did eliminate the threat, for the moment. But he still couldn't go anywhere, and he didn't want to lie here forever. The dragon showed no sign of departing; it was too busy laughing. Striking a funny bone wasn't really all that funny, but the magic didn't care.

He had only one magic stunt left today. That one would have to be something useful, or he was stuck.

He changed—and became a cue card, in the shape of a Q. It seemed impossible to become anything that would be really useful! Printed on the card was advice on the right time to say and do things. So what did this one say? LIE LOW UNTIL THE STORM COMES.

What did that mean? The Factor was still trying to figure it out when there was a crack of thunder. Suddenly it was drenchpouring. The dragon was soaked, which rather quenched his humor, and the Q card floated on the surface of the flooding path. It was borne away from the dragon, carried along by the forming river.

And soon enough it was well clear of the danger. The Factor reverted safely to his natural form. The Q card advice had been accurate, though it had left him soaking wet. Well, that was one way to survive, but he hoped he would not have to do it again. He found a tree to hide in; he would have to finish the day and night here.

In the morning, recharged, gorged on freshly harvested pies—so much better than black bread!—he was ready for action. What now? This business of touring Xanth was turning out to be less fun than he had anticipated. He was tempted to return to the nymphs for another night, but random travel was unlikely to take him there. Still, travel seemed more promising than changing forms. He traveled.

He arrived in a village. It was eerily silent; no one was speaking a word. Was this where the deaf folk lived?

"Hello," he said experimentally to the nearest man.

The man turned to him and held up a sign. HELLO STRANGER.

Surprised, the Factor spoke again. "Can't you talk?"

The man held up another sign: WE BELIEVE IN SIGNS.

So it seemed. "What is there to do in town?"

The man held up another sign. YOU CAN GET A JOB PRINTING SIGNS.

To be sure. "I meant for entertainment."

THAT IS ENTERTAINMENT.

"Not for me."

YOU MUST LEAD A DULL LIFE.

The Factor concluded that he had had enough of this. He traveled again.

This time he found himself in a large enclosure, surrounded by cuddly young animals. They clustered eagerly around him.

"Oh, I didn't see you," a voice said. "You must have just come in." It was a pretty girl.

"I did," the Factor agreed, uncertain what was going on here. He must have exchanged with one of the animals. "I am—the Factor." She looked as if she wouldn't recognize the name, so he didn't have to hide it.

"I'm Petting Sue," she said brightly. "My talent is to attract young animals who like to be petted. Mostly children come. You look older." She took a deep breath, emphasizing her charms. "Do you like petting?"

He considered half a moment. There was more than one meaning for the word, and he didn't care much abut cute animals. But if he petted them, he might get to pet her, later. "I may."

"That's good. The animals feel deprived if not constantly petted." She paused. "You're not a felon, are you?"

Actually some did consider him to be that. "Suppose I am?"

"I have a lamb you can ride. Being on the lamb is better than being punished." She indicated the lamb.

Did she want him to ride the lamb? "I hesitate to put any weight on such a small creature. It might hurt it."

"Oh, anyone can be on the lamb. Try it."

Well, why not. He walked to the lamb and bestrode it. Surprisingly, his legs fit, and he was riding it. His weight didn't seem to bother it at all. "I am on the lamb," he said gravely.

She clapped her hands with girlish glee. "Oh, I'm so pleased. The lamb loves giving rides."

But the other animals still wanted to be petted, so he had to dismount and pet them all. It was a chore, but Sue seemed suitably thrilled.

It was time to get closer to her. "How about you and I—" he started as he petted the last warm fuzzy creature, a miniature sphinx.

"Oh, there's Gourd'n!" Sue exclaimed, and ran to embrace and kiss the man just arriving.

So much for that. She had a boyfriend. Most pretty girls did.

In half an instant Sue was introducing them. "Gourd'n, this is Factor, who has been petting everyone. Factor, this is Gourd'n G'rd'n'r, who grows all the vegetables and things my pets eat. I couldn't get along without him."

Now the Factor saw that the man had a wagonful of produce. Soon he was handing it out to the hungry animals. Indeed, Sue needed him to feed her animals.

It was time to move on. He had traveled magically twice; he had four more to go. He invoked his magic again.

And got nowhere. There was no magic. Something was wrong.

He walked away. Neither Sue nor Gourd'n noticed, though a baby dragon puffed a snort of smoke, sorry to see a good petter go.

When he was well outside the enclosure, he paused to consider. He tried to change form, but that didn't work either. His magic was definitely gone. How could this have happened, after only two magic stunts?

Then it came to him. The limit was not six stunts. That was just the way it had been on his first day outside. The limit had to be random, because he was the Random Factor. He had been limiting himself to six when probably there were more than that on some days. Today there were fewer.

This was a problem. How could he proceed safely, if he never knew the limit? He might conjure himself into a nest of nickelpedes and not be able to conjure himself out, or to change form to protect himself. This made practicing his magic far more risky.

Yet what could he do? It might be useless to limit his stunts, because the limit might be low and he would be caught anyway. It might be better to use them freely, then fend for himself when they stopped, knowing he could no longer depend on them. At least he could always revert to his natural form. Still, it would be nervous business.

Meanwhile, he needed to find food and safety for the rest of the day and night. Maybe he had been depending too much on magic. He remained free and able to explore; those were worthwhile, regardless.

He set off walking again—and paused. Something else was wrong. Not magic, exactly. It was an—awareness. Someone was aware of him. He felt it. Someone was thinking about him. That could be mischief.

He walked to an old beerbarrel tree. Someone had installed a spigot in its trunk, with a mug. That was thoughtful. He took the mug, turned the spigot, and got himself a foaming mug of beer. Then he sat down and leaned his back against the tree as he drank it.

The beer quickly went to his head, making him reminisce. He was originally from the Factory, where factors were produced for export to Mundania, where mathematicians, logicians, physicists, teachers, and other obscure folk used them. It was a dull business, but that didn't bother most of the factors because they had no imagination. They were proud of their mathematical magic. But the Random Factor was different. He was conscious and creative, and he hated being limited. He liked to find wild new ways to do things.

True, sometimes his innovations led to mischief. They still hadn't fixed the randomness he had innocently introduced into quanta. But that was the price of original thinking. There was much more to be gained than lost from thinking outside the box that was the Factory.

Somehow they hadn't seen it that way. So they had confined him in a cell in the dungeon of Castle Maidragon, guarded by the infinitely potent magic of the Three Princesses, where he couldn't corrupt any other factors. All he could do was randomize anyone who opened his cell door. There was some little satisfaction in that, but not nearly enough. Most of the randomness he initiated that way got unrandomized all too rapidly.

But then his randomness had paid off. He had randomly inverted it, so that instead of making others travel or change form, he made himself do it. That was much better, because it brought him relative freedom. Yes, there were problems, but they were really challenges, and he loved tackling them. Already it had introduced him to a number of interesting people and situations, such as the nymphs.

Naturally the Factory wouldn't be pleased. He knew it would set out to confine him again the moment it realized he had escaped. And it seemed it had, because that was surely who was thinking of him. The Factory would probably send out an agent to catch him.

Well, all he had to do was stay clear. But how? The Factory knew how to track him. Every time he did magic, the Factory would pick up on the signal and orient on it. That meant that someone or something would be stalking him. He did not like that. Sure, he could randomly flee the agent, who would take time to catch up again. But what fun would it be to be constantly chased? When would he ever be able to relax?

It would help if he knew who the Factory Agent was, and how he proposed to confine the randomness. But his magic wouldn't tell him that. He needed help.

Well, that defined the problem and perhaps the solution. He needed to find someone who could fathom reality and tell him about the agent. Now was a good time to do it, while he was unable to perform his magic.

Too bad he didn't have the talent of locating worthwhile folk. He would just have to do it the hard way, meeting and questioning people.

He found a reasonably innocuous path and followed it purposefully. Soon he encountered a gnome: a manlike creature about half his height who looked grumpy.

The Factor put on his most winning smile. "Hello, sir. Are you the one I seek?"

"No," the gnome said, scowling, and sought to walk on past.

This did not bode well. "But how can I be sure such a handsome creature is not the one I seek?"

"You can just assume it. Nobody seeks me."

"Why?"

"Because I am Gnome Atter. My talent is to make things unimportant. Such as this encounter."

The gnome walked on, and this time the Factor did not try to engage him further. The little man was right: he was unimportant for this purpose.

The problem was that encountering folk randomly was apt to be tedious. But he had no choice, being who he was. He walked on.

The next creature he encountered was a large white-winged snake, twenty to thirty feet long, with green and orange scales and a cute smile. He let it fly on by, as it was unlikely to have the information he needed.

Then he met a boy and girl. They might be worth questioning. "Hello. I'm the Random Factor. Do you know how to fathom relevant information?"

"Not us," the boy said. "We're twins, named by our uncle. I'm Denephew, she's Deniece. Our talent is telling horrible jokes. For example, a crow, a rabbit, and an ogre walked into a bar—"

"It was an ogress," the girl said. "And they said to the bartender—"

"Very funny," the Factor said, and walked on.

Next was a wise-looking old man who seemed vaguely plantlike. The Factor introduced himself, then asked, "Can you answer a question?"

"I am Herb Sage," the man replied. "I impart wisdom. Your health will improve if you limit your diet to selected herbs."

"Thank you. What I want to know is—"

"I do not give specifics, just generalities."

So much for that. The Factor walked on.

The next was a serious young man. "I am Pathos," he said compassionately. "I make temporary paths to wherever a person wants to go, but they can be used only once."

The Factor was about to walk on, but then reconsidered. "Can you make a path to a person who can answer my question?"

"Sure." A path appeared. "There."

Could be that simple? "Thank you," the Factor said, and followed the path. It was probably a random path, but there was always the chance that the man wasn't a fraud.

He came to two young men sitting at a table. They looked to be of similar age and family, probably twins. The path faded; it had done its job. "Hello. I am the Random Factor. I need some information, and was told you might provide it."

The twin on the left shook his head. "We don't provide information."

"We summon and abolish demons," the twin on the right said.

That wasn't good enough. He didn't need demons, he needed information. But again he reconsidered. "How about a demon of information?"

The twin on the left snapped his fingers. Smoke coalesced, and formed into a demon. "Demon Info here," the demon said. "What's it to you?"

Could this really work? "I need to know who the Factory Agent is."

"A teen girl called Debra."

"A girl? How can she accomplish anything?"

"Forget it, mouse mess," the demon said. "I have to answer only one question." He turned to the twins. "Now that I have done so, I mean to take my pound of flesh from whoever so rudely summoned me." His hands formed into pincers.

The twin on the right snapped his fingers. The demon vanished. "That's how we work," he said. "He summons them, I banish them. But they tend to be surly brutes."

"I met one who wasn't," the Factor said. "The Demoness Metria."

"Did I hear my nomenclature?" a dulcet voice inquired as a shapely column of smoke formed.

"You shouldn't have done that," the left twin said. "When you name them they can summon themselves, and they're not under control."

"So I noticed," the Factor agreed. Then, to the forming demoness: "Did you hear your what?"

"Designation, appellation, title, personage, identification—"

"Name?"

"Whatever," she agreed crossly. "Say, don't I know you? The fandom reactor?"

"Close enough. You teased me cruelly beside the Faun & Nymph retreat, and vanished. I had to make do with a pile of nymphs."

Her eyes snapped little sparks. "Oh you did? What do they have that I don't have?"

"They deliver."

"I can deliver!"

This had prospects. She was a perverse tease, but with the right management might indeed deliver. "I doubt it."

"I'll prove it. Here's a pizza." She produced a hot pie and proffered it.

Really a tease. She well understood what he was after. "That wasn't what I meant."

"Oh, really?" Her forming gown slid down a bit as she inhaled. "I can deliver as well as any nymph."

"Stop wasting my time, demoness. You're married."

"But my aspect Mentia isn't." She shifted form subtly, becoming another demoness who was in no way inferior in sexiness. "What can I do for you, Factor? Something random?"

"You can take me to a private bower and make me deliriously happy all night."

She eyed him. "But you know, I'm a little crazy. Is that a problem?" Her gown was fuzzing out entirely.

"No. I am somewhat random myself."

"Then so be it. Come be crazy." She extended her arms invitingly.

Was this another tease? But if this was a different aspect, with a different personality, it might not be. It was worth the chance. He stepped into her embrace.

There was a wrenching sensation. Then they were in a comfortable chamber, on a bed of pillows. "Where are we?" he asked, looking around.

"In Metria's secret hideaway she stole from a mortal named Esk several decades ago. He sat on her face, and she threw him out."

"Why did he do that?"

"Well, she had the form of a pillow at the time. She told him to get his fat mule off her, and for some reason he didn't understand immediately."

"Her word problem," he said, catching on. "You don't have it."

"I don't," she agreed. "I have my own weird nature."

"Won't she be annoyed if you use her hideaway?"

"Furious," she agreed. She took a luscious breath, her chest expanding marvelously. "We don't necessarily get along well. I can't think why." She momentarily assumed the form of a horned lady devil with a switching tail. "I can be such a bad girl."

"Crazy," he said, and took hold of her. She did not fade out. Instead she went sexily crazy.

By the time the night was done, she had satisfied him that a single demoness could bring a man more crazy bliss than a pile of nymphs. When she tried. It was quite an education.

6
AIR PLAIN

The next clue was "Air Plain." Wira had no idea what that meant; the Demoness Metria had given her only the words. She wanted to follow up on it now because it seemed to relate to air, and they were in the Region of Air, so it should be convenient.

"Air Plane?" Debra asked dubiously. "In Mundania that's a flying machine. I don't think Xanth has anything like that."

"I believe that's plain. Air plain."

"Air is sort of plain," Debra agreed. "But that's not much of a clue."

"I'm sorry I couldn't read the entry," Wira said. "But maybe we'll find it if we look."

"Can we look if we don't know what we're looking for?"

"We'll have to."

So Debra took wing and flew around the area, looking for she knew not what. "This is probably irrelevant," she said. "But I'm aware of something."

"What kind of thing?"

"I don't exactly know. I get an occasional tinge, and I know what direction it's coming from, and think I ought to go there, but there's nothing. It's not a steady feeling; it's irregular."

"A premonition," Wira suggested.

"But what would I have to premonition about? I'm just a girl doing her Service for the Good Magician."

"Could someone be thinking of you? Of your—underclothing?"

"I wonder. My bosom does tingle a bit. Maybe that's it. I once thought being a bare-topped centaur made my curse null, but it's still lurking."

"That's probably it," Wira agreed. "Let me know if it gets worse; it might be significant."

"I will," Debra promised. "Anyway, it's gone now."

Then Wira felt something. "A child is in trouble. That way." She pointed to their right.

Debra swung right, gliding down toward the ground. "There are a few trees here at the edge of the Region of Air. I don't see anything else."

"That one." Wira pointed again.

"Oh, now I see her! A girl in a tree. She looks frightened."

"A girl? It was a boy I sensed."

"We can ask the girl. Maybe she saw the boy." Debra flew to the tree and hovered beside it. "Hello! Can we help you?"

"Oh, I'm so relieved!" the girl replied. "Can you get me down?"

"I can enable you to float down." Debra flicked her tail. "Now let go."

"But I'll fall!"

"No, I made you light. Trust me."

The girl let go. Wira felt her amazement. "I'm floating! Just drifting slowly down. That's amazing."

"It's flying centaur magic." Debra landed beside the girl. "Hello. I'm Debra Centaur, and this is Wira Human."

"I am Ilene, Magician Trent and Sorceress Iris's daughter."

"I remember you!" Wira said, digging out a vial of healing elixir for the scrapes on the girl's body. The tree limbs had not been kind to her limbs. "You came to the Good Magician's Castle a week ago to ask a Question."

"Oh, now I recognize you," Ilene said. "You're the Good Magician's blind niece."

"Daughter-in-law."

Wira felt the girl's embarrassment. "Of course. Anyway, you showed me around the castle, and then up to see the Good Magician. But he refused to help me. I was so disappointed."

"He always has good reason," Wira said. "He doesn't let folk pay the considerable price of his Answers unless they really need them."

"But I did need the answer!" the girl said. "I still do. I'm just getting in trouble without it."

There was something here; Wira could sense it. "Tell me about it," she urged the girl. "The Magician does not share information with me. I knew you were disappointed, but that's all. Maybe I can fathom the reason he passed you by."

"Oh, I don't want to bore you with my problem," Ilene protested. "I'm just grateful that you got me safely down from that tree."

"Please, I do want to know. It is not like him to be unkind to a child."

"I'm no child!" Ilene protested. "I'm eleven years old."

"I apologize. It has been some time since I was that age."

"That's all right." But she didn't volunteer her story.

Wira thought of something. "Would you like a ride on the centaur? You can tell us while we fly."

"A ride!" the girl exclaimed, excited. All girls of that age loved centaurs.

They mounted Debra, who flicked them appropriately light, spread her wings, and took off. Wira could feel by the thinning, cooling air that they were soon well above the landscape. Ilene was of course in rapture. And they did elicit her history.

Ilene was delivered after her parents Magician Trent and Sorceress Iris were rejuvenated. Her older sister was Irene, delivered fifty-two years before, now a grandmother. Actually Irene's grandchildren, the Three Princesses, were the same age as Ilene. But they were Sorceresses, while Ilene had a mere talent, which made her ashamed, so she didn't associate with them. The two half-demon children, Demon Ted and DeMonica, were also her age, but Ilene had no demon ancestry, so did not relate well to them either.

Wira winced. All of Magician Bink's descendants were spelled to have Magician-caliber talents. But Ilene was not his descendant, so had no such guarantee. She had royal blood, but had been delivered after her parents retired from the throne, so was not quite a princess, either. Not even a part-demon. No wonder she felt out of sorts.

Ilene's talent was to make illusions real. That was respectable, but not

Magician class. She had practiced diligently with her mother, converting the Sorceress's illusions of landscapes and creatures to real ones. But here was the rub: without illusions to convert, she could do nothing. Away from her mother, she might as well have been talentless.

So she had gone to see the Good Magician, her reluctant parents allowing her to go. Her Question was: How could she make something of herself? And the Magician had simply said "You have perspective. Use it." And sent her away, unrequited. She had been too ashamed to return home with that nonanswer, so she was here trying to figure out what perspective meant. She had always understood that it was a feature of the magic of things, that pretended to let a person pass them by up close, but the distant ones raced to keep up. A person could see it happening, if she watched carefully. That was not magic she had. Her magic dealt with illusions.

Then she had heard a child crying. She was only eleven, but she was a girl: she had to help a child in trouble. So she had hurried toward the sound. It had looked for a moment as if there were a plain in the hot air, angling up from the ground to distant mountains. Suddenly she had found herself running up that slope. She had looked down, and discovered a tree almost below her feet. This was impossible!

Of course she had fallen. She had managed to grab onto the foliage of the tree, skinning her knees and elbows, and clung there helplessly, afraid to let go. Until Debra had rescued her. "I'm such a washout," she said ruefully.

Wira's awareness intensified. "The boy you heard—"

"Oh, I forgot!" Ilene said. "I was going to rescue him, and only got myself in trouble. He must still be there."

"Still where? Show us."

"Beyond that tree where you found me. On the—the air plain I foolishly imagined."

Debra looped around and winged back toward the tree.

The air plain. This was becoming quite relevant. "You ran up that incline, before realizing that running in air was not your talent, and fell."

"Yes. I'm mortified. How could I have done that?"

"It is almost as if you have a second talent."

"But I don't. I can't. Nobody has two talents."

"But some do have talent with multiple aspects that might seem like several before being understood."

"Making illusions real, and running up imaginary plains? I don't think so."

"I do. That plain was an illusion."

"Yes it was. That's why I fell right through it." Then the girl froze for fully half an instant as a dim bulb formed over her head. "And my talent is to make illusions real!"

"You made it real," Wira agreed. "Until you doubted. Then it disintegrated. Aspects of a single talent. You just need to get perspective on it."

"Perspective," Ilene breathed. "Could that be what the Good Magician meant?"

"It is surely what he meant. You simply need to see your talent from another vantage."

The girl was silent, assimilating that.

They reached the tree. Debra settled on the ground beside it, and they paused to listen.

There was the sound of a small boy crying. Somewhere in the sky beyond the tree.

"You know that illusion is there," Wira said. "I can't see it, but you can. Make it real again."

"I—will try," Ilene agreed, awed.

And soon the centaur started walking up an incline. "What do you see?" Wira murmured.

"An optical illusion," Debra murmured in reply. "Like the puddles you can see on hot days that aren't there. A—a—there's a word—"

"Mirage," Wira said. "A form of illusion."

"That's it! So she can make mirages real. That could be useful on a desert when you're thirsty."

"It could indeed," Wira agreed.

"Now we're coming into a full mirage," Debra continued. "Trees, fields, a stream—an, an, like a nice island in the desert, an—"

"Oasis," Wira said.

"Yes. It's really nice, but up in the sky. This is weird."

"Literal illusions are."

"There he is!" Ilene cried.

"True," Debra murmured. "A boy, maybe seven years old, sitting under a palm tree, looking really lost."

They approached the boy, whose presence she could feel. "Hello," Wira called. "May we help you?"

"I'm lost," the boy said, his voice perking up.

"This is really weird," Debra murmured. "He glows."

They came to stand beside him. "Who are you? Where do you live?" Wira asked.

"I can't say."

"He's looking at me," Debra whispered. "At my—front."

"He's male," Wira reminded her. "Boys lack discretion." Then she spoke to the boy. "How can we take you home, if you don't tell us where to take you?"

That stymied him. He was silent.

This was odd. A lost glowing boy who wouldn't give his identity. "Your parents told you not to give personal information to strangers," Wira said.

"That's it! Because they might hurt me."

"He's still looking," Debra said, not pleased.

"Give him a ride," Ilene whispered. "Then he can't look."

That seemed like a good idea. "Do you know the word compromise?"

He struggled with that. "Each person yields a little."

"Very good! Let's compromise. Tell us your talent, and we'll take you with us until you get unlost."

"Okay. I make mixed metaphors real."

"Why that's like my talent," Ilene said. "I make illusions real."

"Say," the boy said, warming to her.

"You must have really mixed them up to get stuck here."

"Far pastures are greenest by the dawn's early light," the boy said proudly. "Only then I got lost in a pasture."

"It happens," Ilene said. "I'm Ilene, daughter of Magician Trent and Sorceress Iris. I heard you, but then got lost in my illusion when I thought it wasn't real. Does that makes sense to you?"

"Sure. I do it all the time."

"Come and ride with me," Ilene said. She seemed cut out to be a babysitter, and that was fine with Wira, who couldn't do it well blind, and surely with Debra, who couldn't do it well as a centaur.

But there was something else. A glowing boy who made mixed metaphors real: she knew who that was. Nimbus, the son of the Demon Xanth and Chlorine. The heir apparent to the fantastic powers and position of the Demon whose mere incidental body radiation accounted for the whole of the magic of Xanth. No wonder he wasn't supposed to reveal his identity! He was a prime candidate for enormous mischief.

Ilene lifted Nimbus onto the centaur's back behind Wira, then mounted behind him, so she could hold him steady. And Wira discovered something else: she could see him! Not with her eyes, exactly, for she wasn't facing him, but with her awareness of his glow. She remembered that the glow was visible to anyone but his mother, Chlorine. Chlorine wanted an ordinary child, while the Demon Xanth, who preferred to masquerade as a donkey-headed dragon called Nimby, evidently wanted a son with special powers. Chlorine would surely catch on eventually, but by that time might be resigned to having an extraordinary son. That would be for husband and wife to sort out, in due course.

The centaur was now trotting along the plain, as there was no need to fly; they were already in the air.

Wira's musings continued. Yet why was that glow apparent to others, even to the blind? It made the boy all too evident to anyone who knew much about Xanthly lineages. Why tell the boy to conceal his identity, while leaving this giveaway? Wira had half a notion, but wanted to confirm it.

"We'll have to call you something," Ilene said. "Since we don't have your real name, how about a pretend one? Is it all right if we call you Glow?"

"Sure," Nimbus said cheerfully.

"Glow," Wira said carefully, "who told you to hide your real name?"

"Mom."

"Not your father?"

"Dad says no one's going to hurt me. He's not worried."

There it was: no one would hurt the boy because the Demon Xanth was watching. The glow was a warning that only the most foolish or igno-

rant folk would ignore. That explained the seeming conflict. Neither Debra nor Ilene recognized him, being too young or new to Xanth, but they
meant him no harm, so that was all right.

"Dad wants me to get experience," the boy continued. "To get to know
the land and the folk. Because—" He broke off, and Wira knew why: he
was on the verge of revealing his identity by saying too much.

"You should be safe with us until you find your way home," Wira said.
She did not want to be cynical, but it seemed unlikely that anything bad
would happen to any of them as long as they were in the company of the
boy. "We're not lost. We're—exploring."

"Great!" he agreed enthusiastically.

"There's something funny about this plain," Ilene said. "I made it, I
guess, but it seems to have details I don't think I made. I can't quite see
them, but I know they're there."

"I have the same impression," Debra said. "It's as if there is more to
this illusion than you made real."

Wira spread her awareness out—and discovered people. They were all
around, watching the walking party. They were not friendly or unfriendly,
just there. They were—

"The folk of the air plain!" she said aloud.

"Folk?" Ilene asked. "Are they illusory?"

"No, they're real. So I think you can't make them real. They are
merely invisible." Wira paused, working it out. "Not just that. Unde-
tectable, unless you look for them, and know how to relate. No one has,
before, I think."

"I suppose it makes sense that if there is a plain, it can be inhabited,"
Debra said. "By invisible people. Or whatever."

"I wonder whether they know anything we need?" Wira asked. "Such
as the location of my—my vision." Because they were no longer alone,
and the continued privacy of the real mission seemed best.

"Can we ask?" Debra asked, honoring that privacy.

"I'll try." Wira concentrated, attuning to the folk around them as living
entities. *People! I see you! May we talk?*

There was surprise. The folk of the air were not used to people being
aware of them, let alone trying to talk with them. They weren't sure how to
respond.

Please! I am Wira, in search of my lost husband Hugo. Somehow she knew this was not the occasion for the false mission. *I must find him. Can you help me?*

They considered. Then one came close. *We were trying to help the boy, but did not know how, because he is of the solid folk. We know not how to help you either.*

They were answering! *If we can just talk, that may be all we need.*

The air folk considered. *No one has asked before. We will talk with you. First we must take form so your friends can relate to us. But there is a problem.*

This was real progress. *Is it something we can fix?*

The Air person nodded. *If you wish to. The centaur is unclothed.*

Wira smiled. *Centaurs wear no clothing.*

That is the problem. We regard such exposure as objectionable, particularly for our children.

Wira suppressed her faint amusement. She knew solid folk with a similar attitude. "Debra, the folk of the air prefer that you don some clothing."

"But centaurs don't—"

"Can we humor them?"

"I suppose," Debra agreed, nonplussed. "But I have no clothing."

Do you have clothing for her? Wira asked.

Ours would not relate to her.

Can you make illusion clothing?

Yes.

"Oh there's a bra," Ilene said. "And a blouse. Just hanging in midair."

"They are illusions," Wira explained. It seemed it was only the human portion of the centaur that needed to be covered. "Now if you will—"

"Done," the girl said. "Now they're real."

"And Debra, if you will don them—"

"Done," Debra agreed after a bit more than a moment. "They fit perfectly."

"She called you Debra," the boy said. "I want to—"

"No!" Debra snapped.

"What are you talking about?" Ilene asked.

Wira sighed. "Better explain, Debra."

"When men—or boys—hear my name, they want to steal my under-garment," Debra said tightly. "It's my curse. I thought it was gone as long as I'm a centaur, but it seems not."

"I'm sorry," Ilene said. "I didn't know." She spoke to the boy. "Hands off. It's the Adult Conspiracy. I'm bound by it too."

"Aww," the boy said. But he obeyed. It seemed that his mother had inculcated some manners after all.

Then centaur, girl, and boy all took note; Wira could feel them reacting. "People!" Nimbus exclaimed.

"They are the folk of the air, making themselves visible," Wira explained. "It's not exactly optical, because I can see them too." And she could. It was probably what was called mind illusion, where the pictures were projected into the minds of the recipients. Whatever it was, it was a delight, for now she could see the entire scene: people and geography. She seldom had such a chance.

"A whole landscape," Debra said. "Trees, lakes, houses, and people. Amazing!"

"I will take you to Castle Air," a man said. "I am Higgs, the bosun." He indicated his boat. "You can define me if you can spell my name."

"I am Wira," Wira said. "And these are Ilene, Glow, and Debra Centaur."

"Debra," he said, looking at her. "De-bra. Suddenly I have this overwhelming urge to make that literal." He stepped toward her.

"B-O-A-T-S-W-A-I-N," Debra spelled.

"Oh, you got me," Higgs said. "I can't touch you. Bleep."

"I didn't know you could spell that well," Wira said.

"I couldn't, until I had to," Debra said.

They got on his boat, discovering that there was room for them all including the centaur. Higgs saw to the rigging and got it in motion. It set sail across the lake toward the castle.

"Now if you had spelled it B-O-S-O-N," Higgs said conversationally, "it would really have been interesting. No one has ever perceived me in that guise. I don't just sail my ship, I hold the universe together."

"How can you do that, if no one can see you?" Debra asked.

"They don't need to perceive me. My power is there regardless. I bring mass to everything that exists."

Wira did not believe that, but decided not to challenge it. Folk were entitled to their harmless delusions. She was more interested in reaching the castle and learning what the air folk had to say to her.

The motor sputtered. "Oops, I'm low on petrol," Higgs said. "I'll summon the bird." He poked a finger into the air.

"A bird?" Wira asked.

"A petrel."

In a moment a large aquatic bird swooped low. It had a nose shaped like a tube. It put this tube to the boat's motor and regurgitated a bellyful of liquid. Then it flew away.

The motor resumed full power. Its petrol had been restored.

"I thought this was a sailboat," Debra said.

"It was, until it ran out of petrol."

The centaur let that pass. It seemed they did not properly understand this airy realm.

Higgs brought the boat to dock at the castle. There was a welcoming party there consisting of three drummers. They had no drums; they merely beat the air, and the booming of the drums sounded. "Air drumming," Higgs explained. "We have a whole air orchestra, but the others couldn't make it on such short notice."

They got off the boat and followed the winding path to the castle. "I'm feeling faint," Ilene said. "Things are too strange here for me."

"I'll summon a medic," Higgs said. "Though normally they are reserved for older citizens." He put his hand up, and in a moment a man in a hospital uniform flew in with a balloon. He brought this to the girl.

"Whatever this is, I don't need it," Ilene said quickly.

But the medic put the stem of the balloon to her mouth and let it go. Hot air whooshed out of the balloon and into Ilene, inflating her. Then the medic flew away, his job done.

"Are you all right?" Wira asked, alarmed.

Ilene looked surprised as she deflated. "Yes, I'm fine. That medic air took good care of me."

"Ouch!" Debra exclaimed.

Ilene glanced at her. "Something is wrong?"

"I am discovering that centaurs don't much like egregious puns."

"Was there a pun?"

"Never mind. You'd have to be Mundane."

"Ugh!"

"Exactly."

Higgs opened a door at the end of the path. "This is as far as I go. Enter; someone will guide you inside."

They passed through the doorway. Inside was a young man. "Hello, travelers. I am Airon. I can change into the wind."

"You must be a blowhard," Nimbus said brightly.

"Glow!" Ilene said, appalled.

"He means you must be very effective when ships are becalmed," Wira said. "They would really need your help."

"Oh, yes, of course," Airon agreed, deciding to be complimented.

Wira introduced herself and the others. Unfortunately she forgot to fudge Debra's name, and the man eyed her bosom suggestively.

"We need to see the king," Wira said. "We must not keep him waiting."

"Oh," Airon said, as if he had lost track of that. "I suppose not."

Wira was coming to appreciate how annoying Debra's curse could be. Would the man actually have tried to remove her bra by hand, if not intercepted?

Then Airon showed them to the royal assembly room. There were the King and Queen of Air awaiting them. They looked quite royal in their robes and crowns.

Airon introduced them to the king. And of course the Air King eyed Debra's well-filled blouse. "I believe centaurs normally don't wear clothing," he remarked. "We should not enforce our customs on you. Suppose I help you remove—"

"By no means," the Air Queen snapped. "Our customs are inviolate."

The Air King looked disappointed, but dared not argue with his wife on a social matter. She was the arbiter of custom.

Then Wira summarized their situation, concluding with the discovery of the air plain, thanks to Ilene's talent, and their ascent to the realm of the air folk. "We may be bothering you for nothing," she concluded. "It was just a feeling by the words 'air plain' whose relevance I don't know. We found the plain, but I still don't know how it relates to my quest for my lost husband."

"Fortunately we do have a vague notion," the Air King said. "Things do tend to be somewhat diffuse for us, because of our nature, but this is certain: your mystery relates to the air in some manner."

"Or perhaps an heir," the Air Queen said. "The detail is obscure, but the relevance is plain: you must deal with one or the other."

"Or both," the Air King said. "Only then will you achieve your purpose."

"Thank you your majesties," Wira said, thinking of Nimbus, the heir to the Demon's realm. It did seem to be falling into place, though she did not understand how.

"We're sorry to be so foggy," the Air Queen said.

"Now for the fun," the Air King said. "We'll have a feast and a ball."

The Air Queen rolled her eyes. "He does love parties," she murmured. "This will run late; you will need accommodations for the night."

"But we have to move on," Wira protested.

"Tomorrow," the Air King said decisively. "You can't leave tonight; the bosun has departed and won't return until morning."

"We shouldn't argue with a king," Debra murmured. Evidently she liked the idea of a big meal and party. So did Ilene and Nimbus.

Actually so did Wira herself. She had not ever attended a ball, and here, where she could actually see things, seemed ideal. She could enjoy the life of sighted folk, for one evening.

The banquet was fabulous. The Royal Chef brought forth every imaginable dish and several unimaginable ones. Ilene and Nimbus took turns swallowing huge gulps of boot rear, seeing who could get the biggest kick, and gorging on patty cake and eye scream. They were soon patting and screaming with gusto. Wira and Debra, more cautious, nevertheless ate more than was probably good for them.

Then Debra finished with some tap water—and broke into a four-footed tap dance routine. "Oops—I missed the pun," she said, embarrassed.

"But you do a very nice dance," Wira reassured her. Indeed, Ilene and Nimbus paused to watch, then sipped some tap water themselves, joining her.

In the evening was the ball, which was of course held in a room shaped like a huge ball. The royal personnel helped garb them all in elaborate gowns, even the boy: his resembled the king's robe, and he plainly loved it. The Queen took in upon herself to teach him ballroom dancing, and she was a good teacher and he a good learner. Soon they where whirling around the ballroom in style.

The King danced first with Wira. In his arms she discovered that she never made a misstep, though she had seldom danced before; he guided her perfectly. "I know your nature," he murmured. "Only those perfectly pure of heart can see us or our realm."

"I thought it was because you folk made yourselves apparent," Wira said, foolishly flattered.

"We are doing so. But you saw us first. Then we knew we wanted to get to know you better. We facilitated it for you and your associates. You are surely Xanth's nicest person."

"Oh, I wouldn't say that," she protested, blushing.

"Of course you wouldn't," he agreed. "But it is nevertheless true." He glanced around. "And the boy glows. That is significant. He must be protected."

"You recognize him?"

"You don't?"

"I feel he is safer anonymous."

"Surely so," the King agreed, giving her a friendly squeeze. He was a most personable man.

Then he danced with Ilene, who was utterly thrilled. And finally Debra, embracing her human portion carefully. Wira suspected he still wanted to remove her bra, but the Queen was alert and all he could do was touch its back strap through the material of her gown. She had never imagined a man dancing with a centaur, but it turned out to be possible and even graceful in its fashion.

All too soon the evening was over and they were conducted to their suite. "Oh, that was wonderful!" Ilene exclaimed. "I never thought I'd get to dance with a king! Not until I was grown up, anyway." She seemed to be careening between girl and woman, neither fitting perfectly. When she was with Nimbus she was more like a girl, but when she danced with the king she had been much like a woman.

"I danced with the Queen," Nimbus said proudly.

They took turns disrobing, washing, and donning the fancy pajamas the castle provided. "I think I could get to like the royal life," Debra confessed. "I was almost tempted to let the King take off my—" She saw the boy and stifled it. "He was so nice."

They were ready for sleep, but it turned out that none of them were able to relax yet. The events of the day had been too exciting. What were they to do?

"Have you suffered any more of that—awareness?" Wira asked Debra privately.

"On and off. Sometimes my—front—positively itches. There's somewhere I should go, something I should do. But I don't know what. Then it passes. It seems to be random."

"It's almost as if your curse wants you to put on your bra, so as to make men want to take it off."

"Almost," Debra agreed. "One man, anyway."

"Your prospective boyfriend?"

"I'm only thirteen!" Wira could feel her blush.

"Teens can have boyfriends. They just have to stay clear of the Adult Conspiracy restrictions."

"Would taking off my bra be allowed for a boyfriend?"

"Absolutely not." Then Wira reconsidered. "But you are a centaur now. They don't practice the Conspiracy among themselves; it's largely a human convention."

"But I'm human, whatever my present form."

"Say, you're turning a pretty shade of red," Nimbus said, noticing. "I didn't know centaurs could do that."

It was time to distract him. "Maybe we could play a game," Wira suggested. "To pass the time until we get sleepy. Maybe charades."

"I know!" Nimbus said. "Let's play my father's favorite game. Nimbi."

He wasn't aware how close he had come to giving away his identity. Nimby played nimbi?

"Let's," Ilene agreed. "How is it played?"

"Matchsticks," he said. "Lay them in rows. Try to pick up the last one."

"But we have no matchsticks," Debra said.

"Sure we do," the boy said. "There on the mantelpiece."

Debra tried to pick one up, but her hand passed through it. "Those are illusion, part of the decoration."

"No problem," Ilene said. She went to pick them up, and they were real.

The boy laid out fifty matches in five rows of ten each. He and Ilene played the first game. The rule was that a player could pick up any number of sticks in a row or column, as long as there were no gaps in it.

The boy took the top two in the third column. That left the top two rows with two matches and seven matches, and the bottom three with ten matches. Ilene took the whole third row out. That left a gap in the middle of each column. They kept playing until there were only five matches left, two, two, and one. It was Nimbus's turn. "I win," he said, taking the single match.

Ilene studied the situation. "If I take a set of two, you will take the other set and win. So I'll take one match."

"I still win," he said, and took a single match from the other set. That left two isolated matches. She took one, and he took the last, winning.

"If you had seen that coming," Debra said, "you could have set up a winning combination."

"He was thinking ahead of me," Ilene said ruefully.

"I learned from Dad," Nimbus said brightly. "He always wins."

Debra played a game against Nimbus, and lost. Then Wira did, and lost. Then they tried a game with four players, and that messed up the boy's concentration, and Ilene won. They played several more games, and each person won at least once.

By that time they were tired and relaxed enough to sleep. Wira lay down on one bed, while Ilene lay on another with Nimbus, who did not want to be alone. Debra slept standing on her four feet; that was more comfortable for her.

Yes, it had been a fine day, and she had learned things that were worthwhile. She had also added the boy Nimbus to her party, and she suspected that he was the reason for the clue. He must play some part in accomplishing her mission. He was after all the son of Demon Xanth. That was a phenomenal development.

But she hardly seemed closer to finding Hugo. That quietly pained her.

7
GOBLINS

A t least now we have some clues," Happy Bottom said. "They may not lead anywhere, but they're better than nothing."

"They'll help us find Father," Fray said hopefully.

"Surely so," Happy agreed. But Fray could tell that her mother was humoring her, because she was only nine years old and couldn't handle the ugly realities of adulthood.

"What's the first clue, Mother?"

"Peeve."

Oops. What had she done now? She had to try to keep her mother in a good mood, because Happy Bottom could blow up into a terrible storm in hardly more than two and a half moments. "I'm sorry, Mother."

"Not you, dear. The peeve is a thing, not a mood. It's a bird. Somehow it relates."

"A bird?" Fray liked birds; they flew through her substance and sometimes she played with them, tossing them about.

"A nasty bird. It stays at the Golem residence."

"The Golems!" Fray repeated. "Grundy Golem—isn't he the one who insults us as we float by, so we try to tag him with lightning, but he always ducks inside the house and escapes?"

"The same. As peevish as the bird. Fortunately his wife Rapunzel Elf is very nice; maybe we can talk to her."

"Rapunzel! Isn't she the one who sits out on the bank and lets her long hair waft out to dry in the wind? I like her."

"Then you may talk to her. Maybe she will know why the peeve is a clue."

"Yes! She will help if she can."

"Fortunately the wind is right, so we can float there now."

"Goody!"

They diffused into their cloud forms and floated up into the sky. Fray always loved floating; there were so many things to see as she drifted over the Land of Xanth, and the warm air currents were comfortable. The terrain was like a tapestry, with forests and farms and hills and dales. Each had its own air currents and smells. The landscape was endlessly interesting.

They passed over a lake. There were waves on it, and these intrigued her. "Who it is waving at, Mother?" she asked in gaseous cloud talk.

Happy seemed amused. "At you, dear. Maybe it wants you to wet on it."

"Oh, I will!" Fray focused her energy and squeezed out a nice wetting before she floated away from the lake. She hoped the lake appreciated her effort.

"And there is a parade," Happy said.

"Oh, I know what to do with that!" Fray exclaimed. "Father taught me."

"He taught you well," Happy agreed.

They focused, and as they floated over, they rained on the parade. The odd thing was that the folk below did not seem thrilled. Didn't they know that a parade was a summons for rain? Some folk just didn't appreciate the favors clouds did them.

In due course they came to the Golem residence. Now they condensed to their solid forms, because solid folk had trouble understanding normal cloud talk. As solid woman and solid girl, they went to the solid door and knocked. "Remember, we must try to get along with the disagreeable golem and bird," Happy cautioned her.

"I'll try," Fray promised, adding her knock. It was funny the way a solid banging into a solid made a noise.

"It's unlocked, airhead!" a voice called from inside.

Happy opened the door. There on a perch perched the peeve: a small green bird with a sour expression on its beak. "I am Hurricane Gladys," Happy said. "You must be the pet peeve."

"What's it to you, soggy bottom?" the bird demanded peevishly.

"And this is my daughter Fray. Where is Rapunzel?"

The bird eyed Fray. "Fray—does that mean a good fight? You must be a little terror."

"Thank you," Fray said, flattered.

"Are you too dull to know an insult when you hear it?"

"Yes," Fray agreed.

The bird, discommoded for some reason, turned back to Happy. "Rapunzel and Grundy are out visiting their daughter Surprise and grand-daughter Prize. I am holding the fort. What the bleep do you want?"

"Don't curse in front of the child," Happy snapped.

"It got bleeped out, prude. You didn't answer my question."

"We're looking for my father, Fracto," Fray said. "He disappeared, but Wira gave us some clues where to look for him. One clue is you."

The bird was flattered, and for the moment unable to formulate a worthwhile insult. "I'm a clue? I'm clueless."

"We don't know what it means," Fray said. "But you must know."

"How the bleep—uh, bloop—should I know?" the peeve demanded.

"Because you must be Xanth's smartest bird."

The peeve opened its beak, but still couldn't work up a decent insult. "That's not true. The Simurgh is the smartest bird, followed by her son Sim. But I will ponder; maybe there is reason I was identified."

At that point Rapunzel arrived home. She was an older yet still lovely human woman, with tresses that framed her head and body. "Why hello," she said, her hair flaring appreciatively. "Visitors?"

"Two windbags," the peeve said, reverting to form. "Glad Bottom and Fray Cloud."

"The Good Magician's daughter-in-law Wira gave us some clues where to find our lost male, Fracto," Happy Bottom said. "The first one was the peeve. We're not sure why."

"What is the second one?" Rapunzel asked.

"Gwenny Goblin."

"Have you ever been to Goblin Mountain?"

"Never. We have stayed largely in the air hitherto."

"Then that's it: goblins are dangerous. But the peeve knows Gwenny; she was the one who arranged to bring it here. The peeve can introduce you."

"Goblins are dangerous?" Fray asked.

"The males are. But the peeve can handle them. We'll have to give you the bird."

"*Lend* them the bird," the peeve corrected her.

"Of course, peeve," Rapunzel agreed as she fetched it a cracker. "Prize sends her regards."

"Prize is only a year old!"

"But she likes you."

The bird was discomfited again. "Next time you stay home and I'll visit her."

"By all means," Rapunzel agreed. She was a very agreeable person. "So you can go with the Clouds, introduce them to Chiefess Gwenny Goblin, then fly back here. You've been wanting to get out anyway, and you know you like Gwenny."

"I don't like anybody!" the peeve protested.

She kissed the top of the bird's head. "But you dislike some less, don't you?"

That stifled the bird. Obviously Rapunzel was one of the people it disliked less. Fray could appreciate that; she seemed almost as nice as Wira.

So it was arranged. The wind remained good, so they got moving promptly. Happy and Fray diffused into cloud form, and the bird flew along with them.

Progress was slow, because the wind was slow. Soon both Fray and the bird were bored. Then a small flying dragon spied the bird, and came in for the kill.

"Leave me alone, hothead!" the peeve protested nervously.

"Handle it, Fray," Happy said.

Fray was thrilled. She collected her vapors, whipped up some drafts, and generated a charge. Then as the dragon flew by her, she loosed a small lightning bolt at it. The bolt struck it on the tail, setting fire to it. The dragon veered crazily, jetted out black smoke, and spun out of control.

"You know," the peeve remarked, "I could get to dislike you less, too." Fray knew she had made a friend. She liked that.

"You say the Simurgh is the smartest bird?" Fray asked. She had spent most of her life floating in the sky, but had not encountered this particular bird.

The peeve evidently understood cloud talk. "Yes. Wisest and oldest. She has seen the universe end and be restored three times. Her chick is Sim, who will some era inherit her position."

"Her chick? Is he young like me?"

"Almost. He's twelve now."

"I wish I could meet him."

"Maybe you can. See if you can do a Sim-ulation."

"A what?"

"A decoy to bring him in," the bird said patiently. "Form into the shape of a big bird."

"Like this?" Fray wrestled her vapors into a huge bird form.

"Yes. Only bigger in the head."

She worked at it, following the bird's directions. And a big bird appeared, the size of a grown human being, fantastically feathered and colored, flying up to investigate the ulation.

"Sim Bird, you feathered freak!" the peeve called. "Come meet Fray Cloud!"

"Squawk?"

"Fray, daughter of Fracto Cloud. She wants to meet a smart bird. And make yourself intelligible."

"Squawk," Sim agreed. This time Fray understood him: "Hello, Fray Cloud."

"Hello," she said bashfully.

"May I inquire why you summoned me with the Sim-ulation?"

She was worse abashed. "I wanted to meet a really smart bird. The peeve said you are."

Sim oriented on the peeve. "Are you trying to make mischief for an innocent young cloud?"

"No. Merely entertainment along the way to see Gwenny Goblin."

"You like her!" Sim said, amazed. "Peeve, you are becoming soft in your old age."

"Never, poop-for-brains."

"Mother says it started when you helped rescue Prize, the baby who liked you without reservation."

"False, feather-face."

"So when did it start?"

"When the Golem family gave me a good home." Then the peeve paused, disgusted. "You tricked me! I don't admit to liking anybody."

"Except Grundy Golem, Rapunzel Elf, Surprise Golem, Prize Golem, and Fray Cloud."

"False!"

"Who else, then?"

"Gwenny Goblin, Hannah Barbarian—bleep! You did it again!"

"It seems your taste is mostly for the ladies."

"Go back to your hutch, dimwit!" the peeve said furiously. "You're ruining my reputation."

"I'll never tell," Sim said, and flew back down toward the ground.

"I won't tell either," Fray said, delighted to have overheard the dialogue. So the irascible bird wasn't so bad after all. That was worth knowing.

"Well, I *was* bad," the peeve said. "Before I got spoiled. But our coming encounter with the goblins will bring me back to form."

"Are goblins really so bad?"

"Worse." The bird hesitated, then spoke again. "When we encounter them, I will have to speak to them in their language. You must cover your ears, because of the Adult Conspiracy."

"Just what is that?"

"It protects children from being brutalized by bad things. It's for your own good."

"Oh, pooh!"

"That's what all children say," the peeve said. "Until they grow up and join it."

"I'll be different."

"They all say that too."

Fray didn't believe it, but saw there was no use arguing. Adults of any species always thought they knew best.

The wind changed. "We'll have to go to land early," Happy said. "Drop and solidify."

"Yes, Mother." Fray dutifully condensed, and her thickening substance slid down through the air toward the ground.

They landed at the edge of a forest, assuming human form. "Fortunately Goblin Mountain is not far," Happy said. "We should make it by nightfall."

There was a herd of cud-chewing creatures in the way. But before they could circle around them, a cloud of smoke formed. "Ants in rum," it said.

"Ancient rum?" Happy asked.

"Ruminants!" the peeve snapped, landing on Fray's now-solid shoulder. "Go away, Metria."

"Whatever," the smoke said crossly as it formed into a lovely human female. "What are you up to now, peeve?"

"Why don't you go soak your smoke in creosote, demoness?" the bird said politely.

"What would two compacted clouds and a disreputable bird want with a herd of cows?"

"Nothing. Are you satisfied, word-mangler?"

One of the animals heard the commotion and came over. "Get out of here, intruders," it said threateningly, assuming the form of a boy with a bovine head.

"Or what, bullhead?" the peeve demanded using Fray's voice.

"Or I'll gore you to death, you insolent girl!" the bull said fiercely.

Fray retreated, frightened. "Oops, I forgot," the peeve muttered. "I'm not supposed to get you in trouble." Then it spoke to the bull, again using her voice. "I'm thoroughly cowed, O horrendous creature. Please spare me."

"Well, now, that's more like it," the cowboy said. "Just clear on out of here. And watch out for the curs."

"What curse?" the demoness asked.

"It's curfew," the cowboy explained. "To keep the dogs away. If they break it, we have to curtail them."

"To cut off their tails," Metria agreed, getting it.

"Right. Now move on."

They were glad to do so. But no sooner were they beyond the herd than the curs showed up, just a few of them, with docked tails. The cowboy evidently had not been bluffing.

"This is too dull," Metria said, and faded out.

At dusk they reached Goblin Mountain. This was like a monstrous anthill, with many entrances and paths all across it, and goblins busily running along them doing whatever goblins did.

"Head for the main entrance," the peeve advised Happy. "You're too big for the lesser passages. Let me do the talking."

A goblin guard challenged them as they approached the main entrance. "You must be reporting for brothel duty," he said to Fray, who was closer to his size.

The peeve hopped to her shoulder as Fray dutifully covered her ears. "Who the bleep are you, snout-ugly?" it said in her voice. Fray did not let on that she could hear enough through her hands.

"Gatling Goblin, hussy. And who the bleep are you?"

"I am Fray Cloud, here to visit Chiefess Gwenny Goblin. Watch your bleeping language; I'm only nine years old. Now take us to your leader."

"Forget it, slut. Clouds aren't covered." Gatling half turned his head. "Grab them, men. Take them to the interrogation chamber. We'll torture them until they tell us the real reason they're here. Then we'll bake the bird and have some real fun with the clouds."

Goblins swarmed up, laying many hands on them. Fray screamed, but in half an instant goblin hands were across her mouth, stifling her. The same was true for Happy. The peeve was saying something, but it was lost in the scuffle.

They were dragged into the tunnel, and to a deep chamber where goblins ripped off their clothing.

Fray did what came naturally: she vaporized. The goblins lost their grip on her as she converted to mist. Happy Bottom was doing the same.

Then everything stopped. "What is happening here?" a mind-mannered goblin man inquired politely. Fray realized that was incongruous, because goblin males were not polite.

"Nothing, Goody," Gatling said. "Go away."

"Goody Goblin!" the peeve exclaimed, flying to him.

"Peeve! What are you doing here?"

"I brought Happy Bottom and Fray Cloud here to see Gwenny."

"We were just about to make her bottom happy," Gatling muttered.

"Fray is nine years old," the peeve said.

Goody frowned. "You were about to what, Gatling?"

But Gatling and the other male goblins had disappeared, evidently realizing they were in trouble.

Fray recondensed, forming her lost clothing about her. "What were they going to do to us?" she asked.

"Nothing," Goody said quickly. "I'll take you to Gwenny."

Happy Bottom condensed again similarly. "That seems best."

"But they were taking off our clothing," Fray said, sure she was missing something.

"Perhaps it had gotten dirty," Goody said uneasily.

He was right about that. Their clothing had gotten badly smudged by the dragging. But the reformed clothing was clean. The goblins hadn't needed to clean it.

The peeve landed on her shoulder. "Adult Conspiracy," it murmured in her ear. "He's not allowed to tell."

Oh, that again. Fray was getting pretty disgusted with the Conspiracy. But she shut up, knowing that adults never relented on the secrets they kept from children. Sometimes she suspected that adults existed to torment children. So she changed the subject: "Why are you so polite?"

Goody smiled. "It's a long story, but the essence is that I suffered a dunking in reverse elixir as a child and it reversed my nature. Fortunately Gwenny doesn't mind."

They were just then entering a larger meeting room. "Of course I don't mind, dear," a lovely female goblin said, kissing him. All lady goblins were as lovely and nice as the males were ugly and crude, but she seemed especially nice. After all, even the peeve liked her.

Goody disengaged. "This is my wife Chiefess Gwenny Goblin," he said. "These are Happy Bottom Cloud, her daughter Fray, and the pet peeve." But Gwenny was already kissing the peeve's feathered head, and the bird wasn't cussing: proof enough.

"Gatling tried to bleep Happy and Fray," the peeve said. "And he was going to bake me. Until Goody rescued us."

Gwenny's smile faded. "True?" she asked Goody.

"Perhaps it was a misunderstanding," Goody said.

"The bleep it was!" the bird snapped. "You're too bleeping soft-hearted, two shoes!"

"That's why I love him," Gwenny said. "However, I am not like him in that respect." She turned to a goblin orderly. "Have Gatling arrested and strung up for neutering immediately after the trial."

Fray could tell by the appalled look on the faces of Goody and Happy, and by the smug satisfaction on the peeve's beak, that this was a singularly apt and harsh punishment. Gatling would probably never bleep a visitor again, whatever it was. There was steel wire under the soft tresses of the lady chief.

"And to what do I owe the pleasure of this visit?" Gwenny asked Happy.

Happy had trouble answering, evidently still shaken by the fate, whatever it was, of Gatling. So Fray answered. "Father Fracto disappeared. So did Wira's husband Hugo. So we're helping each other look, using clues Wira got from the Good Magician's Book of Answers. The peeve is a clue; you are another."

"This is serious news," Gwenny said.

"It's secret, because something might happen to them if the murderer knew we were looking for him," Fray said.

"Of course," Gwenny agreed. "I suspect the peeve was indicated to get you safely here."

"I failed," the peeve said ruefully. "I've gotten too bleeping soft. In my heyday I could have let loose a verbal barrage that shriveled those goblins' faces off their noggins."

"Indeed you could have," Gwenny agreed. "But you aren't fresh from Hell any more. You are becoming infested with decency."

The bird glanced at her uncertainly. "Are you mocking me, wench?"

"I wouldn't dare," Gwenny said with three eighths of a smile.

"See that you don't," the peeve said sternly.

Gwenny returned her attention to the clouds. "You are surely tired after your journey and, um, experience. You must stay for dinner and the night. I can guarantee there will not be any other ugly events."

"But we haven't found out why you are a clue," Fray said.

"I assure you, I have no part in your father's disappearance, or in Hugo's," Gwenny said. "I am as mystified as you. But the Good Magician's Book of Answers is certainly authoritative. It is what brought Goody to me." She kissed Goody again.

"Ugh," the peeve said. "Spare us your mush."

"Quiet, or I'll kiss you too," Gwenny told it. The bird was quiet. That interested Fray: the mere threat of a kiss could cow a rebellious creature? She would have to try it sometime.

They were conducted to a surprisingly well-appointed bedroom chamber with a perch for the bird.

"How did the Book of Answers bring Goody to Gwenny?" Fray asked.

"He had to find a good home for me," the peeve answered. "Nobody wanted me; can't think why. Along the way he met Gwenny, and she nabbed him and dumped me with the Golem family."

"How romantic," Fray said.

"Ludicrous," the peeve grumped.

Dinner was suitably elegant, with airy cotton candy for Fray and assorted seeds and bugs for the peeve. But as dessert arrived, so did trouble: a pack of ugly goblin males charged in, led by Gatling. "Death to Gwenny!" he shouted, and hurled a pie at her.

"I thought you had him arrested," Happy said as Gwenny ducked and the pie splatted against the wall behind her.

"He got away," Gwenny said. "I thought he had fled the mountain. Instead it seems he hid and fomented rebellion."

"Half the males have joined them," Goody said, concerned. "We're in trouble."

"What of the females?" Gwenny demanded as a piece of cake just missed her.

"They are loyal. They like having a female chief."

"That will do." Gwenny climbed up on the table. "Ladies: form a line between me and the rebels so they have to throw past you to get me. See if you can balk your own men."

The ladies went to it with will and purpose. They scrambled up onto the tables. "Snotnose, what're you doing?" one called to her man. Snotnose was abashed now that he had been recognized. "Pickle-eye, you put down that pie!" another called, and Pickle-eye, similarly abashed, did. "Frogbutt, get your sorry bleep out of here!" A third called, and Frogbutt disappeared.

Meanwhile other women were grabbing bottles of boot rear, cream tsoda, and injure jail and splattering them on the men. One sip of boot rear was enough to deliver a pleasant kick in the butt; a bottle sent the man tumbling feet over rear. The cream tsoda liked to cream whatever it encountered; it was normally used only in little drops, and the bottles wiped out the men they caught. Injure jail was strictly for punishment—and now was the occasion.

But there were too many rebels. They swarmed up to the tables and knocked them down. The women screamed as they fell into the melee, their arms and legs flashing prettily. In fact, several panties showed, causing half a swarm of males to freak out. But their inertia bore them on forward, and the panties got covered by clothing and bodies, ending the freak.

That led to a diversion, because it seemed the goblin men had only one idea what to do with goblin women. But each goblin man wanted his own goblin woman to be reserved for him alone, regardless what he did with the women of other men. Fights broke out, and now pies were being smashed into the faces of other men.

Fray found it fascinating. Just what did grown men do with grown women? Somehow she never quite got to see any detail.

Then half a passel of men broke through the defenses and closed in on Happy, Fray, and Gwenny. They seemed to be doomed. "Vaporize!" Happy said.

They did so, as three men caught Gwenny and bore her down to the floor. She caught one in the puss with a cup of boot rear, causing him to clap his hands to his bottom, but the other two were tearing off her dress. In half a moment her bra was showing, and in three quarters of a moment her black panties. The items seemed to have lost much of their freaking power as the two males fought each other to get at the underwear.

Then Fray was fully vaporous, and charged with electricity. She fired out a jag of lightning. It scored on the rear of the goblin climbing on top of Gwenny. He leaped up, electrified, his bottom burning.

"Haw haw haw!" the peeve laughed. "I guess that reamed your fat donkey, dope!" Then it had to flutter out of the way of a flying pie.

Meanwhile Happy was generating a snowstorm. Snow flung out to coat the men. It melted, but froze again as the cold intensified. They were becoming animate icicles. That cooled their ardor somewhat. Before long they retreated.

Their small party was left victorious amidst a clutter of splatted pies and dirty snow. But already Gwenny was on it. "Arrest them all," she snapped. "They're going to spend time in the dungeon being reeducated."

Fray and Happy recondensed as the cleanup commenced. "Thank you for your timely assistance, ladies," Goody Goblin said. "We apologize for the complication."

"We were glad to have been of assistance," Happy said.

"I haven't had more fun in a decade!" the peeve said. "Did you see how Fray goosed that thug with lightning?"

"I believe I did," Goody said. "It was a nice effort, duly appreciated." He tried to keep a straight face, but smiles invaded the edges until they all had to laugh.

"But what was he trying to do to Gwenny?" Fray asked.

Suddenly Happy, Goody, and the peeve went silent. Darn!

Since no one was talking, she asked another question. "Is time in the dungeon really going to make the rebel goblins better people?"

Gwenny sighed. "Probably not. Neither will reeducation. Soon enough they'll revert to their basic nature, and there will be more mischief. The women always forgive them their trespasses, so there seems to be no permanent solution. They don't like being governed by a woman."

"Why don't you use reverse wood? It made Goody nice, didn't it?"

Gwenny stared at her. "Out of the mouths of babes . . ." she said. "Would it work, Goody?"

"I think so," Goody said, surprised. "Why didn't I think of that?"

"You're not a child," Fray pointed out.

He laughed. "That must be it. But there's no reverse wood close by here."

"Sure there is, dodo," the peeve said. "There's a grove not far south. Humfrey used to send the Gorgon to fetch some when he ran low."

"You could show us exactly where it is?"

"That's what I implied, dumbbell."

"But we'll need to act swiftly," Gwenny said. "Before the men catch on and stage a prison break. We need to dose them before they suspect."

"We'll fetch it," Fray said brightly.

"No, dear," Gwenny said. "The terrain south of here is too dangerous for a child."

"We'll float!"

Goody shook his head. "You couldn't carry it. It would reverse your nature, sinking you. I'll have to do it."

"You're too nice," Fray said. "If it's too dangerous for me, it's too dangerous for you."

"She's right, dear," Gwenny told him fondly.

"For bleep's sake," the peeve swore. "You milquetoasts will never get it done."

"Could you do it?" Goody asked evenly.

"With my flight feathers clipped," the bird said. "*I'm* not too nice to handle it."

"But you're a little bird. You couldn't carry enough."

"All it would take is one chip, stewed in broth and fed to them."

"Why would you bother to do us a favor?" Goody asked.

For a moment the bird was nonplussed, almost non-minused. It plainly didn't want to admit that it owed Goody a favor for helping find it a good home.

"It would be a great joke to convert all those tough goblin rebels," Fray suggested.

"That's it," the peeve agreed immediately.

"And mother and I can go along to protect you from air monsters," Fray added.

"First thing in the morning," Gwenny said. "You all need rest, after this day. Besides, the wind generally blows south in the morning, and north later in the day. You'll need that."

She was right, on all counts. Gwenny was a pretty smart leader, it was turning out. They attended the ball, so that no one would suspect and tip off the rebels. There were few men there, because so many had been arrested, so women had to dance with each other, but Fray learned many of the steps and enjoyed it a lot. Solidified existence wasn't so bad, when she learned its ways.

They turned in early, and Fray was asleep before she knew it. It had, indeed, been one big day. And a really interesting one. If only she had been able to figure out what the males had been trying to do to the females! But all the adults hung on to their stupid Conspiracy to Frustrate Children. She was good and sick of that.

At dawn they set out: two clouds and a bird. They exited through an air vent and floated south; fortunately the wind was just right, as Gwenny had predicted.

Xanth was beautiful as the sun came up beyond the horizon, tinting Happy and Fray a lovely pink. Its rays of light reached out to touch everything below, warming it. Fray felt like dancing for the joy of the morning, but wasn't able to in her natural cloud form.

"There it is," the peeve called. "The reverse grove." It angled down toward a bare stone outcropping. "It's a small isolated colony few folk know about, because of the Good Magician's concealment spell."

"But there's no wood there," Fray protested as she condensed.

"Keep your panties on, kid. You'll see it when you get there."

Dubious, she landed on the apex of the mountain—and discovered that it was actually the top foliage of a copse of three trees. The mountain was a mere illusion to mask the reality.

Happy Bottom landed beside her, and was similarly amazed. "Oooo, this is fun!" she exclaimed, girlishly clapping her forming hands.

"This is business," Fray said seriously. "We must obtain some twigs to put in the peeve's bag."

"Aww, that's no fun," Happy said. "I'm gonna go find me some eye scream to eat."

This was odd. "Peeve, what's the matter with her?" Fray asked the bird, who was hovering without landing.

"It's the reversal. You have become adult, and she's a child. You never know which way reverse wood will work."

"How can I be adult? I don't know the Adult Conspiracy." Then she reconsidered. "And don't want to know. There is excellent reason to protect children from such dangerous knowledge."

"Oh, who cares?" Happy demanded, putting a twig in her hair. "I'm going to go find me a man and pop his eyeballs."

"Mother!" Fray said severely. "Forget that and gather some twigs."

"Awww." But Happy grudgingly obeyed the voice of authority. Their positions had indeed reversed.

Fray glanced again at the bird. "Why are you hovering?"

"To avoid reversal the moment I touch the tree, dummy," the peeve said. "Think I want to become Xanth's nicest bird?"

"It would be an improvement."

Happy wasn't being very effective, so Fray gathered the twigs herself. Someone had to be responsible, after all; children couldn't be depended on. When she had several she took them to the peeve and fitted them carefully into the little bag it carried by a string. "There. Now fly back toward Goblin Mountain. We'll follow when we can catch a fair wind."

The peeve pumped its wings—and dropped to the ground. "Ooops. The bag's too close; it's grounded me."

That was no good. Fray made a swift adult decision. "Then we will walk back. It's not too far. I'll carry you." She put out a wrist, and the peeve obligingly perched on it. The bag of twigs dangled below her arm, but she could feel its power.

They walked north. Soon they came to a little shop run by a gnome. The creature was quick to spot an opportunity. "We have a sale on beauty aids," he called. "Come get them while they're cheap!"

"Oooo!" Happy cried, running to the shop. "What do you have?"

"Watch out," the peeve muttered. "That's a rip-off outfit. I've seen them before."

"Mother, we can't afford to waste time or attention on diversions," Fray said.

"This is a beauty mark," the gnome said smoothly. "Put it on and you will be the most beautiful lady extant."

"Oooo!"

"Mother!"

"Or these hair clips," the gnome said quickly as Happy hesitated. "They will cut your hair to just the right length."

Fed up, Fray walked across and caught her mother by the ear. "No cosmetics until we complete our mission," she said. "Gwenny Goblin is depending on us."

Reluctantly, Happy went.

But soon they encountered another man. He was human and halfway handsome. Happy approached him immediately. "I'm Happy Bottom. Let's summon a stork or two, stranger."

"Mother!!"

The man was taken aback, but only one step. "I'm Curtis. I'm interested, but I have the talent of not being able to finish what I start."

"I'll finish it for you," Happy said, opening her shirt.

Fray was too appalled to speak immediately. Happy had become a child in a woman's body, and was exploiting its features without fear of consequences. That was downright dangerous.

"Mother," the peeve said in Fray's voice. "If you don't get moving this instant, you'll get no dessert!"

Happy began to cry. Curtis, surprised and nervous, quickly made a retreat.

"Thanks, peeve," Fray murmured. "How come you are being so helpful?"

"It's this blessed bag of twigs. It's making me uncomfortably nice. I'm horrified to think what it might do if it were any closer."

"That will do. But we've got to get that reverse wood twig out of Mother's hair before she gets in real trouble."

"You'll have to do it. All it can do is make you more adult responsible."

"That's true." Fray reached up and tried to jerk the twig from Happy's hair. But her hand became vapor the moment it touched; she had been reversed another way. "Now what, genius?" she asked with adult irony.

"Maybe if she turns cloud, it will drop to the ground. Then she'll be herself again."

"A worthwhile notion," Fray agreed. "Mother, why don't you try diffusing for a while? It should be less tiring."

"Okay," Happy said with childish acceptance. She dissolved into vapor, and the twig dropped away.

"Now condense again," Fray said. "The wind remains wrong."

"Don't tell me what to do, child!" Happy snapped. Then she paused reflectively, sunlight bouncing off her shiny surface. "What just happened?"

"You were reversed by reverse wood, Mother," Fray said. "You were acting childish."

"Horrors! We can't afford that. We have a mission to accomplish." She solidified and marched resolutely north.

It was good to have her mother back. But a small part of Fray was sorry, too. Had she kept her mouth shut, she might finally have seen exactly how storks were summoned.

They reached Goblin Mountain by mid-morning. This time Gwenny and Goody were out at the entrance to intercept them before the uncouth goblin males did. "Did you get it?" Gwenny asked anxiously.

"Right here, you charming creature," the peeve said, jerking the string holding the bag.

"Excellent. We shall cook up the broth immediately. Goody knows how to do it."

"I do," Goody agreed, taking the bag in his hand, releasing the peeve.

"Hey, you're going to get reversed, dolt," the peeve said.

"No. I am already reversed." Goody walked back into the mountain with the bag.

"Oh, while you were away, I think I thought of the reason I was identified as a clue," Gwenny said to the Clouds. "So I could help you succeed in your quest. Here is my insight: A report arrived saying that the Random Factor has escaped his cell and is on the loose. You are looking for Fracto. That's an anagram: Factor, Fracto. There has to be a connection."

"The Factor escaped—and Fracto got caught," Happy said. "Could they have somehow switched places?"

"That is my thought," Gwenny agreed. "I think you should check Castle Maidragon."

"Daddy's in the Factor's cell?" Fray asked.

"We don't know that, dear," Gwenny said with adult caution. "But it does seem possible."

"We'll go there on the first fair wind," Happy Bottom said, showing a flash of actual happiness for the first time since Fracto had disappeared.

"This should be fun," Fray said. "I've never seen that castle up close. Are you coming, peeve?"

"Not me," the peeve said. "My job is done. I just want to go home and resume insulting passersby."

Gwenny ruffled its feathers. "After you get through insulting our goblin males. They really need your attention."

The peeve nodded thoughtfully. "They do. And I need the practice, to recover my edge."

Things were looking quite positive.

8
ESCAPE

In the morning Hugo exchanged minds with Bathos Bat, and made ready to explore more of the environment.

Brunhilda was there. "I will fly with you," she said. "Maybe I can help."

"I'm not Bathos," he told her. "I'm Hugo." He wasn't at all sure he wanted her along.

"I know who you are. You're the one with the marvelous talent."

"No, that remains with my body. If you go there now, you can gorge on fresh ripe fruit."

"Only while Bathos occupies your body. Once you obtain your freedom, and depart, he will revert to his normal pathetic self."

"That's unfair," Hugo protested desperately. "He has a fine talent."

"If you don't shut up, I'll kiss you, like this." She kissed him before he could dodge.

She had done it again. The kiss stirred his desire and gutted his protest. She wanted to make him her love slave, and knew exactly how to do it. If he tried to protest further, she would do it immediately. She didn't care that he was a human man.

He made his way to the cave entrance, and she paced him. He took wing, and she matched him perfectly.

It was probably useless, but he had to try. "What would you want with a human man anyway?"

"A bushel of fruit every day," she replied without hesitation. "What more could any fruit bat want?"

"But I must get home to my wife, whom I love."

"She will learn to make do without you, in time."

"But I could never be a—a husband to you. We're of different species. We couldn't summon the stork together."

Brunhilda shrugged in air. "Stork summoning is overrated, not that bats bother with it. Your alien form makes you safe in that respect; you won't expect constant physical attention. As my love slave you will obey my every whim regardless of your species. I can see advantages."

"I can't. I just want to be home with Wira. She's the only one I'll ever truly love, and I can summon the stork with her."

Brunhilda sighed. "You're getting independent again. I see I'll have to kiss you."

"No!" he cried supersonically. He winged straight into blank air, trying to escape.

But she paralleled him without seeming effort. "I love it when you attempt bravado. It makes the conquest that much sweeter—and I do have a sweet tooth. All the same, I'd better kiss you."

"There's a dragon!" he cried.

"Why do you think I'll fall for that familiar ruse, you cute thing?" She oriented, making ready to kiss him while on the wing. That was surely not all she could do in flight.

A jet of fire almost toasted her rear. "Because it's true," Hugo said, diving clear.

"For pity's sake," Brunhilda said as the dragon opened his ponderous and mottled jaws to take her in.

Then she kissed the dragon on his hot upper lip. It was no token effort; she plastered the monster with a huge wet one lasting a moment and several instants. Evidently it required a more heroic effort to affect a creature that size.

The dragon veered crazily, losing elevation. Little hearts swirled in the vortex of his descent. That answered the question of whether her power worked on other creatures: she had just rendered the dragon into her love slave.

"Now where we we?" she inquired, rejoining Hugo.

"We were searching for a way for me to escape my confinement in that cell," Hugo said. "I don't even know where that castle is."

"Oh, that's no problem. It's the human Castle Maidragon, named after its caretaker, Becka Dragongirl. I thought you knew."

"Castle Maidragon!" he exclaimed, amazed. "I have heard of it! Why didn't I think of it?"

"Because you don't have a good female to keep you in proper order. As my love slave you will remember whatever I tell you to remember, and not much else. Mainly, my favorite fruits. Let's see to that now." She swung in close to him, to plant the kiss.

He dodged so hard that the universe spun for half a moment. When his orientation cleared, he was hovering in a glade surrounded by several old oak trees. There was some sort of ceremony taking place there.

"Oh my soul," Brunhilda said behind him. "It's a wedding! I just love weddings."

A robust, handsome human man stood before the group. "We are here to celebrate the union between Forrest Faun and Imbri Nymph-mare," the man intoned. "I am King Emeritus Trent Human, here by re-quest to officiate, being long familiar with the bride. All be seated, please."

The small group sat on the greensward. Hugo and Brunhilda settled also, so as not to make a commotion. "I know Magician Trent," Hugo mur-mured in bat talk. "Maybe I can tell him my plight, and he can help me."

"After the wedding," Brunhilda said firmly. It seemed there was just something about females and weddings.

"A spot recap," Trent said. "Imbri has been known to us for decades, first as a Night Mare bringing bad dreams to those who deserved them. Then she was briefly the Mare King of Xanth, when the Horseman was taking us all out in turn. She finally dispatched him, rescuing us all, but in the process lost her body. Thereafter she became a Day Mare, bringing pleasant dreamlets, and some of us may have preferred her that way. Then the Good Magician assigned her to assist Forrest Faun, here, in his quest to find a new faun to represent the tree of his lost friend Branch Faun. He did not succeed, but Imbri kindly consented to assume the role of nymph, saving the tree."

Trent looked around. A number of human eyes were wet; it was part of the magic of weddings. They made folk cry for no reason. "Since then Imbri's original body has been recovered, and also Branch Faun. Her association with the tree has enabled her to assume nymph form. Now she will marry Forrest and share his tree, so that Branch can have his tree back. Meanwhile Branch is serving as Best Faun, and his favorite chasee as Nymph of Honor. I trust that no one present takes exception to that."

For some reason, no one did. "Step forward," Trent said. Forrest Faun did so, and so did a lovely nymph whose long black hair swished around like a horse's tail. "I now pronounce you Faun and Nymph, to share your long lives and tree henceforth. You may kiss."

They kissed, and even Hugo found his eyes wet. Little hearts orbited them so swiftly that some spiraled out to land in the audience, causing appreciative ooohs. As they touched people and popped, they left minidaydreams of gamboling fauns, nymphs, and spirited horses. It was beautiful.

"Oh, I have to get married," Brunhilda breathed.

It was time to move on. Hugo took wing and flew toward Magician Trent, hoping to attract his attention and somehow establish his identity. Trent would certainly be able to help.

But Brunhilda caught him from behind. "Not so fast, love slave!" They swirled out of control, the universe spinning again.

And there they were, back under the dragon's nose. They must have suffered some kind of magic vortex that carried them to the romantic wedding, and then back here. Had that been another random event?

Random! Now he remembered: it was the Random Factor who occupied the lowest cell of Castle Maidragon. Hugo had somehow switched places with the dread Factor!

The dragon sniffed him, and revved up some fire. "No, no, honey," Brunhilda said, petting him on a nostril with the tip of a wing. "This bat is not for burning. I'm about to enslave him too."

The dragon did not seem entirely pleased, but had to go along with it. That was, it seemed, what love slavery was all about. How was he going to escape it?

"I have to notify someone of my picklement," he said.

"Oh, all right," she said, humoring him. "My kiss hasn't recharged yet anyway."

That was right: she couldn't invoke that magic kiss after exhausting it on the dragon. So this was his window of opportunity to escape her, and his confinement in the Factor's cell. He didn't know how it had happened, but he knew he had to get out while he could.

"Maybe the dragon can help," Brunhilda said. "Dragon, what's your name?"

"Dragoman Dragon," the beast replied.

She almost fell out of the air. "You speak my language!"

"I ought to," Dragoman said. "I'm a professional interpreter. I speak many winged monster dialects."

"But you were going to toast and chomp us!"

"That was before you kissed me, you passionate vamp."

"I'm not a vampire bat, I'm a fruit bat."

The dragon lifted half a brow, evidently realizing that her vocabulary was limited compared to his. "Seductive creature."

"That's better," she agreed, mollified.

"But with your linguistic expertise, why waste it on stupid chomping?" Hugo asked. "Any dull creature can do that."

"A dragon's got to eat."

That did seem to make sense. "Well, that will have to wait, sweetie," Brunhilda said. "We have to talk with someone to tell them that Hugo here is really a human being in bat form."

"A human being! Oh, he really needs chomping!"

"No way," Brunhilda said sternly. "I need him."

"Please? With toasted acorns and hot peppers?" the dragon pleaded.

"I said no. I might even marry him."

"I'm already married," Hugo reminded her.

"I'll toast and chomp his present wife," Dragoman offered. "Then he'll be free to marry you."

"Well," Brunhilda said, considering.

"No!" Hugo said. "I'll never conjure another fruit for you."

"Then what good will you be to me?"

"None."

"So you might as well let me toast him," the dragon said reasonably. "Then *I* can marry you. We'll make winged monster history."

Oops. Hugo had walked into that one.

"We'll see how you feel once you're my love slave, Hugo," she decided. "I think I can persuade you to conjure fruit, considering the alternative."

"When pigs fly," Hugo said, realizing as he said it that he was walking into further mischief.

"I know a flying pig," she said. "Pigasus, who as food is hambrosia."

"I'll toast that pig!" the dragon said, slavering eagerly.

"For now, just lead us to someone Hugo can contact," Brunhilda said. "Preferably human."

"Do I have to?"

"Yes, dear reptile, if you ever want my favor."

Dragoman issued a fiery sigh. "Then get on my back and we'll go find a human."

"And don't toast that human until we're sure he's of no use to us," Brunhilda said sternly.

"You're a harsh mistress," the dragon complained.

"Thank you," she said, flattered.

They clung to Dragoman's scaly back. He accelerated, looking for humans to contact. "But you know, humans aren't necessarily the smartest creatures."

"Oh?" Hugo asked, annoyed. "Who is smarter?"

"Dragons, for one."

"Give me one example."

"Gladly. You know of Clio, the Muse of History?"

"Everyone who is anyone knows of Clio," Hugo said.

"Would you consider her to be a smart human?"

"Yes."

"Smarter than a dragon?"

"Yes!"

"Well, she isn't. She got into a pun fathoming contest with my kind, the dragons, and won."

"So she was smarter."

"No. She was too stupid to know she had really lost."

Both Hugo and Brunhilda paused at this. "Did she win or lose?" Hugo asked after most of a moment.

"She lost, but thought she won."

"And the dragons didn't question this?"

"We wanted her to win."

Hugo paused the rest of the moment, which gave Brunhilda the chance to speak next. "Why have a pun contest if you don't want to win?"

"That might be complicated for bat brains to fathom."

"Guano!" she swore. "Tell it."

"She wanted to take half a slew of dragons from Dragon World to Xanth, where they would become real. Naturally we dragons approved. But we couldn't simply give them to her; she had to earn them. Dragon protocol, paragraph 62, footnote B, relating to necessary appearances. But then she was losing, so we changed the score, and telepathically altered her mind so she never questioned it. We did it at the Poop Deck pun, to be sure she wouldn't poke her delicate nose in it. So she thought she won, and she took the dragons to Xanth, and here we are. But we were smarter."

"Not if you altered her mind," Hugo protested. "That's cheating."

Dragoman's whole body inflated with fire. "That's *what?*"

"A difference of opinion," Brunhilda said quickly as she kicked Hugo in the wing.

The dragon blew out the fire in a harmless cloud. "So there you are."

"There we are," Hugo agreed weakly. Brunhilda was right: it was dangerous to question the integrity of dragons, at least from up close.

"Ah, there's a human family," Dragoman said. "Fly down and talk with them, while the bat girl and I discuss romantic plans."

It occurred to Hugo that Brunhilda might have gotten herself into more than she had bargained for, but he was hardly the one to protest. He took off and glided down, while the dragon flew on.

It was indeed a human family: a somewhat asinine looking man, a somewhat monkey-faced woman, and three children, evidently having a picnic. He landed on the table next to the stack of sandwiches.

"Eeee!" a girl screamed with four e's. "A club!"

"You mean a bat, Upp," the larger boy said.

"Get rid of it!" she screamed, retreating so fast she fell over backward.

"Ree Sette, look what you made your sister do," the mother said severely.

"Well, she is Upp Sette," Ree said. "That's her nature."

"True, Marmie," the man said. "Don't blame Ree."

"Well, he'd better use his talent," Marmie said. "Ree Sette, undo that scene."

Ree looked rebellious, but obeyed. He gestured—and suddenly Hugo was back in the air away from the table and the Sette family was going about its picnic undisturbed. The scene had been reset.

But he hadn't managed to communicate. So he tried again. This time he flew in to land beside the smaller girl, what had not freaked before. Maybe she liked bats.

She did. "Ooo, nice! I'm Sunny Sette, getting pretty in the evening. Who are you?"

Hugo realized belatedly that he lacked a way to talk to humans. He couldn't speak Human in bat form, and they did not understand bat talk. How could he make them understand?

Maybe he could trace words in the dust of the tabletop. He started spelling out HELP.

"Asse, Sunny's got something," Marmie said.

Asse Sette, evidently a man with resources, came around the table. "That's a bat," he said. "It may be rabid."

"No, it's slow," Sunny said.

"He said rabid, not rapid, dummy," Upp Sette said.

The little girl began to cry. She had been upset, of course.

Marmie sighed. "Ree."

Then the scene was back to what it had been before. Hugo considered, and concluded that he was unlikely to get anywhere with this family. He flew back to rejoin Dragoman and Brunhilda. "I couldn't get through," he said.

"That's all right," she said. "I thought of a better way. We'll fly back to Castle Maidragon, and Dragoman will talk with Becka Dragongirl and tell her about you."

Hugo's bat mouth fell open. "This is brilliant!" he said. "Why didn't I think of it?"

"Because you're not female," she replied smugly.

"Because you're not a dragon," Dragoman said, as smugly.

It seemed they had him there, though Hugo did not see it quite the same way.

They flew back to the castle. There was no dragon in sight. "She must be in her dull human form," Dragoman said. "You'll have to send her out."

So it was up to Hugo after all. He left them and flew into a turret window. And promptly got lost in the labyrinth of the castle. There were passages, stairs, chambers, and courts galore; where was Becka?

Finally he blundered into what seemed to be a child's playroom. There was a two-year-old boy there, playing with salamanders and fire. Evidently his parents knew about it, because the room was fireproofed.

Could he talk to the child? He settled down in front of the boy.

"Bat," the child said. Suddenly Hugo was surrounded by a ring of fire. He lurched back into the air before his wings got scorched. This was no good.

The boy started crying. That brought his mother: a pretty blonde with brown eyes. That would be Becka. "What's the matter, Ben?" she asked, picking him up.

"Bat gone," he wailed.

She glanced around. "There was a bat in here? They're supposed to stay in their cave."

It was time for Hugo to make an appearance. He flew to the nearest chair and perched on it somewhat clumsily, for his body wasn't made for it.

"So there *is* a bat," Becka said. "Why aren't you in your cave?"

And how could he explain? He started to trace the first letter of his name: H. He walked up and down on the seat of the chair, then across between the two verticals.

"Brusk!" Becka called. "There's a sick bat in here."

Brusk appeared. "Yes, dear. I'll take it out."

That wasn't what he wanted! Hugo tried to protest, but in a moment Brusk had a net and was stalking him.

Hugo took wing and tried to fly around the man, but Brusk reached quickly out and managed to touch a wingtip. Suddenly Hugo was hard and heavy. He dropped to the floor with a clunk.

Brusk put the net over him, then touched him again through it. Now he was very light and soft. That was Brusk's talent: to make things hard and heavy or soft and light. Hugo was caught.

Brusk carried him outside. He poked the net over a battlement and let it open. "There you are, bat," he said. "Now go home. You don't belong in the castle."

There was nothing for Hugo to do except fly away, defeated.

"So it didn't work," Dragoman remarked. "I knew it. As a human you aren't smart enough."

"And you are?" Hugo demanded.

"To be sure. Observe and learn, if your puny intellect is capable of it." He flew down to land by the castle's front gate.

"He's such a dynamic creature," Brunhilda remarked.

Dragoman inhaled hugely, then bellowed out a roar that could surely be heard throughout the castle.

In a moment and a half Becka appeared at the gate. "Is there a problem?" she called.

Dragoman blew three smoke rings. That was evidently a signal.

Becka nodded. Then she transformed into her dragon form. She had purple-tinted bright green scales. She spread her wings, pumped them once, and glided across to meet Dragoman snout to snout. "What's so urgent, Dragoman?" she asked in dragon talk.

"This bat's a man. You have to let him out of the dungeon cell."

"That cell confines the Random Factor," she said, alarmed. "Anyone who opens that door gets randomized in some distressing way."

"He says he got switched. Now he's a man called Hugo."

"Hugo?"

"The Good Magician's nonentity of a son."

She pondered half a moment. "I remember now. He does have a son or two, along with five and a half wives. But what's your interest in this?"

"I want his girlfriend. If he returns to man form, she'll be mine."

"That does seem to be a suitably cynical dragon motive. But how can I believe this isn't some ploy by the Random Factor to get me into his clutches so he can do something horribly random to me? I don't believe he's been near a woman in decades."

Dragoman nodded. "I hadn't thought of that. Maybe you had better talk to him yourself."

"Maybe I'd better. Where is he?"

"Here!" Hugo called.

"What's that noise?" Becka asked.

"You don't understand bat talk?" Dragoman asked.

"I'm a dragon, not a bat. You hadn't noticed?"

"I noticed. A lovely one, too. If you ever are on the prowl for a male dragon—"

"Never mind. You know I'm married." She changed back into human form, signaling her disinterest in any dragon liaison. "You understand bat talk?"

"I understand all flying monster talk," Dragoman said proudly. It was clear that Becka understood dragon talk in either form, and Dragoman understood human.

"Then you translate. Tell him I need to ascertain whether he's really who he says he is."

"Right," Hugo agreed.

"He understands you," Dragoman said. "He knows human; he just can't speak it now. I'll just translate his answers."

"Good enough." She turned to Hugo. "Who is your wife?"

"Wira. She's blind." The dragon translated that, and asked, "Is that a trick question?"

"No. Everybody knows the Good Magician's sons are married. Who is the Good Magician's wife?"

"This month, the Gorgon. She's my mother. He has five and a half wives, who rotate monthly."

The dragon translated, and added, "I didn't know that. Your excellent magician must be quite the man. How old is he?"

"Answer that," Becka told Hugo.

"Physically or chronologically?"

"Both."

"Physically he keeps himself at about a hundred by using measured doses of youth elixir. Chronologically he is one hundred and seventy-four."

"Who wrote the Book of Answers?"

"The Good Magician wrote it himself, mostly during his first century.

He studied all Xanth, compiling answers. That's why contemporary things can be missing, until he adds them."

Becka shook her head. "I don't think anyone outside his immediate family would know that. He guards his knowledge. You must be who you say you are. Go back to your human body and I'll let you out."

Victory, so rapidly! "Thank you. I'll be there."

Becka returned to the castle, and Dragoman took off to circle around to the bat cave. "So now you can be mine," he said to Brunhilda.

"Except for two things," she said thoughtfully. "First, I want the fresh fruit Hugo can provide me."

"I can show you where there's a secret secluded fruit tree grove that no other bat knows about," Dragoman said.

She considered. "Show me."

The dragon veered and winged in an unknown direction. Soon he landed by a secluded grove in a niche offshoot of the Gap Chasm. It was overgrowing with richly flourishing fruit trees of many kinds.

"Hmm," the dragon said, annoyed. "Someone's been picking the fruit recently, but there are no tracks or smell."

"A mystery," Brunhilda said.

"This must be where I conjure my fruit from!" Hugo exclaimed. "I've taken a lot in the past few days, for Bathos. I never knew where it came from."

"So this is the source," Brunhilda said, pleased. "So I don't need you any more."

"You don't need me," Hugo agreed, relieved.

"So you can marry me," Dragoman said.

"Not quite so fast, fireface," she said. "There is still the second thing."

"What is that?" Dragoman asked.

"Bathos Bat. When Hugo trades to get his human body back, Bathos will be a bat again, and will want me. And he *is* a bat."

"I'll chomp him!"

"No, he has a useful talent. I might need it some time."

"What for?"

"To make out with you, for one thing. Short of a quadruple strength accommodation spell, you and I are never going to make physical love, now are we?"

"I'll find the accommodation spell!"

"No, it would be easier to exchange minds with Bathos and tryst with me as a bat. I'm sure Bathos would like to be a dragon for a while, too."

The dragon considered. "How do you like being a bat?" he asked Hugo.

"Actually, it's all right. It enabled me to contact Becka Dragongirl to arrange my escape from the cell."

"Could you make out with Brunhilda?"

"I'm married!"

"If you weren't married, could you make out with her?"

Hugo got the dragon's drift. "Yes, enthusiastically. She kissed me too, you know. She's some bat."

Dragoman nodded. "Good enough. But will Bathos agree to let me have his body for that?"

"He will if I kiss him," said Brunhilda. "He'll be my love slave, and will do anything I ask."

"Then you can keep him. You're right: he will be useful. Now let's go make the exchange."

They flew back to Castle Maidragon and the Bat Cave. Dragoman dropped them off and hovered outside, too big to enter. They made their way to the crevice that opened to the cell.

There was his body, sacked out amidst a pile of half-eaten fruit. It seemed that Bathos had not yet quite conquered his hunger.

Bathos! Hugo called mentally. *I'm back.*

"Go away," Bathos said, tossing a ripe pear at the crevice.

It is time to trade back. I have made contact with the proprietress of the castle. She will let me out.

"She's a pretty girl, isn't she? Maybe I'll make time with her. I'm sure this body can do it."

What was this? *You can't. She's married.*

"Well, there'll be others. And gobs of fruit. How I love it!"

"What's happening?" Brunhilda asked. She did not understand human talk, and lacked the mental connection.

"He's balking about changing back."

She paused half an instant. "Oh he is, is he? After we have it all arranged? I'll deal with that." She squeezed through the crevice and dropped into the cell. She spread her wings and circled the chamber. Then she swooped into the human body and planted a recharged kiss on its mouth.

The body staggered, hearts and planets spiraling wildly around it. She had staggered it with the potency of the kiss.

Hugo pounced, mentally. *Trade back now! Brundilda wishes it.*

And he was back in his own body, his belly full to the verge of sickness. But he wasn't Brunhilda's love slave; that enchantment had remained with the person rather than the body. That was a relief.

Brunhilda remained in the cell, watching him. "I'm myself, Hugo," he told her. "Human. Go deal with Bathos."

She understood his manner if not his words. He waved as she headed for the crevice and squeezed through. She would handle Bathos and Dragoman, making the best of an interesting situation.

He got to work cleaning himself up. His clothing was a loss, but he didn't want to exit the cell nude. Maybe he would be able to borrow something.

Soon there was a knock at the door. That would be Becka. "Yes," he called. "I am Hugo. But the bat who used my body made a mess, and I have no clothing. Can I borrow something?"

She was evidently reassured that he wasn't the Random Factor. "Oh, don't be concerned," she said as she unlocked and drew open the door. "I've seen it be—" Then she caught a full glimpse of him, perhaps two glimpses. She froze in place, her eyes staring blankly.

She had freaked out. One flash per eyeball had taken both out. Hugo hadn't realized it happened to women too. Maybe the case had to be truly egregious. Hastily he picked up his sodden bundle of clothing and held it over his soiled midsection. Then he snapped his fingers.

She recovered, unconscious of her time in freakdom. "I'll fetch some clothing. You'll want a shower, too." She beat a swift retreat.

Hugo shook his head ruefully. There was nothing between him and Becka, but he would have preferred to have made a better appearance.

Soon Brusk appeared, carrying an armful of clothing. Evidently Becka was making sure not to be flashed again. "Follow me," Brusk said, turning around. It seemed he wasn't that keen on Hugo's filthy forty-three-year-old body either.

He followed the man to a magical shower stall. Soon he was luxuriously washing. Then he dried and donned the clothing. It didn't fit him well, probably being some of Brusk's, but was far better than his own.

Now at last he met formally with Brusk and Becka. "So that's why the bat was inside," Becka said. "That was you."

"That was my identity borrowing the bat's body," Hugo agreed. "While the bat used my body to gorge on fruit. He's a hungry fruit bat, you see."

"But just how did you get in that cell?" Brusk asked.

"I don't know. One moment I was in the cellar of the GMC, and the next I was in that cell."

"GMC?"

"Good Magician's Castle. I'm so used to it I abbreviate it. Anyway, the conjecture is that somehow the Random Factor managed to exchange places with me."

"But that means the Random Factor is on the loose," Becka said, alarmed.

"I fear it does," Hugo agreed.

"I'd better call the Gorgon," she decided. She went to the magic mirror hanging on the wall. "Mirror, mirror, on the wall—"

"I heard," the mirror said. "I'm flashing her now."

Hugo wished it hadn't used that word.

The Gorgon's veiled face appeared in the mirror. "Yes?" Then she saw Hugo. "Hugo!"

"Mother," he agreed.

"At least you might have told me where you were going," she admonished him. "Wira's been beside herself." The mirror obligingly put two small images of Wira in a corner, beside each other. "Where are you?"

"At Castle Maidragon, mother."

"Visiting with Becka? For shame! Not only are you married, so is she."

"Mother, it's not—"

But then her smile, unable to remain suppressed, twisted her veil. "I'm glad you're safe, son. What happened?"

"We think the Random Factor switched places with me. Is he there?"

"The Random Factor! No, he's not here. There's only a nebulous dead body here. I trust you didn't do it?"

"I didn't do anything. Are you sure that's not the Factor?"

"If it is, he's dead, or dead to this world. I don't think it is."

"Doesn't father know? There should be something in the Book of Answers."

"The Book of Answers has been scrambled; Humfrey's struggling to put it back into order." The Gorgon paused. "But you know, that's something the Factor could have done. So maybe he was here, and left the body."

"But whose body is it?"

"We wish we knew. It's a mystery. We were afraid you were being framed for it."

"I'm not a murderer!"

"We know, son. We've kept it quiet until we can exonerate you."

"May I talk to Wira now?"

"She's not here. She's out looking for you."

"Where is she? I want to be with her."

"We don't know, dear. I'm sure she'll check in in due course."

"I want to find her!"

"And she wants to find you. Something about an overdue signal to the stork, I think. Why don't you return here, and be here when she returns?"

"I suppose I'll have to," Hugo agreed, disappointed.

"I'll take you there," Becka said. "You obviously don't mind riding dragons."

"Not when they're going where I'm going," Hugo agreed. But he was sorely disappointed that he wouldn't be back with Wira immediately.

9
PASSION

A re you satisfied?" the Demoness Mentia inquired.

"I am prostrate," he confessed.

"You are what?"

"Worn out, tired, exhausted, utterly sated—" He paused. "You haven't reverted to Metria, have you?"

"Whatever," she said with mock crossness. "I merely thought you used a dirty word."

"I did not. Anyway, you certainly proved your point. Are you going to vanish now that you've done it?"

"Naturally. That's what demonesses do."

"I can't interest you in a continuing relationship?"

"What continuing interest would I have in a mortal? There was a challenge, I rose to it, now it's done, and there's no point in staying."

"You demons don't have a conscience," he said, remembering.

"Well, Metria got half a soul when she married, so I have part of a soul too. That gives us some conscience. It's a nuisance. What do you care? You have precious little conscience yourself."

"I couldn't do my randomizing if I had much of a conscience. It would make me be concerned about the consequences of my actions to others. So I have it parked somewhere out of the way."

"Why are you interested in a continuing relationship? You're random,

not crazy. I'm the crazy one." Her head shifted shape until it resembled
her bare bottom. Her bottom surely now resembled her head. She was indeed a little crazy. "Otherwise I wouldn't have wasted a whole night making you delirious," her voice said from under her skirt.

"I want something from you, of course."

"I already gave you a night of it. That's enough."

"Something else."

"Oh, with my features reversed? That would be different, all right. But
what would be in it for me?"

This wasn't getting him far. "What can I offer you that would enlist
your cooperation taking me somewhere and helping me meet someone?"

Her head and face reformed where they belonged. "Someone else?
Who?"

"A girl."

"You want me to set you up with another woman?" she asked, sparks
jumping from her hair and little lightning jags from her eyes. One might
almost have supposed she was annoyed.

"It would be complicated to explain."

"I'm a little crazy, not a little stupid," she snapped, her teeth striking
further sparks.

"But you'd have to keep company with me long enough to hear my
explanation."

She nodded. "True. That would be deadly dull. So oo-toodle, as my
other self would put it." She began to fade.

"There's a small mystery," he said desperately.

She remained half faded. "Metria has an insatiable curiosity. She must
be done with her morning routine by now. I'll swap out with her. It's been
a while since I emulated her form and seduced her husband. That *really*
annoys her."

Her half-faded form subtly shifted. "What's this stupid conundrum?"

"This stupid what?"

"Puzzle, enigma, riddle, maze—"

"Corn?"

"Whatever," she agreed crossly. "Hey, wait half a moment! That's
not it."

"Mystery," he said.

"That's it. Anyhow, that's maize, not maze, when its corny. So what's your deal? Mentia says she already gave you triple the bliss any mortal man deserves, just to make a point. She was crazy to do it."

"Naturally," he agreed. "Now I have a stupid, minor, inconsequential little mystery to fathom, and I could use your help to accomplish that."

"Is it interesting?"

"Dull."

"You cunning one-eyed card! You know I don't believe you."

"Cunning what?"

"King, queen, jack—"

"Knave?"

"Whatever. What's your mystery?"

Now was the time for truth, as she would catch on quick enough otherwise. "You know I'm the Random Factor."

"No corn there," she agreed.

"I tried to escape from the Factory some time ago, and they confined me in the dungeon of Castle Maidragon. I escaped, but now they're after me. They've sent an agent to fetch me back. I don't want to go back; it would stifle my random nature. So I need to know how this girl proposes to do it."

"Girl?"

"Maid, damsel, young woman, servant, female—"

"I mean how's a mere girl going to catch you and bring you back when you can randomize out of it?"

"Exactly."

"What?"

"Precisely, correctly, properly, accurately, veraciously—"

A puff of steam blew her head off. "I mean how's it going to happen?" the head called from on high.

"That's what I want to know. It's a mystery. Can you help me?"

The head settled back into place. "What kind of help do you want?"

"I want to go to her and investigate without her knowing who I am or what I'm doing."

"So why don't you?"

"She'll know who I am the moment I use my magic. Then she'll nab me. Unless I know how to stop her."

"This is intriguing," the demoness agreed. "Very well, I will help you fathom this corn. What's your tack?"

"My what?"

"Procedure, technique, plan, course, angle of attack—"

"Approach?"

"Whatever. Answer the question."

"First you'll have to take me there, so I don't have to use my magic, though my magic couldn't work that way anyway. Then you can pose as my girlfriend or wife—"

"I knew it! You just want me to proselytize!"

The Factor considered momentarily, and decided not to question that. He treated it as the word she had intended. "No. Your crazy half already did plenty of that. I need an innocent identity, and a married man traveling with his wife would seem to be that."

"A pretend wife." She considered. "I can do that. But there's a wonder."

"A what?"

"Suspicion, mistrust, issue, doubt, dubiousness—"

"Problem," he said. "Your problem with words."

She nodded.

She had a point. The moment she opened her mouth, anyone who knew her or had ever heard of her would catch on to her identity. "Maybe you could be mute," he said.

"Be what?"

"Silent, quiet, still, soundless, stifled—"

"Gagged?"

"Whatever," he agreed crossly.

"Me? I never shut up! How could I make mischief if I were gagged? The thought gags me. I'm not gaga over it."

"It won't work if you mess up words. Maybe it will have to be Mentia after all."

"That smoky hussy? Never!"

"But obviously you can't do it."

She considered two thirds of an instant. "How about Woe Betide?"

"How about what?"

"My child identity. When a sphinx stepped on me long ago I fractured into three forms. The third is a five-year-old waffle."

Her problem was getting annoying. "Waif?"

"Whatever. She doesn't have a vocabulary problem. But you have to honor the Adult Conspiracy in her presence."

"But surely she knows everything you and Mentia know. She would remember the night I just had with that sultry demoness. That would completely fracture the Conspiracy."

"She's in de Nile."

This one threw him. "The what?"

"A river in Mundania. Not. Pretending something doesn't exist."

"Denial!" he said, getting it. "You know, that would work. We could be father and daughter, because the mother was toasted by a dragon. Completely harmless. What do you think?"

Metria dissolved into smoke. In more than an instant but less than half a moment she reformed as a cute little tike. "Matches?" she asked, proffering one. "They grant you your fondest wish."

"I want to abolish that agent."

She clouded up. "That's a mean wish."

He backed off. He didn't want trouble that would alienate her. "I take it back. But what about your name? How can you be anonymous?"

"Be what?"

Was this really Metria? No, probably just too big a word for the waif. "You need a pretend name. It's a game. So no one will know who you really are."

She clapped her little hands. "A game! I'll be Trace, 'cause I'm only a trace of my grown-up self."

"Very good. Trace it is. And I'll be—" He paused, considering. "Fabian. You will pose as my daughter, and when anyone asks you about your mother, you cloud up and say she went away because of a dragon."

"Goody," she agreed. "I like being half an orphan."

"Now we need to go to join Debra. Can you find her?"

"Let me look." She fuzzed into smoke, which then faded. That was something else she would have to stop: acting like a demoness. Soon it reformed. "Yes."

"Can you take me there?" He knew the adult demoness could, but this one was much smaller.

"Sure."

"Then do it, but don't take me right there. Take me nearby, so Debra doesn't see me travel and know you are a demoness. After we get there, don't do any demonly things. Better hide those magic matches, too."

"Okay." She fuzzed back into smoke. This time it spread out to encompass him. Then there was the half-familiar wrench, and they were elsewhere.

"Thank you," he said as the smoke retreated and condensed back into the child. "That was very good, Trace."

"Ooo," she said, pleased.

"Now remember, you're a girl, not a demon."

"Got it, Daddy," she said winsomely.

"Where is Debra?"

"Around that copse."

He looked around. "What corpse?"

"Copse. A thicket of small trees. I'm small, so I relate."

But she had an adult vocabulary, when she wanted it. "So let's join them." But then immediately he had a second thought. "Let's spy on them first. Go into the copse and see what you can learn."

"Okay!" the child disappeared into the copse.

Soon she was back. "I couldn't see them, but I could hear them. They said something about finding the Factor—"

"The Factor!"

"And the Nameless Castle. Only they don't know where it is."

They were looking for him? That meant that Debra was coming directly after him. But what was this about the Nameless Castle? What did that have to do with it?

But he doubted that the girl knew what he looked like, because he had been confined for so long in the dungeon cell. So he would try to bluff it out.

They walked around the copse. And there was a woman, a young centaur, and two children. This set him back; which one was Debra? She was supposed to be a teen girl. These were too old, too young, or not human. He couldn't just ask, because that would give away his advance knowledge.

"Why didn't you tell me one was a centaur?" he whispered to Trace.

"You didn't ask."

Even as a child, this demoness could be annoying.

"People!" the little boy exclaimed, spying them.

Commitment. "Hello," the Factor called. "May we join you?"

"That depends on who you are," the woman said.

"Fabian. And my half-orphaned daughter Trace."

"A girl," the boy said somewhat disdainfully. "I'm Glow."

Trace smiled at him. It was almost bigger than she was, and surely owed much to the adult demonesses' experience. The boy visibly melted.

"I'm Ilene," the girl said. She looked to be about eleven.

"I am Wira," the woman said.

"And I am Debra," the centaur said.

She was a centaur! How could that be? Had the demon been wrong?

"Transformed human," Debra added.

Oh. "You weren't satisfied in your original form?" he asked.

"She is carrying me," Wira said. "I am blind."

What was the agent doing with a blind woman? This was one curious business. "My regret," he said politely.

She ignored that, surely fathoming that he hardly cared. She was evidently the leader of this little party. "Where are you going?"

He suffered a sudden flash of genius. "I promised Trace a tour of the Nameless Castle."

That got the woman's attention. "You know where it is?"

"Yes," he lied. Not only did he not know, he had no idea what it was. But he had a plan.

"Well, then," Wira said. "May we travel with you?"

Exactly. Now he just had to find it. "Of course," he agreed. Then, to Woe Betide: "Trace, didn't you have to do something in the woods before we get going?"

She glanced at him, and understood. She had to get out of sight so she could turn demoness and locate the Nameless Castle. Then she could quietly tell him, and he would lead the party there.

"I guess so," she said. She made her way into the copse.

"What happened to your wife?" the girl, Ilene, asked. It was the sort of question girls did ask.

"She ran afoul of a dragon," he said. "We don't like to speak of it."

"That's so sad," the centaur said sympathetically.

That surprised him. That was the Factory Agent who was going to capture him? The oddest thing was that he rather liked the look of her, especially her front. He almost wanted to touch it. But of course that would not be wise, for several reasons. She was a centaur, she was underage, and she was the agent. He had to learn her secret weapon and somehow nullify it. So he had no business liking any aspect of her. She was dangerous. Yet she was a winsome creature, quite unlike either the nymphs or the demoness.

"So who's taking care of your little girl?" Ilene asked.

"I am. It's quite a job."

"Surely so," Debra agreed with further sympathy. And again it got to him. It would be so easy to believe that she really was a nice girl who really did care. He couldn't afford that. He had to fathom her secret weapon, then figure out how to nullify it. Before she discovered who he was.

Trace returned. "Done," she reported matter-of-factly. She meant that she had located the castle, because of course as a demoness she had no natural functions unless she wanted them.

"Then it is time to be on our way," he said, picking her up in a fatherly manner.

"It's in the sky," she whispered in his ear. "Floating over the eastern Gap Chasm now."

He turned to the blind woman, Wira. "There is one problem. The Nameless Castle is out of reach at the moment."

"Not out of Debra's reach," Wira said.

"Oh, of course. She can fly there. However—"

"You can't," the little boy, Glow, said.

"Readily solved," Wira said. "Debra can carry you there, if you show her the way. Then she'll know, and fetch the rest of us at leisure."

Ride the centaur? Suppose she knew his identity, and this was a trap to get him on her so that she could carry him helplessly back to the Factory? She had given no indication that she knew, but of course she wouldn't. Not until her trap sprung.

Yet if she didn't know, that would give him a far better chance to discover her weapon. He would have to gamble if he wanted to win. And riding on her could be a rather pleasant experience. He decided to gamble. "Excellent," he said, evincing no doubt.

"Good enough," Debra said. "Just let me flick you light." She stepped up close to him, turned about, and flicked him with her tail.

Suddenly he felt astonishingly light. That was the magic of winged centaurs, he remembered. They did not fly by powerful wingbeats, but by lightening themselves and their burdens. It was a convenient system.

"Now mount," she reminded him.

He did so, putting one hand on her back and jumping. He sailed right over her. She reached up and caught his foot as he passed. "Easy does it," she murmured as she set him down on her back.

"Thank you," he said, embarrassed. "I haven't done this before."

"Understandable. Now hold on to my mane."

He took hold of her luxurious hair. "Got it, I think." Her mane was continuous with her beautiful hair. He wanted to stroke it. In fact he wished he could reach around her torso and stroke something else. What was stirring him?

She spread her wings and flapped them as she leaped into the air. They were thus readily airborne. She spiraled up until they were well above the forest. "Now where to?"

"It is floating over the eastern Gap Chasm," he said. "Perhaps anchored there for the time being."

"Anchored in the air," she said, laughing.

He liked it when she laughed. He wished he could see her front, which surely shook in a really interesting manner. At the same time he knew this was flirting with destruction, because she was the agent of his doom.

And he realized that this might be no coincidence. She might have been crafted by the Factory to be exactly the kind of maiden he liked. So that he would be attracted, and come to her, so she could take him in. So he was in more than one kind of danger.

Yet why should they have sent an underaged maiden? It griped him at times, but he did honor the Adult Conspiracy to Keep Interesting Things from Children. If she was supposed to seduce him into mischief, she should have been of age. It wasn't as if the nymphs or demoness had had any trouble on that score. Surely they had adult maidens to send. It didn't seem to make sense. That bothered him, because he was sure the Factory was not being nonsensical. Factory folk were always supremely programmed. That's why they couldn't abide his randomness.

Unless she was merely an advance scout, sent to locate him and report him to the Factory, which would then send out a competent agent to haul him in. Maybe they didn't want to waste the time of a full-fledged agent, so wanted to make sure of him first.

Yet the demon had said she was the agent. Could the demon have been wrong? Or was the answer incomplete? Could she be older than she claimed, the seeming youth a mere cover to conceal her real nature? Maybe to keep other men from bothering her until she could orient on the right one, and then turn older, reeling him in? He didn't dare gamble. He would have to treat her like the real agent, until he knew for sure.

"You became suddenly quiet," Debra remarked. "Did I laugh inappropriately? I did not mean to give offense."

Which was an entirely appropriate response for an innocent girl. Which made him think he should try to verify the state of her innocence. The real agent would be anything but innocent. "I had an inappropriate thought," he said.

"Oh? I don't think I understand."

"When you laughed, I wished I could have seen your front."

She considered. "I still don't—" She paused. "Or maybe I do." She blushed, her entire human section turning red, as far as he could see.

"And I wish I could see it now," he said.

"You are embarrassing me something awful," she said, the red deepening.

"Centaurs are not embarrassed by natural functions, and male interest in the fronts of females is natural."

The blush became a flush that heated her skin; he could feel its radiation. "I am not really a centaur. Please, I don't want you thinking of me like that."

She was certainly innocent. He doubted any person could fake such color.

Then it came to him: *she didn't know she was an agent.* So she really was young and innocent.

"I apologize," he said. "I shouldn't have told you my thought."

"But I don't want you to lie to me." Her color was starting to fade.

And indeed he did not want to lie to her. He wanted her to trust him, and he wanted to be trustworthy for her. He hated the fact that it was necessary to deceive her. He would have to step carefully.

"You appear to be a young grown woman," he said. "Or filly, as the case may be. Grown men have private thoughts about grown women, finding them attractive. But I know you are several years short of grown, so I should not have expressed my thought. I apologize, and will try not to do it again."

"Centaurs don't honor the Adult Conspiracy," she said. "And I'm from Mundania, where most young folk know what's in it even if they're not supposed to. So you really didn't say anything wrong."

Yet she had blushed furiously. She might know the content, but she wasn't used to it. "Still, it was unkind, and I regret it." And he did.

"It wasn't even unkind," she said. "It just caught me off guard. I never thought—as a centaur I am better formed than I was as a human, so it didn't occur to me that—even though I have caught others looking. So— Oh, I'm all confused!"

"That's why the Conspiracy exists. To protect young folk like you from concepts they aren't yet equipped to handle. Your reaction proves it. I'm sorry I was so unpleasant."

"But I did ask. You did say it was inappropriate. So it was really my fault."

She was getting to him. "Don't say that! I was trampling on your innocence. I'm sorry and I wish I could take it back." The weird thing was that he meant it. She was either a phenomenal actress, or truly as innocent as she seemed.

"No, I need to learn how to handle things. I'm sorry I blushed. I'll try not to, next time."

"There won't be a next time."

She paused, then shrugged. He wished he could see that, too, from the front. "I don't quite know how to say this, so I'll surely mess it up. But I'd like there to be a—a next time." Her blush was returning.

He was surprised. "You want me to say something crude again?"

"Yes," she whispered. "I hate it, but I like it. I know that's crazy."

She wanted to come across as a girl, but womanly instincts were manifesting. Adults could handle their mature urges, while teens tended to misplay them. It was the classic struggle of teendom. Adults were not supposed to take advantage of it. Yet he was sorely tempted. There was just something about her that drew him in, making him like her. That might be cynically crafted, but it nevertheless worked. He cursed himself for falling into a trap he could plainly see, but continued falling. Still, he temporized. "I shouldn't."

"Do you really want to—to see my front?" she asked timidly. "When I laugh?"

What was left but the truth? "Yes."

She half folded her wings and glided down toward the ground. "Then think of something funny to say after we land."

"I don't understand."

"To make me laugh. While you're watching." Her blush intensified again. "Oh, I'm so disastrously naughty! If I had panties I'd be flashing them at you. And I don't even know you."

She wanted to impress him. Which meant that she was as eager to have a relationship as he was, probably for no better reason. She was attracted to him, as he was to her. Even though there could be nothing between them, and not merely because of her age and species, and his need to avoid the trap she represented.

"We hardly know each other," he agreed, mainly because it was the right thing for a proper man to say.

"Yes. That makes it worse." She came down in a glade, and her legs ran as she touched the ground, so that there would not be a sudden stop.

"This is crazy," he protested. "For all you know, I could be a—a really bad man."

"There's something about bad men," she agreed. "Maybe you'll show me what it is."

He dismounted and faced her. As a centaur, her human portion was significantly higher than he was. "I can't think of anything funny to say. This is dangerously serious."

"That's hilarious!" she said, laughing. "I think I'm hysterical." She continued laughing, unable to stop.

The effect was every bit as impressive as he had anticipated. He feared this was disaster, but couldn't help himself. "Get down on your knees," he said.

"Crazy!" she said, folding all four knees. That brought her head down parallel to his.

He stepped up, put his arms around her bare torso, drew her close against him, and kissed her.

She kissed him back, fiercely. The passion of it flared, encompassing them both. They remained there, timelessly embraced.

At last they fell apart. The Factor sat on the ground before her, not trusting his balance. She remained kneeling, her mane and hair flaring as if electrically charged. He saw the swirling hearts sailing up and away, a dissipating cloud.

"I shouldn't have done that," he said.

"What is it?"

"We have entered a dangerous new dimension."

"What is it?" she repeated.

"It's love. Forbidden love."

"Forbidden love," she echoed. "I never expected it." She pondered half a moment. "But why is it forbidden? I don't mean because I'm too young. Time will take care of that, and I may be only thirteen, but I know love when I feel it. Or because I'm a centaur. I'll be a girl again soon enough. Or because you're a stranger. You aren't any more. I don't care about any of that. There's something else, much worse. I know it, I feel it. What is it?"

He would have to tell her the whole truth, though it damned him. Because he had abruptly fallen in love, and he couldn't deceive her any more. "You won't like this."

"I can't stand not to know."

"It will force us to separate, probably forever. It might be better to hide it, so we can be together, at least for a while."

"I love you," she said simply. "Nothing can change that."

"I love you," he said. "And that is part of the problem."

"You're married!" she said with sudden alarm.

"No! I have been with women—well, nymphs and a demoness—but you're all I want, henceforth."

"So you're experienced. I want that, because I'm not. If that's the worst of it—" She paused. "But it isn't, is it. You know I truly won't like it."

"Yes."

"Tell me anyway. But kiss me again, first."

Now he laughed, ruefully. He got up, stepped up, embraced her, and kissed her again. This time the floating little hearts were so thick he could feel them brushing his shirt and her bare back. When they separated, after a brief eternity, he saw that one heart had gotten tangled in her mane. And in his own hair. After a moment the two hearts managed to free themselves, came together, and merged into one larger heart which floated away on the breeze.

He sat down and talked. "I am the Random Factor."

"The what?"

She didn't even know of him! "I worked at the Factory some time ago, but I was random, and messed up their business. So they confined me in the dungeon cell of Castle Maidragon, where I wreaked random magic on anyone who opened my cell door. I had no choice; I was cursed to do it, so that no one would try to free me."

"Why didn't you simply escape when it was open?"

"It wasn't the lock on the door that held me. It was the enchantment. But then I randomly reversed myself and escaped. I knew they would send an agent after me, to confine me again. You are that agent."

"I am not!" she protested angrily.

"Where were you last year?"

"In Mundania. I didn't like it so I came to Xanth."

"Exactly how did you do that?"

She considered, surprised. "I don't know. I just—found myself here, not long ago."

"Doesn't it seem more logical that your memory of Mundania is artificial, and that you came into existence when you appeared in Xanth?"

She started to protest, but then her mouth fell open in surprise. "It does."

"It is your job to locate and capture me, so I can be confined again. Which means we can't be together, because either we'll be apart because I'm fleeing you, or because I'm confined in a dungeon cell."

"But I wouldn't do you any harm! I couldn't!"

"You won't have a choice."

"Of course I have a choice. No one can make me do something I really don't want to do."

"You have been conditioned to think that. But when the time comes, your innocent-girl persona will fade and you will do what you are programmed to do."

"Horrible thought!"

"It is why I came to you. I had to find out what your secret weapon was, so I could nullify or escape it. I fear I have discovered it, but not escaped it."

"Love," she said. "We were supposed to fall in love."

"Yes. But that would be just the precursor. That will keep me close to you, or bring me back to you if I flee. There has to be something else, as obviously you have not bound me yet in any physical manner."

"There's something," she said thoughtfully. "Sometimes I have an awareness and a sense of direction, as though there's somewhere I should go. But then it passes."

"It's when I do my random magic. You can sense that, and know where it occurs. But what are you supposed to do?"

"I think it has something to do with my curse."

"Your curse?"

"When I wear a bra, and any man hears my name, he wants to come take it off me. To de-bra me. But I don't know how that could affect you."

"I'm a man. I'd want to take it off you."

She smiled ruefully. "And I'd let you. You've already seen my breasts. You're seeing them now."

"And they fascinate me," he agreed. "Maybe I'm supposed to touch them, and that will invoke the confinement spell."

"You already have. We were plastered together when we kissed. Twice."

"No. They touched my shirt. I touched only your back, and your mouth."

She glanced down at herself. "Then maybe you should touch them with your hands, and find out. I'm sure they won't hurt you."

"I am not sure," he said.

She laughed again, and again he was fascinated almost to the point of freaking out. "Let's settle this. I'll fetch my bra." She reached into her arrow quiver, which somehow had not intruded when they kissed, and drew out a cloth halter.

"I don't know," he said warily.

"I want to know too," she said. "So I can avoid whatever it is that will trap you." She put on the bra and hooked the two sides of it together in front.

"Don't do this," he pleaded, unable to remove his eyes.

"I have to."

"That's what I fear."

"My name is Debra," she said firmly.

He started toward her, his hands reaching for the filled bra. Suddenly he knew what the threat was. "Take it off!" he cried desperately. "Now!"

Startled, she did. The cloth fell away just as his hands reached her breasts. He wound up with two amazing handfuls, but no bra.

Debra smiled. "See? You're not confined."

"It's the bra," he said. "When I touch it, that will invoke the spell. I felt its power. Your curse is just a nuisance to you or any other man, but deadly to me. That's your secret weapon."

She looked at the material, now lying on the ground. "Maybe you're right. I did feel a horrible power as you came near it. That faded when I got it off." She smiled. "You can let go any time now, you know."

Now he blushed. "Sorry." He let go of her breasts. "At least now we know. It's that bra that will destroy me, if I ever touch it. And if you wear it, I will be compelled to touch it."

"I'll burn it," she said, picking it up.

"I don't think that will do it. Any bra you wear will carry the magic."

"Then I'll never wear a bra again."

"I suspect you'll have to. Don't you want to already?"

"Yes," she said, surprised. "I'm starting to, well, itch." She put the bra back in the pack.

"The curse. It didn't bother you before, but now you know what you're supposed to do, and it will force you to do it. That's why we must separate."

"Oh Random, I don't want to!"

"Neither do I. But you exist to destroy me. I must hide from you."

"You're right," she said tearfully. "I truly don't like this."

He nerved himself, and said what had to be said. "I love you. I think I always will. But I must leave you. Maybe in five years, when you're of age, your curse will fade, and I can safely join you."

"I'll wait for you!" she cried.

"I fear not. You must pursue me, and I must flee, because I can't stand to hurt you. We must be apart, as long as your curse exists."

"But if they turn off my curse, they'll have no reason to keep me in business," she said. "I might cease to exist."

He viewed her with horror. "Oh, Debra, I couldn't stand that! I have to believe that somehow, sometime, we can be together."

"Somehow, sometime," she echoed. "I have to believe it too. But at least we have this moment. Kiss me again."

He did, and once more reality compacted into the two of them in the center of the universe, all else being incidental. The orbiting hearts were almost suffocatingly thick.

Then they separated, and she got back to her feet. "Now I'll go," he said sadly.

"We must locate the Nameless Castle," she reminded him.

He formed half a smile. "Is that a chore or a pretext to stay together a little longer?"

"Yes," she said with the other half of the smile.

"The Nameless Castle it is," he agreed. He mounted her back, she flicked them both light again, galloped forward, spread her wings, and sailed into the air.

"The dream realm," she said suddenly. "Can we meet there? I know I'll be dreaming of you."

"And I of you," he agreed. "Maybe we can. We don't have to wait for night; any gourd will facilitate it."

"It's a date." She was silent half a moment. "Does the Adult Conspiracy exist in the dream realm?"

"Oh Debra, what are you thinking of?"

"You know better than I do."

"I don't know. Dreams can be quite naughty, so maybe the Conspiracy doesn't exist there. We'll just have to find out."

"I can be my own form, there," she said.

"But no bra."

She laughed, this time turning at her supple waist so as to present a stunning side view of her chest as her face faced him. He couldn't help it: he kissed her a fourth time, stifling the rest of her laugh.

Suddenly they were sailing straight upward into the sky. "Oh, that makes me light-headed," she gasped as they broke.

"So I noticed. Don't hit a cloud."

"You know, if you started to fall off, you might have to grab me around the torso," she said.

"But then I would touch your—" He broke off. "You're such a tease!"

"I wasn't teasing," she said, blushing.

What an invitation! "In that case—"

"Oh, there's the castle," she said.

He looked. There was a cloud floating above the Gap Chasm, which they had intersected during their distracting dialogue. On the cloud rested a fancy castle. The Nameless Castle. "Yes."

"I understand that's where the Demon Xanth lives now, with his mortal wife Chlorine."

The Demon Xanth! Who would surely want to keep things in good order, so would side with the Factory. He couldn't go there.

"Now you know where it is," he said with infinite regret. "Now I must depart. Randomly. I love you."

"Oh, not yet!" she protested tearfully. "We have so much more to talk about, so many more kisses to share."

"I must, or I never will," he said. It was the truth.

"Please!"

He invoked the random location exchange before he could change his mind. His last sight was of her adorable tear-wet face. That would haunt him forever.

10
REGROUPING

D ebra blinked, and he was gone. But there was something
in his place, balanced on her back. It looked like a portion of a statue, a bust of a girl, with only the head and
body above the waist showing.

Well, he was the Random Factor. He did things randomly. As she understood it, he himself had no control over it; he merely initiated the action and something random happened. So he had switched places with
this statue, and now was wherever it had been. Maybe on someone's
mantelpiece.

"And what do you have to say for yourself?" she inquired rhetorically.
The last thing she needed at the moment was half a statue.

"Come all ye fair and tender maidens," the statue said. "Take warning
how you court young men."

Debra almost dropped out of the sky. "You're talking!" she exclaimed.

The statue eyed her as if she had said something stupid, or at least less
than completely intelligent. "Of course I'm talking. I'm a maiden head.
When invoked I warn maidens about bad boys."

And she had inadvertently invoked it. Fair enough. "How did you
come here?"

The eyes glanced around. "That I don't know. Heights make me nervous. If I fell I'd break into seventy-three pieces and some gravel. But I'm

sure a man has something to do with it. Men are if not the root of all evil, at least the stem of it. It's not safe to love any of them; you're in for heart-break." She glanced more carefully at Debra. "And from the look of you, you are heartbroken now. It's a man, right?"

"But it's not his fault," Debra said. "He loves me."

"That's what they all say, until they get into your pants. Never trust a man!"

"No, this is different. He wants to be with me, but can't. It's compli-cated."

The bust gazed at her with the pity reserved for the self-delusional. "It always is, when they're married."

"He's not married!"

"Or gay. Or impotent. Or terrified of commitment. There's always a reason, but it's never the one they tell you. But girls never learn. It's such a tragedy."

This was getting nowhere. "Maybe I should take you home. Where is that?"

This set the bust back. "I really don't know. I've always been on the shelf. No one listens to me, for some reason. I'm sure it's a man's fault."

"Then I'll just have to take you with me." Debra made a smooth turn and headed back the way she had come. She didn't need to stop at the Nameless Castle; she would do that when they delivered Nimbus there.

"That's very kind of you," the bust said. "But remember—"

"I'll be wary of men," Debra agreed. Actually her experience was quite limited, but she had matured considerably in the last hour. She had been a mere girl or filly with a spot curse; now she was a woman in love. That was a different creature.

In due course—she had carefully avoided the undue courses that were offered along the way—she returned to the glade where Wira and the chil-dren waited. They all stared as she landed. "Where's Fabian?" Ilene asked.

"Look at the bare statue," Nimbus said.

"It's a bust," Debra explained, lifting it down.

"Wow! A bare bust." His small male eyes were goggling.

"Hands off!" the statue snapped as he reached.

"Fabian is gone," Debra said. "I have this instead. It's complicated."

"I think you had better explain," Wira said.

"Not before the children."

"Did you drop him?" Ilene asked.

She would have to tell part of it. "He is someone called the Random Factor. He—"

"The Random Factor!" Wira exclaimed. "He's dangerous!"

"You know of him? I didn't."

"He's confined in the dungeon cell of Castle Maidragon. He does terribly random things to anyone who even opens his door."

Debra didn't argue that case. "He's out. He switches places randomly with other people or things. In this case, the maiden head."

"He told you this?" Wira asked.

"Yes. He comes from the Factory, but they don't like him because he's random. So they want to confine him again."

"Why did he approach us?"

"He believes I am an agent sent by the Factory to bring him back. He was—scouting."

"But you're just a girl with a curse."

"So I thought. But he may be right. My curse may be meant to trap him. So he had to go."

Wira clearly realized there was more, but that it was indeed complicated. She was sensitive to feelings, and surely was picking up on Debra's. So she shifted the subject slightly. "His little daughter Trace remains here."

"Oh, fudge," the child swore. "Just tell me how you're going to trap him, and I'll be gone."

"You're not what you seem," Wira said.

"I'm Woe Betide. I was trying to help him solve the mystery."

"Woe Betide," Wira repeated. "The child aspect of Demoness Metria. We have met before."

So she was a demoness. Debra had not suspected. "I can explain that particular mystery. When I don a bra, and men hear my name, they want to take it off. But if the Random Factor touches it, he will be caught by its magic, and confined again. That's the trap. So he had to depart before that happened."

"Okay," the tike said, and faded out.

"Did you locate the Nameless Castle?" Wira asked.

"Yes. I can take us there now."

"Then we had better do it. Thereafter we can talk."

When the next youngest child was gone. That made sense. "All aboard," Debra said.

She flicked each of them light, and herself, and they mounted. Soon they were airborne.

"Whee!" Nimbus exclaimed. "I love flying."

"You've flown before?" Ilene asked.

That made him pause. "I guess."

Debra found that interesting. There was something about the boy, and not just the way he glowed. He was still concealing his identity.

They approached the Nameless Castle, perched on its cloud. "Home!"

Debra landed carefully on the fluffy white edge of the cloud. It was spongy, but firm; her hooves did not sink through its substance. Naturally it wasn't an ordinary cloud; it could not have supported the castle otherwise.

Nimbus jumped down and ran toward the castle. "Mom! Dad!" he cried happily. "I'm home!"

A lovely young woman emerged from the castle as Wira and Ilene dismounted. She swept the boy into her embrace. Behind her came an amazing oddity: a dragon with the head of a donkey. A giant pet?

"You found him!" the woman said to Wira, clearly recognizing her as the senior figure. "Thank you so much! I was so worried."

"We didn't feel it would be right to leave him lost," Wira said. "I am Wira, the Good Magician's daughter-in-law, and these are Debra and Ilene."

"Of course we know of you, Wira," the woman said. "I am Chlorine, and this is my husband Nimby."

"Nimby," Wira repeated, seeming daunted though she could not see the dragon. "I—also know of you."

"But Debra and Ilene do not," Chlorine said.

"Actually I do," Ilene said. "My father told me long ago." She too seemed oddly daunted.

"Am I missing something?" Debra asked.

"Nothing important," Chlorine said easily. "Come in for a visit; we really appreciate your help in recovering our son."

"Oh, we don't need to stay," Debra said. Then she caught Wira's sightless look. "Or maybe we do."

"You must be hungry," Chlorine said. "We'll have a feast for you."

"Actually we're still full from last night's feast with the Air Folk," Wira said. "But we'll be happy to visit briefly."

They entered the castle, which seemed even larger inside than outside, and amazingly ornate. Debra was becoming quite curious about it, and its inhabitants.

They came to a lovely courtyard filled with exotic plants. Chlorine bade them sit in comfortable couches in the center, while Nimby and Debra remained standing.

"But doesn't the furniture get wet when it rains?" Ilene asked.

"It doesn't rain on the furniture," Chlorine said.

The girl looked puzzled, so the woman glanced at the dragon. Suddenly it was raining on the plants, but none fell on the couches. The rain ended in a circle just beyond the couches.

"Oh," Ilene said, looking abashed.

"You have done us a considerable favor," Chlorine said. "We will do each of you favors in return."

"There's no need, really," Wira said. "We just did what seemed right."

"So will we," Chlorine said. She caught Ilene's eye. "What would you like?"

The girl hesitated, but realized that it would be impolite to refuse. "I'd just like to visit with Glow every so often, because we have similar talents."

"Glow?"

Ilene seemed flustered. "He wouldn't tell his name, so we had to make up one for him. So we used that, because he glows."

"But Nimbus doesn't glow," Chlorine said.

"Yes he does. He—" Ilene, abashed again, went silent.

Chlorine looked at Debra. "Glow?"

"He does," Debra said. "Even Wira can see it."

Chlorine looked at Nimby, but the dragon avoided her gaze. "So it's like that," she said, frowning. "And I thought he was merely named after his father. I wonder what else I don't know about him." She looked again at the dragon, who still avoided her gaze.

"We didn't mean to make any trouble," Wira said.

"We'll settle this later," Chlorine said grimly to the dragon. Then she returned to Ilene. "You want to visit. If Nimbus is interested—"

The boy ran across to hug Ilene.

Chlorine nodded. "So it shall be. We'll give you a magic air pass that will bring you here any time you invoke it. It will be good for Nimbus to have a friend." She glanced at Nimby again, and this time the dragon wiggled an ear. A piece of paper appeared in the air, floating down to fall into Ilene's surprised hand. "Do not share it; it is for you alone. Now I believe Nimbus wants to show you the punnery."

"The punnery?" Ilene asked blankly.

"It is where all the really bad puns are sent, so they won't appall innocent folk. Nimbus loves to play with them." She grimaced. "It's a job to clean him up afterward. There's nothing quite so smelly as a squished pun, especially when he gets it in his hair."

"Ugh!" Ilene said as the boy caught her hand and dragged her off to a corner of the garden.

"Have some of this potato," Nimbus told Ilene.

She looked at it suspiciously. "Are you sure this is potato? It doesn't smell very good."

"It's potato, I swear. It's served at banquets."

"All right." Ilene touched her tongue to it. "Yuck! It's awful."

"It's potato ogre rotten. Served at ogre fests."

"That's not funny!"

The boy looked woeful. "I'm sorry. Let's watch the race."

"The race?"

"The E race. See here are the e-racers. See which one wipes out more scenery."

The cars looked like blocks of rubber. As they moved they left trails of smeared nothingness. "Erasers," Ilene said, getting it.

Debra smiled. Ilene seemed to have shamed the boy into behaving. For a while.

Chlorine turned to Wira. "And what would you like?"

"I just want to find and rescue Hugo."

"There is no need. Call home." She produced a magic hand mirror.

"But I can't use a mirror," Wira protested.

"Then I will do it." Chlorine faced the mirror. "The Gorgon, please."

In a moment the Gorgon's snake-framed veiled face appeared in the mirror; Debra saw her. "Oh, Chlorine," she said. "What can I do for you?"

"You can tell Wira about Hugo."

The Gorgon's gaze went to Wira. "It's true, Wira. My son has been rescued. He's looking for you. He was in the Random Factor's cell."

"The Random Factor!" Debra exclaimed involuntarily.

"Oh, thank you, thank you!" Wira said. "That's all I want."

"Becka Dragongirl will carry him back here tomorrow. I'm sure he's eager to rejoin you."

"Oh, yes!"

"Thank you," Chlorine said to the Gorgon, and the mirror went blank. "So you must ask some other favor."

"But there's nothing else I want."

"How about your lost sight?"

"We just said I was looking for that, so folk wouldn't know we were looking for Hugo. I never actually—"

Chlorine glanced at Nimby. He wiggled an ear.

Wira screamed and clapped her hands to her face.

Chlorine plucked a cloth out of nowhere and dropped it over Wira's head. "I apologize. I forgot that sight would be alarming to someone who isn't used to it. But you can cover your eyes and learn to use them gradually, at your own pace."

"She really can see now?" Debra asked, amazed.

"She really can. I trust you will continue to help her until she gets used to vision."

"Oh yes, of course!"

"Now what about you, Debra?"

"Oh, I don't need anything."

"What, nothing?"

"Nothing possible, anyway."

"This threatens to be interesting. Tell us your story."

"Oh no, it really doesn't—" The dragon wiggled an ear, and suddenly Debra knew she had to tell all completely everything without reservation. That dragon was weird, and not just because of his ridiculous head.

Debra told everything, from her appearance in Xanth to the present. It just poured out of her. "So you see, it's hopeless love," she concluded. "I can't be with him without destroying him, and that's the last thing I want. Not even if I were of age."

"And if you don't get to him, in time you may be abolished yourself," Chlorine said.

"Yes, I think so. I'm not sure I'm really real. I think they just modeled me after a thirteen-year-old Mundane girl and gave me the bra curse. I exist to trap him, and I can't stand to do that."

"We don't like to interfere in the ongoing history of Xanth," Chlorine said. "But we can do this much: we can make you real. Then the Factory won't be able to abolish you. The rest of your adventure you will have to work out yourself."

"Make me real?" Debra asked numbly.

"Yes. Nimby did it for Grundy Golem, and later in effect for Umlaut, who married Grundy's daughter Surprise. Of course you could still be killed, so don't be careless."

"I won't be careless," Debra said, somehow unable to doubt the truth of the statement.

The dragon wiggled an ear. Debra felt something weird and wonderful infuse her, and knew that she was indeed real. She seemed to be floating on a sea of amazement.

"I feel—more mature," she said in wonder.

"Nimby made you a real eighteen-year-old girl, apart from your transformation to winged centaur form," Chlorine explained.

"But I'm only thirteen!"

"Nimby advanced the model. It was as easy to make you be of age as it would have been to make you underage. There was no need to make you wait five years in frustration."

Debra was amazed. She looked at Wira. "Is this possible?"

"Oh, yes," Wira said. "Believe it."

"Who *is* Nimby? Or *what* is he?"

"Now it is time for you to go," Chlorine said. "Wira wants to get back together with Hugo." She faced the punnery. "Nimbus! Ilene has to go now."

"Awww," the boy said, from a stand of wormwood trees. The long wooden worms were standing upright, forming a small forest.

Ilene turned to face them. Her mouth had disappeared, leaving her teeth bare.

"Oh, he tricked you into trying that shade lipstick," Chlorine said. "That's strictly for ghosts." She held up the mirror so the girl could see.

"Eeeek!" Ilene screamed with four e's, which was pretty good for a girl her age. Nimbus rolled on the ground with laughter at his joke.

"Cold cream will take it off," Chlorine said, producing a bottle of cream with icicles on it.

Ilene accepted it gratefully and poured out a frozen cube. She rubbed that across her lips, and they came back into sight.

Debra trotted over to pick her up. "Horsefeathers!" a loud voice said, startling her. It seemed that some of the plants could talk, at least in the punnery.

Sure enough, there was more. "Get thee to a punnery!" the voice said as she passed. She didn't answer, knowing it was a pun on nunnery, which was in turn sometimes a crude name for a Mundane house of ill repute. These puns were not only thick, they were obnoxious. Which was of course why they were confined here. Her new maturity gave her adult understanding of such things.

Necessary confinement? Like the Random Factor, only for different reasons. She might be real now, but she still had to stay away from him—and feared she could not, for already her love was making her long for his company. Her change of age had not changed that. Her love was, if anything, even more thorough now. She was no longer a girl; she was a woman.

Ilene mounted. "Thanks," she said. "Watch your step!"

Too late. Debra had already put a hoof on a low-lying pun. Now the thing was squished all over her foot. She tried to scrape it off, but foul pieces of it clung, while the boy laughed some more. Boys did find that sort of mishap hilarious.

"Actually, the punnery is a lot of fun," Ilene said. "As long as you are careful."

"I'm sure it is," Debra agreed tightly.

Back in the center of the court, she picked up Wira, and was escorted out of the Nameless Castle. Wira still had the cloth over her head.

Once they were safely airborne, Debra posed the question again: "Who are those people? How do they rate a floating castle to themselves? How can they grant magic favors to passing folk, and collect atrocious puns for their garden? And what is with the idiotic donkey-headed dragon she says is her husband?"

"Some time back," Wira said, "the Demon Xanth, from whom all of our magic leaks, indulged in a wager with other Demons. He assumed the form of a dragon ass, and was allowed to speak only once. Thereafter he had to win a single tear of love or grief from a mortal who did not know his nature. That mortal turned out to be Chlorine, who was neither lovely nor smart, but knew what she lacked. He gave her that, and they traveled together, and in time she did shed her last remaining tear for him. That freed him and gave him the victory. He had fallen in love with her, so he married her, and they took over the Nameless Castle, which was vacant at the time. Now they remain largely clear of mortal business, but on occasion help out folk who don't know their natures."

"The Demon Xanth," Debra said. "I never suspected!"

"Precisely."

"But you knew; that's why you took Glow—I mean, Nimbus—there."

"Yes. He might be kidnapped or harmed if others knew his identity. I had to get him to the safety of his home."

"Why can't Chlorine see his glow?"

"She wanted an ordinary child. Nimby cheated, so concealed it from her."

"Nimby. That's an odd name for an odd creature."

"It stands for Not In My Back Yard. He doesn't have to keep that form, but likes it because he had it when he met Chlorine. She organizes things, but the power is all his."

"And now you can see, and I'm real and of age, and Ilene has a pass to visit anytime."

"Sometimes it pays to do the right thing."

"So it seems," Debra agreed. "But my dilemma remains. Real or unreal, I don't want to hurt the Factor."

"You know the love you feel is a product of the enchantment. It did not come naturally."

"I know. I was shameless in approaching him. I don't wear panties, so I flashed him with my bra. I laughed so he could see my breasts bounce. I did everything I could to make him desire me, my age no inhibition. I'm not like that in real life. I think."

"And it seems it worked. He does desire you."

"He kissed me, and everything changed. After that, age, species, and mission didn't matter. We just want to be together."

"That's so romantic," Ilene said.

"It's the trap," Debra said. "I'll destroy him if we come together again, and we can't stay apart."

"There are antilove spells on the Good Magician's shelves," Wira said. "All you have to do is drink one vial and you'll be out of love."

"No!"

"But it will solve your problem."

"No it won't. I'll still be determined to find him and destroy him. Only my love for him holds me back. I don't want to give it up."

"That's so romantic," Ilene repeated.

"We had better return you to your home," Wira said to the girl. "Before we return to the Good Magician's Castle."

"I suppose so," Ilene agreed. "It's been a great adventure."

Debra flew to the girl's house. Her parents weren't there at the moment, but it was no problem; Ilene was safe there. "Thank you so much!" she said as she dismounted. "I hope someday I have a love like yours. Either one of yours."

"You're welcome," Debra replied, halfway bemused. She had love, yes, but it was sadly conflicted.

They set off for the castle. "I apologize," Wira said as they flew. "I wasn't thinking. I wouldn't take a potion to wash out my love for Hugo, no matter how convenient it might seem."

"That's all right. At least you'll soon be back together with him."

"Soon," Wira agreed. "For the first time I'll be able to see him."

Debra laughed, the action reminding her of the Factor for some obscure reason. "I hope you like what you see."

"I know I will. It will be a challenge, learning to use my eyes. I'll probably keep them closed most of the time, at first, to make it easier."

"And one of your first solid sights will be of him."

"Oh, yes!"

"It's ironic, that the make-believe quest succeeded before your real one. You weren't really looking for sight, so to speak."

"One must be careful what she asks for," Wira agreed. "You weren't looking for maturity."

"All because we helped a lost boy we chanced to encounter."

"I am not certain it was chance. The clue led us to the air plain, where he was. It may be that the Book of Answers knew that Hugo was somehow associated with the lost boy."

"That seems horribly far-fetched."

"Answers sometimes do seem that way, yet always make sense in the end. It may be that I needed to regain my sight in order to rescue Hugo."

"But he rescued himself, and is on the way back. All you had to do was wait for him."

"That is odd," Wira said thoughtfully. "I've never known an Answer to be irrelevant."

"Maybe the scrambling got the Book confused."

"Or maybe it isn't over yet. That makes me nervous."

That in turn made Debra nervous. Her own situation was complicated enough without Wira's complicating also.

In the afternoon they arrived back at the Good Magician's Castle. The Gorgon welcomed them. "The dragongirl should be here soon with Hugo. She flies swiftly." She turned to Debra. "And you can return to your natural form, with our appreciation for your help. The Good Magician has made progress reorganizing the Book of Answers; he may be able to give you your Answer now."

Debra was suddenly excited. "To get rid of my curse?" For that might make her able to be with the Factor without ending his freedom.

"Of course, dear. But first the counterspell." She fetched a vial from a dingy shelf. "Drink this."

Debra did. Immediately she started changing and shrinking as the several parts of her compacted to her smaller human form. In no more than two and a half moments she stood before them, bare. She was, indeed, more fully formed than she had been as a girl.

"Oh!" she said, suddenly self-conscious. She felt quite exposed without her wings.

"We have many outfits," the Gorgon said. "Each wife maintains her own wardrobe. I'll adjust one of mine."

"Thank you," Debra said faintly.

It required some taking in, for the Gorgon was considerably more shapely than Debra, but soon she had a passable outfit, complete with a hat in the form of a coiled snake with attached veil. It dipped a bit too low in front, and showed too much thigh, but was better than being bare. It was good to be herself again, though emotionally she knew she would never be the same as she had been. Love had transformed her, and as yet she could not be sure it was for the better.

The Good Magician, however, wasn't yet ready to try for her Answer, so she continued as a guest of the castle, feeling a bit out of sorts. Fortunately there was a bowl of sorts on the kitchen table; they were like chocolate bits, neatly sorted. The Gorgon was an excellent hostess, and Debra felt quite at home that evening, and for the night she had her own room. Meanwhile she was getting used to her own original body again.

It took her a while to sleep, but that was all right; she daydreamed naughtily of the Random Factor. How she wished that could be real!

Then she fell asleep, continuing the dream. She was in bed with him, eager to do whatever the Adult Conspiracy forbade by day. Could it be bypassed in the dream realm? She intended to find out.

And suddenly she was out of the dream and out of sleep, but she couldn't remember why. It seemed the Adult Conspiracy had abruptly clamped down, erasing whatever had been about to happen. "Bleep!" she muttered.

The worst of it was that in her dream she had forgotten that she was now of age, so the Conspiracy no longer applied. She could have been completely naughty without guilt. Well, she would not make that mistake again.

It took her some time to get back to sleep, and this time she didn't dream of him. Bleep!

They expected Hugo in the morning, arriving by air, but the first to arrive was a pair of clouds, borne by a favorable wind. They coalesced and formed into the solid forms of Happy Bottom and Fray.

"I saw you coming," the Gorgon said. "I have a hurricane watch." She showed the watch on her wrist: a circle with an arrow pointing toward Happy.

"I haven't been a hurricane in years," Happy said. "Now I'm just a dull married cloud, a misty spot low-pressure zone dependent on the wind instead of making it."

"But you still have the potential to rev up to hurricane status," the Gorgon said.

"If I ever have to. But that takes a lot of energy. The glory of hurricanes tends to be brief and seasonal."

"What brings you here?"

"We were going to check Castle Maidragon," Fray said brightly. "In case Daddy is there. But the wind took us here instead."

"We hope you don't mind," Happy Bottom said.

"We don't mind," Wira said. "We have learned that Hugo was there at Castle Maidragon, not Fracto. He's on his way home now."

"That reminds me," Happy said. "Gwenny Goblin figured out that Fracto and Factor are an anagram. So they might conveniently have switched places. But if it was Hugo who switched, that's not a good clue."

"Fracto and Factor," Debra said. "That can't be mere coincidence."

"I wonder," the Gorgon said. "Maybe you should look at the body. As clouds you must have seen many folk; you might recognize it."

"We can do that," Happy said. "As long as we're here."

"I'd like to see it too," Debra said.

"Welcome," Wira said. "We never can know what will be revealed."

They went down to the cellar, a trip Debra never could have managed in her centaur form. There in a dusky corner was the body. She helped the Gorgon and Wira drag it out into the light.

Happy screamed. "That's my husband!"

"Daddy!" Fray cried almost simultaneously.

The Gorgon looked at Debra, amazed. The look bounced off Debra's own amazement. This was Fracto?

"Cumulo Fracto Nimbus," Happy said. "In condensed form, as we are now."

"Nimbus," Debra repeated. "That's the boy's name."

"Did we get the wrong Nimbus?" Wira asked. "Was it supposed to be the cloud on the air plain?"

"Was the Book of Answers wrong?" Debra asked.

"Unlikely," the Gorgon said. "The confusion is more likely ours."

"Unless both Nimbuses relate," Wira said.

"Like Fracto and Factor," Debra said. "We just had to understand the devious hints."

"Who cares?" Happy Bottom said. "We must wake him and take him home."

"Why didn't he wake before?" Wira asked. "We thought he was dead."

"He's locked into sleep," Happy said. "It must be a stasis spell. Do you have an antidote?"

The Gorgon smiled under her veil. "The very best. Sleep-stasis spells are normally broken by the kiss of one who loves the sleeper best."

"That's easy!" Happy dropped down and slopped a wet and windy kiss on the body's face.

Fracto stirred. His eyes opened. "Happy! What kept you?"

"I'll explain later, dear. Let's revert to form first."

"Gladly!" He started to vaporize.

Happy looked around. "Thank you so much!" Then she vaporized too.

"Great adventure," Fray said, and did the same.

Before long the mist of their presences had floated out of the cellar. They had made it safely into the sky. Wira, Debra, and the Gorgon were left standing in the cellar, sharing a pleasant bemusement.

"Let's see how this fits," the Gorgon said as they returned to the main floor. "The Random Factor does random magic. So he exchanged randomly with another person, who happened to be Hugo. Thus Hugo wound up in the Factor's dungeon cell, and the Factor was here in our cellar. Then he made another random exchange with Fracto, only this wasn't quite as random, because of the anagram, and Fracto wound up in stasis where the Factor had been."

"Maybe he loses some of the randomness when he does it too frequently," Wira said. "Can randomness wear out?"

"Maybe so. But it doesn't explain the scrambling of the Book of Answers or the stasis spell on Fracto."

"Or the clues," Debra said. "Or the way they led us to find Nimbus. Unless—"

"Unless the randomness spread out," the Gorgon said. "Here a scramble, there a stasis spell, and elsewhere a lost boy because his name connected to Fracto's name. Not completely random, but still random enough to make a mystery and a lot of mischief."

"And it seems that my involvement wasn't random at all," Debra said. "The Factory acted the moment the Factor escaped, generating me and sending me here so that I would be chosen to participate in the search for the Factor. Except that we weren't looking for him."

"Yes we were," Wira said. "Because Hugo was hidden in his cell. We just didn't know it."

"And the Factor knew the Factory would send an agent to capture him," Debra said. "So he checked it out, to see if he could nullify it. Only he fell in love with me instead. And I with him. Which really messes things up."

"At least Nimby made you real," Wira said.

"Real but still in hopeless love."

"This is an ugly complication," the Gorgon said. "Now it won't be enough for you to abolish your curse, because the Factory might simply send another agent to capture him. The problem is bigger than the two of you."

"And we can't just let them suffer," Wira said. "At least everything else has simplified."

"Someone's coming by air," the Gorgon said, glancing at a sensor. "That must be the dragongirl. I remember when she first came here as a querent."

They went up to the landing roof. Sure enough, the colorful dragon was gliding in. But alone.

Debra felt a sudden clutch of apprehension for Wira. Where was Hugo?

The dragon landed and converted into the girl. "Something awful has happened!" she exclaimed. "Hugo can't go home yet."

They stared at her, shocked. Whatever could account for this?

11
EXCHANGE

T he Random Factor found himself sitting on a mantelpiece. He dropped to the floor, as he did not fit well on that shelf. Fortunately there was no fire in the fireplace below. This would be where the Maiden Head normally rested. He always knew on some level what he exchanged with, though he did not actually see it; it was just part of the process. He was glad it was something innocuous; he would not have wanted Debra to suffer.

Ah, Debra! What a strange turn his life had taken. He had met the agent the Factory had sent, and come to love her, without even a love potion or a fall into a love spring. It had just happened. Oh, he knew it was part of the enchantment the Factory had set her up with. He had been surprised by it, and so caught by it. Yet for all that, it was real, and he knew it was mutual. She could have caught him merely by leaving her bra in place for him to touch; instead she had flung it off and he had caught her breasts. That had transported him in a different but harmless fashion. She did love him too.

It had started with the kiss. He had seen her laugh, and just had to kiss her. Then the little orbiting hearts had enclosed them, and it was love. They had been destined, or enchanted, to fall in love at their first opportunity. He with her, so that he could not avoid her. She with him so that she would constantly seek him out. That was the first half of the trap. Now they both wanted to avoid the second half. The cursed bra.

How could they escape it, when they couldn't stay away from each other? That was the awful, wonderful challenge. The Heaven and the Hell of it. Some sadist at the Factory had shown real imagination.

Where was he? This was somebody's private residence, a room in a house. The Maiden Head must have been part of a collection of artifacts. There might be others.

He inspected the rest of the mantelpiece. There was a small wooden box. What was it? It was surely magic, so shouldn't be touched ignorantly.

Then he saw the plaques. Ah. The one where he had appeared said Maiden Head, of course. The box was marked Fresh Err. That would be a pun for fresher, but hardly the whole story, if the Maiden Head was any guide. Another box was labeled Err Conditioner. Maybe something that altered the quality of the surrounding air.

But that wasn't enough information. He might be misunderstanding their nature. He'd best not touch them yet.

He walked around the room. There was a door to the outside, and a window. He looked out the window and saw a village street. So this was in a metropolis. He did not want to attract attention by going outside. He went on.

He found a curtained-off corner containing a basin and chamber pot. Standard equipment; better than the trench he had had to use in the dungeon cell.

Next was a small antechamber leading to a bedroom alcove beyond. There was a bed in it, and—a sleeping woman.

The Factor paused, beset by odd emotions. She was an attractive one, with nice hair and a nice figure. Her face was buried in the pillow and wasn't visible, but it was surely pretty. Her nightdress rode up some to show her full thigh. This was the kind of woman he liked to sport with for an hour or a night.

And he wasn't interested. He was in love with Debra, though he had encountered her only as a centaur. She was the only one he wanted to be with. That was what mixed his emotions. He had truly been changed by love, and this was the inadvertent proof of it.

He passed the bedroom on by, not disturbing the woman.

Then he found a closet door. It was labeled Imagination. What could that mean?

He considered. It seemed most likely that the sleeping woman had set up a safe place to store her imagination while she slept, and this was the place. It was surely securely locked.

He turned the knob. The door unlatched.

He hesitated. Did he really want to intrude on someone else's imagination?

He shrugged and opened the door. It wasn't as if he intended any harm.

It was murky inside. He put one hand in to feel what was in it, but there was only space. So he stepped in, keeping one heel back so the door could not close and lock him in. He was wary of prison cells since his experience in the dungeon. Of course he could transfer out, now that he knew how to do it, but he preferred to do so in his own good time.

His eyes adjusted to the dim illumination. He was in a chamber of considerable size; in fact it seemed larger than the whole universe, though it was probably just his imagination.

He paused. Imagination? That was what it said on the door. Could this really be the closet of imagination? If so, anything he could imagine would be here. Maybe even something useful. Such as a way to nullify Debra's curse.

That thought made him extend the pause, making it a long pause. What would nullify that bra curse? A bra-vo? Bra-zen? Bra-zil nut? Brae bonnie girl? That was intriguing. He didn't know, and didn't dare guess.

He took off a shoe and wedged it to keep the door open. Then he moved on in.

He spied a plaque on a shelf. It said Ab Cent. But there was nothing there. Oh.

Next to it was what appeared to be a Mundane dollar bill, with the face of a king on it. The plaque said Bucking. Oh, again. Beside that was a mundane penny standing guard: Cent-inel.

The Factor stifled a groan. These were mere puns. He wanted something with more substance.

Still, where there was one king, there might be another, and kings had special powers. So he checked further, and found them. There was an entire shelf filled with models of assorted kings. One was a crowned mule-like animal with a load of keys and a questioning look, labeled Ass King. The Factor pondered, and in half a moment got it: Don Key asking a question. Another was a human monarch standing before an overnight residence in the shape of a Mundane printer doused in black fluid, labeled Inn King. Again he pondered, and got it: inking. Another was a crowned dog with its mouth open, looking somewhat tipsy, labeled Bar King. Also a slender king reading a serious tome: Thin King. A king peeking voyeuristically into a toilet chamber: a Loo King. There were others, but the Factor had had enough; these kings were not what he needed.

Farther along was a cup of what looked and smelled like hot tea. It smelled very good, and he was inclined to drink it. But he distrusted it. Sure enough, the plaque said Fatalitea. That would be lethal.

Then he spied a jar of De Ogreant. That would repel ogres, a useful function. But his problem was with a curse, not an ogre.

Next was a mirror with a pencil and paper pad before it. The plaque said Mirror Writing. So he wrote a word on the pad: olleH.

That wasn't what he had written. Then he saw the reflection in the mirror: Hello. He had written backward; it showed the word forward. That was nice incidental magic, but still not what he sought.

He came to a bookshelf. On it were several books. The title of one leaped out at him: Dream Dictionary. If that was really a dictionary of dreams, it could be quite useful. He had agreed to meet Debra in a dream, and he fully intended to do it. This book might help him find a compatible dream setting. Such as a very private bedroom.

He took the book down from the shelf and opened it. The title page said "This dictionary is the property of the Night Stallion, for use cataloging all the dreams used to torment deserving sleepers."

This was quite a reference! How had it gotten here? The Night Stallion surely missed it.

He picked up the book and turned to depart the Closet of Imagination. He saw the distant outline of the door; he had come farther into the closet than he realized. And framed in the light of it was the woman. He recognized her immediately by her superior shape; she was the one who had been sleeping. Alas, she was sleeping no more. She must have seen the shoe blocking the door open, and realized someone was in there.

"elloH," he said awkwardly.

She didn't smile. "The rule is that you can enter my imagination and take out one thing, use it, and return it. What do you want with that book?"

"An ideal dream setting. But how do you come to possess it?"

"This is an imaginary copy, of course. The Night Stallion has the original."

The Factor nodded. "Then I will use it now, and return it." He opened the book, riffled through the pages, and stopped randomly, of course.

A scene opened out across the facing pages. It showed a lovely land of milk and honey, where a number of couples were embracing and kissing. It was of course the Honeymoon, the other side of the moon that had not been turned to spoiled green cheese by the constant vision of the ugliness of Xanth. This was ideal. He would meet Debra in this dream, or take her here once he found her elsewhere in the dream realm. Somehow they would get together; he knew it.

He put the book back on its shelf, then returned to the door. The woman still blocked it.

"It is time for introductions," she said. "I am Venus Vila."

She was one of the vily! That was mischief. The vily were all females, living in the deepest forests and greatest heights, and they didn't much like men. He would have to tread very carefully, and be ready to transfer randomly out on half an instant's notice.

But he waited, because he couldn't be sure how many transfers he had today, and didn't want to risk using up his last one unnecessarily. "I am the Random Factor."

Now she paused. Evidently she knew of him, and was now as wary of him as he was of her. "What are you doing here?"

"I escaped my dungeon cell. I am here randomly."

"Of course. What is your intent?"

"To move randomly on."

"Let's converse a bit. We will surely never meet again. I will do you no harm if you do me none."

"Agreed." For the vily were dangerous. This was a temporary truce. She did not realize that he was no longer doing random things to those people he encountered. He was not actually dangerous to her now, but it did not seem expedient to clarify that. But what did she want with him?

"You saw me sleeping, and passed me by," she said. "Why?"

"I did not come here to molest innocent women."

She burst out laughing. "You're a man, aren't you? Try again."

"You weren't sleeping." He had just realized this.

"So? You gazed at me, and considered, and passed me by. I want to know why."

She had seen him look, with her face buried? Maybe she had acute hearing. "It's a personal thing."

"To be sure. Stop being evasive."

"It's not your business," he snapped.

She frowned. "Beware. We are at truce, but there are limits."

"Don't try to threaten me, woman. You know my powers."

"You are bluffing. You have lost your power."

"Merely changed it. Now I apply it to myself instead of to others. You can't threaten me, and I wasn't threatening you. This dialogue is becoming pointless."

"No it isn't. You have power, nerve, and discretion. You are not in awe of me. I think I will marry you."

"No."

"As a general rule I hate men. They are brutal, uncouth, and interested in only one thing." She touched the nightgown at the juncture of her nice legs.

"Two things," he said, looking at her nice breasts, outlined by the filmy clingy material.

She smiled briefly, acknowledging his brutal uncouth male nature. "But they have their uses. The stork won't answer without one, the stupid bird. You are surprisingly worthy, and not unhandsome. So I'll make your life pleasant just long enough, then make it miserable when it's time to get rid of you."

What she said was true. The vily could be fantastically alluring when they tried, and insufferable when they didn't try. But he had another agenda. "No."

She paused, the word finally sinking in. "I don't understand."

"I won't marry you. I won't even get into bed with you. I'm not interested in a relationship with you."

"Ludicrous. No man denies a vila when she chooses him." Her nightie fell open to reveal a body of unmatched splendor. "What have nymphs or a demoness to offer that I don't?" She made a slight bob on her heels, whose effect on her torso was anything but slight.

The Factor's eyeballs started to glaze. He quickly closed them. "No," he said a third time. How could she know about the nymphs and demoness? Considering that his appearance here was random, she was remarkably well informed as well as well formed.

"This is amazing. But you can't oppose me that way." He heard her approach. He didn't move because he would have to open his eyes, and she would nail him then.

She came to stand immediately before him. She took his hands and placed them about her half-bare body. His fingers touched the back of her panties, and went numb. But still he resisted. "No."

She drew herself in, flattening against him. He did not move. She kissed him, and his lips went numb. But still he resisted.

"Something's wrong," Venus said, stepping back. "Such resistance is unnatural. I will make you a deal: tell me how you managed it, and I will let you go without further persuasion."

"Deal," he agreed, relieved. She had not tempted him when seemingly asleep, despite her artful partial exposure, but had certainly done so when she turned up the heat.

"You may open your eyes now. I have turned it off."

He opened his eyes. She was now fully garbed, showing nothing particularly suggestive. She was keeping her part of the deal. "Thank you."

"Now tell."

"I love another. That spoils me for incidental liaisons."

"This must be recent."

"It happened today."

She nodded. "Stay the day and night. I can see it's a long story." She set up a table and began serving vegetables. Most vily were vegetarians, because they cared so strongly for their local animals.

The offer was worthwhile. He was hungry and tired. He told her the story at length.

Venus shook her head. "You know you'd be better off with me, no matter how difficult I make your life. Because I'm temporary and we both know it."

"I know. But I don't have a choice. Debra is all I want."

"So I have verified. It's too bad for me, and for you." She considered. "If you were to cooperate, I could probably distract you long enough to take the edge off the spell of love for her. Then a drink of love potion admixed with reverse wood sawdust—"

"No."

"Even though you know this is part of the trap set by the Factory. You were a fool ever to approach her."

"I was," he agreed.

"But of course men are fools about women. That's one of the few redeeming features they possess. Well, you'll share my bed tonight, and be on your way in the morning."

"I'm not—"

"I have only the one bed and won't make you sleep on the floor. I promised not to seduce you. I won't make a move." She smiled obscurely. "Of course if you make a move, I won't resist. Consider it further proof of your love for her."

She had put it in a way he couldn't argue with. So that night he shared her bed. He wore pajamas she provided—evidently she had entertained men here before—and she wore her well-closed nightie. The bed was not large and they were jammed together, but thoroughly covered. Soon she was asleep with her head on his shoulder, leaving the pillow to him.

It took him time to nod off. The events of the day still roiled his mind. But at last he slept.

He found himself in the dream realm. He knew that the hypno-gourd proffered daytime access to the dream realm, but that was programmed and usually started with the haunted house. This was a real dream, so it started where he chose, and that was on the Honeymoon.

There were the loving couples, hugging and kissing each other, heedless of the other couples and himself. He walked around, observing fountains of milk and honey, becoming restive. All this loving was making him eager for some of it himself—but where was Debra? Shouldn't she be here, since he was dreaming of her?

But she might not be asleep. That would explain her absence. So he might just have to wait for her. Or she could be in some other dream setting.

Then a dreamy bulb flashed over his head. He hadn't dreamed of Debra, he had dreamed of the ideal setting, the Honeymoon, that he had researched in the Dream Dictionary. He should have dreamed of her first, then together they could have sought this setting.

Well, he would dream of her now, in effect conjuring her to him. He concentrated, and she formed, somewhat in the manner of the demoness. "Debra!" he said gladly.

"Factor," she answered, recognizing him. Then she glanced down at herself. "I'm in centaur form."

"That's the only way I have known you. Are you all right? You seem a bit vague."

"Well, I'm not asleep. This is a daydream, very distractible."

"Where are you? I don't want to get you in trouble."

"That's sweet of you. But there's no problem; I'm spending the night in the Good Magician's Castle, because he doesn't have my Answer yet. I'm hoping he will tell me how to abate my curse, so I can be with you without capturing you."

"I hope you get that Answer! It's awful being apart from you."

"Where are you now?"

"I'm in bed with Venus Vila." The moment he said it, he wished he hadn't.

"You are where?"

"Oh Debra, please trust me! It's not what you might think."

"I do trust you, Factor." She hesitated. "May I call you by your first name? I hate being so formal."

"Call me Random," he agreed. "Here is what happened: when I exchanged away from you, I landed where the Maiden Head had been, which was on the mantel of Venus Vila. She let me stay the night, but there's only one bed. I assure you—"

"I said I trust you, Random. I just wish it could be me in that bed with you."

Then, suddenly, there was a bed, and they were on it together, she in her straight human form.

"What happened?" he asked, amazed.

"I think I just fell asleep and passed from daydream into real dream. And my wish just came true."

"Oh, it did!" He kissed her. "I love you, Debra!"

She kissed him back. "I love you, Random. But you know, in my own form I'm not nearly as, well, busty."

"I don't care about that. I'm sure your bust is just fine. I'd love to see it."

"Immediately," she said. "I fell asleep with my clothes on." She brought her hands up. "Let me get my shirt open—"

Both of them froze in mutual horror. "You've still got your bra on!" he said. Then, involuntarily, he reached for it.

"No!" she cried.

Then she was gone. The shock had awakened her, leaving him alone in the bed. Then it too faded, as it was part of her dream, rather than his. He landed on a cushion of honey.

Then he woke, and found himself lying beside a different woman. The vila. With no bra.

She stirred. Hastily he closed his eyes and pretended to be asleep. Soon enough he was really asleep.

In the morning Venus got up and washed, unconcerned about whatever he might see. Or maybe she was continuing her effort to seduce him while pretending not to.

Unfortunately Debra had been correct: her natural body was nothing compared to the splendor of Venus Vila. But fortunately it didn't matter; he still loved only Debra.

Later, after breakfast, Venus questioned him. "What happened in the night? I thought you were going to embrace me, but then you pretended to go back to sleep."

She was uncannily observant. "I had a bad dream."

"So the Night Mares located you. You surely deserved it. What was it?"

Did it matter? She had a right to know, according to their truce. "I was dreaming of Debra."

"Your enchanted enemy agent love, of course. But wouldn't that have been a good dream?"

"I was about to see her bare bosom, but it turned out she was wearing her bra."

"Which you couldn't touch, lest it damn you to eternal confinement in the dungeon," she agreed. "So of course she took it off. Then what? Did she turn out to be breastless?"

"She reacted automatically, and woke up, disappearing from my dream. So I never got to see it."

"You should have taken the Fresh Err from the mantelpiece. That enables a person to undo his last mistake. Or the one beside it, the Err Conditioner. That merely softens the impact of the mistake."

"You mean I could have gone back in the dream and told her to remove her bra before she got into bed with me?"

"Yes. Then you could have fondled her breasts all you wanted without risk." She paused, inhaling impressively. "I understand that men like that sort of thing."

He averted his gaze before his eyeballs glazed. "Except that the Adult Conspiracy forbids it. She's underage."

"She's underage? You didn't mention that before."

"I must have overlooked it."

"Exactly how old is she?"

"Thirteen."

"Thirteen! She's a child!" And the vily were especially protective of children.

"She looks like a woman to me."

"You beast. You could have clasped me anytime, but you passed me up for a child?"

"It seems I did."

"That does it. The truce is off. I'm going to destroy you." She changed into a poisonous snake and struck at his leg. He barely whipped it out of the way in time.

She became a Mundane bear and reached for him, about to crack his ribs into bone kindling. He ducked and retreated as the huge claws barely missed him.

Her lovely human form reappeared, gloriously unclothed. His eyeballs started to smart. "But I'll forgive you if you renounce the child and marry me this instant."

His smartest course was to accept. But he couldn't. He was in love. "No."

"Then I'll toast you and eat you for dinner." She became a huge fire-breathing dragon.

"But you're a vegetarian!" he protested.

"I'll make an exception for a child molester." The dragon's belly swelled as she inhaled for a horrendous burst of fire.

He had no choice. He randomly exchanged.

He found himself in midair with a man on his back. Before either of them could react, they crashed into the rotten upper foliage of a huge zombie tree. Then they slid down through the festering mass of it until they slurped to the ground, landing in a pile of rancid goo. It was disgusting, but soft, so no one was hurt.

"This is a plumpkin pie," the man said, tasting a spatter of goo. It made him look fatter already.

The Factor tramped squishily out of the sludge and looked at the sign beside the tree. It said WAVE WAR MEMORIAL PARK. That figured. A dead tree in a park for the dead people.

He realized that he had just exchanged places with a flying dragon. He was wondering increasingly whether his random exchanges were truly random, since he had just faced a dragon. Maybe they were random only within certain parameters.

"Who are you? What happened?" the man asked.

"That may be complicated to explain. I am the Random Factor."

"You!" the man cried. "You changed places with me!"

"No, I changed places with the dragon. I probably saved you from being eaten."

"That was Becka Dragongirl! She was taking me to the Good Magician's Castle to be with my wife. I'm Hugo. I was locked in your dungeon cell."

"Well, now she's facing Venus Vila. What's this about your being in my cell?"

"You escaped by putting me in there. I had an awful struggle getting out."

It was beginning to make sense. "My first exchange took me to the Good Magician's Castle. I exchanged with a middle-aged man. You're that man."

"You bet I'm that man! Have you any idea the mischief you caused?"

"I got into some mischief of my own. I exchanged with what turned out to be a cloud to get out of there, and finally was free. Only to fall in love with the agent sent to send me back to prison. Now I'm captive in another manner."

"You didn't mean to do anyone any harm?"

"All I want is to live my own life in my own way, with the girl I love."

"But you messed up my love in the process."

The case wasn't worth arguing. "We need to get cleaned up."

"On that we agree. I can't face Wira like this."

They trekked through the forest until they found a spring. But they had the caution to observe it before plunging in. Sure enough, a wasp and a butterfly paused to sip at its fringe, and immediately got to work summoning whatever kind of stork bugs did. It was an incidental love spring.

"Maybe I can do better," Hugo said. He concentrated, and a huge watermelon appeared before him, followed by another.

Each of them plunged into a melon, and the water quickly washed off the grime. But they had to forage for new apparel; their old clothing was beyond salvage.

Then Hugo conjured tasty smaller fruits for them to eat.

"That's a nice talent you have," the Factor said.

"It helps. Now how am I going to complete my journey, and what's Becka going to do?"

"I think Vily Village is not far from here. She should be able to fly back and find us before long."

"Vily Village? Is that on the map?"

"I doubt it. They are very private folk."

"Maybe we could go there and they would help us."

"That would be risky. One of them wanted to marry me. She might decide to marry you."

"But I'm already married."

"And I'm in love. She hardly cares. I don't want to go back there."

There was an odd sound. Something was coming. It was a sort of swirl of jingling fragments with wings. Some weird kind of bird.

"I know that from Father's reference tomes!" Hugo said. "That's a jinx! It brings bad luck to whoever it encounters."

"I can transfer out of here. What about you?"

"I'll hold it off with fruit. Cherry bombs, if I have to." Small red balls appeared in his hands.

"Good enough." But the Factor waited, not wanting to risk a transfer unless quite necessary.

Hugo threw a cherry at the jinx, but had the bad luck to miss it. He threw another, but this one was also jinxed. Which was to be expected.

Meanwhile the bird was coming right at them. It was time to go.

The Factor exchanged.

He found himself throwing a cherry at a bird. It missed. He was too old and out of condition to aim well. He threw himself to the ground and the bird passed just over his head and went on.

He sat up. There, sitting beside him, was himself.

"Oh, no!"

"What?" the Random Factor asked.

"Look at your body."

The Factor looked. "Oh, no!"

"Exactly. We have exchanged bodies or identities, however you see it. You're in my body; I'm in yours."

"That jinx! That must have done it."

"It must have," the Factor agreed. "This is new; I haven't done it before, and didn't know it was coming. This exchange does neither of us any good. I don't want your body, and I doubt you want mine."

"I agree. Quick, change us back."

"I can't. My exchanges are random and seldom if ever repeat or reverse."

"But I can't return to Wira this way!"

"And I doubt Debra would understand either."

They gazed at each other with mutual dismay. "It seems we have a problem," Hugo said.

"We do," the Factor agreed.

"Maybe my exchanges with Bathos Bat facilitated my exchange with you. By providing a model for the jinx to invoke." He explained about the bat.

"That could be," the Factor agreed. "My exchanges don't always seem completely random. But hitherto they were limited to others, or to myself. This is like a fluke cross between them that won't happen again."

"Especially if I'm the one doing them," Hugo said. "If the talents stay with the bodies."

"We had better find out."

Something darkened the sky nearby. It was a dragon.

"All we need now is to be hunted by a dragon," the Factor said.

Hugo, in his body, gazed up. "No, that's Becka, returning to find me. But she won't recognize me. You had better hail her."

"And get toasted? I'll pass."

"She'll think you're me. Hail her."

The Factor realized that did make sense. He jumped up and waved his arms. "Here, Becka!"

The dragon spied him and came gliding down to the ground. "Now I'll try to explain," Hugo said. "You'd better introduce me, though."

That, too, made sense. The Factor addressed the dragon. "There is a problem. We have exchanged bodies. I am actually the Factor. This is Hugo." He gestured to the other body.

The dragon hesitated, then became a young woman. "Is this true?" she asked Hugo.

"It is true. Do you want some proof of my identity?"

"Yes."

"I tried to contact you when I was a bat. You had me netted and taken out. Then I got Dragoman Dragon to talk to you, and you went and let me out of the dungeon cell. I was naked and dirty. You freaked out when you saw me."

"I did not freak out," she said hotly. Then she smiled. "But you have made your point. The Factor would not know those details. So can you change back?"

"It is random," the Factor said. "It would probably be better to find some other way to make the exchange. Maybe the Good Magician would know how."

"The Gorgon says his Book of Answers is scrambled. So he can't help."

"Then we seem to be stuck," Hugo said. "I don't want to return to Wira like this."

"Nor I to Debra," the Factor said. "Though that is already complicated."

"How so?"

The Factor briefly explained the problem.

"I wonder," Becka said. "Could you touch her bra in your present body?"

The Factor exchanged a surprised glance with Hugo. "I don't know," the Factor said. "That depends on whether talents and curses go with the spirit or with the body."

She nodded. "Maybe we'd better find out."

"But there's no telling what my random talent will do. It might make the situation even worse."

"Then try for Hugo's talent. That's relatively harmless."

Hugo held up one hand. Nothing happened. "My talent isn't working."

The Factor held up one hand and thought of a grapefruit. A giant grape appeared. He had conjured it.

"So the talents stay with your bodies," Becka said. "If the curses do too, then you can be with Debra without worrying about her bra."

"But this body is forty-three years old," the Factor protested. "I'm sure she wouldn't like it."

"And I wouldn't like my body being with another woman," Hugo said. "I certainly don't want to approach Wira in this one. And who knows—I might do something disastrously random and mess things up worse."

"But you have to do something!"

"I think we should stay together until we figure out how to change back," the Factor said. "Only then can we address our other problems."

"I think you're crazy," Becka said. "But I'll fly on to the Good Magician's Castle and tell them you aren't coming."

"That seems to be best," Hugo said with evident regret. "We'll remain here for the time being."

"That will help," Becka said. "Because if you go randomly elsewhere, I won't know where to find you."

"Actually Debra can locate me," the Factor said. "When I do my random magic. Or when he does it. I think."

"On my way." Becka changed back to dragon form, spread her wings, and took off. They were left behind.

"Meanwhile," the Factor said grimly, "I think we had better educate each other about our respective talents. I'll need to know how to use yours for food and defense, and you'll need to know how to avoid doing something drastic with mine."

"I'm afraid to use yours at all," Hugo said.

"Aspects of it are relatively safe. You can do random form changes, and if you get tired of that, you can revert to your natural body. Just stay clear of the location exchanges or identity exchanges. Also, don't use the talent unless you need to, because you can do it only a random number of times a day. You don't want to run out at an awkward moment."

"Awkward moment," Hugo said. "Such as being about to get toasted by an unfriendly dragon."

"Exactly."

"How can we stay together if I exchange locations?" Hugo asked. "I don't want to do it, but I want some way to make it halfway safe, just in case."

The Factor pondered. "We must be closely linked, each having part of the other, whether body or mind. Maybe if we are in physical contact with each other when invoking an exchange, we'll go together."

"And if we don't?"

"Let's hope we do. Our problems are bad enough already."

They discussed things further, while the Factor conjured more fruit for them to eat, and Hugo learned exactly how to invoke each aspect of the random talent. They were passing time, waiting for Becka to return with word from Wira and Debra.

Then there was a rustle. Both men looked. The Factor relaxed. "It's only a birdlike lizard."

"The bleep it is!" Hugo said. "I recognize it from the Good Magician's pictures. That's a cockatrice! Its gaze will turn us to stone."

The cockatrice heard them talking. Slowly its head turned to orient on them.

"Take us away!" the Factor said, grabbing Hugo's arm.

Hugo invoked the location exchange aspect. There was a wrenching as the Factor was carried along.

12
DREAMS

S o that's the situation," Becka Dragongirl concluded. "Hugo doesn't want to join you when he's in the wrong body. He believes you wouldn't understand."

"I don't care about his body," Wira said. "It never was much anyway. I love him for himself." But she knew as she spoke that this wasn't strictly true; she was familiar with Hugo's body, and would have trouble doing anything serious, such as signaling the stork, with a different body.

"It may not be just that. He has the Random Factor's powers now, and hardly knows how to use them."

"While Random conjures fruit," Debra said wryly.

That was perhaps significant, Wira thought. Debra was calling the dread Random Factor by his first name.

"I can show you where they are," Becka said. "Then I have to get home to my own family."

"You can't carry two," Wira pointed out.

"I could become a winged centaur again," Debra said. "If there's another potion."

"But if you still have the curse—"

"I'll leave the bleeping bra behind. I just want to be with Random."

"And as a centaur you don't necessarily have to abide by the Adult Conspiracy," Wira said. "Apart from the fact that you are now of age."

Debra didn't answer, but she blushed. That was answer enough.

"Then let's go reassure them," Wira said. "Maybe when the Good Magician completes the reorganization of the Book of Answers he'll be able to find a solution to the problem of their exchange of identities. Meanwhile we can bring them here to the Castle."

"And persuade them that we love them regardless," Debra said.

The Gorgon located another potion, and Debra took it. This time she removed her clothing first, so as not to ruin it by her expansion. She shook herself. "Actually I rather like this form," she said. "It's talented, and it looks good."

Wira suspected that it was the enlarged bosom she really liked, but didn't comment. "You can flick me light and carry me," she said. "I still can't see well enough to trust myself out alone."

Soon they were following Becka's dragon, winging across the landscape. Wira was getting better at seeing it. Her vision was complete; the problem was that there was such a welter of things to see, coming at her all at once, that it could be an indecipherable jumble. She was trying to train herself to focus on one thing at a time, tuning out the rest. But it was tricky, because her eyes tended to track anything that moved, when that wasn't what she wanted to see. Normally sighted folk had had their whole lifetimes to adjust, to refine their awareness; she was decades behind. Still, it was interesting as the blue of the sky and green of the forest cruised by.

What would Hugo look like? She was curious to see, even if it wasn't him in his body. She would have to verify it by touching his face, of course, but in time she would surely get to know him visually as well as by sound and touch. Once they solved the problem of the bodies.

The dragon swooped down. Debra followed. They were arriving! Wira found herself holding her breath.

They landed in a pleasant enough glade. But it was empty.

The dragon sniffed the ground, then converted to girl form. "They were here," she said. "I smelled their traces."

"But why did they leave?" Wira asked, troubled.

Becka turned dragon and sniffed the ground more thoroughly. She changed back. "Now I know. There was a cockatrice. They had to flee it."

"Can you sniff out their trail?" Wira asked.

"There is no trail. They must have transferred out, using the Factor's magic. Evidently they went together."

"But that's purely random! They could be anywhere!"

"I'm sorry," Becka said.

There was nothing to do except thank the dragongirl, and return to the GMC. Wira was quietly crying during the flight back, and she suspected Debra was too.

That night Wira remained troubled by the situation. She had been so close to getting Hugo back, then suddenly he was gone again. Even if she found him again, he would be in the wrong body. She still wasn't sure how she would feel about hugging or kissing him in the other body, let alone summoning the stork with him. Intellectually she knew it was proper, if unusual, but emotionally there was a problem. Even if she had no prior visual image of him, she knew him very well by touch, and touching was what she had in mind.

And she didn't even know where he was. If she could just find him— find them both, and bring them here to the castle—there was surely a spell or three that could help. Perhaps even a cure. So how could she find him?

A bulb flashed over her head. She stared at the afterglow, amazed. That was a bright-idea flash! She could see it now.

She focused on the idea. Physically the two men were lost, but the dream realm covered everything. She could dream of him and find him. Unless she found the wrong man, because of the identity exchange. But since both men shared the problem, she needed to dream of both; they should be together, wherever they were.

What about Debra? It was her problem too. But she had an answer for that too; her flashing bulb had illuminated a lot.

She got up and went to the Good Magician's storage shelves. She closed her eyes and felt for the shared-dream spells; it remained easier to find things this way than to confuse the issue by using her untrained eyes. She took one down and held it in her hand. It was a dusty stoppered vial, stored for decades. She should have cleaned this shelf more often, but hadn't wanted to risk knocking over anything, lest it break and splatter its magic on the floor.

She went to Debra's room, which was actually a stall; it wasn't feasible to keep changing forms back and forth, as they would run out of conversion spells. "Debra," she murmured.

The answer was immediate. "Yes, Wira. Are you sleepless too?"

"Yes. But I have an idea."

"I thought I saw a flash. I thought it was distant lightning. It must have been your idea bulb."

"I have a potion to induce shared dreams. I'll take it soon, and when I dream, others will be able to share it."

"So we can search for the men in the dream realm!" Debra said. Her maturity had made her quick to catch on to things.

"Exactly. So when you do sleep, seek my dream, and we'll seek the men together, and learn where they are."

"I will!" Debra said gladly.

Wira returned to her room and lay down. She popped the cork on the vial. Greenish mist puffed out and formed a little cloud. She breathed the cloud, and sank immediately into sleep.

She found herself hovering above the castle, waiting for Debra. It was sometimes possible to fly without wings in dreams. Not that she needed to, as she could simply wish herself to wherever she wanted to go. But she didn't want to go alone, as she remained uncertain of her sight. She had always had it in dreams, but this was different.

Debra appeared, flying up from the castle. "Ah, there you are," she said. "Did you flick yourself light?"

"Couldn't," Wira said, smiling. "No tail."

"Now how do we locate the men? Can we just think of them, and join them?"

"We can, or we can use your ability to orient when they randomly move. Which way did they go?"

"I forgot about that," Debra said. She focused. "That direction."

Wira joined her, and the centaur stroked powerfully in the direction she had indicated. Before long they came to a mountain village.

"That's not on the map," Wira said. "Curious. I believe it is Vily Village."

"Aren't the vily dangerous? We should make sure this is where we want to be."

"True," Wira agreed. "We can pause long enough to inquire."

They landed in the valley beside the mountains, a fair distance from the village. There was a woman concentrating on the air before her. "Hello," Wira said.

The woman jumped. "Oh! I didn't see you. I thought I was dreaming."

"You are. This is a communal dream. I am Wira, and this is Debra Centaur."

"A communal dream. That's new to me. I'm Alison; I'm trying to perfect my talent."

"You seem to be focusing on empty air," Debra said.

"Not exactly. My talent is to make a small or large force field in the air, permeable or tight, with different shapes, colors, or textures." As she spoke a blue haze appeared in the air before her, coalescing into a black box. "Only what use is a black box? I want to make a sharp sword or something else that might defend me if a dragon threatens. But it's hard to squeeze it that much." The box flattened, but fell apart before it became a sword.

"Air is hard to control," Wira said. "A force field must be even harder. I suspect you'll just have to keep practicing."

"But it's a remarkable talent," Debra said.

"Do you know anything about that village in the mountains?" Wira asked. "We think some friends of ours are there, and we're concerned."

"That's Vily Village!" Alison said. "Don't go there; the vily don't like regular people."

"So we understand. But if our friends are there, we need to rescue them."

"I don't know how you could do that, even in a dream. You're more likely to get yourselves in trouble."

"That is our concern," Wira agreed. "Do you know anyone who might have good advice?"

"Well, there's Carter, who once had a vila girlfriend, before she tried to destroy him, but he's hard to pin down."

"Why?"

"Because his talent is the ability to steer conversation any way he wants, to or from any subject. He won't want to talk about the vily."

Wira considered. "You're probably right; he wouldn't help us. Is there anyone else?"

"There's Young, with the talent of redirection; he can bounce a talent directed at him to somewhere else, or to another person. He's had some brushes with the vily." Alison paused. "Oh—I just remembered he's away visiting his cousin."

Wira suppressed her annoyance. Potentially good contacts were proving to be elusive. "Anyone else?"

"There's Cary. He's had vily friends, on and off."

"On and off?"

"That's his talent. You can't ever tell what he's going to do. I don't think he knows himself. It always turns out different."

This was getting them nowhere. "Thank you," Wira said.

"I'm glad to be of help," Alison said, focusing again on her force field. She was evidently unconscious of any irony.

They walked on, so as not to make the dream seem too memorable for the woman they had talked to. "I don't think dreaming people are as helpful as we had hoped," Debra said.

"Yes. It was a bad idea. Let's just brace the vila directly."

"If I didn't know how nice you are, I'd suspect you of being annoyed," Debra murmured.

Wira had to laugh as they took flight again. "Point the way."

Debra did, and they flew up to Vily Village. "This house," Debra said. "They're in here." She landed beside it and transformed to her human form, which she could do on her own in the dream.

Wira knocked on the door. After two thirds of a moment it opened to reveal a ravishingly beautiful shapely attractive seductive sexy woman wearing a translucent negligee. Even Wira's eyes heated, though more with envy than fascination. "Go away; I'm busy at the moment." The door closed.

"We can't go away," Wira said. "This is our dream." She put her hand on the latch and opened the door.

"Hey!" the woman exclaimed. "Who are you?"

"I am Wira, Hugo's wife," Wira said firmly. "This is Debra, the Random Factor's beloved."

"The child!" The woman gazed at Debra. "But you're no child. You're at least eighteen."

"Correct," Debra agreed. "Now who are you?"

"I am Venus Vila. He said he wanted to molest a child."

"I did not," Hugo's voice called from the interior of the house. "I said I was in love with her."

Wira was shocked. "In love with whom?" she demanded, pushing past the vila.

"No you don't," Venus snapped. She transformed into a manticora, with the body of a lion the size of a horse, the wings of a dragon, and the deadly multisegmented tail of a scorpion. "No woman intrudes on my demesnes without my permission." Her voice sounded like a cross between a trumpet and a flute. She had a human face, but her mouth contained three rows of teeth. A fearsome monster indeed.

"In my dream I'll intrude where I choose," Wira said. Normally she preferred to be nice, but the idea of Hugo loving another woman, let alone a child, appalled her. She had already had her temper rubbed a bit raw. A ripe stink horn appeared in her hand. That was another thing about controlled dreams: she could shape some of the details as desired.

"Bleep," the manticora swore, easing back. That species had sensitive smell, and there was hardly any stench worse that that of a ruptured stink horn.

Wira entered the main room of the house. And stopped, appalled anew. "What is this?"

For there was Hugo, lying naked on the vila's bed. The disturbed covers suggested that the vila had just vacated it to answer the door. "I can't get up," he said.

"You look as though you're getting up well enough," Wira snapped. "I ought to jam this stink horn where it counts."

"That's Wira!" a strange voice called. "My wife."

Wira looked. There, tied to a tall board, was a strange man. "What are you talking about?"

Debra came up beside her. "That's Random!"

Then Wira remembered. "They switched bodies."

"Even in the dream," Debra agreed. "So the one on the board is Hugo in Random's body, and the one on the bed is Random in Hugo's body."

"What's he doing naked in the vila's bed, regardless?" Wira asked.

"I used a dream catcher from my closet," Venus said. "They were trying to sneak off to some hussy's communal dream, but I nabbed them on the way and bound them to bed and board."

"That's *my* dream!" Wira said. Now she saw that Hugo's body was actually tied to the bed. He had spoken literally when he said he couldn't get up.

"And now I'm seeing to it that this miscreant can't seduce any more children," Venus said. She had reverted to her human form. "Once I'm through with him, he'll not seduce *any* female."

"I'm not a child!" Debra exclaimed. "I'm eighteen."

"You told me you were thirteen," Hugo said from the bed.

"Well, I'm not. I was going to tell you, but you exchanged out." Actually she had been thirteen then, but it did not matter now. She paused, glancing at the man on the bed. She winced. "Where are you, anyway, outside the dream?"

"Inside some anonymous empty beerbarrel tree where the demoness took me before; I remember it."

"Some demoness?" Debra asked dangerously.

"Before I met you!" Hugo's body cried. "I told you about that."

"So you *thought* you were seducing a girl of thirteen," Venus said. "So you're still guilty."

"*I* was doing the seducing," Debra said. "Get over it."

"A willing girl is no excuse. That's why the Adult Conspiracy exists. He should have known better."

"But that's Hugo's body on your bed," Wira said.

"It's the Factor occupying it."

"Whatever you do to Hugo's body will punish Hugo once they switch bodies back, not the Factor."

The vila considered. "True. So I'd better do them both, to be sure I get him regardless of the body he's in."

"No!" Wira and Debra said together.

"You're both entirely too forgiving." Venus marched toward the bed.

"No," Wira repeated, running to intercept her.

"You can't stop me," Venus said, becoming the manticora again.

Wira jammed the stink horn into the monster's mouth. It ruptured, making a foul-smelling noise.

"Ugh!" the vila gasped, a purple stench issuing from her face. She vanished from the dream, choking.

But the stench remained. "Stay where you are," Wira said. "Get out of the dream. We'll go there tomorrow."

"I don't know if we can stay there," the Factor's body said. "It's Demoness Metria's hideout, and if she comes there we'll have to transfer out."

"And Demoness Mentia may be crazy enough to tell her," Hugo's body said.

"Then we'll make a new dream," Wira said, and vacated the dream just before the spreading stench suffocated her. Just the mere thought of a whiff of it was enough to make her gag. She had not been at all nice to Venus Vila, which she regretted. But she couldn't let the female hurt the men.

She reformed her dream well outside the house, realizing that she didn't know where the beerbarrel tree was. She hoped Debra could find it.

Debra appeared nearby, in centaur form. "What an awful thing you did to that murderous vila!" she said, trying to frown. Then a half a giggle squeaked out.

Wira tried to remain serious. "It was most unkind," she said. Then the other half of the giggle got free.

That did it. They both hovered in the air, laughing until they gasped.

At last they settled down to business. "Can you orient on their bodies outside the dream, from within the dream?" Wira asked.

"I thought I was doing that before." Debra focused. "Yes. That way." She pointed.

They flew that way, roughly east. After a time and several moments they found the beerbarrel tree and phased through its wooden wall. Debra converted to her straight human form.

The men were there, but they weren't asleep. They were up and talking. ". . . stink horn," Hugo's body said.

"Don't start me laughing again," the Factor's body said. "I never thought Wira had it in her to do a thing like that. She's always been the nicest person I know."

"I'll try to be nice again, for you," Wira said.

"I love Debra," Hugo's body said. "But if I didn't love her, I think I'd love Wira. She's such a woman."

"Oh you would, would you?" Debra demanded.

"They can't hear us," Wira said. "Because we're here only in our own dream."

"Yes, I loved her from the first time we met, in the dream realm," Hugo (in the Factor's body) said. "Her talent is sensitivity, and she's just wonderful despite being blind."

"Blind?"

"That's why she was in the dream realm. Her family put her to sleep, because they felt a sightless person was too much of a burden. So I got her, and that was my greatest fortune."

"This is worth hearing, I think," Debra remarked.

"It wasn't like that for me," the Factor (in Hugo's body) said. "It was more like an enchantment. I've never been in love before. I wouldn't trade it, even though I know she was sent to destroy me."

"What were they saying about her age?" Hugo asked. "Is she underage?"

"She said she was thirteen. It didn't matter; the spell of love holds me. That's what set Venus Vila off, and I can't say I blame her, though I'm glad she didn't have the chance to unman me, or you, as the case may be. But in the dream Debra said she was eighteen. I don't understand that."

"It is a significant distinction."

"Yes, indeed. But academic, since she has to wear a bra so I can be compelled to take it off, and the moment I touch it I'm doomed."

"Can't you just tell her not to wear it?"

"Oh, I did, and she tries not to wear it. But the spell compels her, as it does me. Sooner or later she'll put it on, and I'll try to take it off. So I have to try to stay away from her, though all I want is to be with her."

"But you're in my body now," Hugo said. "Our talents go with our bodies, so maybe the curse does too. That means you could touch her bra in my body and not get fried."

"We've been over this before. It's impossible to be sure. It might be that if you touch her in my body, you'll be caught forever. Because you'll still be locked in my body, and my body will be caught."

"I hadn't thought of that," Hugo admitted. "But I wish I could kiss Wira again, even if I have to use your body."

"I'd let you," Wira breathed. "Now that I understand."

"I wonder," Debra said. "Suppose Random in Hugo's body touched *your* bra?"

Wira stared at her. "If the curse goes with the body, that would be safe. But if they are wrong—"

"Then Hugo in Random's body could touch my bra. But I think they are right, and that Random in Hugo's body could touch mine. So there would be no danger."

"Would it be the same in the dream?" Wira asked. "Or could the curse be invoked, and all it would do would be to break up the dream?"

"Dreams are dreams," Debra said. "We may dream of being hurt, but then we wake and we aren't. So I think we could experiment safely in the dreams. Then we would know, one way or the other, for real life."

"If we can stand to have the wrong men touching us."

"I think we can, for something this important."

The men had missed the women's continuing dialogue, but it probably didn't matter. They were now settling back to sleep.

"Let's make sure they join us," Wira said. She floated down and kissed the Factor's body.

Suddenly Hugo was with her in the dream. "Oh, Wira!" he cried, holding her with the Factor's arms. "How I've longed to be back with you."

"Even in the wrong body," she said, smiling.

"Even in the dream," he agreed. "But maybe in the dream we can switch back to our own bodies. If Debra can change between centaur and human in the dream, we might switch too."

"Not yet," she said. "We want to verify the curse in the dream, where we think it's safe, before getting together physically."

"Verify the curse?"

"We think you can't touch Debra, because the Factor's body carries the curse. We need to know for sure."

"I don't want to touch Debra!" Then he paused. "Wira, you're looking at me!"

"I can see, now," she agreed. "And not merely in dreams."

"But—"

"It's a devious story. Does it turn you off?"

"No! I'm just—surprised."

"My turn," Debra said. She dropped down to kiss Hugo's body's mouth.

Then the Factor was with them too, in Hugo's body. "I'd know your kiss anywhere!" he said. "I love you, Debra."

"I love you too," she said. "But I have to ask you to do something odd."

"Odd?"

"Touch Wira's bra."

"But it's only your bra I want to touch—and I dare not."

"It may be different in the dream. Try Wira first."

"But she's Hugo's wife."

"And you're in Hugo's body. She understands."

"*I* don't understand."

"We're verifying my curse. If it applies only to your body, well, you're not in your body. But you should be able to touch Wira, regardless."

"She'd never understand."

Wira stood straight and removed her shirt to reveal her bra. "I do understand."

"I suppose—if that's the way it is."

"We need to know," Wira said.

The Factor approached her. She braced herself, stifling an incipient scream. His hands reached for her bra. "Are you sure?"

"Do it," Wira said.

"You look ready to explode."

"My bra's not *that* tight," she said, forcing a faint smile.

Debra got an idea. "If it's just the bra that's magic, you don't have to be wearing it when he touches it."

Wira nodded, relieved. "Yes." She undid the snaps and removed her bra. She held it out to him. "Touch it."

He touched the strap of her bra with one finger. Nothing happened. He put both hands on it. Still nothing. He backed away. "It's not enchanted," he said.

"It's not supposed to be," Wira said, glad to put it back on.

"Now touch mine," Debra said grimly, removing her shirt. Her bra was better filled than it had been before her age advanced. "I don't have to take it off, for you."

He went to her and put both hands on her bra, trying to remove it.

Nothing magical happened. In three quarters of a moment he had it off her. "You look—"

"Older," she said. "I'm eighteen now, remember."

"I'm still here," the Factor said, half surprised.

All four of them paused, splitting the other half surprise among them. What did this mean?

Then Wira figured it out. "The curse goes with the body. That's Hugo's body. The real test is what happens with the Factor's body."

"So we have to do it again," Debra said grimly.

"But I felt the compulsion," the Factor said. "I had to go remove her bra."

"Was that the curse, or just being male?" Wira asked.

He considered. "Being in love."

"And we know the bra makes any man want to remove it," Debra said. "That's not the same as the trap."

Wira turned to Hugo, in the Factor's body. "Touch mine," she said.

"But if it goes with the body—"

"Not my body. I'm just the control case. And I don't need to remove it, for you. We've been married seventeen years."

He came to her cautiously. "I love you, Wira. But this makes me nervous."

"I know who you are despite your body. That helps."

He touched one strap, then another. Nothing happened.

She flung her arms about him and kissed him. "Now the other bra," she said.

"But if the curse—"

"This is a dream," she reminded him firmly. "What happens here isn't really real. We need to find out, before we try anything awake."

He nodded. Then he oriented on Debra, who had not yet put her bra back on. She held it out at arm's length, dangling.

Wira saw him tense as his eyes fixed on the bra. It was as if something else took over his body. He walked to it, ignoring Debra, and took two handfuls.

There was a crackle of electricity and a cloud of smoke. Hugo disappeared, along with the bra.

Debra stood there bemused and bare-topped. A wisp of smoke curled up from where the bra had been. "Now we know," she said, shuddering. "I think I would have vanished too, if I had not become real. If we both had been awake."

Wira was inclined to agree. They had certainly verified the curse.

"Where is he?" the Factor asked.

"Awake," Wira said, gesturing to the pile of pillows that formed his bed. The others looked.

There was the Factor's body sitting up, looking dazed. He appeared to be unharmed.

"Now we know," Debra said. "It's definitely the body."

"Which means I can be with you now, in this body," the Factor said.

"And Hugo can be with me, in your body," Wira said. "As long as we all know exactly what's what. It's hardly ideal, but until the curse is abated, it's much better than nothing."

"Let's get out of the communal dream," Debra said. "Then we'll come here for you, awake. Don't transfer anywhere before then."

"For the chance to be with you, without the curse, I will stay," the Factor agreed.

"Kiss me, then wake up," Debra said.

He stepped toward her.

There was a flash of smoke in the beerbarrel tree chamber. "What is this extrusion?" the smoke demanded.

"This what?" the awake Hugo asked.

"Imposition, infliction, unwanted, shoved in, poked inside—"

"Intrusion?"

"Whatever," the demoness said crossly, forming out of the smoke. "What are you doing here, Factor?"

"Hello, Metria," Hugo said. "I was—sleeping."

"In my secret den?"

"It's complicated."

She looked around, and spied Hugo's body, still asleep. "With him? I didn't know you were friends."

"It's complicated," Hugo repeated.

Metria sniffed the air. "I smell Mentia. What was she doing here?"

"You'd better get back awake and try to explain before she gets revved up," Wira told the Factor. "That demoness can be dangerous when she's riled."

"I agree." He kissed Debra again, then concentrated. In a moment Hugo's body faded from the dream and stirred awake.

"What was that slut Mentia doing in my hideaway?" Metria demanded more forcefully.

"Well, she is an aspect of you," the Factor said. "She's surely entitled."

"The bleep she is!" She sniffed again. "Now I remember: I turned the Factor over to her to seduce. But she wasn't supposed to do it *here*. This is a confounded damage."

"A confounded what?"

"Harm, hurt, injury, insult, affront—"

"Outrage?"

"Whatever! You stank up my whole hideout!"

"Sorry about that," the Factor said, clearly not sorry.

"Not you, idiot. Him!" She turned on the Factor's waking body.

"It wasn't me," Hugo said.

"You liar!" Flames danced along her body. "I have half a mind to defoliate you!"

"To what me?"

"Boil, smolder, combust, scorch, char—"

"Incinerate?"

"Whatever!" The flames intensified.

"Now don't be hasty, demoness," the Factor said. "Defoliation isn't a proper synonym. It means to remove the leaves from trees."

"You stay out of it, moron!" she snapped.

"Half a mind is all you seem to have," the Factor said in Hugo's body. "You don't know anything."

"Don't antagonize her!" Wira cried. But the men couldn't hear her, being out of the dream.

The flames started shooting out of Metria's nose. "Ploop!"

"What's that, half-brain?"

"Floop, sloop, sleep, freep, bloop—"

"Bleep?"

"Whatever!" Thick black smoke was pouring out of her mouth. "Get the whatever out of my nooky!"

The Factor nodded. "Nooky does seem to be what set you off. It means—"

"She means nook," Wira said, knowing it was useless. There was a world of difference between the words.

The demoness exploded into a ball of fire. That ignited the furnishings and quickly spread to the wooden wall that was the outer trunk of the tree. Long-lost beer vaporized in jets of steam. Suddenly everything was burning.

"We've got to get out of here," Hugo said.

"You can't get out, ploophead! I sealed the door."

"We do have to move," the Factor said.

"But if you transfer, we won't know where to find you," Debra said. Her words, too, could not be heard.

The fire surged inward. The men linked hands so they could transfer together. "Isn't that saccharine," Metria said.

They paused. "Isn't that what?" Hugo asked.

"Honey, winsome, alluring, attractive, tasty—"

"Sweet?"

"Whatever. Now burn!"

They vanished. In their place was a small collection of odd coins.

"What the ploop is that?" the demoness demanded.

The coins circulated half a moment. Then one answered. "We are special pennies. I am a quies-cent; I don't move much. My friends are reminis-cent, who likes to remember the past, omni-cent, who knows everything, ex-cent-ric, who is an odd fellow, and magnifi-cent, who is a wondrous thing."

"I wouldn't give two cents for the lot of you! Where are the boys?"

"What boys? We came alone. We're small change."

"I'll throw you out!" The demoness swooped them up in one hand. "Ouch! You're burning hot!"

"What did you expect, demoness? Your house is on fire."

Indeed it was. There was a poof and the old dry tree trunk exploded into an eighth of a slew of burning fragments.

"Now see what you made me dew," Metria said.

"Made you what?" the penny asked.

"Lily, plant, serve, shift, execute, act—"

"Do?" the penny asked.

"Whatever. You ruined my retreat."

"Non-cents. You wouldn't have done it if you had any cents at all. You probably stole the two cents you refused to give."

"That does it, copper face! I'm going to heat you until you melt."

"I think we're done here," Wira said to Debra. "It's time to exit the dream."

"It didn't go well," Debra said.

"We'll just have to track them down again. Where are they now?"

Debra focused, then pointed.

"But that's toward Castle Roogna."

"Maybe they'll stay there, if it's not on fire."

Wira laughed, but it was a feeble laugh. She hoped they did stay there.

They let the dream collapse, like their hopes of a quick resolution and reunion.

13
CONE

Hugo transferred them out before the closing fire could burn them to death. He found himself in a dark cellar, aware of several small coins. Those were more of what they had exchanged places with.

But he still heard the fire, immediately above, and smelled smoke. "Where are we?" he asked, alarmed.

"In the beer cellar," the Factor said. "This time the random exchange was a very short distance."

"Then we'd better get out of here!"

"Wait!" the Factor cried.

But Hugo was already implementing the exchange. This time there was an unusual wrench, as if he was being somehow turned out of his body.

Then they were sitting on a broad pavement, and orange cones were coming at them. Both of them jumped up and dodged before any cones struck them. "What's going on here?" Hugo demanded as he dodged.

The Factor reached out and caught a cone as it missed him. He held it up. On it was printed the word NUNDRUM. "A cone named Nundrum?"

Hugo groaned. "Cone-nundrum. A pun."

"But why are they trying to collide with us?"

"In Mundania they have some sort of game they play with cars, dodging stationary orange cones. Here it seemed we have to dodge the moving cones."

The Factor looked about. "This is an odd landscape. It seems longer than wide, and one side is thicker than the other. I don't recall a place like this."

Hugo looked. Indeed, one side seemed to diminish to a point in the distance, while the other grew large. Ahead and behind the land seemed to curve grandly downward. "Oh, no!"

"What's the problem?"

"I think this is another world."

"Another what? And don't play Metria with me."

"A world of Ida. One of them is in the shape of a giant water-filled cone."

The Factor looked at him. "And we're among cones, and exchanged with some. This makes uncomfortable sense."

Hugo dodged another cone. "However, it makes it easy for us to return. We don't have to exchange; we can simply let our soul substance dissolve."

The Factor dodged his own cone. "Our what?"

Hugo realized that the Random Factor had not learned about Ida's moons. "Princess Ida has a moon orbiting her head. That's Ptero, and on it is every creature who exists in Xanth, or who is likely to exist. When Xanthians visit, they have to leave their bodies behind, and just their souls go to Ptero. The souls condense into the little bit of material substance they have, forming likenesses of the people they are. So you and I are really tiny bits of condensed souls. When they are ready to return, they just let those souls diffuse, and float back to their sleeping bodies."

"But you said we're on a cone, not Ptero."

"On Ptero is another Princess Ida, with another moon. And so on. I'm not sure what number Cone is, but it's very small. It doesn't matter; we can return from any of those worlds."

"But we exchanged with two cones. They must be on Xanth now."

Hugo considered. "I wonder if they took our bodies? Then we might have trouble returning, because our bodies would be cones."

"I have a worse notion," the Factor said. "Suppose our bodies got burned up in the fire? Then we won't be able to return to them at all."

Hugo stared at him, horrified. "It's bad enough being in the wrong bodies, but this would be awful!" In his distraction he remained still too long, and a cone collided with him. "Ooof!"

"We left them while the fire was burning. I tried to make you wait, because we might have escaped that cellar before the fire reached it. But if our bodies are unconscious there, they'll burn when the cellar does."

"Maybe the fire didn't get that far," Hugo said desperately.

"We shall have to hope that's the case. But I'd rather be certain before I risk my life trying to return to it."

"So would I!" Hugo got up and avoided another cone. "Let's get out of here so we can concentrate."

"We're already concentrated souls." But the Factor started walking.

Soon they were off the plain, and the orange cones were no longer coming at them. "We need more information," Hugo said.

"How can we get information, without going back to see?"

"On each world there's a Princess Ida. Maybe she'll know."

"So where is this Princess Ida?"

Hugo concentrated, remembering. "I think she's—she's in the apex of the cone, inside. Under the sea."

"What sea?"

"That's the water in the cone. I think visitors can breathe under the water, so that shouldn't be a problem." Hugo strove to remember what little he knew about it. "But there's a—a thick jungle in the way, and some weird activity at the rim. We'd really do better with a local guide."

The Factor sighed. "So we'll get a local guide. Where?"

"Maybe we can find one."

They didn't find a guide. They found a castle. It was pretty, with shiny gray walls and colorful flags flying from assorted turrets. It seemed to be unguarded; it didn't even have a moat. On its front gate were blazoned the words CASTLE NAMETAG.

But there was something odd about it, apart from the name. "This thing is made of cardboard," Hugo said, surprised, as he tapped the wall. It had the dull hollow sound of compressed paper.

"What do you expect, on a world with a pointed tip, filled with water, orbiting the head of Princess Idle?"

"Ida. Princess Ida." But Hugo did wonder.

"So let's go in and see if they have a guide we can borrow."

"Suppose it's a fire-breathing dragon's castle?"

"It would have burned up long ago." The Factor put a hand on the painted gate and pulled. It swung open on rolled paper hinges. Hugo had to join him, not daring to get separated, because it was Hugo's body the Factor was risking.

Inside was an arched hall decorated with poster paint, leading into a painted court. The court was filled with cardboard statuary and paper plants.

"Where are the people?" Hugo asked nervously.

"Who cares? All we want is a guide."

Hugo wasn't easy with the man's attitude, but didn't argue. Then he heard a faint clamor from somewhere above. "What's that?"

The Factor listened. "Sounds like a party."

So it did. They hadn't come here for a party.

In the center of the courtyard was a circular corrugated cardboard stairway spiraling down. From it came a faint hiss. "What's that?"

"A warming teakettle, for all I care."

Hugo wasn't quite satisfied with that answer. "It sounds alive."

"That's all we need: a living teakettle."

Hugo was getting annoyed with the Factor's insensitive responses. "I'm going down to check."

"It could be a simmering dragon."

"In a cardboard castle?" Hugo got a certain private satisfaction from turning the Factor's logic against him. They needed each other, but they really weren't friends.

They stepped down around the spiral, which led into the depth of the foundation rock. The hiss grew louder, and more plaintive. It was definitely from something alive.

"Oh be quiet," the Factor snapped.

The hiss halted.

Hugo exchanged a glance with the Factor. The thing was responsive?

Then, silently, they walked down the passage from which the sound had come. And there in a hard cardboard cage was a tightly coiled winged snake. Its wings were bound to its body by twisted paper cords, and its mouth was held closed by more cord. It looked miserable.

"You poor thing!" Hugo exclaimed, going to the cage.

"Don't risk my body near that monster," the Factor said.

"Monster? This is a poor suffering winged snake. No creature should be treated this way."

"I've seen that monster before," the Factor said. "I was looking for information on the Factory agent, and I passed that flying snake along the way. I'd know it anywhere."

"But that was back in Xanth!"

"So what is it doing here?"

"It can be here too. Everything in Xanth is also in the Worlds of Ida. Here they are mere ideas; in Xanth they are real. Only a few possible creatures get to assume reality." Hugo paused, gazing at the bound snake. "Did it attack you, in Xanth?"

"No, it just flew on by."

"So it's not vicious. I'm going to free it." Hugo walked up to the cage.

"Why bother? It's not what we're looking for."

"Because I hurt when I see others hurt. I feel their suffering." Hugo put his hands to the cage door and worked it open.

"Ludicrous," the Factor said. "I'm surprised your wife puts up with it."

"She's worse than I am," Hugo said. "I mean, *better* than I am. She's more sensitive. She can charm wild creatures just by being near them. I think that's why I loved her from the start." He put his hands to the cord binding the snake's muzzle.

"And doubtless why she married you," the Factor said drily. "You're two of a kind."

Hugo paused. "Yes, I suppose we are. I always wondered what she saw in me. She's such a wonderful woman, while I'm such a nobody."

"Wonderful my foot! She was *blind*."

Hugo paused again. "What does that have to do with it?"

"Why tie yourself down with a blind woman? You did her a favor marrying her."

Hugo was becoming considerably annoyed, but he did not want to make the Factor angry and perhaps have him run off with Hugo's body. "If I did her a favor, what's wrong with that?"

"You might have married a luscious princess and lived happily ever after. You don't need to do favors for stray characters with liabilities."

Hugo resumed work on the binding, carefully freeing the snake's mouth. "Don't bite me," he murmured, smiling.

I won't.

Hugo's jaw dropped. The snake understood him—and had spoken to him telepathically! Unless he was losing his mind. "Did I imagine that?"

"No, that's a real feathered serpent you're handling, idiot," the Factor said. "It won't bite you until you free its wings so it can get away."

Him I might bite, the snake thought. *You, never. You are the kindest person I have encountered. Hello, Hugo; I am Era Demon.*

"Why didn't you communicate before?" Hugo asked it.

"What do you mean?" the Factor demanded. "I've been talking to you all along, dumbbell."

I was verifying your intentions. Sometimes the nametaggers tease me cruelly, pretending they will free me, then binding me worse.

"The nametaggers?"

"Yes, this is Castle Nametag," the Factor reminded him.

All they're interested in is playing name tag.

"Playing name tag?"

"What nonsense are you talking about?" the Factor demanded.

Shut Your Mouth! the snake thought violently.

The Factor's mouth snapped shut, astonished.

Hugo removed the cord from the snake's wings. "If you're a demon, why didn't you just dissolve into smoke and float away?"

I'm not that type of demon. I'm a winged monster demon. I can change shapes, but only when I'm free. The nametaggers know that, so they keep me bound.

"Well, you're free now," Hugo said. "Do you need help getting out of that cage?"

No. The snake slithered forward, uncoiling. It turned out to be several times the length of a man. Its scales were green and orange, its wings white, and it had a really cute smile now that it was free. *But I am not entirely free yet.*

"We'll lead you out of the castle," Hugo said. "Then you can fly into the sky."

I will not be free until I have repaid you the significant favor you have done me. You need a guide to Princess Ida. I will be your guide.

"Oh. Well, yes, we do need a guide. But that wasn't why I freed you."

I know. You freed me because you have empathy.

"Empathy?"

You feel the feelings of others, as does your wife. You make a wonderful couple.

"What is empathy?" the Factor asked.

He lacks it. But he's in your body. I can if you wish provide him a mental/emotional link so that he understands.

Hugo nodded. "Yes, that might help."

"Great fishes and little gods!" the Factor exclaimed. "Suddenly I understand! So that's why you freed the monster!"

"That's why," Hugo agreed. "I suffered when he did. Now he has volunteered to be our guide to Princess Ida."

"Then let's be on our way." The Factor set off for the spiral stairway.

But now the way was blocked. A crowd of men and women stood there, human in body but without regular heads. From the neck of each rose a tag. On each tag was printed a name.

"The nametaggers," Hugo said.

"To be sure," a sturdy male with a tag saying JAMES agreed. Hugo wasn't sure where the sound came from, but the tag vibrated as the man spoke.

"He freed the monster!" a shapely female said. Her tag was printed MARY.

"So we'll recapture it and put him in a cage too," a third one said. His tag said ROBERT.

Beware! Era thought. *They have means.*

"What means?"

It relates to their game. If they touch you with a tag, you are null until you fetch another name. Don't let a tag touch you.

This was bad. The three of them couldn't possibly forge through that pack of taggers without getting tagged. "We don't dare transfer yet," Hugo said. "Factor, you'll have to fight them with fruit."

"With fruit?" the Factor asked incredulously. "So they'll gorge to death?"

"Cherries. Pineapples," Hugo clarified. "Watch how you handle them."

"Oho!" A handful of cherries appeared in the Factor's hand. "Say, you freaks want a bit of fruit? Try this!" He flipped a cherry toward the throng.

The cherry flew down to land at the feet of the nearest man. It exploded into red fragments, leaving a puff of reddish smoke. The nametaggers, surprised, backed off.

"What, you disdain that?" the Factor asked. "Here's another." He flipped a second cherry, which banged closer.

Beware, Era thought. *They are coming from other directions.*

So they were. The trio was now surrounded. How could they avoid getting tagged?

"Oh, really?" the Factor asked. A pineapple appeared in his hand. "How would you like a taste of this?"

The nametaggers fled. They had seen a pineapple before.

"Well done," Hugo said. Normally he did not wish anyone harm, but after seeing what the nametaggers had done to Era, he was annoyed.

"Let's go," the Factor said, holding the pineapple threateningly.

They started down the hall to the stairs.

They are lurking.

"Give me a pineapple," Hugo said.

The Factor tossed it to him, and conjured another. Hugo caught it, but his knees felt weak. Cherries were impressive, but pineapples were dangerous.

They made it to the stairs. "Go on up," Hugo said. "I'll guard the rear."

There was not room here for the serpent to fly, but he had no trouble slithering rapidly up. The Factor followed. Hugo wielded his pineapple, facing back.

The nametaggers appeared, running toward him. "He doesn't have the nerve," one cried.

Hugo didn't have a choice. He heaved the pineapple at the crowd, and turned to run up the stairs. He had hardly gone five steps before the pineapple detonated. The blast blew him up several more steps—but it also blew out the steps behind him. Losing support, the ones above him began to dangle. He struggled to mount them, but the footing was bad, and he found himself slipping back down to the floor.

Then a green and orange cable slapped against his chest. It was the serpent's tail. He grabbed it. It lifted, hauling him along with it. When he reached the next flight of steps he was able to put his feet down and resume running up the stairs.

Then he smelled smoke. The pineapple had set fire to the cardboard foundation! That was more damage than he had intended to do, but he couldn't stop it now. If only the taggers had let them go in peace.

He followed the others to the ground floor and out of the castle. Behind them the flames were spreading. They got well clear, then turned to look back, panting.

The castle was going up in flames, literally. Sections of burning cardboard were flying into the sky, and smoke was pouring out. The castle was doomed.

"I hope the nametaggers manage to get out safely," Hugo gasped.

"You would," the Factor said.

A group of people was forming outside the castle. It did seem that the taggers were making it. But they would have a long hard haul rebuilding their castle. It probably served them right, but Hugo was sorry anyway.

"We'd better get on our way before we are discovered," the Factor said.

Good advice. They walked on away from the conflagration.

Too late. "There they are!" a tagger cried.

"Run!" Hugo cried.

"I've still got my pineapple," the Factor said.

"I'll take it," Hugo said. "The two of you get away, as before."

They did so. Hugo stood facing the taggers, holding the pineapple aloft. That brought them to a rapid halt; he heard faint screech-marks.

Then the tagger named James stepped forward. "You world travelers have escaped our justified retribution," he called. "But not entirely. I have a curse I saved for an appropriate occasion. Now it is yours: you can move only upworld." He gestured, and there was a kind of shimmer that sailed at Hugo, touched him, and passed on to catch the others. That was all.

James turned away, so Hugo did also. He walked to catch up with the others. "They have given up the chase."

But they cursed us, the green snake thought.

"I don't understand it. I felt no effect."

I do. It prevents any of us from going downworld. You two can't return to Xanth. I can't return to my alien home. All we can do is remain here on Cone, or travel farther upworld.

"But I want to rejoin Wira!"

Only if she comes to you. You can't go to her. That's a powerful curse.

Hugo wasn't sure how to react. He had never imagined such a curse. "You mean we can't even transfer back to Xanth, assuming our bodies are there and free?"

That is what I mean. Would it help if I told you how noble I find you? Twice you have risked your life to enable us to escape danger.

"I just do what it is right to do."

Without any thought of personal gain. That's noble. I think it's a function of your empathy. We did not offer to do the same for you.

Hugo didn't argue the case. "I still want to consult with Princess Ida."

I will scout the route, Era thought. He spread his lovely white wings and took off. He was a beautiful creature in flight. *Thank you.* Hugo realized that the serpent had read his thought.

"I could get to like this talent," the Factor remarked. "Those fruits are something."

"No way," Hugo said firmly. "I want my body back. And my wife."

Era returned. *The best route is circuitous but safe. However, there's no way to avoid the forest near the rim.*

"What's the matter with the forest?" the Factor asked. "We have forests in Xanth."

Not like this.

Hugo decided not to inquire. They would find out soon enough.

Night came while they were still on the safe route. Hugo wasn't sure exactly what made day and night here, as there seemed to be no sun, just the huge nebulous head of the lower-world Ida around which Cone revolved. The cone spun around its long axis, and that dim head was dropping out of sight.

The Factor, following Hugo's instructions, conjured a greatfruit. The thing was the size of a small tent, which was the point. They hollowed it out and camped under its protective husk. The Factor also conjured an array of fruits for them to eat.

"Why did the nametaggers imprison you?" Hugo asked the serpent as they settled down to sleep.

Jealousy.

The two men looked at the serpent, not comprehending.

Every person on this planet is a crossbreed, Era explained. *The two of you will stand out, because you are obviously not crossbreeds, but proba-*

bly you'll be left alone. But I am more of a crossbreed than most, and they resent that. They are mere two-type crossbreeds: human beings and name tags. They feel inferior.

"You must have bird ancestry, and snake ancestry," Hugo said. "But that seems to me like a garden-variety crossbreed, if you'll pardon the expression."

I can assume the form of any of my ancestors, for a while. The winged dragon disappeared, replaced by a straight snake. Then by a straight hawk. Then a young cat, really a kitten. And a mature panther. A large scorpion. A spider. A hummingbird. A stallion. A gargoyle, and a winged humanoid with batlike wings. Then the man split into three copies of himself, all identical. "But this takes a lot of energy," the three men said together. He reverted to what was apparently his natural form, the winged snake.

"That is impressive," Hugo said, amazed. "I didn't know that anyone in Xanth could have so many forms."

As I said, I'm essentially a demon. I'm from another universe. All I want is to live a long, full, fruitful life in peace. But the moment folk discover my nature, there's trouble.

"I appreciate your problem," Hugo said. "Maybe Princess Ida will know of a world where you can be yourself in peace."

That would be nice.

They slept. Hugo was a bit surprised that sleep was much as usual, despite his being made of soul stuff. He didn't think to try to dream of Wira, and didn't know whether she was asleep now, so there was no dream contact. That was too bad.

In the morning they ate more fruits, then resumed their trek toward the great rim of Cone. And soon enough encountered the Forest. And stood, daunted. These trees were something else.

The monstrous tree trunks were closely spaced, each larger and gnarlier than the others. Their massive branches intersected and formed giant knots of wood. About halfway up toward the distant sky the main trunks actually expanded and formed wooden ledges. On these high ledges were houses where the forest denizens evidently lived. However, there seemed to be enough space between the trees at ground level to allow them to pass.

No such fortune, Era thought. *Farther in they grow so close it's a veritable wooden wall. However, I located a tunnel.*

"That will do," Hugo said.

The snake flew to the side. Soon they came to the tunnel, formed by trunks and branches that had not quite been able to make a perfect link. *It passes all the way through.*

"Good enough." Era was certainly doing his part.

A crossbreed appeared. It seemed to have kraken tentacles and horse hooves, with a vaguely human head. "Pay the thumb tax," it said. "You have four thumbs between you; the snake doesn't count."

"I don't know what you mean," Hugo said. "We're just passing through."

"Ignorance is no excuse. Pay, or we'll not let you pass." The creature indicated the trees, where several enormously ugly creatures perched.

I think I found someone, Era thought. *I sent her a signal.*

A girl approached. Her body was human, but her skin was green, and her hair resembled tufts of grass. She smelled fragrant. "Hello. I'm Citronella, a crossbreed between grass and human. Can I help you?"

"Go away, weedhead," the kraken creature said. "I'm collecting the thumb tax."

"I don't believe in that tax," Citronella said.

"Nobody asked you."

The kraken's attitude suggested that Citronella was worth cultivating. "Hello. I am Hugo Human, from Xanth, and this is the Random Factor, also from Xanth. The winged snake is Era, from another realm. He contacted you telepathically, hoping you could help us. We just want to pass safely through this forest."

She nodded. "I can help you. But I have a price."

This was not necessarily good. "What price?"

"One kiss."

Not good at all. "We're both committed."

"Not you. Him." She looked at Era.

The snake had been hovering nearby. He almost dropped out of the air. *Me?*

"Yes, you're so cute," Citronella said. "You can rustle in my grass anytime."

"Disgusting," the kraken said.

"Deal," Hugo said.

Era flew up, hovered before Citronella, and gave her a solid green kiss. Little tufts of grass circled their heads before dissipating.

"That was great," the girl said. "Now I'll exercise my talent."

"What is your talent?" Hugo asked.

"I get rid of pests of any type." She focused on the kraken. "Begone, vermin!"

"Traitor!" But the kraken walked away.

"Thank you," Hugo said.

"Oh, I wanted to mess up the kraken anyway. I'd have done it for nothing." She walked away.

Era slithered into the tunnel, leading the way again. The men followed. It became awesomely dark, but they followed the sounds of the slithering and had no trouble.

Eventually they emerged on the other side. And stared.

They were at the brink of the vast sea that filled the great cone of Cone. It was as wide across as a world. And around its edge were countless crossbreed couples interacting intensely.

"Stork summoning," Hugo breathed. "Right out in the open. Everywhere."

That's the way of it on Planet Cone, Era explained. *The land creatures are able to breed only with the sea creatures, so they meet at the fringe and do it. They don't fool around; neither can survive long out of their element.*

"But there are children here too!"

Of course. They can't be deserted, lest some drown or dehydrate. There's no Adult Conspiracy here.

So it seemed.

"Actually it's interesting," the Factor said, watching the nearby couples closely. "They have some remarkable techniques."

Hugo had noted that. In part it was because different crossbreeds needed to adapt to each other in different ways. But they also seemed to have a certain experimental enthusiasm that led to unusual positions.

But they had business to accomplish. "We had better trek on down to Princess Ida," Hugo said.

There should be no further significant barriers to your progress, Era thought. *I think I will remain on land if you can spare me.*

"But you have reason to talk with Ida too," Hugo reminded him. "To find a world where you can live normally."

On reconsideration, I may be able to make it on this one. I'd like to discover whether Citronella really likes me as I am. I could assume another form for her, so she wouldn't have to trek to the sea to, well, breed.

"Oho!" the Factor said. "So you have a selfish motive."

Era blushed along his length. *It seems I do.*

Hugo laughed. "Then by all means go to her. You have more than repaid us for our service to you."

I am not sure of that. I brought the curse on you.

"We'll manage," Hugo said with more confidence than he felt. "Farewell, Era."

The snake flew gratefully away.

"You say we can breathe the water?" the Factor asked.

"That is my understanding. That visitors can, not being entirely bound by the local planetary rules." He put his face in the water and tried to breathe, half expecting to choke.

Instead it worked; the water tasted like thick air. So he plunged on in. In a moment and a half the Factor joined him.

They found themselves in a new realm. They seemed to be at the top of a steep mountain slope that was much like the dry side. There were massive seaweeds that resembled trees, and people working angled fields. There were even some small ponds. Hugo decided not to ponder that too intensely, lest he become confused. "Let's keep moving," he said, and was gratified to find that he could speak normally.

"The denizens have gills," the Factor said. "We don't."

"We must be enabled by the magic of our alien status."

They found a path and followed it down. Unlike the outside of the planet, there were no special threats or challenges here; the people seemed to be peaceful and satisfied to let the visitors pass on through. Still, it took time to walk the length of the planet, even downhill, and they had to camp for the night. How there could be day and night under the deep sea Hugo wasn't sure, and preferred not to inquire.

"Empathy," the Factor said as they chewed on fruit. "It is a strange concept. I think I'm beginning to feel it."

"That's good," Hugo said. "Though it may simply be leakage from my body."

"I think Debra would like me better with it."

"She surely would."

"I wonder where she is now?"

"With Wira, on their way here, I hope."

"Maybe Princess Ida knows."

"Maybe she does." This seemed to be about as close as they could get to personal dialogue; they were in each other's bodies, but even though the Factor was learning about empathy they still weren't really friends.

They slept.

Next day they finally made it to the apex of the cone. There was a modest residence, no palace, with a nice little garden. Their path led right to it.

Princess Ida turned out to be a normal human woman with the head of a horse. A crossbreed, of course. Around her head orbited a moon in the shape of a dumbbell.

"You understand," she said after listening to their story. "That curse is binding. You can't return downworld. That means that your beloveds will have to join you here, and remain. Are you prepared for that?"

"No," the Factor said.

"Is there a Good Magician's Castle here?" Hugo asked.

"I am not aware of any. Not everything is duplicated on every planet, except for myself, and I'm not the same on each. So I suspect you would not be able to set up a similar lifestyle here."

Hugo sighed. "I was afraid of that. I am not at all sure she would like it, so far from the Good Magician."

The Factor considered. "To be with Debra, in this body, so that the curse does not apply, I believe I am prepared to make the sacrifice of remaining on this world. I shall be satisfied to wait here for her, and see how she feels about it."

That made Hugo consider. "Your body is younger and more handsome than mine. If Wira should be satisfied to be with me in this manner, I would be satisfied too."

"Then perhaps you have your solution," Ida said. "All you have to do is wait for your women to catch up with you here."

They nodded. They thanked her and left her house.

There was a guest house nearby for travelers. The Factor conjured some nice exotic fruit to trade for their residence there, and they took temporary possession.

"It's hardly perfect," the Factor said. "But it seems that some compromises have to be made for love."

Hugo was not entirely satisfied. "Wira and I were about to summon the stork when you switched me out."

"Sorry about that. It was nothing personal. I just didn't want to be stuck in another cellar."

"I'm not sure I want to signal any storks with her in your body."

"I see your point. But of course we hope to solve that problem too, in time. First we get together with the girls; then we work with them to get switched back. There must be a spell, somewhere."

"There must be," Hugo agreed. But he remained ill at ease.

They slept—and there was Wira in the dream. She rushed to him and kissed him. "I used some more of the communal dream potion," she said. "It doesn't work across worlds, but we're on Cone now, and so are you."

He kissed her back. "We're near Princess Ida's residence. We'll wait here for you."

"There's a problem," she said. "We followed the direction Debra knew. But it led us to the tip of the cone, and there's nothing here."

Suddenly he understood. "You're on the outside! We're on the inside. The straight line direction took you close, but you have to go the other way. To the rim and into the sea."

"That explains it," she said ruefully. "We reckoned without this world's special shape."

"We'll wait here—or come to meet you halfway." He laughed, embarrassed. "Maybe at the brink of the sea, where all the couples meet and, er, relate."

"So no one will care if we do the same," she said, blushing.

"You don't mind that I'm in the wrong body?"

"I understand the situation. Hugo, I just want to be with you and love you."

"I feel the same. So does the Factor, with Debra. But maybe we had better check with Debra."

Debra appeared in the communal dream. "I feel the same. I *can't* be with Random in his own body; you know why. So yours will do, until we find a way to nullify the curse." She glanced at the Factor, who was also present.

"Until we find a way," Hugo agreed. He knew the curse needed to be nullified, because Debra evidently slept in her bra, and that bra made his hands itch to take it off. Because he was in the Factor's body, that could be deadly.

"We don't have much dream potion left," she said. "So we won't be in touch this way often, just as necessary."

"I understand. And I need to explain something too: we're under an additional curse the nametaggers put on us. When we transfer, we can only go upworld, not back to Xanth."

Wira frowned. "That's bad. But maybe we'll find a way around it. Meanwhile, don't transfer."

"We won't," he agreed. "We need a curse nullifier, if we can find one."

She began to waver. "Oops, it's running out. We must go. Remember—the rim of the Hypotho-sea."

"The rim," he agreed. "We'll start walking in the morning."

"So will we." She stepped quickly up and kissed him, then faded. Debra did the same with the Factor.

"The Hypotho-sea?" the Factor asked.

"That's what she called it. It makes sense: the sea where the hypothetical water creatures exist."

They sank back into pleasantly dreamless sleep.

Suddenly there was a looming cacophony. It sounded as though half a passel of unruly monsters was banging at the door and windows.

"I don't like the sound of this," Hugo said, jolted awake.

"Neither do I," the Factor said. "Who would be raiding us?"

"In the name of the nametaggers you wronged," a monster's voice shouted at one window.

"And for the thumb tax you cheated us out of," another monster's voice added at the other window.

"We will hereby devour you," a third monster cried at the door.

"They must have made a foul deal with the sea monsters," Hugo said nervously.

"To gain their vengeance on us," the Factor agreed.

The door crashed inward. Three monsters jammed in the doorway, trying to get in together. Both windows shattered as more monsters hurtled against them. Each was more bug-eyed, tentacular, and sting-tailed than the others. Any one monster could have eaten them both, and there were many.

A pineapple appeared in the Factor's hand. "No!" Hugo cried. "That will blow us up along with them, in this confined chamber."

"Then you transfer us out of here," the Factor said, coming to grab his arm.

Hugo needed no further urging. He transferred them out. As he did so, he saw the pineapple slip from the Factor's hand. That would drop to the floor and explode among the converging monsters.

Fortunately, the two of them were gone from this world before that happened.

Unfortunately, they could only be in another world, much smaller than the one they left. And the women would not know, until they set up another communal dream.

They would have to start all over again.

14
HEIR APPARENT

Thomas T hey flew to Castle Roogna in the morning, hoping for the best. Debra landed in the orchard, then trotted toward the castle, carrying Wira. Their dream had gone bad, but at least she retained the ability to orient on the Factor's body when he did magic, and this was where he had gone.

A girl appeared before them. She had brown hair and eyes, and wore a brown dress. Also a little crown. She looked about eleven. "Hail, centaur," she said. A brown harmonica appeared in her hands. She played a note and a small brown hailstorm formed.

"Stop it, Harmony," Wira snapped. "This is Debra, helping me with a vital mission." Then, to Debra: "This is Princess Harmony. She's a lot of impertinence."

Harmony was abashed. "I didn't know it was you, Wira." She paused, gazing at the woman with surprise. "You can see!"

"It's a long story," Wira said. "Portions of which are covered by the Adult Conspiracy."

"Oh, fudge!" the girl said. A plate of fudge appeared in her hands. The harmonica had vanished. "Have some. It's fresh conjured."

"Thank you, Harmony," Wira said. She reached down to take a piece, and so did Debra. It turned out to be excellent fudge. "Apology accepted,"

Wira said. She evidently understood this girl quite well, and was not at all in awe of her. Debra realized that Wira had probably babysat her on occasion.

A second girl appeared. This one had green-blonde hair, blue eyes, and wore a green dress. She also wore a crown. "Anything interesting gets covered by the Conspiracy," she said. "We're ill and fatigued of it."

"And this is Princess Melody," Wira said.

"Twins!" Debra said, surprised.

"No," both girls said together, giggling.

"There's a third," Wira explained. "Rhythm. They are triplets, each more mischievous than the others."

The third princess appeared. She had red hair, green eyes, a red dress, and a crown. A red drum appeared in her hands. "Present," she said, and beat a brief drumroll.

"We are looking for my husband Hugo and another man," Wira said. "They may have appeared here rather suddenly."

The three princesses circulated a glance. "No," Melody said.

"They're not here," Harmony agreed.

"And never were," Rhythm concluded.

Wira sighed. "Let me explain, girls. Debra is able to orient on them when they do magic. They came here last night. We need to catch up to them."

"They're not here," Melody said.

"We'll show you," Harmony said.

"Now," Rhythm concluded.

Then Melody sang a note. Harmony's harmonica reappeared, and she played a matching note. Rhythm's drum reappeared, and she beat a beat.

Castle Roogna became transparent. There were people all through it, going about their business. None of them were Hugo or the Random Factor. It was astonishing magic.

"Can this be believed?" Debra asked quietly.

"The princesses are all Sorceresses," Wira said. "Any one alone is as strong as any other Magician or Sorceress. Any two square it. The three together cube it. If they are sure our men are not in the castle, it is surely true."

"I think we have a problem," Debra murmured. "I know they came here."

Three little lightbulbs flashed over the princesses' heads. "Princess Ida!" Melody said.

"They're on one of her moons," Harmony agreed.

"And she's in the castle, so the direction is toward her," Rhythm concluded.

Wira sighed. "I fear that may be true."

"I don't understand," Debra said.

"Princess Ida is Queen Ivy's twin sister," Wira explained. "A little moon orbits her head. That moon is a world in itself, called Ptero, where all the folk who exist or might exist dwell, most of them hoping for a chance to come here to Xanth and be real. It follows its own rules of magic. If the men went there, we'll have a horrible job locating them."

"But if we go there, I should be able to track them," Debra said.

"Yes, if they transfer again. But then they'll be somewhere else."

Now Debra understood the gravity of it. "This may not be fun."

"Not fun at all," Wira agreed. "It is apt to be a long and perhaps difficult chase. I think we're going to need help."

"We'll go!" the three princesses said together.

"Would your mother let you?" Wira asked evenly.

Their enthusiasm collapsed. That was answer enough.

"Maybe we'd better talk with Princess Ida," Debra suggested.

"Yes. She's a sensible woman."

They crossed over the moat, using the drawbridge. A huge green head lifted from the water to inspect them. "It's okay, Sesame," Melody said. "We're going to see Princess Ida."

The head nodded and sank back beneath the water of the moat.

The princesses showed them into the castle, which had reverted to normal solid colors. Soon they were ushered upstairs, and to the modest chamber of the queen's sister. Debra was surprised that there was so little ceremony, but of course with three Sorceresses and a smart moat monster around they hardly needed guards or protocols.

Princess Ida was an older woman of thirty-eight, undistinguished except for her crown. And the small ball circling her head. "I'm so glad to see you, Wira," she said. "And you have achieved your vision at last!"

"I'm still working on it," Wira said. "Mostly I close my eyes to keep things familiar. This is Debra, temporarily in centaur form so she can fly me where I have to go. We have a serious problem."

"I'm so glad to meet you," Princess Ida said to Debra.

"I'm sorry I did not know of you," Debra said, embarrassed. "I am told that that—that ball is an entire world. I am amazed."

"Things can be amazing," Ida said. "What is this problem?"

Debra expected Wira to describe it, but the woman demurred to her, oddly. So she plunged in, telling everything she thought was relevant. "So now it seems that Hugo and Random are not only in each other's bodies, but on your world of Ptero," she concluded. "I think we can find them, but—"

"I'm sure you can," Ida agreed. That was oddly reassuring, as though it became true as she spoke.

"But my ability functions only when Random does his magic," Debra said. "So if we go to Ptero, we'll have to wait for them to move, and then they won't be there any more. So I think we need some other way."

"You surely do," Ida agreed. "Perhaps there is someone else who can locate them without the need for them to do magic."

"I suppose so," Debra agreed uncertainly.

Ida glanced at Wira. "Are there others who might help?"

"We have checked out all those indicated by the live spots in the Book of Magic," Wira said. "All except one I don't understand, because it doesn't refer to a person. That's 'Air Apparent.' "

"I think we figured that out," Debra said. "That was Fracto Cloud in his condensed form. Remember, we thought he was a dead body."

"Air become apparent," Princess Ida agreed. "That certainly could have been a clue."

"Yet it lingers in my mind," Wira said. "As though it isn't yet done."

"I wonder," Debra said. "Happy Bottom and Fray helped us search, and thought their role was done when they identified Fracto. Maybe it wasn't done."

"That certainly could be the case," Ida agreed. She seemed to be a most amicable person.

"So maybe we should check back with them. We may need one of them along, in compacted form, to complete this mission. Maybe not Fracto, who I understand is irascible, but Happy seemed nice when we met her."

"I agree," Ida said.

Wira glanced at her appraisingly. "Then I think I do too."

"Oh, it's just a wild conjecture," Debra protested.

"It will do," Ida said.

"And I don't see how a compacted cloud could help us handle the world of Ptero. But if the Book of Answers suggests that is the case, then maybe we should try it."

"I agree," Ida said.

"But it also might be a pun for 'heir apparent,' in which case it would be someone else. Such as Sim Bird, heir to the knowledge of the universe, or Nimbus, heir to the phenomenal powers of the Demon Xanth. So it is possible that one of them is the one we want."

"You are thinking like a centaur," Ida said.

Debra blushed, surprised both by the compliment and the fact that she considered it a compliment. She had actually spoken more thoughtfully than she was accustomed to, so the centaur form might indeed be affecting her mind. That seemed to be no bad thing.

"Thank you, Princess Ida," Wira said. "We will go see whom we can enlist, then return here to tackle Ptero. We appreciate your help."

"You are more than welcome, Wira. You deserve to have your happiness back."

They left the chamber and the castle, unobstructed. "Where to now?" Debra asked as Wira mounted and she took wing.

"You have spelled it out," Wira said. "First the Region of Air, then the others."

"But I was just conjecturing! It might be nonsense."

"It's not nonsense. It's an approach that should facilitate our success."

"We have no certainty of success," Debra said sourly. "Only my half-baked ideas. I'm almost embarrassed to have spoken them to the princess."

"You did very well, Debra."

"I still think you could have presented our case more clearly and succinctly. Why did you leave it to me?"

"There is something else about Princess Ida. She is the Sorceress of the Idea. Her moon is a world of ideas, but that is only part of her talent. Whatever idea she accepts is valid."

Debra laughed. "Oh, surely even she makes mistakes on occasion."

Wira remained serious. "Here is the way it works: ideas become reality when Ida accepts them. But they have to be the ideas of folk who do not know her talent. That may be nature's way of preventing her from changing the reality of the universe to suit herself."

"You knew this, but I didn't. So I may have been spouting nonsense." Then she paused. "Wait half a moment. Ideas become real, when—"

"Exactly. Now we know we are on the right track, because it became right when you suggested it and Ida agreed. All we have to do is follow up."

"That's why you left it to me!" Debra said. "Because I was ignorant!"

"Because you didn't know the significance of the situation," Wira said. "I could not suggest anything, because she would be unable to make it real. But you could, and you came up with some good ideas, fortunately."

Debra shook her head. "Well, I hope they are good, because it seems we are stuck with them."

They crossed the Gap Chasm. A small cloud floated there. It spied them and formed a smiley face.

"Fray!" Debra called. "We're on our way to talk to your mother."

The smile faded. An arrow symbol formed, pointing down.

"Very well," Wira said. "We'll land so we can talk."

Debra spiraled down to land at the brink of the huge chasm. The cloud condensed and formed into the nine-year-old girl form. "Mother sent me out to play so she can blow hot and cold with father," Fray reported. "They're blowing up a storm. I don't think they want visitors today."

"The Adult Conspiracy," Wira murmured. "It's surprising how that gets around."

"It's a nuisance," Fray said. "I don't know what they're doing that has to be so secret."

"I recently joined the Conspiracy," Debra said. "It is intended to protect children from things that might damage their bodies or spirits. It is better to let it be."

"Did you say that before you joined it?" the girl demanded rebelliously.

"No, I was all set to violate it."

Fray laughed, surprisingly. "I almost violated it too."

Both Debra and Wira looked at her, dismayed. "You did?" Wira asked.

"Sure. When the goblin men were attacking at Goblin Mountain. They were grabbing the women, pushing them down to the floor, and tearing off their clothes. I know all I had to do was stay still and let them catch me, and I'd find out what it was all about."

"You didn't," Wira said, appalled.

"I didn't," Fray agreed. "Mother told me to vaporize, and I did, and they couldn't get me. But whatever it was looked pretty brutal. Then later mother had some reverse wood, and she was getting all childish, while I got adult and stopped her from having any naughty fun." She grimaced. "So why are you headed there?"

"We think we need an air apparent," Debra said. "That is, folk like you are air, but when you condense you became apparent. So your mother may be able to help us."

"*I* could help you," Fray said. "Mother's too busy making weather with father."

"But our mission may be dangerous. Your mother might not want you going on it."

"She'll let me go," Fray said confidently. "As long as there's at least one adult along."

"How can you be sure of that?"

"Ever see a cloud tantrum?"

Both Debra and Wira had to smile. Even a small thunderstorm could be devastating on occasion. "Maybe she will do," Debra said to Wira. "She has spirit. The idea didn't specify age, and children can do some things adults won't."

Wira addressed Fray: "We have to check on a couple of other folk. Why don't you go home and get your folks' permission, and we'll meet you at Castle Roogna."

"Goody!" the child exclaimed, and vaporized.

"I hope we don't regret this," Wira said as they took off for the most likely place to locate Sim Bird: Mount Parnassus, where the Simurgh dwelt.

"One thing about Parnassus," Wira said. "You can't fly there. The Simurgh has a no-fly zone."

Debra shrugged. "Then I'll trot. It will be interesting to see it. Is it true that there are wild women there, and a giant serpent?"

"The maenads and the Python," Wira agreed. "Both are extremely dangerous."

"And me having to fake expertise with my bow."

"Maybe we can talk our way past the maenads. We're women, after all. But the Python may be a challenge."

"It's nice to see your confidence," Debra said, shuddering.

"We have our men to rescue."

That stiffened Debra's resolve. "We'll get through."

She glided to a landing near the base of the twin-peaked Mount Parnassus and trotted forward. There was a convenient path leading up the southern peak. But not far along it they heard the whoops of an approaching war party. "Show no fear," Wira said tightly.

"I have no fear," Debra said with half a smile. "Only terror."

The savage women burst into view. They were naked, shapely, and wild-haired. "Food!" one screamed, spit dripping from her pointed teeth.

"Not today," Debra said firmly. "We have come to see the Simurgh."

"Who cares? You've got good meat on you." They crowded closer, salivating.

"We are on a mission relating to men," Wira said. "We have to catch them so we can deal with them appropriately."

The maenads milled about. "Are they tasty?" one asked.

"Delicious," Wira said.

"Bleep." The maenads moved on. They evidently weren't supposed to interfere with female hunting missions.

"Delicious?" Debra inquired when they were alone.

"When you have been party to the Adult Conspiracy longer, you will understand."

They continued up the mountain. Suddenly a monstrous serpent slithered into view. "Morsels!" it said.

Debra's bow was in her hand, an arrow nocked, the string drawn. She wasn't aware of taking it; it just happened. She was surprised that she had the strength to hold the taut bowstring. The arrow's head tracked the serpent's left eye.

"Oh, come on now, filly," the Python said. "Do you think you can threaten me with that tiny barb?"

"I have others," Debra said evenly.

The Python lifted his head high. "I am the nemesis and delight of all women," he said. "I rouse their desire as nothing else can. After I possess you, I will consume you both."

The weird thing was, the big snake was doing it. His gaze held Debra in a temporary trance as he talked. She was unable to move.

The Python slid smoothly forward. His jaws gaped, seeming almost wide enough to take in the centaur.

Then he paused. "Shouldn't you be wearing a bra?"

The curse worked even on the Python? Well, he was male.

"Forget it, snake," Wira said. "You can't fascinate me. I can't see you."

Startled, the serpent focused on her. "You're that blind woman," he said. "What are you doing here?"

"Coming to see the Simurgh. Now get out of our way."

"Unlikely." The gaze flicked back to Debra.

The first arrow was suddenly sticking out of the serpent's nose, and the second was nocked. "A warning shot," Debra said. "Next one strikes your eye."

The Python considered. His forked tongue flicked out, wrapped around the arrow, and yanked it out. Then he slowly backed away. In two and a half moments he was gone.

Debra shakily put the bow away. "You distracted him just long enough," she said. "How did you break the fascination?"

"I closed my eyes. I really don't use them to find my way. That was a nice shot."

"I did loose an arrow!" Debra said, belatedly realizing. "I put it right where I wanted. I would have scored on his eye too. I thought I didn't know how."

"It seems the body does provide that talent. Too bad you lost an arrow."

"It was worth it."

They moved on up the slope until they came to the cleared summit. There was the biggest, largest, hugest possible tree, with a monstrous bird perched on one of its stout branches. The bird had a head crested with fire, feathers like veils of light and shadow, and wings like mist over a mountain. This was the Simurgh, the Keeper of the Tree of Seeds.

They paused in place, awed by the magnificence of the great bird. Then Wira spoke. "Oh Simurgh, I am—"

I KNOW WHO YOU ARE, GOOD WOMAN. The thought was almost mind-blowingly powerful.

"And this is—"

The bird's gaze oriented on Debra, as potent as that of the Python, but different. She realized that the bird was plumbing the depths of her mind. A CONSTRUCT FROM THE FACTORY. The eyes blinked with surprise. MADE REAL BY THE DEMON XANTH, AND FALLEN IN LOVE WITH THE ENEMY MAN.

Debra fought to speak, and managed it. "Random is not my enemy!"

There was a freighted pause. NOT ANY MORE, the Simurgh agreed. BUT YOU MAY STILL BE HIS ENEMY.

"I won't wear a bra!" Debra said.

Wira spoke. "We came to ask—"

MY CHICK NEEDS TO KNOW EVERYTHING. HE IS INDEED MY HEIR APPARENT. THE TOUR OF WORLDS WILL BE GOOD EXPERIENCE. HE WILL JOIN YOU AT CASTLE ROOGNA.

That was it. They found themselves at the base of the mountain without quite remembering how they had gotten there. There was one more person to enlist.

They set off for the Nameless Castle. "Do you think Chlorine will let Nimbus go?" Debra asked.

"I suspect Nimby will. He wants his son to get worldly experience."

"Worldly," Debra echoed, appreciating the pun.

They arrived at the Nameless Castle in the early afternoon. Debra landed on the edge of the cloudbank—and there were two children.

"Mother is having half a fit," Nimbus reported brightly. "But she's letting me go, provided Ilene comes along too, to babysit."

"I reminded her I'm only eleven," the girl said. "But she says I have the illusion of being older. I don't think I quite understand that."

"You can make illusions real," Debra said. "If you had the illusion of greater age, you might make it real, at least for a while."

"I hadn't thought of that," the girl said, surprised.

"I was part illusion, until Nimby made me real," Debra reminded her.

"He also made me older. So I appreciate the concept. When you need to be older, maybe you'll be able to make the pretense, then make it real."

"That seems far-fetched."

"Chlorine surely knew. Sometimes things you believe do come true. We just this morning talked with Princess Ida."

"Oh, yes, she's very nice."

"It seems we have our complement," Wira said. "If you are ready to go—"

"We are," Nimbus said, reaching up to her. She lifted him up to sit in front of her. Ilene got on behind her. Debra flicked them both light and took off.

"We're so glad they let you come with us, Nimbus," Wira said.

"Aw, they just wanted to relax a while."

"Relax?"

"They can't talk much when I'm around."

"I don't understand."

"Mom said the Nameless Castle is a palace. Dad said then let's put wheels on it."

"Those are metaphors," Wira said. "She meant that it's a very fancy castle. He meant that it was time to move it elsewhere."

"That's a mixed metaphor!" Debra said. "Wheels on the palace."

"Yeah. So next thing the castle was rolling almost off the cloud. Dad barely caught it in time."

"You made it literal," Wira said. "That's your talent."

"To make mixed metaphors real," Ilene said. "They were pretty upset."

"I can imagine," Wira said. "Maybe you had better stifle it while we're on this mission."

"Why should I? I want to have fun."

"Nimbus!" Ilene snapped.

"Aww, okay."

Debra nodded to herself. The boy knew to mind Ilene.

"Will you tell us what your mission is, this time?" Ilene asked, changing the subject.

Wira explained how they had found and lost their two men. "So now we have to go to the World of Ida," she concluded. "With the heirs or air apparent."

"But don't you have to leave your body behind to go there?" the girl asked.

"Yes, of course. But Princess Ida will see that our bodies are safe."

"What about the men's bodies?"

Debra felt Wira stiffen, and Debra did too. "The men—they had to leave their bodies behind," Debra said.

"In the burning tree," Wira said.

"But they exchanged with some fancy pennies."

"If those pennies came from a World of Ida, their bodies couldn't have gone."

"That what I wondered," Ilene said. "I didn't mean to make trouble."

"You didn't," Wira assured her. "We missed something we should have understood right away. If the men remained mostly in that tree—"

"There must be a confusion," Debra said quickly. She couldn't bear the thought of the men's bodies burning.

"We'll have to go check that tree," Wira said grimly.

Debra veered to fly to the tree they had visited in the dream. No more was said; neither of them dared.

They landed near the tree and walked to its site, dread threatening. Dread confirmed: there was nothing but a pile of ashes there.

Ilene dismounted. "Let's take a walk, Nimbus," she said.

"But I want to see—" he began, before her warning glare cut him off. "Walk it is," he agreed.

"That girl does show signs of maturity," Debra murmured.

"We have to look," Wira said, contemplating the ashes.

"We have to," Debra agreed.

They found a nearby fan tree and picked large fans. They waved these, blowing the ashes away. Soon the ground showed, with the scorched cents lying on it.

"Those are talking cents," Wira said. "I wonder—?"

"Do you have common cents?" Debra asked the coins.

"We're not common," a penny replied.

"I can see that. Did you happen to see any—any bodies here?"

"No, but we know where they are. In the beer cellar."

"Do you mean wine cellar?" Wira asked.

"This was a beerbarrel tree, not a winebarrel tree. It has a beer cellar."

The woman and centaur exchanged a look of burgeoning hope. "A cellar!" Debra said.

They inspected the ground, and discovered a square panel embedded in the center. It had a heavy ring set in its metal. They hauled on the ring together, and slowly the panel came up. There was a dark hole below, with steps leading down.

"Time for some help," Wira said. "Ilene! Nimbus! We need the illusion of light here."

In less than a moment the two were there. "I can't make illusions," Ilene said. "They have to exist first."

"Isn't my glow an illusion?" Nimbus asked, gazing eagerly into the hole.

"Maybe it is," Ilene agreed. She focused, and the boy's faint glow became bright.

"Still, I had better go first," Wira said. "I don't need light, and I don't want to put the children at risk." She closed her eyes and started down the steps.

"This is fun," Nimbus said. "Maybe there's hidden treasure."

"It seems safe," Wira called from below.

Nimbus and Ilene went down, his glow illuminating everything. That helped, because Debra was far too large to join them. "What's down there?" she called.

"Ninety-nine bottles of beer," Ilene called back.

"And some orange cones," the boy added. "Dodging around."

This hardly made sense. "Cones?"

"There are words printed on them," Ilene said. "Nundrum."

Debra groaned. "Cone-nundrum. A pun."

"I found the bodies," Wira called. "They're alive!"

Debra was so relieved she sank to her knees. "Thank you, fate," she breathed.

After some discussion they figured it out. The men had randomly exchanged with the collection of coins, which had been in the cellar with the beer, left over from some game beer drinkers had played. Then they had exchanged again, with the cones, which had come from one of the worlds of Ida. They probably hadn't realized that they were going to that world;

they just hadn't wanted to be stuck in the cellar of the burning tree. But as it turned out, they were safe there; the massed beer bottles insulated the chamber against the heat, and the cellar was undamaged. The men could have waited, and been rescued by now, had they realized.

"But at least they are safe," Wira said. "I think we should just leave their bodies here until we catch up to their souls and somehow bring them back. However, we should take the little cones, as an indication of where the men went."

Debra agreed. They exited the cellar, closed its door, and carefully piled the ashes back over it so that no one would know the cellar existed. Then they set off for Castle Roogna, greatly encouraged.

"I just thought," Debra said. "Do we have more of that communal dream potion?"

"Yes, I packed a vial. But we'll have to be cautious about using it, as we may not be able to return for more when that runs out."

Fray Cloud and Sim Bird were already at the castle, being entertained by the three princesses. Then the group of six of them went up to see Princess Ida.

"Cones," Ida said. "The fourth world is Cone; that might be where they came from."

"The fourth world?" Debra asked.

"There is what seems to be an endless chain of worlds," Ida explained. "The first is Ptero, where time is geography."

"Geography?" Debra asked.

"Folk age as they go west, and youthen as they go east, so they can be any age they want, but they can't travel beyond their assigned lifespans. They call it To and From."

"Couldn't they travel to the north or south pole and return on another meridian, without suffering aging or youthening?"

Ida considered, surprised. "I suppose they could. That might greatly increase their freedom to travel."

"But we aren't going there," Wira said.

"Yes," Ida agreed. "On the word of Ptero is another Princess Ida, with another world orbiting her head. That is Pyramid, with four triangular faces, blue, red, green, and gray. On the blue face is another Ida, with a donut-shaped world orbiting her head. That is Torus. The Ida on that world has a cone-shaped world orbiting her head. That is Cone, where I think these cones came from. Is that correct, cones?"

The two cones dodged back and forth as if avoiding a speeding object. That was their confirmation.

"I hope my sense of direction works once we're on that world," Debra said. "Because even a very small world is a very big place."

"I hope so too," Ida said. Debra realized that the princess could no longer make her conjectures come true, because now she knew Ida's talent.

"If it works on Xanth, shouldn't it work on Cone?" Fray asked.

"Yes, it should," Ida agreed. "In fact, I'm sure it does."

Because Fray, only nine years old, didn't know about Ida's talent. Debra breathed a silent sigh of relief. The child was already proving her usefulness.

"You will have to leave your bodies here," Ida said. "But your souls will condense to form similar bodies with similar abilities. Cone is the fourth derivative, extremely small, but it will seem full size to you. I hope you are able to persuade your men to return."

"How do *we* return?" Debra asked.

"You merely release your bodies, which are made of soul stuff. Your souls will puff into full size and return here, and to your sleeping bodies. The men should be able to do the same."

Debra didn't like the sound of that. "Should?"

"They did not arrive there by any normal route. That might complicate their return."

"There has to be a way," Wira said.

Princess Ida did not comment. That did not ease Debra's misgivings.

They lay on assorted couches, and Debra settled on the floor. Then Ida brought each a small vial to sniff as she opened it. Each person settled down, unconscious. So far this seemed to be mostly imagination.

Then it was Debra's turn to sniff. She did—and found herself rising out of her body. This was weird! But soon she formed into her centaur shape, albeit diffuse, and saw the others resuming their shapes, only on a miniature scale. Princess Ida was the size of a mountain.

Wira beckoned, then set off flying toward the little moon orbiting Ida's head. The others followed. The closer they got to it, the larger the world became. Debra realized that they were getting smaller, reducing to the scale of the world. As they approached it, it seemed as if they were coming toward a full-sized world.

They accelerated, until it seemed they were going to crash into the ground. But then they swerved to zoom along just above the surface, the six of them flying in a line with Debra at the end, going to—

Castle Roogna! And into it, like spirits flying through matter, and up to the room of Princess Ida. And there she was, with her tiny pyramidal moon with its colored faces. They oriented on that, and soon it was expanding the same way Ptero had, becoming the world it was.

There was the Ida on its blue face, on an isle in a lake, with her donut moon. They oriented on that, and found that Ida, and there was her moon, shaped like a cone. That was the one!

They zoomed in on the cone world, and came to rest at last on its outside surface. This was girt by fields and jungles and other routine features.

But where were the men?

Debra focused. "That way," she said, pointing toward the distant rim of the cone. "I think. My sense is a bit fuzzy, but that may be because we're on a different world."

"Are you sure?" Wira asked. "Has the Factor transferred recently?"

"No, I'm not sure at all. He hasn't transferred. So I must be imagining it. My feeling is gone now."

"I may have an idea," Sim said.

"Aren't you Xanth's smartest young bird?" Ilene asked admiringly. "Your idea is surely great."

Sim paused, evidently taken aback by this compliment. A few feathers turned pinkish. "That is irrelevant."

"I doubt it," Wira said. "Let's hear your idea."

"It occurred to me that we might craft a device to indicate the proper direction. Nimbus's talent is to make mixed metaphors real. Suppose we mixed some for him?"

"That might be entertaining," Wira said. "But what we need is a direction."

"Precisely. One metaphor is Time's Arrow. Another is factoring a human equation. Time isn't really an arrow, and factoring is a mathematical process, but as metaphors they can facilitate understanding."

Where was he going on this? But Debra kept her mouth shut.

"True," Wira said. "The key would be in the mix, if that's not metaphorical itself."

"Suppose we mixed them and came up with the Factor's Arrow?"

Wira frowned. "I'm not sure I—"

"There," Nimbus said, glowing more brightly.

There was an arrow in the air, pointing toward the narrow tip of the cone. A literal mixed metaphor.

"That's where Random is!" Debra exclaimed jubilantly.

A glance circulated somewhat haphazardly. Could this really make sense?

Wira shrugged. "Let's try it."

Debra fixed the direction in her mind, and they started off. They couldn't go in a straight line, because there was a hill and forest in the way, and the forest looked rather ominous. So they allowed the terrain to guide them, and followed the curve of the hill beside the forest.

And came to a smoldering ruin. It looked as if someone had piled up a mountain of cardboard and set it afire. People were working around it, using insulated hooks to catch and pull the pieces clear of the main mound. This would be the start of the rebuilding effort.

The people spotted them. Three forged toward them.

All of them stared in astonishment. Instead of heads, the people had name tags! The tags said JAMES, MARY, and ROBERT. They were, respectively, sturdy, shapely, and neutral. "Who are you?" James demanded, the tag vibrating.

"We are visitors from Xanth, just passing through," Wira said.

"From Xanth!" Mary said.

"Yes. We're looking for two men, also from Xanth. Have you seen them?"

"Oh, yes," James said grimly. "They burned down our castle."

Oops. Debra glanced nervously around. These angry people might have a grudge.

Wira had evidently come to a similar apprehension. "Thank you," she said. "We'll be moving on now."

"I think not," Robert said grimly. Then, to the others: "Tag them!"

Mary stepped forward and tagged Wira. Robert tagged Sim. Robert tagged Ilene. The three who were tagged went still, standing without speaking.

Debra acted immediately. She leaped with all four feet to the side, avoiding getting tagged. Nimbus and Fray, the youngest members of the party, were on her back; they had the sense to hang on. She was able to outrun the two-footed folk.

"Something has happened to them," Debra said tersely. "Do either of you have any idea what?"

"Maybe," Nimbus said. "I think they're nametaggers. I heard about them once. Whatever they tag is null until it finds a new name. But I think it just stuns outsiders."

"We have to rescue them," Debra said.

"You can't escape us, centaur," James called angrily. "We're sending the flamma-bull after you. You can't outrun him!"

That sounded bad. They needed to get well away—but if they did, what would happen to the three who had been tagged?

The bull appeared. He was a fine-looking bull the color of intense flame. In fact, flames were rising from him. Now she got it: flamma-bull, the flaming bull.

"I can help!" Fray cried. "In a little time."

"Then do it," Debra said grimly. "I'll try to distract him meanwhile." She drew her bra from her pack, glad she had forgotten to leave it behind. She wasn't sure the curse would work on a bull, but it was worth trying. After all, it seemed to have affected the Python.

Fray vaporized. She became a cloud, expanding rapidly.

"I need some color," Debra said. She spied a patch of redberries growing between greenberries and blueberries. She scooped some up in her bra, then swished them in it so that the red stained the cloth. Now she had a bright red double flag.

The bull charged, his flames brightening. Debra held the bra out to the side and waved it tauntingly. The bull caught it with one horn and jerked his head. That yanked it out of her hands and set fire to it. Now she was weaponless.

But Fray had gained altitude and wind. She made a small rumble of thunder and squeezed out some rain. It dropped on the bull, making his flames sizzle. He made a bellowing moo of outrage and tried to charge the cloud.

Fray was still gathering force. She dumped more rain on the bull, wetting on his head. More flames sizzled, and his head went up in steam. That made him realize he was getting doused. He got sensible and charged away before losing the rest of his flames.

"Get the others!" Debra called to the cloud.

Fray went to it with a will and a half. She expanded until she covered the nametaggers, who were in the process of carrying away the three they had tagged. She wet on them voluminously, though Debra suspected she didn't know what the word meant. That dampened their enthusiasm. They dropped the three and sought shelter in the forest. Fray encouraged them by sending a few small bolts of lightning after them.

Debra galloped back to where the three were lying. Now the rain was pouring down, soaking them all. Small sparks scattered, and the three stirred. The spell had been shorted out!

"Follow me!" Debra called, leading the way. Wira, Ilene, and Sim, dazed, obeyed, staggering after her. Sim seemed to be better able to repel the water, while Ilene was stronger on her feet; the two got together and helped each other move. Debra led them out of the storm and away from the nametaggers, to safety.

In time Fray recondensed, becoming her apparent air form again. "That was great!" Nimbus exclaimed, hugging her. "Wonderful talent!" She looked surprised but pleased.

"I agree," Wira said. She was bedraggled, with matted hair and clothing, but still the most mature member of their party. "And you handled the problem very well, Debra."

Now it was Debra's turn to be surprised but pleased. "I just did what I had to do. Fray really was the one."

"I regret I did not anticipate the nametaggers' ploy," Sim said, fluffing out his feathers. "I'm supposed to be smart."

"Nobody could have known," Ilene said.

He nodded, appreciating her defense of him. The two were of similar age, and seemed to be drawing closer to each other.

"Everyone behaved appropriately," Wira said. "Now let's get dried out."

The others were glad to agree. They located a spring and took turns washing themselves and their clothing. Debra found some brush to make a lean-to, and Ilene harvested some fresh berries from the colored berry patches. They were all glad to have come through their adventure without harm.

Next day they walked and flew south to the top of the cone, where the arrow had pointed. Debra carried Wira, Ilene, and Nimbus, suitably lightened, while Sim flew alone, generating a powerful wake that towed Fray Cloud along behind.

"He's such a smart, handsome bird," Ilene murmured.

"He has to be, to be the Simurgh's heir apparent," Wira said. "Che Centaur tutored him for years."

But when they reached the tip, there was no one there. It was a barren hump. "How could the arrow be wrong?" Wira asked, flustrated.

"That's an interesting mood," Sim remarked. "A mergence of flustered and frustrated, fit for the demoness Metria. But there is surely an explanation. Perhaps tonight will be appropriate for one of your communal dreams."

They set about making camp again, and Sim and Debra flew back to fetch some pies from the nearest pie tree. "If you don't mind," Sim said when they were alone. "I have a private question."

"Ilene is a nice girl," Debra said immediately. "She does like you; it is apparent."

"But I am a bird."

"Xanth's most beautiful bird," she agreed. "And smartest. Women are drawn to such qualities. Remember, all the creatures of this world are crossbreeds. Romance across the species is the social norm."

"But she's only eleven years old."

"And you are twelve."

"I'm an heir apparent."

"She's the heir to fairly illustrious folk herself, being the daughter of a former king and queen."

"So—?"

"So it's a feasible match, if the two of you agree. There is no suitable female of your species, so you have to look elsewhere. You do have several years to study the situation before any adult commitment would be expected."

"And if it should become love?"

"More power to you both. Love has happened to stranger couples. I'm in a position to know."

He nodded. "Thank you."

That night Wira used some of the dream-share elixir, and Debra joined her in a dream that sought the menfolk. Debra remained in centaur form in her dream; it seemed she had to focus to avoid mirroring her physical body. Well, this would do for this purpose.

The men were in a pleasant cottage, in contrast to the crude shelter of the women and children. At least they were safe. They were, it turned out, inside the tip of the cone, instead of outside; the arrow had pointed true, but a detail had been missed.

Wira rushed to kiss the Random Factor. Debra was startled, until she remembered that now Hugo had the Factor's body. So she went to kiss Hugo's body. It was safe to do that now, with or without her bra.

"It's good to see you again," Random said, his hands unable to stay away from where her bra would have been. The curse made any man who knew her name want to touch her bra, and this was as close to it as he could safely get. "This may be the only way; we fear our bodies were burned up on Xanth."

"No they weren't," she reassured him. "We found the beer cellar intact, and your bodies there."

"That's a relief. It gives us faint hope. Now if we could just nullify your curse."

"Would you still love me then?" she asked teasingly.

"Oh, yes! My love may have been inspired by the curse, but I know it's eternal."

"That's nice." That seemed inadequate, but this whole situation was unusual, with her in the winged centaur form making out with the body of her friend's husband. As she had told Sim, love could be strange.

All too soon Wira drew the dream to a close. They agreed to meet next day at the brink of the Hypotho-sea.

But before the night was over, Debra woke with a start. She had received the signal. The men had transferred out of this world!

"Something must have forced the issue," Wira said when Debra told her. "We shall simply have to orient on their next stop. It is merely a delay." But there were tears in her eyes.

Debra understood completely. They had come so close to reunion. Now they had to start over.

15
MOTES

The Factor looked around. They were on a small rocky irregular world. Around it were other little worlds, floating to the sides and above. In fact this was a swarm of fragments, each big enough to hold a village but not much more. Some were barren, some had turf and trees, and some did seem to have human houses. "What is this?" he asked, perplexed.

"This would be Motes," Hugo said. "Magicians Bink, Dor, and Dolph visited it once in a dream, and the Zombie Master. It was a most interesting report; the Good Magician made a long note on it."

"A collection of fragments?"

"Orbiting the head of the Ida on the world of Tangle," Hugo said. "Each world is different, and some are pretty strange. I don't remember them all, but know that one is Zombie World, with all zombies, and another is Dragon World, in the shape of a giant dragon, and all the imaginable varieties of dragons exist there. Motes is just along the way."

"Like islands in a sea," the Factor said. "Do you suppose the women would like to live on one of them?"

Hugo considered. "Maybe if it were a nice one. We can look around and see what's available."

"It is interesting that we are able to breathe here. This tiny planetoid should not have enough gravity to retain an atmosphere."

Hugo laughed without humor. "How fortunate that this realm is magic, rather than Mundanian science. There is light without a sun, and air without atmosphere."

"They should be along in another day or so. Debra knows when my transfer magic is invoked. We can use that time to explore and locate a suitable island."

Hugo shrugged. "Might as well." He looked at the mote they stood on. "I wonder what we exchanged with this time?"

"A couple of small plants," the Factor said. "That's why the ground is bare where we stand."

"I wonder whether we have bodies there also, as it seems we do on Xanth proper? All the soul stuff left over when we went to this infinitely smaller world."

The Factor considered. "I suspect they simply dissolved into background material."

They jumped to the nearest other mote. Science might not be operative here, but gravity was not strong, and they were able to do it readily enough. This one was completely barren, and they didn't linger.

The next was a larger fragment, with several houses on it, and men working in small fields. They approached a man who was loading a wagon, in his fashion. He had a stout short-legged goat, on which he piled a bale of hay. Then the goat levered itself up until it stood higher than the wagon. The man then rolled the bale from the goat's back to the floor of the wagon. The goat's legs shortened, bringing it down for the next load.

"That's a remarkable goat," Hugo said. He was by far the more social of the two of them, and knew how to talk to people. The Factor had never much cared about people, before falling in love.

"He's Billy Jack," the man said proudly. "There's no load he can't lift."

"We're new visitors to this realm," Hugo said. "We're looking for a fragment where a few people might live in comfort. Can you direct us to any prospects?"

The man hesitated. "You don't want to stay here long. Best to move on soon."

"That's not convenient," the Factor said. "Why should we move on?"

The man's lips tightened. "It's your decision."

"Where should we look?" Hugo asked. "We don't want to impinge on anyone else's territory."

"Try the Tell-A-Path."

"Telepath? Where is he?"

"Tell-A-Path," the man repeated. "Over there. Tell it where you want to go, and it will go there."

They looked. Not far away was a passing path. It looked ordinary, but so did many magic things. "Thank you," Hugo said.

"But you don't want to stay," the man repeated.

What was his problem? Were the decent territories limited, so that they were trying to discourage new settlers? Yet the man did not seem unfriendly. It was more as if he were simply offering good advice. Curious business.

They walked to the path. "We want to find a nice planetoid suitable for four people," the Factor said. "Two men and two women."

The path glowed briefly, acknowledging. They got on it and stood, perplexed. "Which direction?" Hugo asked.

"Either way," the man called.

Maybe that made sense. There was bound to be more than one route to wherever they wanted to go.

They picked a direction and walked. The path went to a hillock and stopped at the top. But there was a faint glow in the air beyond, pointing to another planetoid. So they jumped, and landed where the path resumed on the adjacent mote. This was another small barren one, and the path soon moved to another. They seemed to be moving toward the outside edge of the cluster of motes. Was it just meandering, or did it really have somewhere to go?

They paused at a mote where a number of people were busy fashioning assorted nets. "What's this?" the Factor asked.

"We're networking," the closest worker answered. "Making every type of net: fishing, magic, inter, whatever."

"I always wondered where nets came from," Hugo remarked. "Now I know: from the networks." Then he spied a woman who was painstakingly weaving an extremely fine net. "What's that?"

The woman looked up at him and smiled. "I'm Ruby. It is my talent to make a net that will stop wiggles."

"But nothing stops wiggles!"

"That's why this net is needed. But the work is slow; it will require decades to complete it."

"Let's move on," the Factor said, bored.

At the base of a hill they met a woman walking the other way. She was looking to the side and didn't seem to see them. "Hey, watch where you're go—ooof!" the Factor said. For the girl had just collided with him.

That started a small chain reaction. The Factor fell back into Hugo, and all three of them fell into the brush bordering the path. They wound up in a heap, the girl plastered rather indelicately across the two men.

"Oh, I'm sorry," she said, scrambling up and tucking her clothing back together so that no bra or panty showed. On one level the Factor regretted that. "I didn't see—" Then she broke off, because a cart was zooming down the hill. It was loaded with bricks, and was surely quite solid. It whistled by them and on out of sight.

"That cart would have wiped us out," Hugo said. "If you hadn't pushed us off the path."

"Yes, I think so," she said. "That's my talent."

Both men stared at her. "Your talent?" the Factor asked.

"I'm Tovi. I'm a small-scale klutz. I'm forever bungling things. But often my mistakes lead to larger scale benefits, purely by coincidence."

"I'm Hugo, and this is the Factor," Hugo said. "Your mistake just saved us from getting squashed."

"Yes, that's the way it works. But I should have looked where I was going."

"We're glad you didn't," Hugo said. "Thank you for saving us."

"As long as you're not mad," she said.

"We're not mad," Hugo said. "As a matter of fact, maybe you can tell us what life is like, here on Motes. Why wouldn't we want to stay?"

"I'd better be moving on before I klutz again," she said nervously. She did so, leaving them halfway bemused.

Then they came to a planetoid that seemed ideal. It bore a sign saying OASIS—VACANCY. It had a nice spring-fed pond with quacks swimming on it, several handsome shade trees, and a fair number of pie bushes. It looked like exactly the kind of mote the women would like.

"Thank you, Path," Hugo said. He was odd that way, treating even inanimate things like people. But his courtesy was wasted; the path was gone. It had done its job.

"We can build a house," the Factor said. "Everything's here."

"Two houses," Hugo said. "I have to keep your body away from Debra."

"Two houses," the Factor agreed. He was quite satisfied to have his body avoid the curse. This Hugo-body might be forty-three years old and not handsome, but with it he could do anything he wanted with Debra, and he wanted to do everything. Until such time as they thwarted the curse and exchanged bodies back, this was a satisfactory alternative.

They got to work. On the far side of the mote was a brick mine with many fine bricks. This must have been where the self-propelled cart came from. They cleared places on either side of the duck pond and started moving bricks there. It turned out to be a larger job than they had realized, and long before they were done night closed. So they lay down beside their separate piles of bricks and slept.

It was funny, the Factor thought, how he now was interested in things that had never occurred to him before. All he had wanted was freedom to do his own thing, randomly. That had included fine times with nymphs or demonesses, or even a vila, had the timing been right. Now he wanted to please Debra, and that meant trying to anticipate her needs and desires and accommodate them. She would want a nice house. He wasn't sure what else she would want, but he would try to find out and do whatever it was.

Yet somehow he felt a deep foreboding. Not because of the danger Debra represented for him; they understood that and were on guard against it. This was something else, and it was slowly intensifying. It stopped him from sleeping.

"Do you feel it too?" Hugo asked from the darkness.

"Yes. What is it?"

"I don't know. But I am wondering what that man with the goat meant when he said we wouldn't want to stay here. And why such an ideal little world as this is vacant. There is something we don't know, and now I think we ought to find out before we go further with our preparations."

"How can we find out?"

"There should be an Ida here. There's one on every world. She seems most likely to know."

That did make sense. "Can that trip wait until morning?"

"I don't think so."

"I agree," the Factor said grimly. "Whatever it is, it's coming closer. I don't want it to find us unprepared."

"What can we do in the dark?"

"Hide!"

So they made their way to the trees, and climbed, hiding in the upper foliage. But the foreboding remained. Whatever was coming seemed to be orienting on them, and it seemed to know exactly where they were. They could not stay here.

They studied the night sky, but could not see anything other than faintly glowing motes.

"I dread traveling at night," Hugo said. "We might jump and miss a mote, and float helplessly in space."

"Nonsense. I could simply conjure one of your fruits and throw it, and the reaction would push me the other way, assuming that principle is not too scientific for this realm. We can get where we are going."

"But suppose the menace we fear is lurking in the dark spaces between motes?"

That made the Factor pause. Then a bulb flashed over his head. "The Tell-A-Path! We can tell it to show us a safe route to Ida."

"Great. But where is the path?"

"Over there." For the path had appeared when named, and now wandered past the trees they were in. It seemed not only to go where told, but to start where needed. It was an obliging path.

They climbed down and approached the path, which glowed brightly enough to make everything on it visible. "Take us to—" Hugo started, and paused. Someone was already on it.

It was a young woman with long red hair and blue-green eyes. She jumped when she saw them, rather prettily, because her hair and skirt flared, showing nice bare shoulders and nice nude knees. "Oh! I didn't see you two handsome men out there in the darkness. I was just walking along this wonderfully obliging path on my way to harvest a peach for a midnight snack." The path glowed for a moment, evidently appreciating the compliment.

"We were just about to ask the path to take us to Princess Ida," Hugo said.

"What a smart idea! She can surely help you, though I don't see why two such competent men should need any help."

The Factor exchanged half a glance with Hugo. There was something winning about this girl.

"Hello," Hugo said, waxing social. "I am Hugo, and this is the Random Factor." He didn't bother to try to explain about their exchanged bodies. "My—his talent is conjuring fruit. I'm sure he has a nice peach for you."

The Factor took the hint and conjured the loveliest ripest juiciest possible peach. He held it out to the girl.

"Oh thank you!" she exclaimed, accepting the fruit. "You are so thoughtful. I am Besanii. My talent is flattering people and things."

They might almost have guessed, the Factor thought.

"The path may have known that we could provide your peach," Hugo said. "So it led you to us."

"Yes, it usually takes the most direct route. But why are you seeking Princess Ida, if I may ask, at this late hour? It must be fantastically important."

·   The two men exchanged the other half of their glance. "We fear some undefined nemesis," Hugo explained. "We hope that Ida can explain it."

"Oh, no," Besanii murmured.

"There is a problem?" the Factor asked.

"No, not at all, no problem at all," Besanii said quickly. "Thank you so much again for the peach and I'll go now." She turned so swiftly that her hair and skirt flared again, showing more than bare shoulders and knees, and hurried away.

There was definitely something odd here. "I think she knows about the nemesis," Hugo said, when his eyes recovered from the momentary flash of panty.

"And won't or can't tell us," the Factor agreed, as his eyes recovered from the flash of bra. "Just as that farmer and the klutz girl didn't tell us."

"Maybe there are others on this path," Hugo said.

"Who may also refuse to clarify the danger. I suspect we're best off going directly to Ida."

"I could use some shoes," Hugo said, looking at his bare feet. "I lost mine in the tree."

"Ask the path."

"Good idea. Path, I—" He broke off, and the Factor saw why. There was a pair of sandals growing next to the path that surely had not been there a moment ago, and certainly not two moments ago.

Hugo picked them, shook them, set them down, and put his feet into them. And flipped forward so hard he landed on his back.

"There's no need to do stunts," the Factor said, concerned about such treatment of his body.

"I didn't," Hugo protested, climbing back to his feet. "I just put them on, and suddenly I was flat."

"Let me see those." The Factor took the sandals, removed his shoes, and put his feet into the sandals.

And flipped entirely over, landing on his back.

"I see you tried on the flip-flops," a man said. In their distraction they had missed his approach.

"Flip-flops," Hugo said, disgusted. "I was looking for more sedate footwear."

"There's a pair of lady slippers," the man said, halfway stifling a smile.

"At this point, I'll take them," Hugo said. He picked the slippers and put them on his feet. "These are light, soft, and comfortable."

"Who are you?" the Factor asked the man gruffly.

"I am Bill," the man said. "Bill Fold. I can fold anything, living or dead."

"Thanks, we don't need folding," Hugo said.

"I'm looking for my girlfriend, Besanii, so I can enfold her. She makes me feel so great, and I love it when she jumps. Have you seen her?"

Hugo started to answer, but the Factor stifled him with a gesture. "We may have," he said. "Suppose we trade information?"

"Sure. What do you want to know?"

"There's some sort of malign entity that—"

"Forget it," Bill said, quickly retreating.

"There's definitely something," Hugo said. "Maybe we need to be more subtle."

"Very well. You tackle the next traveler on this path."

That traveler was already appearing, as if the path was providing him. He looked like a perfectly ordinary man, but at this point the Factor didn't trust that.

"Hello, stranger," Hugo said. "I'm Hugo. I wonder if you could direct me to the nearest monster?"

That was as subtle as a coconut bouncing off a head and spilling cocoa all over.

"In a manner," the man said. "I'm Troy. My talent is invoking monster qualities, such as ogre strength or nymphly grace. But unfortunately I can't control the quality summoned. So I'm apt to get ogre stupidity or nymphly shallowness instead."

"That's fascinating," Hugo said, evidently emulating Besanii's flattering technique. "But I was thinking of approaching a monster more directly."

"Oh, you wouldn't want to do that," Troy said. "Not without my brother's help. His talent is to confuse monsters, so they can't aim well. You know, a dragon's blast of fire will miss you, or a werewolf's teeth will bite your shoes instead of your leg." He glanced at Hugo's lady-slipper clad feet. "Speaking of shoes—"

"Sore feet," Hugo said quickly. "We sense some sort of monster in the vicinity, and would like to locate it more specifically. Would you happen to know—"

"Oh, *that* monster. I would not." And Troy abruptly departed.

"I think we have a problem," the Factor said. "Obviously there is a monster, but the locals are in some sort of denial."

"I wonder," Hugo said. "Suppose it left them alone on condition that they not tell travelers about it?"

The Factor nodded. "We had better hope that Princess Ida is not similarly intimidated."

They gave the path their destination, and followed it from mote to mote. It turned out to be an extended trip, winding sinuously about.

"I thought the path went directly to the destination," Hugo said.

"There's a qualification," the Factor reminded him. "We asked for a *safe* route."

"That does make sense," Hugo agreed. "But somehow I don't find it wholly comforting."

They came to a section of small motes. Some were hardly larger than fossilized men and women. In fact they were statues of people and animals, their faces forever fixed in expressions of utter horror. There was also a bad smell associated with them.

"I'll be glad to get beyond this stinking region," the Factor muttered.

"This makes me even more nervous, for some obscure reason," Hugo said.

The Factor was nervous too. Why would anyone make a statue of a horrified person, coat it with smelly mud, and leave it to float free amidst the swarm?

As sunless morning dawned, they were approaching a large mote in what seemed to be the center of the swarm. There was a nice house with feminine curtains at the windows. The path wended its way directly to its door.

They knocked. The door opened. There was a woman whose head seemed somewhat lumpy, in the manner of an irregular mote. About her head orbited a tiny planet. This was definitely Ida. "Why hello, travelers," she said.

"We are Hugo, son of the good Magician and the Gorgon," Hugo said immediately. "And the Random Factor, beset by a deadly curse. We're in each other's bodies. We think we need your advice."

Princess Ida nodded. "Of course you do, with all that and the Mote Monster on your trail. Come in."

They entered her house and made themselves comfortable in her padded chairs. "Moat monster?" the Factor asked.

"Mote. We'll get to that in a moment. Describe this curse."

"It's a bra. I don't dare touch it."

Ida kept her face straight. "Time and experience are normally effective in abating male freakouts by bras and panties. There is no need to struggle."

Hugo stepped in. "He has no problem with ordinary bras. This particular one is cursed to instantly transport him into confinement the moment he touches it. And he has an urge to touch it."

"Men do. Perhaps he needs to develop a relationship with a woman whose undergarments are not cursed."

"I love her," the Factor said simply.

Ida nodded sympathetically. "Then you do have a problem. But this is out of my bailiwick; I don't have the ability to abate curses."

"That's not really the problem," Hugo said. "Since we are in each other's bodies, and the curse applies to the body rather than the person, he can approach her in my body without danger. I'm the one who must not touch her bra. Since I am married, I am happy to stick to Wira's bra, which is not cursed."

She nodded again. "That leaves the Mote Monster. This is a thing who consumes motes, digests them, and ejects them somewhat the worse for wear. It likes the taste of new things better than old excreted things, so pursues travelers who happen by this region. Naturally travelers don't wish to be consumed; it is bad for their health."

"Naturally," the Factor agreed somewhat weakly.

"We saw some statues," Hugo said. "I wonder—"

"They are coprolites. The compacted remains of digested people who failed to escape the monster."

"We felt foreboding," the Factor said. "As if something were stalking us. But the natives refuse to talk about it."

"The natives avoid the monster by moving from mote to mote when it comes by. But they prefer not to aggravate it by warning travelers, because the monster *can* catch them if it really tries. It's a kind of truce. They know that it will ignore them as long as there is fresh meat to pursue."

"And we are fresh," Hugo said, shuddering.

"Yes. It seems there is something about newcomers. Perhaps they have exotic flavors. Naturally you wish to escape consumption."

"We do," the Factor said.

"You must move on. Either by diffusing back to your source world—"

"We can't," Hugo said. "Another curse limits us to upworld travel."

"Then by traveling upworld," she agreed.

"We can't," the Factor said. "We must wait here for our women to catch up."

Ida shrugged. "My mote alone is protected, because I am part of a larger chain. The monster can't consume it or me. You can be my guests until your women arrive."

The Factor exchanged most of a glance with Hugo. "I don't think we can do that," Hugo said. "The women will arrive where we did. They will be vulnerable to the monster there. We shall have to be there to protect them."

Ida shook her head. "There is no protection against the Mote Monster!

It can swallow entire motes of any size, together with whatever is on them. You must avoid it."

"And let it eat Debra and Wira?" the Factor asked. "This is out of the question."

"Then I am unable to help you," Ida said regretfully.

They departed her house and headed back the way they had come, crossing from mote to mote. "What now?" Hugo asked.

The Factor's mind was in turmoil. He had never before really cared about anyone else, but since love had invaded his being, he couldn't stand to let Debra be hurt. "Maybe we can become decoys."

"Decoys?"

"Tempting the monster with our fresh flesh, leading it away from where the women will arrive."

"I see," Hugo said. "But what's the point, if it eats us?"

"Maybe we can fight it. Really big pineapples might daunt it."

"Might," Hugo agreed. "Now that my body can conjure perfect fruits, some really potent pineapples are feasible. If we can blow it up, then the women will be safe."

"Then that seems to be our program. In fact, if we can destroy it, we won't have to worry about it bothering the women. We can go after it immediately."

"We'll stalk the stalker," Hugo agreed. "Conjure me some clusters of cherries; I can use them to distract it while you heave a pineapple into its maw."

The Factor conjured several cherry clusters. Hugo accepted them carefully, fastening the stems to his belt. Then the Factor conjured large pineapples, and carried one in each hand. They were ready to tackle the monster.

Then they saw it, coming at them from dead ahead. It was a huge floating thing vaguely resembling a thundercloud. Black bulges were on its heaving surface, like blisters filled with smoke. It was about as ugly as the eye could handle.

"Where's the maw?" the Factor asked nervously.

"That seems more like a demon—a big one," Hugo said, as nervously. "It may not need a maw. The Good Magician's Book of Answers lists some really strange monsters." He pondered half a moment, trying to remember. "Pyroclast—something like that. Huge and burning hot, formed of gases and floating ashes. Its mere touch will burn a person to death."

"That must be why Ida said we couldn't protect ourselves from it. We can't fight it in any ordinary manner."

"Well, we have to try."

"I will try," the Factor agreed. He wound up and hurled a pineapple as high and far as he could. The fruit sailed into the looming cloud and disappeared into it. "Well, so much for that."

Then there was a muffled boom as the pineapple exploded from the heat, and a puff of smoke gouted back toward them.

"We need a bigger bomb," Hugo said.

"What is there?"

"I never conjured one, but I understand there's a fruit-like mushroom that can pack a monstrous explosion."

"That's what we need," the Factor agreed. He concentrated, made a supreme effort, and conjured a large ball-shaped mushroom. He looked at it, disappointed. "That's it?"

"Throw it!" Hugo said. "It's radioactive!"

The Factor didn't know what radioactive meant, but he hurled the fungus into the monster. There was a pause.

Then there was an explosion like none he could have imagined. The monster was blown apart, and where it had been there formed a whirling new cloud in the shape of a giant mushroom, rapidly expanding.

"Don't look at it!" Hugo cried. "Get under cover!"

The Factor trusted the man's judgment in this respect. The two of them dived behind a boulder just before the mushroom cloud reached them. That was just as well, because there was a fearsome blast of heat and light. It was like being in a thunderstorm made of fire.

Finally the effects faded. They picked themselves up and looked around.

"That's some bomb," the Factor said shakily.

"I never dared conjure it," Hugo said. "For one thing, most of my fruits were imperfect, because of that mediocritree seed in my hair. The thing might have detonated in my hand."

"You have a good talent. It did the job. Now let's go intercept the women."

They had forgotten the winding route, but that was no problem; the Tell-A-Path reappeared when needed and guided them there.

But there was a problem along the way. "What's that?" Hugo asked.

"What's what?"

"That," Hugo said, pointing. "It looks like a mini–Mote Monster."

The Factor looked. It was an unshapely blob floating across the path before them. He poked a finger at it. It opened a mouth just a bit larger than its body and snapped at the finger, almost catching it.

"It *is* a mini–Mote Monster!" the Factor said, alarmed.

"Maybe it had offspring," Hugo said. "I'll feed it a cherry." He perched a cherry on the end of a stick and poked it at the thing. The cherry was the same size as the monster.

The monster snapped up the cherry, doubling its size. Then it exploded, smoky shrapnel flinging out in every direction plus a few additional directions. The two men had to shield their faces from the blast.

"Cherries don't agree with it," the Factor said.

"There's another."

Sure enough, there was a pea-sized monster floating by; as they oriented on it, a slightly larger monster floated in from the other side. The larger one opened its maw and gulped down the smaller one, expanding to one and a half times its former size in the process.

"This makes me nervous," the Factor said.

"We may have blown the big one into smithereens," Hugo said. "But now each smither is merging with others, growing larger."

"That is my thought. That may be why there is no real defense against the monster; it is a form of demon, and can reconstitute when fragmented. We may simply have rejuvenated it."

"And the little ones are hungry," Hugo said.

They looked warily around. In the near distance was a churning cloud of sand and pebbles. The sand was getting eaten by the pebbles, and the pebbles eaten by larger pebbles. The process was proceeding entirely too rapidly for comfort.

"At this rate, we'll have the original monster back within hours," the Factor said.

"We could blow it up again, but never actually destroy it," Hugo said. "That means—"

"That means we can't stay here."

"We had better get to the women before the little monsters do."

They hurried, but so did the monsters. By the time they reached the spot in the motes where they had arrived, they were being pursued by a dozen head-sized monsters. By six double-head sized monsters. By three quadruple-heads.

There was no sign of the women. "They can't transport instantly, I think," Hugo said. "They have to follow the trail of worlds, and I don't know how many there are between Cone and Motes."

"We shall simply have to wait," the Factor said. "And guard our site."

They waited and guarded, summoning cherries, pineapples, and edible fruits as required for defense or food. They took turns sleeping, because though the approaching monsters were fewer, they were larger. Cherries, then pineapples blew them up, but that was obviously a temporary reprieve, because the fragments were quickly gobbled by other little monsters. There were now little monsters scattered all through the Motes, all merging in their fashion, and soon enough the last and worst of them would be coming hungrily here. The Factor hoped they would not have to expend another mushroom; he agreed with Hugo that those fruits were dangerous.

They were both awake and alert when a mountain-sized monster loomed, orienting on them. This was probably too big for a pineapple, but too small for a mushroom. "We need a small, new, clear, mushroom," the Factor said. "A tactical weapon."

"Conjure the smallest one you can," Hugo suggested.

The Factor did, producing a fungus hardly thicker than a furry hair. He blew on it, wafting it toward the monster, but it drifted to the side ineffectively.

"Put it in another fruit," Hugo said. "One you can throw."

The Factor conjured an apple. He cut a hole in it and set the mushroom there. Then he hurled the apple at the monster.

The monster didn't wait for the apple to arrive. It surged forward and gulped it down.

They held their breaths.

There was a submerged rumble. Then the monster split in two, with mushroom-colored smoke puffing out. The two halves were pushed apart by the force of the mushroom cloud, disappearing to either side.

"But they'll be ba-a-ack," Hugo muttered.

Meanwhile other, smaller fragments were still coming in. Sooner or later one was bound to catch one of the men by surprise, and gobble down a finger, hand, or foot before it could be stopped. The situation was desperate.

Suddenly a party of six appeared: a woman, a girl, two children, a centaur, and a big beautiful bird.

"Wira!" Hugo cried, running to embrace her.

"Debra!" The Factor ran to do the same with the centaur. But even as he did, he was conscious of where her bra should be. The curse remained, stifled by his change of bodies, but lurking.

Debra put her arms around him and hauled him up to reach her face. They kissed. It was the most glorious sensation he could imagine. "This time you waited for us!"

"What is that?" the girl asked, staring at the mote.

"I believe that is the fabled Mote Monster," the bird said. "Mother has spoken of it, but I have not seen it."

"That is only part of the Mote Monster," the Factor said, reluctantly releasing Debra's delightful mouth. "We have to get out of here."

"You can't leave us now," Wira protested.

"There's no time to explain. We can't remain here."

"No explanation is necessary," the bird said. "And no separation. We must form a cluster, and you can transfer us all together."

Whoever that bird was, he seemed pretty smart. The others heeded him, and they quickly formed a cluster. "I'll need to be in touch-contact with each of you," Hugo said. "Maybe you had better hold on to my hands and feet. We don't want anyone left behind."

They all took hold of Hugo's limbs, with Wira hanging on to his head, as the Mote Monster loomed. Then, abruptly, they were elsewhere.

16
LOOP

"Oooo, nickelpedes!" Nimbus exclaimed, delighted.

"Stay away from them!" Ilene snapped, hauling him clear.

"Aww, you're acting just like an adult," he complained.

"We must have exchanged with several of them," Wira said. "That's why we're at their nest, and they are disturbed. They don't know what happened to their associates."

"You sympathize with anything," Hugo told her fondly. "Even nickelpedes."

"Of course." She kneeled and communed with the fearsome bugs, and they seemed reassured. They retreated into their burrows.

Sim Bird was finding this to be an educational excursion, which was of course the point of his attendance. But he hadn't counted on the additional curse the two men had incurred: being able to travel only upworld. That did not apply to their own party of women, children, and a bird, except in one significant respect: Wira and Debra were not about to return to Xanth proper without their men. Since Ilene—such a nice girl!—and Sim were committed to help the women, that ethically locked them into that limitation too, as well as the children Fray Cloud and Nimbus Human/Demon. So they really needed to find a way to free the men of that upworld curse.

But how was that to be accomplished? Only an experienced counter-cursor could do it, and how was one to be found? They couldn't be certain that one was aboard any particular world.

Meanwhile, here they were on—where? Sim had an encyclopedic memory of all the Worlds of Ida that had been discovered by Xanthians who had visited them are returned to make their reports. Trapezoid, Shoe, Implosion, Puzzle, Octopus, Tesseract, Fractal, Green Goo, Plane, Spiral, Pincushion—their names were legion, and each was fascinating in its own right and left. But this was none of these. It had a halfway shiny silvery surface, and was extremely convoluted. Like Dragon World, except that this wasn't that.

"I believe I'll fly up and survey the landscape from above," Sim said. It was fortunate he had taken the trouble to learn to talk human, because humans tended not to understand squawks, however superior they might be.

"Just so long as we're safe," Wira said. "This world seems rather barren."

"Nothing seems barren, as long as I'm with you," Hugo told her. They kissed.

They were still so much in love, after years of marriage and their recent separation. Sim wished he could have a relationship like that.

"May I go with you?" Ilene asked. "Debra could make me light enough to carry."

This was of course sheer foolishness. "Certainly," he agreed, more pleased than seemed sensible.

"Who's going to watch me?" Nimbus demanded rebelliously.

"I will," Fray said. "I can handle it for five minutes. Maybe even ten."

He pushed out his lower lip. "Aw—"

But he never got the remaining www's out, because she kissed him. "Now don't fuss, or I'll kiss you again."

He shut up immediately, looking cowed, perhaps even horsed.

Sim saw Wira and Debra exchange a knowing glance. He had learned to decipher such glances reasonably well. This one indicated that they thought Fray had female potential. She was in the process of becoming ready to be a babysitter. She was already learning how to handle males of any age. This was impressive, considering that she was merely a condensed cloud: visible air.

Soon he was carrying Ilene as he spiraled upward. It was awkward for his talons to hold her comfortably, so she was holding on to him, clinging to his back between his wings as if riding a centaur. He was aware of the gentle pressure of her thighs; she was on the verge of becoming a woman. Of course it wasn't appropriate to think of that, considering her age. The Adult Conspiracy applied to all humans and most crossbreed humans.

"I'm only one year younger than you," she said, as if reading his mind.

"Birds mature faster," he said, feeling awkward.

"Not necessarily. Nimbus sees me as adult. That's illusion, of course."

And her talent was making illusions real. Suddenly she felt remarkably mature. "I think you are teasing me," he said wishing he could look directly at her to see how mature she looked.

"Not necessarily," she repeated. "Even the smartest males can be stupid about women. I think you are *the* smartest, so you may be quite stupid in this respect."

Of course that logic was fallacious. Nevertheless he felt the tips of his feathers blushing. She was definitely flirting with him. He tried to remain fully rational, but he loved it. If nine-year-old Fray Cloud was learning how to handle males, Ilene was that much further along, and evidently knew it.

So, being stupid in exactly the way she defined, he changed the subject. "I believe we are high enough now. We need to survey this world to determine its nature."

"Yes. Meanwhile there is something else I wanted to talk to you about. You should have superior insight."

"Having established that I'm stupid."

She laughed and ignored it. "I am trying to help Nimbus perfect his talent. As I see it, making mixed metaphors real is potentially far more than an ordinary talent."

"That would not be surprising. Nimby surely wants his son to have the best. But since Chlorine doesn't want more than an ordinary boy, the power has to be subtle."

"Yes. When Princess Ida agrees to something, it becomes true— provided it is suggested by someone who doesn't know her talent. That is a formidable limitation. But Nimbus lacks that limit. He can't make up mixed metaphors himself, but others can make them for him, even if they know his talent. That makes his companions quite powerful, limited only by their ability to shape their notions into mixed metaphors. Do you agree?"

She had worked it out well. "Yes. Therefore his companions should be cautious about their metaphors."

"I am his chief companion. Should I explain to him the way I see his talent?"

"I think not. It would place a considerable burden on you, as he would demand ever more potent metaphors to exploit. He is after all a child in a way that you and I are not."

"That's what I thought. Thank you, Sim." She kissed the feathers of the back of his neck.

Sim was electrified, but tried to mask it. "We were about to examine this world."

"Of course."

They looked. All he saw was a complicated array of surfaces and angles, with two very large projections almost like deadly pincers. This was a highly irregular world.

Ilene screamed.

Startled, Sim almost lost his altitude. "What's wrong?"

"This world!" she cried. *"It's a nickelpede!"*

Now suddenly he saw it. He had been looking at details, and overlooked the larger nature of it. Ilene had viewed the whole. Nickelpedes were perhaps Xanth's most ferocious small monsters, gouging out nickel-sized discs from any tender flesh they found. This had to be the source of the idea of them. It explained why they had landed in a nest of nickelpedes; that was no coincidence.

"Nickelpede World," he said. "We don't want to stay here."

"We must tell the others," she said. "Before this world strikes."

They spiraled down. As they approached the group they saw a series of flashes and heard pops. Hugo—or Hugo's body—was conjuring cherries and throwing them. Perhaps for the entertainment of the children.

Then his sharp eyes spied better detail. They were throwing cherries at charging nickelpedes. They were not small ones, but large and ferocious. The world was already striking.

They landed. Ilene jumped off his back and ran to warn them. "This is Nickelpede World! We have to get off it now!"

No one argued. This was obviously no place to stay. Nickelpedes were voracious, and they would have no chance.

They grabbed on to Hugo in the Factor's body, as before. There was a wrench, and they were somewhere else. They seemed to be on a massive leg of an eight-legged world.

Nobody moved. Standing right before them was a monstrous slavering spider. Her ferocious mandibles clicked. Sim had studied assorted animal languages, so understood what she was saying: "What did you do with my children?"

He clicked his beak in mandible language as well as he could. "We are travelers. We must have exchanged places with them."

"Well, bring them back, tidbit," she clicked.

"I'm afraid we can't do that," he replied.

She made a clicking sigh. "Then I suppose I'll have to adopt you. You will learn to feast on fly juice."

Sim translated that for the others. They reacted with horror. "This must be Spider World," Hugo said. "We don't want to stay here."

But the spider mother was already forming a lasso of sticky silk. "Or maybe I'll eat some of you instead," she clicked. "There should be a fair amount of nutritious juice in some of you." She flung the loop around them and jerked it expertly tight. They were securely caught.

"I'm going home!" Nimbus said. "I'm dissolving."

"Not without me," Ilene said, casting a regretful look at Sim. "I'm your babysitter."

There was a pause during which nothing happened.

"It doesn't work," Nimbus said, starting to cry.

Ilene put her arms around him comfortingly. "It's true," she said to the others. "We can't vacate."

"The curse must have extended to the rest of us, when we traveled with the men," Sim said, horrified. "Now we're all caught."

"Hang on!" Hugo cried. Actually they were all being squeezed against him as the loop tightened.

There was the wrench, and they were elsewhere, standing among huge ants. Sim noted peripherally that this world seemed to be shaped like a gi-ant. A gi-ant.

"We must have exchanged with some ants," the Factor said. "Maybe the spider mom will find them adoptable."

"Let's move on," Debra said tightly. "Now."

They moved on. Sim hoped they would get out of the bug realm and find some more compatible planet.

And they stood on a feathery surface. Could it be? "Let me check," Sim said.

"Me too," Ilene said.

In three quarters of a moment they were airborne, and in another moment and a quarter they confirmed it: "It's shaped exactly like a bird!" Ilene said.

"Bird World," Sim agreed. "This interests me. We must have exchanged with some feathers."

"There would be others of your kind here," she said thoughtfully. "Including females." She was mature again, though the others had not seemed to notice it. Evidently she had made the illusion of greater age real mainly for him.

For some reason he suspected she might be against remaining on this world. "Yes."

"We could put it to a vote."

"That seems fair." But he knew she was hoping the others would vote to move on.

And actually, did he really want to remain here, where he would be just one bird among many? The average bird was not particularly smart.

They glided down to rejoin the others. "It's Bird World," Ilene called. "Do we want to stay?"

They discussed it, and concluded that no, they did not want to remain on a world limited to birds. "Of course, if you really prefer it . . ." Wira said to Sim. She was always sensitive to the perspectives of others.

"I think not," he said with mixed feelings. "For assorted reasons."

"OoOoo!" Ilene said, kissing him on the beak.

That reason too.

The next was Centaur World. Now it was Debra's turn to take stock. "But I'm not really a centaur," she concluded. "I just want to return to my own form and fail to dazzle someone with my bra." She kissed the Factor.

They passed assorted obscure worlds, none of which seemed satisfactory for long-term residence. Then they landed on one that most resembled a fluffy cloud.

"Cloud World!" Fray exclaimed, delighted. But then she thought it further through. "Mother's not here. Daddy's not here. I want to be shooting the breeze with them, not strangers."

The next world was like a giant building. "Oh, no," the Factor said. "It's the Factory! Move on before it captures us!"

They didn't argue. In 1.3 moments they were on their way again.

The next was not exactly a landbound realm, and not exactly a cloudbound one. It was in between, with a formidable pearly gate rising from cloudstuff. A plaque on the golden bars said WELCOME TO HEAVEN.

Five of them tried to exchange three and a half glances. At least half a glance got lost in the shuffle. "Heaven?" Debra asked.

"Or a representation of it," Wira said. "Does it matter? It should be a perfect place to stay."

Sim wondered, but kept his beak shut. This was for the humans to sort out among themselves.

Wira knocked on a bar. "Is anyone home?" she called.

An angel appeared, flying over the gate. "Yes?"

Wira turned to Sim. "Maybe you should speak for us, as you may be more objective about this particular world."

Sim nodded. "We are world-hopping, looking for a world where we can settle down. Is this one open?"

"That depends," the angel said. "We have rather stringent requirements for residents. However, those who don't make our standards will surely qualify for our companion realm, whose entrance is behind you."

They turned and saw what they had missed before: a dark river and another gate. The sign on that one said WELCOME TO HELL.

"Oh, my," Wira murmured.

"What are your requirements?" Sim asked.

"These relate to the condition of your souls. We assess them in the course of the tours, and decide."

"Tours?" Sim asked.

"All prospective residents are provided with tours of each realm, so they understand exactly what they are getting into before they commit. It seems only fair."

"Then let us take those tours," Sim said.

"Excellent. Let me fetch my companion tour guide." She flew across to the other gate. "Beau! We have a tour group."

"The angel associates with a demon?" Ilene asked, amazed.

Already the angel was returning with a demon. This one had vestigial horns and a softly tufted tailtip, and wore spectacles. He was not a very ferocious example of his species. But of course demons could assume whatever form they preferred. "It is time to introduce ourselves," she said brightly. "I am Angela Angel. This is Demon Beauregard. We met at a love spring." She blushed prettily. "It was accidental. We both thought it was regular water."

"The irony is that neither angels nor demons need to drink," the demon said.

"Not water, anyway," the angel said.

"She drinks nectar and eats ambrosia," he said.

"He drinks strong spirits and eats devilsfood."

"We had been arguing about lifestyles," Beauregard said. "Our feet touched the edge of the spring. Then things changed."

"Now we hardly care where we exist," Angela said. "So long as we are together."

"So we're making ourselves useful while we sort this out," the demon said.

"While we try to convert each other," she concluded.

"This interests me," Sim said. Actually everything interested him, but he didn't find it necessary to clarify that. "I am not completely conversant with human mythology, but aren't angels and demons fundamentally incompatible?"

"We thought so," Beauregard said. He kissed Angela.

"It is our understanding," Angela agreed, kissing him back.

"But there's just something so softly feminine about her," the demon said, stroking a softly feminine curve.

"And something so naughtily masculine about him," the angel said, pressing herself against a naughtily masculine ridge.

"I am amazed by the variety of things we are finding on these chained worlds," Sim remarked. "An angel/demon romance. On Motes there were man-shaped coprolites."

Beauregard looked really interested. Angela swooned.

"Coprolite," Sim repeated carefully. "Fossilized animal manure. Not copulate."

"Oh," the demon said, losing interest. "Of course. I misheard."

Angela recovered. "Naturally I don't know either word. Angels would never do anything like that."

"Not unless they convert and come to H*ll."

"But if a demon converts and comes to Heaven, he'll be free of that sort of ugliness."

It was evidently that neither had succeeded in converting the other yet. "Do you have plans for the future?" Sim asked.

"Oh, yes," Angela said. "We'll have a sweet little girl with a gentle song."

"Or a shapeshifting boy with big ambitions," Beauregard said.

They were still at odds. Sim wondered how they would work it out. He remembered references to one Demon Beauregard, a friend of Magician Humfrey, who had been around for eons. But of course both angels and demons were pretty much eternal. In that respect, at least, they were a fair match.

"It is time for the tour," Angela said. She lifted one fair hand, and the pearly gates opened. "Behold: Heaven." There was a trumpet fanfare.

Beyond was a wonderland of opalescent clouds with nacreous fringes. Or, in ordinary language, opal-colored with pearly edges. Perched on them were winged humans garbed in white robes, holding harps, singing musical hosannahs. It was all quite lovely.

"This is it?" Wira asked.

"Yes," Angela said. "Isn't it wonderful? We spend eternity in this perfect delight."

"There is no stork summoning?" Hugo asked.

"Heavens no! Nothing like that."

"What about games of nimbi?" Nimbus asked.

"Games are decadent; we don't play any."

"Kissing?" Ilene asked.

"Of course not." Angela glanced regretfully at Beauregard, who remained studiously silent. "It is suggestive of some base design. Not that I am capable of imagining any such thing."

"It would take me about ten minutes to be thoroughly bored," the Factor muttered.

"Boredom isn't allowed. Everyone is simply divinely happy to be in this perfect place."

"Perhaps it is time for us to tour the other realm," Sim suggested.

They departed Heaven, whose shining gates clanked shut behind them. Now the demon came to life. "Hell has all the things H*ven lacks," he said, leading them to a small bridge. "Do not misstep; the River Styx will not let you return if you touch it."

They were careful. When they were across, a demoness appeared in a puff of smoke. Her scanty red costume barely covered her evocative torso. "Fresh meat, Beau?" she inquired saucily.

"Visitors taking the tour," Beauregard replied. He turned to face the group. "This is Demoness Lusion, who likes to fascinate visitors. She is about to depart."

"The hell I am, boyfriend."

"*Ex*-boyfriend. We were through—"

"The moment you dipped your toe in that blessed love spring," Lusion said bitterly. "I don't accept that. She tricked you."

"I did not!" Angela protested. "We don't practice subterfuge."

"In contrast to your machinations," Beauregard told Lusion. "That love spring opened my eyes to your nature. Now let me conduct my tour in peace."

D. Lusion formed a smoky smile. It was plain that she was jealous and unscrupulous. Sim knew that was mischief, but wasn't sure how to stop it.

Lusion oriented first on the men. "So did they show you anything like this in H*ven?" She struck a pose that threatened to burst a button in front and a zipper in back.

The eyeballs of the adult males began to sweat, and those of young Nimbus warmed. Even Sim's avian eyeballs widened in guilty appreciation. It was some pose.

"Talk of overstuffed sausages," Angela murmured.

"Nothing like that, Lusion," Beauregard said. He faced the group. "Her point being that Hell is much more into temptation than H*ven is."

"I have not yet begun to tempt," Lusion said. "Ladies, look at this." There was a groan behind her. It was from a table so overloaded with pastries and drinks that its legs were paining it. "Every cake is sinfully sweeter than the others, and every drink will send you rapturously floating. Here in Hell you can feast continuously."

Now it was the eyeballs of Wira and Debra that sweated, while those of the children had entirely locked into place. Sim moved between them and the table, spreading his wings to interrupt their gazes. They recovered their vision, somewhat guiltily.

"And horribly fattening," Angela said.

Meanwhile the smoky gaze of the demoness oriented on Sim. "So you think you're immune, featherbrain?" She became the most beautiful bird-of-paradise. Sim was stunned.

"How come that bird can show up in Hell?" Ilene demanded querulously.

"It's a delusion," Angela explained. "She's faking it."

"You stay out of this, angel face!" Lusion snapped. "Or I'll give Beau what you can't, like this." She resumed the form of the supremely sexy woman, this time with translucent clothing. "And that will be no fake." She advanced on him, jiggling dangerously.

"Forget it, Lusion," Beauregard said. "I love her, and you can't change that."

"Well, I don't see her joining you in Hell." Lusion turned to Angela. "How about it, frigid virgin? Care to show your heavenly undies here?"

Angela quailed. "You uncouth, horrible creature!"

Lusion formed a smile that threatened to burn her teeth. "It's a fair question, Beau. If you really want to have a family, you will have to summon the stork with her. She's going to have to bare her pristine panties sometime. It's not going to happen in H*ven. You know that."

That shut Beauregard up. He did know it.

"I'll even put it to the visitors," the demoness continued. "Am I right?"

"This is Hell," Wira said. "We don't want to side with the evil-spirited demoness."

"But we have to," Debra said. "She's hellishly correct."

The two men reluctantly nodded.

"It is true," Sim said. "By your human conventions, the route to the storks passes through the panties." That, unfortunately, was all he knew about it. He was still technically a child, and bound to ignorance by the dread Adult Conspiracy. That really annoyed him. What supreme secret did those human panties conceal?

Angela burst into tears. They sparkled like blessed little stars.

"You utter—" Beauregard started.

"Female dog?" Lusion inquired, becoming one. "Better that, than a sterile doll."

Beauregard focused on her. Two jags of lightning stabbed out of his eyes. They struck the demoness on the face and chest. She puffed into a noxious cloud, her shapely legs dissolving last. Sim knew that Lusion wasn't really hurt; the demon had simply banished her for the moment.

Beauregard turned to embrace Angela. "I'm sorry, beloved. She's a creature of Hell. You can't silence her."

"Yes I can," Angela said, wiping her eyes. "I'll do it. I'll bare my— my—"

"Don't let her taunting get to you," he said. "She's just jealous of your heavenly status, and wants to bring you down."

"But she's right," Angela said. "I love you, and I know your nature. I can never satisfy you as an angel."

"I love you regardless."

"And I love you. Now I'm going to prove it." She reached for her skirt.

"Are we satisfied that neither realm is suitable for us?" Sim asked quickly.

"Yes," the four adults said in chorus.

"Farewell, Angela, Beauregard," Ilene called. "Thank you for the tour."

The angel and the demon didn't notice. They were embarking on the next level of their relationship, and had tuned out the rest of the universe. Sim hoped it worked out well, but wasn't sure how it felt to be a fallen angel. Yet at least she had the courage to do what she had to do, and that might augur well for the future.

They formed their formation of eight and transferred out.

"Aww," Nimbus said. "They were going to make a scene."

"She was going to show her panties," Fray said. "You know you're not allowed to see that."

"Mice!" he swore rebelliously. Sim saw Wira and Debra exchanging a glance. Nimbus was a typical boy.

Meanwhile the others were gazing at the new world. This one seemed to be in the form of a giant tree, and was covered with forests. "Obviously the World of Tree," Sim said. "This may be a prospect."

"I wonder what the demons of Hell will think of a collection of small trees," the Factor remarked. "Or perhaps acorns." Because that was what they must have exchanged with.

They explored the local environment. There seemed to be no animals, but there were insects, especially bees. Flowering trees liked bees, so that made sense.

"This is really nice," Ilene breathed. "Don't you think so, Sim?"

She was engaging him in dialogue, making him constantly aware of her. He recognized the syndrome, and was powerless against it. Had they both been older, she would have conquered him on Cone, the crossbreed planet, except that one of them was not a sea creature.

"I wonder," Hugo said. "If we are locked into an endless journey from which we can never return, we might be foolish to give up a world like this. It would be a gamble to seek a better one farther along."

"And we might find one like Hell, with nasty demonesses to fascinate you," Wira said. "We wouldn't want that."

"Of course we wouldn't," he agreed, the pupils of his eyes forming momentarily into evocative demoness shapes.

"So we need to do some serious thinking," Debra said. "I believe I could accept this world, if it is as it seems."

There, of course, was the question. Was this world really as peaceful and pleasant as it appeared?

"I'm hungry," Nimbus said. "I want a pie tree."

The Factor conjured a luscious chocolate cherry. "Try this."

The boy eyed it. "Will it explode in my face?"

"No. This is an edible cherry."

"Mice!" he said, disappointed. But he accepted the cherry, which looked absolutely delicious.

"Conjure me an air potato, please," Fray said.

The Factor did. She took it and joined the boy under a giant acorn tree, chewing on its vapory substance.

"I believe we could all use a rest," Wira said. "It has been a challenging excursion."

The others agreed. They went to join the children under the tree. Hugo sat down and leaned his back against the trunk, and Wira sat on his lap and kissed him. Debra folded her four legs under her so that her human portion was no higher than the Factor stood, and soon was giving him a double-breasted braless smooch. They might all be tired, but they had special ways of resting in mind.

"I will look around," Sim said, feeling slightly awkward.

"I will join you," Ilene said.

Sim saw another of those subtle glances pass between Wira and Debra. They were well aware of the girl's quest, and perhaps approved.

"Of course," he agreed, not at all loath.

He took her on his back and spread his wings, flying around and up. Then he remembered: "You didn't get lightened."

"I have the illusion of lightness," she said.

So she had made the illusion real. "You have more of a talent than I judged," he said appreciatively.

"I am still learning to use it." She was back in her semblance of maturity. He could feel the shapeliness of her body in contact with his.

A daring idea occurred to him. "When you make your illusion of being older real, does that include the Adult Conspiracy?"

"Why, I hadn't thought about it," she said, surprised. Then, after a startled pause: "Oh, my! So that's how they signal the stork! I never would have thought of doing that particular thing."

"What thing is that?"

"Well, a man and a woman get together, and—you're twelve, aren't you? I can't tell you."

Bleep. Sim had learned an extraordinary amount about Xanth and the universe, but not that particular thing. He was most curious, but it seemed she had inherited the Conspiracy along with the adulthood. Still, maybe he could gain peripheral information. "Is it feasible between a bird and a human?"

"Oh, yes. In fact you don't even need an accommodation spell. It's just a matter of—" She kicked his side with a well-fleshed leg. "You tried to trick me! That wasn't nice."

"I'm sorry," he said, though in truth he was more frustrated than sorry.

"However," she murmured, "if you ever achieve the illusion of maturity, I might make that real and then show you some interesting things."

How he wished he could achieve that illusion, if only long enough to learn the secret! But he saw no way. The Conspiracy was immutable.

They were now high above the forest. The trees extended everywhere. They had landed on the crown of the planetary tree, and its furry surface was solid forest. Except for one spot, or line. "What is that?" he asked.

She peered down. "It looks like a cultivated path leading to a special glade with a domed hothouse."

"Perhaps we should investigate."

"Yes. It has the aspect of being important."

They flew to the glade, glided down, and landed beside the dome, which turned out to be huge. A flower-bordered path led to its main door. They went to that door and knocked, quite uncertain what to expect.

The door opened. No one was there; the path simply wended its pretty way inside. So they followed it on into the greenhouse. This was a vast interior, with a large skylight above.

Here the plants were more exotic, as if unable to thrive in the more moderate climate outside. Small trees bore huge flowers, and bushes supported unusual fruits. "This may be where the trees are developed, for the rest of the planet," Sim said.

"And maybe for the rest of the Worlds of Ida, including Xanth itself," Ilene said. "My big sister Irene can make any plant grow; she would be delighted to see this."

"Did I hear my name?"

They looked up, startled. There on a pedestal was Princess Ida, in a manner. She wore a crown, and a tiny planet orbited her head, but she was nude and as shapely as a nymph. "Hello," he responded belatedly.

She flung her gorgeously long hair about and kicked up a long leg to cross it over the other. The process would have freaked Sim out, had he been human; as it was, it brushed him back. She *was* a nymph!

Ilene, of course, was not at all fazed. "We are Sim Bird and Ilene Human," she said. "We are part of a party visiting this world."

"Yes, of course," Ida said. "You will want to remain here."

Sim recovered his voice. "We are considering it. We are under a curse that prevents us from returning to our origin world of Xanth. We can travel only upworld."

"I'm sure that's true," Ida said. Sim realized with foreboding that even if it hadn't been true before, it was true now, because Ida had accepted it. They were truly cursed.

"But some members of our party might be bored with just trees," Ilene said, obviously thinking of Nimbus. "So we can't be sure we want to stay here."

"That will not be a problem," Ida said. "You need to remain here. This world needs more nymphs and fauns for its trees, and it seems you will serve."

"We can't commit to this," Sim said. "We must consult with the rest of our party."

"They are in sleep under the acorn tree, and will not be roused until you commit."

Sim exchanged a wary look with Ilene. This was clearly not the nice Ida they had known on Xanth. This was the Tree World Ida, with a different agenda.

"We must go to them now," Sim said.

"You cannot," Ida said. "The dome is locked."

"The skylight isn't," Sim said.

"That is illusion. The dome is solid."

Illusion. "Mount, Ilene," Sim said tightly.

She got on his back immediately. He spread his wings and launched into the air. He spiraled up toward the skylight, trusting that Ilene knew what to do.

He reached the skylight and flew up through it. It had become real. Ilene had done her thing.

He flew rapidly back to where the other members of the party were. They did turn out to be sleeping. "There must be some pacifying potion in the air," he said.

"We must rouse them and get them moving," Ilene said. "Quickly, before it affects us." She was a sensible girl.

He landed. "We may have to try holding our breaths."

"If they don't wake, we must drag them to the Factor's body and pile them on," she said.

"But if Hugo is sleeping too, that won't help."

"It may."

The others refused to be roused. So Sim helped Ilene drag the others to the Factor's body. It was difficult, but they managed. Now there was a human pile, still sleeping.

"Touch him too," Ilene said tersely, putting one foot on the body's shoulder to ensure her own contact. Then she carefully used her thumbs to draw up the man's eyelids, making him appear to be awake. It was of course illusion.

Then Sim understood. She was making the illusion real. "Hugo," he said urgently. "Transfer us out, immediately."

"But—" Hugo said. Then he got a peek under mature Ilene's lifted skirt, and started to freak out.

"Now!" Sim snapped.

There was a wrench, and they were elsewhere.

"You are some girl," Sim told Ilene appreciatively.

"Thank you," she said, managing a hurried blush.

After that the others began to wake. They were free of the air that had put them down. Sim explained what had happened.

"We owe you our freedom," Wira said. "Thank you."

Hugo shook his head. "I think I dreamed I saw—" He looked at Ilene, who was back to her normal appearance. It seemed that once she had learned to handle a given illusion, making it real, she could summon and abolish it at will. "Nothing," he concluded, embarrassed.

Sim decided not to explain; it would only generate mischief. He trusted that Ilene would remember to revert promptly in the future, when not distracted by the need to save the others from unkind captivity.

Ilene caught his eye briefly and let half a smile escape. In that instant she seemed eerily mature again. She was, indeed, some girl. He began to wonder whether her developing talent was really below Sorceress level.

They looked around at the world they had landed on. It was a greenish gourd-shaped mass, with a huge hole nearby.

Gourd-shaped? With a peephole? "This world is not for us," Sim said grimly. "It must be Gourd Moon."

"A dream world," Debra agreed. "We'd never escape that." She smiled briefly. "It would be a bad dream."

They transferred again. This time they came to a world shaped like a tapering four-sided shaft of stone. All across its surface were smaller projections of stone.

"An obelisk," Sim said. "A monolith."

"Somehow I don't think this is our world either," Wira said.

"I wonder," Hugo said. "We have been traveling randomly upworld, skipping countless intermediate worlds. Is it possible we're missing the best ones? In which case we might do better by doing it the conventional way, through Princess Ida, one at a time. Eliminating the randomness."

Wira kissed him. "You're a genius, dear!"

It was his turn to blush, silenced. It was not the kind of compliment he was accustomed to receiving.

"That depends on the nature of Princess Ida," Sim said. "We have learned that they are not all nice people."

"If she's bad, we can transfer again, as we have been doing," the Factor said. "It remains our escape option."

Debra kissed him. "You're a genius, dear," she said teasingly, emulating Wira.

He shook his head. "How I wish you weren't cursed, so that I could have at you in my own body."

"So do I. In my own body too."

"Actually your centaur body is more fully formed. It doesn't need a bra."

She made as if to slap him, and he made as if to flinch. They liked teasing each other. Their relationship clearly made Debra more confident, and the Random Factor more human. And was Sim's own relationship with Ilene doing the same for the two of them? It seemed likely.

"So let's try for Princess Ida, cautiously," Wira said.

"I can survey the terrain," Sim offered.

"Not without me," Ilene said. "Ida might be another nymph. Or worse, a lovely bird."

"Don't contact her at all," Debra advised. "Just locate her."

That made sense. Ilene went to Debra for lightening, so that the others would not realize she had discovered how to do it herself through illusion realism, then got on his back. He took off and ascended.

"Which way?" Sim inquired.

"Well, I could try this way," Ilene said, sliding around so that she was clinging to his front. She was light enough now to do this without falling. She was of course fully mature again. He could feel the twin pressures of her, well, bra under her blouse. Her clothing seemed to mature along with her body.

"You'll be dangerous when you're older," he said.

"I *am* older, for now." She kissed him on the beak. "And some time, when you present the appearance of maturity, I'll make you older too. For just long enough."

She was teasing, but also not fooling. He desperately longed for that temporary maturity, for she had pretty much won his avian heart. She was human, yet there was no other bird of his species, other than his mother, as Debra had reminded him. The notion of a crossbreed couple no longer seemed at all irregular.

"Maybe the pinnacle," he said.

"You're so smart."

And she had virtually complete command of his interest. Intelligence had nothing to do with it.

He flew north toward the apex. There at its tip was a curtained window, as if a lady lived there. The curtain was decorated with pictures of a crown and a tiny orbiting moon. "That's bound to be Princess Ida," he said.

"Bound," she agreed, working her way around to his back. "We must tell the others."

He turned back, flying toward the spot their party had landed. "Ilene, if we do find a suitable world—"

"I will remain with you, of course."

"But if we find one where there are good human men—"

"Would any be as pretty or smart as you?"

"Well, no. But they would be human."

"And if there were a beautiful bird-of-paradise, like the one the demoness emulated, and she cocked her crest at you?"

"Never! I already love you." Oops; how had that slipped out?

"I think we have answered each other," she said.

Indeed they had.

They returned to the group and reported what they had seen, omitting their other dialogue, though its general nature could hardly be secret from the women. Women were simply too canny about romance; they could not be fooled. At least the younger children would be innocent.

Wira gazed along the broad avenue that was this facet of Obelisk. "I think that is too far for us to walk."

"I could carry some of you, if Debra makes you light," Sim said. "She could carry the others."

Wira nodded. "That seems to make sense."

Soon Debra was carrying the Factor, Wira, and Hugo, while Sim carried Ilene, Fray, and Nimbus. Fray could have reverted to her cloud form, but would not have traveled fast enough to keep up, even were the wind right. He led the way north.

"Did you kiss her?" Fray asked.

So much for the innocence of children.

"I kissed him," Ilene answered. "He couldn't stop me; he had to keep flying."

"That's so romantic!"

"Ugh," Nimbus said.

"Oh?" said Fray. "Suppose I kiss you? Are you going to jump off and fall until you squish on the metal ground?"

"You wouldn't dare!"

"No, *you* wouldn't dare. Take that." She kissed him.

"Double ugh!"

"Okay, I'll do it again." She kissed him again.

Sim felt Ilene's knees tighten against him. She knew that Nimbus secretly liked getting kissed. The two were forming a couple that might amount to something a decade or so later.

They glided down to land beside the window at the pyramidal apex. Wira knocked on the pane.

A door appeared beside the window, large enough to admit them all. They entered. They had been standing with their heads away from the planetary surface, but as they entered the doorway their heads pointed toward the tip. Gravity had changed, as magical things could.

They entered a large chamber. There on a throne sat Princess Ida, resplendent in a royal gown. She wore a crown, and a tiny ball circled her head. "Welcome, travelers," she said. "I am Princess Ida, governess of Obelisk World. Please introduce yourselves."

They did so, and told their story. "So you see, we got trapped by a curse," Sim concluded. "Now we are looking for a world where we can comfortably settle, and we thought we could check less randomly by going through you, if you don't mind."

Ida nodded. "You surely would not be satisfied here; almost our sole interest is creating monuments. But my moon Earth may prove to be more hospitable."

"Earth!" Wira exclaimed.

"You have heard of it?"

"It is next to Xanth, our home realm."

"Oh, I don't think so. Earth is governed by the Demoness Gaia, and has very little magic. I am not sure what lies beyond it."

The group exchanged several mixed glances: wonder, surmise, and maybe hope. Were they coming up on another Xanth? Just how similar to their own could it be?

"We'll try it," Wira said.

"As you wish. You will have to leave the bulk of your souls here, and they may be difficult to recover if you decide to return. They will soon dissipate and be lost."

"We can't return," Hugo said. "We are cursed."

Ida shrugged. "Then I hope you discover your compatible world."

They linked hands and let their substance sublimate. Soon they were orienting on the new planet, which loomed larger as they approached. It was blue, with huge seas and oddly shaped masses of land.

They were able to direct their landing, and chose a peninsula that strongly resembled Xanth. It might not *be* Xanth, but it seemed the most likely route *to* Xanth.

They aimed for Castle Roogna, though aware that there would be no such castle here. Just so long as there was an equivalent.

They landed in what turned out to be the big village of Summer Haven. They did not try to speak with any natives; the language of Mundania was indecipherable to Xanthians. They scavenged for blankets to cover Sim and Debra, knowing that Mundania did not have many man-

sized birds or winged centaurs. Fortunately the local people were all hur-
rying about their own business, paying no attention. Most were in the
Mundane vehicles called cars, zooming madly from red light to red light.
Sim wasn't sure what the magic of the lights was, but it evidently had considerable stopping power.

And there, on a private estate, was a castle. The natives did not seem to
notice it, but it was right where Castle Roogna existed in Xanth. That had
to be it.

They went to the front gate. It was open, so they trooped into the estate
and made their way to the castle. No one was around, so they entered it
and went to where the chamber of Princess Ida ought to be.

They found the room. But its door was locked. So they knocked.
"Princess Ida!" Wira called.

"Hello!" the answer came. She spoke Xanthian!

"We need to see you. Will you let us in?"

"I don't have the key."

She was locked in? Something was wrong here.

Finally Debra lifted a front hoof and stomped the doorknob. It broke
off, and the door swung open.

There was Princess Ida, with a little blue globe-shaped moon orbiting
her head.

"But Ida," Wira said. "How is it that you are confined? This can't be
right."

"They think I am crazy," Ida said. "Because I don't speak their language."

"You speak *our* language. We're from Xanth."

"Oh! Isn't that one of the derivative moons? How did you manage to
get here? I hardly ever get visitors."

"It's a long story," Wira said. "But you—how can they call you crazy?
How do they explain your moon?"

"They can't see my moon."

There was half a silence. Obviously the Mundanes had a serious per-
ceptual problem.

"Why don't we take her with us?" Fray Cloud asked. "She wouldn't be
crazy in Xanth."

"Is that possible?" Debra asked.

"It is possible," Sim said. "Our Princess Ida finally learned how to visit some of her own worlds. Provision has to be made for her moon, and she can't remain indefinitely, as her body remains behind, but she can visit."

"Let's do it," Debra said.

They set up Ida on her bed comfortably, with her moon satisfied to continue orbiting her head in that position. Then they dissolved their bodies, and Ida's soul joined them. They floated as a group toward the next World. They were completing some sort of loop, traveling from Xanth to Xanth. But what would they find there, really? Sim concealed his nervous misgivings. After all, what choice did they have?

His misgivings were soon confirmed: the next world was not Xanth. It looked a lot like Earth, yet couldn't be, because they had just come from there.

They were standing at a deserted field near a town. They knew where Princess Ida should be, but were surveying the region before just walking in on her. The last world especially had instilled caution.

A man spied them from a distance and approached. "You have to be from Xanth!" he called.

Surprised, Sim answered him. "How do you know this?"

"I love Xanth," the man said. "I've read about it all my life, it seems. I felt your presence the moment you arrived; maybe its my talent. Where else would you find a winged centaur, a huge pretty talking bird, Princess Ida, and a lad who glows? I am David Scalise, and I will help you any way I can."

Sim introduced himself and the others. "We are travelers," he said. "Trying to find our way back to Xanth. It is bound to be one of the Moons of Ida, especially this close to Earth. What world is this?"

"This is Moondania, and it has no magic. I understand it is very similar to Earth, with Princess Ida in the same place." He looked at Ida. "I'll be happy to guide you there. I've never had a pretext to intrude on you, I mean her, before."

"Thank you, David," Sim said. "This facilitates things." They accompanied the man to Ida's residence.

But this time she wasn't crazy. Her problem was different. They stood and stared, at a loss.

She had no moon.

They stared at that absence. How could they travel on upworld if there was no world to go to?

"I confess I have had strange dreams of exotic other realms," Ida said. "But a moon orbiting my head? This is unbelievable."

"Look at mine," the Ida of Earth said. They were now on her moon, yet it also still orbited her head.

The Ida of Moondania stared. "This is amazing! How do you keep it in place?"

"It is just there. It is an idea made tangible."

"What do we do now?" Wira asked Sim. She looked halfway desperate.

Sim opened his beak, and closed it again. He was stumped.

"I know," Fray said. "Make her an illusion moon."

Sim looked at her, then at Ilene. Was this possible? Could they make a moon that was more than an inert ball of matter? Yet what Princess Ida believed—*any* Princess Ida—was true almost by definition. Did Fray know that? He hoped not, because a new idea had to be suggested by a person who did not know this aspect of Ida's talent.

"Yes, we should do that," Sim agreed carefully. "But without magic it may be a challenge."

"Mirrors," Debra said. "I may not really be from Mundania, though somehow I think I am. Maybe even this Moondania. I remember that special effects can be done with them."

"They can," David agreed.

"Let's have Earth Ida stand before a mirror, here," Debra said. "So her world shows, and Moondania Ida can stand here where it reflects."

They did so, and after some careful repositioning and adjustment of the surrounding light, they made it seem as though the world was orbiting the second Ida's head. "It's illusion, of course," Sim said, glancing meaningfully at Ilene.

"Now it's real," Ilene said promptly. "Oops. I saw it in shadow, and made it irregular. It looks like a peninsula."

"It's Xanth!" Fray exclaimed, delighted. "Home!"

"Your home world?" the Moondania Ida said. "I'm sure it is."

And there it was. Earth Ida stepped away from the mirror. Her spherical moon went with her. The Xanth-shaped moon remained orbiting the other Ida's head. Ilene's talent had made it real, and Ida's belief made it authentic. He hoped.

"Let's move on," Wira said. Sim knew she was afraid that if they delayed, the Xanth world would fade away. It might be a manufactured world, but would surely be more compatible than the others they had encountered. "Princess Ida can come too."

"I can?" Moondania Ida asked, surprised.

"I'm sure you can," Earth Ida reassured her.

They explained how she could do it. "But will my body be safe?" she asked dubiously.

"I will be happy to watch your body," David said. "If I can have the chance to visit Xanth myself, in my turn."

"Oh yes," she answered, and kissed him. He looked thoroughly dazed. He would surely do his utmost to keep her safe.

Then they were on their way, as a party of ten. Again, Sim concealed his private misgivings.

17
QUESTION

They landed on a field not far from Castle Roogna, surrounded by innocent buttercups. All of the butter seemed quite ripe and fresh.

Fray glanced around. It certainly looked like Xanth. It had the same landscape, the same pie plants, the same punnish features. But it had been crafted by illusion, and imperfect illusion at that. Could it really be real?

"Perhaps I should look around," Sim said.

"I'll go with you," Ilene said immediately. She was sweet on him, and didn't mind showing it.

"I think we saw enough as we condensed coming here," Wira said. "I believe there are serious questions we should address before we go farther."

"There are," Sim agreed somewhat guardedly. Fray could tell he was nervous. Why was that?

"Every world we have visited is very much smaller than the prior world or worlds," Wira said. "So that a diminishingly tiny fraction of our souls is enough for us to form seemingly complete solid bodies. This was the case here. So how can it be the original Xanth?"

"Exactly," Sim agreed. "It has to be a derivative. Yet if it is a perfect imitation of the original, it should do."

"Will it?" Wira asked grimly. "If it is perfect, there may be duplicates of all of us here. How will we interact with them?"

"It is possible to get along with a duplicate," Ida 1 from Earth said, glancing at Ida 2 from Moondania. Indeed, the two seemed to be relating well to each other.

"And you both will want to meet the version of you who is here," Debra said. "But I wonder: will the Random and Hugo who are here be in their own bodies? Will the Debra who is here be dangerous for Random? How can we find out?"

Fray saw that these were complicated questions. They could not simply return to their prior lives, because those lives might already be occupied. There might be another Fray floating happily in the sky. They needed to know the situation before they went anywhere.

"Check the bodies," Nimbus said.

"Bodies?" Fray asked him.

"The ones we left behind."

A glance ricocheted around their circle. "If this should somehow be the original Xanth," Ilene breathed.

"There will be bodies," Wira agreed.

"Unless this world emulates the bodies also," Sim said. "It could be a perfect derivative."

"Or a perfect copy we made real," Ilene said. "How can we tell?"

"It may never be possible to be certain," Sim said. "There could be an endless chain of loops going from Xanth to Xanth, each one infinitely smaller than those below and infinitely larger than those above."

"Does it matter?" Fray asked.

Another glance circulated, catching most eyes. "Yes," Wira said. "I set out on this quest to recover my real husband, not a copy."

"I'm your real husband," Hugo said.

"In another man's body. That's not ideal."

"I agree: let's check the bodies," the Factor said.

"Which ones?"

"Ours," Hugo said.

"We are now a party of ten," Wira pointed out. "That will be complicated."

Hugo nodded. "Yours first, then. Castle Roogna is close by."

They organized for travel, with the younger children riding Debra, Sim flying with Ilene, and the five adults walking.

As they approached the castle, the three princesses appeared. "You're back," Melody said.

"From Ida's Moons," Harmony added.

"And we didn't see you arrive," Rhythm concluded.

"It's complicated," Wira repeated.

Then they saw the two Idas. For once in their little princessly lives they were silenced.

They went to Princess Ida's chamber and knocked. She opened the door and looked at them, surprised. "How can you be out there?"

"It's complicated," Fray said mischievously. "Wait till you see who else is with us."

They crowded into Princes Ida's room, and she saw the two other Idas. "You're from the moons!" she exclaimed.

"We are," Ida Earth said.

"But to us, *you* are on a moon," Ida Moondania said.

"But how can you be my size? You should be tiny, or so diffuse as to be ghostly."

"I have been pondering that," Sim said. "If this is a derivative Xanth, a tiny fraction of their souls can condense to be full size for the tiny world this is, compared to theirs. The same would be true for the rest of us: our origin world is almost unimaginably larger than this one. So we have no problem with size. Only if we were to travel in the other direction would we lack sufficient matter to function on the worlds below us."

"But your bodies are here!"

"Yes. That may be the proof or disproof of my thesis. If those really are our bodies, then we may indeed have completed a loop."

Ida showed them to their bodies, which were sleeping in various poses in adjacent chambers. Fray's own was there, compacted to be visible, looking sweet in repose.

"Oh, I want mine!" she said, going to it.

"Caution," Sim warned. "If that is actually the body of a derivative person, you could be repulsed."

But Fray was already plunging into her body. She was the same size at it, but when she touched it, the two of them drew together, overlapped, and merged. There was a moment's disorientation.

Then she sat up. "I'm me," she announced.

That glance reappeared and caromed violently around the circle. "Are you sure?" Wira asked.

"Sure I'm sure. This is my condensed body, the air apparent. I'd know it anywhere."

"Is it possible that you just think you are you?"

"Sure I think I'm me! I *know* I'm me."

"That must be the case," one of the Idas said.

Sim had been starting to open his beak, but now he closed it.

"It must be the case," Debra said. "Yet how can it be?"

Something was skew. They were being too adultish. "What am I missing?" Fray demanded.

Wira smiled wanly. "I suppose it is fair for you to know, now, dear. What Princess Ida believes is true, so long as an idea is suggested to her by a person who does not understand her magic. You facilitated things along the way, and now your certainty in the identity of your original body has been endorsed by Princess Ida. That means it is true."

"Sure it's true. So what?"

"With each journey to a new world, we became very much smaller, discarding the great majority of our soul substances. This seems the smallest of them all. How could we be the same size as the natives—if this is actually our world of origin? It's a paradox."

"Actually I have a theoretic answer to that," Sim said. "But it sets up another difficult question. If the worlds of Ida are a closed loop, each one can indeed seem much smaller than its predecessor, yet this would be illusion. All of them would actually be the same size."

"But Moondania World is tiny compared to Earth," Ida Earth said. "It orbits my head, the size of an eyeball. I could never support it if it were the same size as my home world."

"And Xanth world orbited my head, once it became real," Ida Moondania said.

"Nevertheless, perspective could make them seem much smaller than they are," Sim said. "We have been amazed that each world seems full size, once we land on it. That may be reality, while the smallness may be illusion. Mathematically it is feasible."

"Yes, it is," the Factor said. "What is your other difficult question?"

Fray wondered too. It was hard to see what could baffle a person who could believe that infinitely tiny worlds were all the same size.

Sim paused thoughtfully. "If we assume that the illusion is in the size, and that each world is real on its own terms, then this could be the real Xanth."

"Sure it is," Fray agreed.

"But this world seemed not to exist when we first encountered Princess Ida on Moondania. It came into existence when we made an illusion copy of it from Princess Ida of Earth's moon. Ilene did that conversion."

"It's my talent," Ilene agreed modestly. It was clear that she loved hearing Sim intelligently expound.

"Yes it is," Sim agreed. "But what level of talent could copy an entire world with all its people in perfect detail? And shouldn't that world be a perfect copy of Earth, its model?"

This time a silence passed around the group. What the bird said made sense, even to Fray.

"It was an imperfect copy," Ilene said. "I think there was shadow just as I focused on it."

"Yet it turned out to be a perfect rendition of the original Xanth. Coincidence could hardly account for that. This was not copying, it was creation. What level of talent could do that?"

Ilene stared at him, openmouthed. "All I did was try to copy her orbiting world. I don't have creative talent."

"Yet here is Xanth, where there was none before."

"I can't explain it," Ilene said. "I just know I'm not a Demon or something; I can't create whole worlds."

"In which case I have an alternate hypothesis. Suppose you did not create or copy a world. Suppose you merely made an existing connection real, that had been interrupted? That would explain why the world you copied did not match the one you copied from."

"That must be it," Ilene agreed uncertainly.

"It must be," Ida agreed. This was opinion, and not a magical confirmation.

"So perhaps we have an answer, or set of answers," Sim said. "Yet questions remain. We still don't know for certain whether this is the original Xanth, or a tiny derivative, one of an endless chain of derivatives. It would be comforting to get that question settled, one way or another."

"Yes it would," Wira agreed a trifle grimly. "If the worlds are all really the same size, how is it that we have to leave most of our bodies behind when we go to the next?"

"That is an excellent question. I have noted that effect myself, when Clio the Muse of History arranged to import dragons from Dragon World. They had to animate local organic substance in order to exist here. My tentative conclusion is that each person or creature is connected to his home world, and is unable to transfer any significant mass to others. Traveling downworld means that only enough mass exists to animate the soul, which is not mass-hungry. But traveling upworld is more compatible, and more is retained." He glanced at Fray. "You seemed far larger in relation to your original body than you would have had you returned to it via the downworld route."

"*If* it is her original body," the Factor said. "We need to be certain."

"I should think you would prefer to abate Debra's curse, and your exchange of bodies. If these are not the same bodies, there may be no curse, and the two of you can reanimate your proper ones."

Hugo and the Factor exchanged a weighty glance.

"And if the curse remains?" Hugo asked.

"That will suggest that this is the original Xanth, or resembles it so closely as to make no difference."

"That is hardly perfect," Wira said. "I don't want a perfect copy of my husband. I want the real one."

"Let's try it," Hugo said. "But you ladies and children will have to do it first, because this is where your bodies are."

"They are," Wira agreed. She approached her body, and quickly merged. "It feels the same," she said.

Debra went to her centaur body, and animated it with a similar result. Then Ilene, Sim, and Nimbus animated theirs. All agreed that they felt the same.

"But does the curse remain?" Wira asked.

"We can find out," Debra said. She produced her bra and started to put it on. She glanced at the Random Factor, who remained in Hugo's body.

He walked toward her. He reached for her bra.

"Don't touch it!" Wira cried. "We're not sure."

But she was too late. "I can't stop," the Factor said tightly. His hands grasped the bra and pulled it off. Debra was resplendently bare-breasted again. He had de-braed her.

Nothing happened. An expression of hope struggled to take over Debra's face.

Then Fray remembered. "It's the bodies," she reminded them. "He's in Hugo's body. That doesn't count."

This time a nod passed around the group. "She is correct," Sim said. "The Factor's body has to test it."

Debra recovered her bra and put it on again. This time Hugo, in the Factor's body, approached her. He reached toward the bra.

"No!" Wira cried, grabbing his arm just before his hand touched.

"But dear, we have to find out," Hugo told her.

"Not at the expense of your life or freedom."

"Yet how else are we to know?"

Wira pondered. "At least put on gloves."

Ida-Xanth produced a heavy pair of work gloves, and Hugo donned them. He reached again for the bra.

There was a spark jumping from the bra toward the hand. But the gloves prevented it from making a complete connection.

"I think that proves it," Wira said sadly. "The curse tried."

"It might have been the magic of static electricity," Sim said. "If so, it has now been discharged, and should not happen again."

"We still do need to know," Hugo said. He removed the gloves.

"But if you are banished, whatever will I do?" Wira asked desperately.

"It's a gamble," Hugo said. He kissed her. "If I am confined in a cell, come to rescue me, somehow. We have to know."

Fray realized that he was a really brave man.

Hugo returned to Debra. He reached for her bra. No spark jumped. He removed it. Nothing happened.

Wira fainted. Fortunately the Factor in Hugo's body caught her before she fell.

"So this is not the original Xanth," the Factor said. "The curse is gone. If we could just exchange bodies back, all would be well."

"Not necessarily," Sim said. "We forgot that this is not the Factor's original physical body. It is his soul-solidified body, which is another matter."

And this time a sigh circulated. Of course he was right. They had not proved anything.

"Which means that this could still be the original Xanth," the Factor said.

"It could indeed," Sim agreed.

"We need to return to our bodies," Hugo said. "And find out how to exchange back."

"And maybe have me destroy my beloved," Debra said.

"The alternative is to remain in our wrong bodies," the Factor said. "That's not ideal."

A bulb flashed over Fray's head. "Maybe you could get the Transformer Magician Trent to change your bodies so they looked right!"

Yet another glance circulated. "With the right souls, and the right appearance, that might be satisfactory," Sim said. "And it would effectively abate the curse."

"But we'd always know that the bodies were wrong," Debra said. "We have gotten along so far, expecting to be on some other world, but here on Xanth it doesn't seem the same."

"I wonder," Wira said. "Would it be possible to negotiate with the Factory to get the curse lifted? Then there would be no need to avoid it."

"Never," the Factor said. "The Factory wants to make me a slave to its system, exactly like all the others. You wouldn't like me then, Debra."

Debra considered. "Yes. Even though I was crafted to bring you back, I don't want you that way."

"So we still don't have a sure answer," Sim said.

"Let's go animate your real bodies," Wira said bravely. "Maybe we'll figure out something along the way."

"Perhaps the children should be allowed to go home," Ida-Xanth said. "To their families."

There was a pause. Then Nimbus, the youngest, spoke. "Not until we know they're our real families."

There it was. Fray agreed. She did not want to return to some other Fracto and Happy Bottom. She had to be sure they were hers.

"Then perhaps the other Idas can stay and visit with me," Ida-Xanth said. "I'm sure we have much to compare."

"We do," Ida-Earth said. "They think I'm crazy."

"They don't even notice me," Ida-Moondania said. "I'd like to see some real magic before I return to my dull moondane world."

"That can be readily arranged," Ida-Xanth said.

Soon Fray, Nimbus, and Wira were on Debra, suitably lightened, while Ilene rode Sim. The two men seemed stuck, not wanting to overload the others, but not able to travel to any particular destination nonrandomly.

"This is our opportunity to demonstrate some magic," Ida-Xanth said. She snapped her fingers. "Princesses! You may enter now."

The three eleven-year-old princesses came into the chamber. Obviously they had been listening at the door. Fray admired that.

"These two men need help traveling," Ida-Xanth said. "Are you willing to help?"

"Sure," Melody said.

"We'll help them fly," Harmony added.

"With winged hats," Rhythm concluded.

They hummed, played a note on a harmonica, and beat a beat on a drum. Suddenly the two men had winged hats.

"But won't they fly up without us?" Hugo asked.

The wings on his hat spread and flapped. Hugo rose into the air. The hat did not separate; it remained firmly on his head. Evidently its magic kept it close. It did not even seem to be hauling him up by the head. It simply enabled him to fly comfortably.

They thanked Ida and the young princesses and departed Castle Roogna. Soon they were all in the sky.

When this adventure was done, Fray thought, she'd be glad to return to her natural form and float freely in the sky. But for now she had to keep her condensed state, so as to interact with the others, and because this one wasn't dependent on random winds to get her places.

Actually it wasn't bad being condensed. She had gotten to have a marvelous adventure that would wow her cloud parents, and gotten to know solid folk in a way she never would have otherwise. Debra and Wira were nice, and Ilene and Sim. Even the men weren't bad, and she sort of liked

Nimbus. She had kissed him to shut him up, as a threat of punishment, but that had had a backdraft, affecting her more than him. True, he was a mere boy, two years younger than she was. But he was the son of the Demon Xanth, which impressed her, and he had a marvelously confusing talent, and that cute little glow. She would be sorry never to see him again, after this. But of course what would such a boy want with a mere cloud? In time he would grow up and find some distressingly solid girl, who wouldn't even be jealous of Fray. But right now he was sitting in front of her, and her arms were around him to help keep him steady so he wouldn't do something foolish like jump off Debra's back in mid-flight. It was easy to imagine that they were close because they liked each other, though she knew that was only half true.

In two and a half periods of time they reached the pile of ashes that was the men's burial place. They landed, Sim with Ilene, Debra with the three of them, and the two men in their almost comical winged hats.

Fray let go of Nimbus, and he jumped to the ground. Actually the danger of his falling has been slight, because they all had been lightened for the flight. She followed—and he reached up to catch her and help her down. She was so surprised she didn't think to protest. "Thank you."

Then he pulled her close and kissed her, catching her with her astonished mouth open. "Now we're even," he said, and giggled.

He walked away, leaving her dumbfounded. Had it been his little joke, or had he really wanted to kiss her back? She was truly confused.

"He likes you," Wira murmured. "But he's embarrassed to show it. Boys—and men—are like that."

Oh. Evidently Wira had had enough experience with men to decode their mysteries.

Meanwhile the men were busy delving into the ashes. Soon they uncovered a trapdoor, opened it, and revealed steps leading down.

And there they were, lying as if asleep. "Now do we take our own bodies?" Hugo asked. "Knowing the risk?"

The Factor considered for a good seven eighths of a moment. "Yes. I'd rather have the risk in my own body, than be forever in yours." He went to his own body and touched it.

Nothing happened. He was unable to get into it. Hugo tried with his body, with no better success. "So we can't exchange back this way."

"It seems we have to return to the bodies we left," Wira said.

The men shrugged and went to their own bodies. In barely one and a half fractions of a moment they had merged. Now all the members of their party had been restored.

"Now for the curse test," the Factor said. He approached Debra, who obligingly put on her bra. He removed it with no trouble.

Then it was Hugo's turn. He approached Debra in the Factor's body. "No!" Wira cried. "I know it's going to destroy you! Even if this isn't the original Xanth."

Hugo looked at her. "I have a gut feeling you're right. The curse remains. We don't dare risk it again."

"Then maybe Fray's solution is the best," Debra said sadly. "We can go to Magician Trent for transformations."

"This bothers me," Sim said. "There remain mysteries here. I think we should fathom them before making any significant decision."

Fray saw the others looking at him warily. Sim was only twelve years old, but he was a very smart bird. "What remaining mysteries?" Wira asked guardedly.

"For one thing, what started the chain of events that brought us here?"

"That's easy," Hugo said. "The Random Factor randomly changed himself so he could affect himself, and switched places with me, then with Fracto. That put Wira in motion to find me, and me in motion to escape, and Happy Bottom and Fray in motion to rescue Fracto. One thing led to another."

"And the Factory crafted me to recover him, the moment he escaped," Debra said. "Thus the curse, and, incidentally, our love."

Sim nodded. "That does seem to be where it started. But how was it possible for the Factor to change himself, when he had never been able to before? His randomness never applied to himself until that moment. How could his talent change?"

"That's true," Wira said. "Talents don't change themselves, not even randomly. Something else must have changed him."

"Not the Factory," Hugo said. "It doesn't want him free. Anyway, I don't know anything that can change a person's talent, other than—" He halted.

"Other than what?" Wira asked.

"A Demon!" Fray said, seeing it.

"This is my conjecture," Sim said. "Which in turn raises the question, which Demon, and why?"

Wira shuddered. "We don't want Demon involvement. They are way too powerful, and way too indifferent to mortal concerns. They care only about their status games."

"Which suggests that we are participating in a Demon game," Sim said. "This is what concerns me most. What are the stakes, and what is the bet? Such things may make a difference in our fate."

Fray feared he was right. She understood that the Demons normally did not interfere in the affairs of mortals, except to use them in trifling ways to settle games. She had heard about the one involving Roxanne Roc, a fine creature of the air, who had been put on trial for saying a bad word in the presence of the Simurgh's egg she had been incubating for five hundred years. The bet was whether any mortal jury would convict her. Another had involved the Demon Xanth himself, who had to assume the form of a dragon ass, Nimby, and win a single tear of love or grief for him from an unsuspecting mortal. He had won that, and married the one who shed the tear, and Nimbus was the result. But no Demon had interfered after the initial settings; the mortals had had to settle them themselves.

"Let me see if I understand this," Debra said. "A Demon must have touched Random, and changed the nature of his talent, and the Demons have some sort of bet on where that will lead? And it's not finished yet? And it won't be finished until something we do settles the Demon bet?"

"That is my conjecture," Sim agreed.

"What are the stakes likely to be?" Wira asked.

"They can be anything from a kiss to the destruction of a world," Sim said. "This is why we have a right to be nervous."

"And what is the bet likely to be?" Ilene asked.

"It can be anything from whether a given person steps on an ant, to whether the Factory manages to recover the Factor."

"Or whether we make it back to our original home," Hugo said.

"Or whether we succeed in returning to our own bodies," the Factor said.

Fray thought of something. "The Demon Xanth governs the Land of Xanth. The Demon Earth governs the planet Earth. They are next to each other, and folk cross between them all the time. But when we came through the loop, there was another world between: Moondania. And Princess Ida of Obelisk said that Earth was governed by the Demoness Gaia, not the Demon Earth. They don't match!"

The others gazed at her silently.

"Did I say something stupid?" Fray asked.

"On the contrary," Sim said. "You just pointed out something we all missed: there is a misalignment. Which suggests in turn that this is not our world of origin. In this portion of the chain of worlds, there is a world between Earth and Xanth, and Xanth is a planet itself. We may have our answer."

"May?" Wira asked. "Why not?"

"It is possible that we simply have misunderstood the relation of Earth and Xanth. Or that when Ilene made real the illusion planet we crafted, that changed the lineup."

"So this could be the original Xanth, but a link has been added in the chain," Debra said.

"And this could be part of the Demons' bet," Hugo said. "Like maybe whether we figure out where we really are."

"Or something entirely different," Wira said. "And the alignment of worlds is merely an incidental complication along the way."

"A matter of indifference to the Demons," Debra agreed.

"I am getting very nervous," Ilene said. "How can we know what to do that won't mess everything up horribly?"

Sim's beak curved into a smile. "We might ask the Demons."

"Which Demon, dear?" Ilene asked, smiling back.

"I know!" Fray said. "The new one. The Demoness Gaia. We can invoke her."

Both Sim and Ilene winced. "We were speaking ironically," Sim said.

"We wouldn't dare invoke a Demon," Ilene agreed.

Oh. This time Fray realized she had been stupid. She had misunderstood their adultish humor. She didn't even know what irony was. "Then not," she said.

The air shimmered. So did the ground. "Uh-oh," Hugo said. "Sometimes just mentioning a Demon is enough."

A form coalesced from the shimmer. It was like a human woman with a head like a cloud, who glowed like Nimbus, only more so. Her bosom was like two boldly shaped mountains, and her limbs were like those of trees, but she was the most beautiful possible creature.

"Hi, Gaia," Nimbus said. He had evidently seen her around before this adventure, maybe when the Demons held some sort of conclave.

"Hello, Nimbus Xanth-son," Gaia replied with a voice like windblown mist. Then she oriented on Fray. "Why did you conjure me, cloud girl?"

"I—I didn't mean to," Fray faltered. "I thought you could answer our questions, but maybe I shouldn't have."

"What questions?" the breath-of-spring voice asked.

Fray wanted to flee, but knew she couldn't. She had to answer, whether foolishly or sensibly. "Did you—were you the one who—changed the Factor's talent?"

"Yes," the trickling-brook voice said.

This wasn't over. She had to ask the next question. "Why?"

"Why do you think?" the soft-wind-through-fragrant-flowers asked.

"To—to make us—" What was next? "To make us conjure you."

"Yes!" the dawn-after-horrendously-dark-night voice said. "Earth! Xanth! Show yourselves. Two steps have been accomplished."

Two more Demons appeared. Fray recognized one as Earth, because his head was a slowly spinning blue-fringed planet. The other was the Demon Xanth, whose head was like a luxuriant peninsula. Then he assumed his dragon ass form, Nimby.

"Daddy!" Nimbus cried, running to him for a hug. He had no fear at all of the dragon, and indeed the dragon accepted his embrace and licked his face.

Demon Xanth looked around. "Have these mortal folk treated you well?" Fray was startled; she had thought the dragon couldn't talk. She was learning things at a startling rate.

"Oh, sure," the boy said carelessly. "Ilene made sure of that. She's on the way to becoming a Sorceress, you know." The boy frowned. "Her talent's better than mine."

"Not necessarily," the dragon said. "She has worked harder than you to perfect it. Yours will get there when you apply yourself."

"Oh." The boy wasn't much interested in applying himself. That, too, would surely change as he aged. "And Fray's sorta cute."

Fray felt herself blushing storm-gray.

Demon Xanth looked at Demoness Gaia. "Clarify the situation."

"There was a Demon contest millennia ago," Gaia said with her wash-of-ocean-surf-at-dusk voice. "It was wrongly decided. In order to correct that wrong, three requirements obtained. First, the break in the loop had to be repaired. That has been accomplished. Second, the relevant Demon had to be invoked. That has been accomplished. Third, the issue had to be decided by an ignorant mortal." She gazed intently at Fray with her storm-swirl eyes. "You."

"Me? But I'm just a little condensed cloud! I don't know anything."

"Precisely," Gaia agreed with her summer-zephyr voice.

"You are the air apparent," Xanth explained. "You were fated to make this decision concerning the heir apparent."

"How can I decide anything when I know nothing?"

"You will ask the Demons for information," the first-refreshing-chill-of-fall voice answered. "We alone will answer you; the other mortals are mere spectators."

Fray looked around. The others were standing there as if posed for a picture, aware but expressionless. She realized that they were in suspenders animation, or whatever. It was all up to her, whatever it was.

She tried to focus her air head, but there was nothing significant inside. "Why me?" she asked stupidly. "I mean, I know I'm ignorant, but so are lots of folk."

"Because you invoked me," Gaia replied with her school-wonderfully-closed-because-of-winter-snow voice. "Without knowing the significance."

That did seem to make sense. "What do I have to decide?"

"Which Demon possesses Earth. The heir apparent."

"Isn't that Demon Earth?"

"No. He is an impostor," the first-new-flower-of-spring voice said. "Earth is mine."

"I don't understand."

"Originally the world of Earth was mine," Gaia's sheer-joy-of-existence voice said. "All creatures existed in their natural states in imperfect harmony. Then the usurper Demon came and challenged me to a contest game for my world. I won, but he pretended he had won, and tried to assume the name and likeness of Earth. This led to a fissioning of the world into two aspects, Earth and Moondania, with the latter between Earth and Xanth. This has had complications."

A bulb flashed over Fray's head. "Like the way Xanth seems to overlay Mundania!" she exclaimed. "So that folk can cross over without going through Princess Ida. The Waves and all."

"True," Gaia said with her sunrise-over-the-massive-gray-mountain voice. "I suspect those intrusions annoy the Demon Xanth."

"Actually they make it interesting," Xanth said. "I married a mortal descendant of one of those Waves, and you already know our son." He glanced at Nimbus, who glowed brightly for half an instant. "But dealing with Demon Earth has been a nuisance."

"What's your side of it?" Fray asked Demon Earth. She was becoming bolder as she accepted that she really did have to learn enough to make a decision that could change everything, or at least make a difference.

"I contested for her planet, and won, but she refused to vacate, so I got only part of it. Moondania."

"Shouldn't that be Mundania?" Fray asked.

"Mortals mispronounce it, just as they do the day Moonday. Call it what you want. It is only an aspect of a world that should be mine entirely. All you need to do to abolish this schism is agree that I am the proper heir."

"When did this—this schism—happen?"

"About ten thousand years ago."

Fray almost wet her shoes. "I thought it was recent!"

"It was," Earth agreed.

She realized that to the eternal Demons, ten thousand years was like yesterday. So all of the history of Xanth had occurred during this schism. But then she thought of something else. "But Princess Ida got her moon only a dozen years ago."

This time Demon Xanth answered. "The schism caused the loss of a moon-connection or two, so that there was none on Moondania or Xanth. But the loop of worlds always existed. It was merely the local ones that were isolated. Then Ida got the idea of a moon, and the connection came to her. Now her image handles all the moons as connections to the adjacent worlds. When she passes from the scene, there will come another

gatekeeper to handle the links. With the restoration of the connection between Moondania and Xanth, the loop is again complete. Which means it
is time to settle the issue."

It seemed to make sense, sort of. "What was the contest?" she asked
Gaia. "The one that was supposed to decide who got the world of Earth?"

The Demoness smiled with her cloud head, and there was a flare of
glorious brilliance. "We have mentioned it. It was the proper pronunciation of Moondania. We listened to the mortals, and the first one said
Moondania."

"The first one said Mundania," Demon Earth said.

"You each heard it differently!" Fray said.

"Well, it was in a different language, ten thousand years ago," Earth
said. "But the pronunciation was quite clear."

"Yes it was," Gaia said with her surging-surf-by-a-lovely-beach-resort
voice. "Moondania."

And Fray had to decide which pronunciation they had actually heard?
Her head was filled mostly with air, but even she knew that this was serious mischief. Apart from the dubious merits of the case, what would happen to the world of Xanth if she favored Earth? Or Gaia? Their little
traveling group had problems enough, without ruining a world or two as
well. How could she risk bringing disaster on them all?

She remembered something that adults had been known to do when
faced with conflicting purposes. "Can't you compromise?"

"Compromise?" Demon Earth asked, frowning. "Demons don't compromise."

"It is unDemonocratic," Gaia agreed with her divine-music-of-the-
spheres voice.

Which was the challenge. Each Demon was so powerful that reality
was whatever he or she decided it was. Only when two Demons collided
was there a problem, as in this case. How could she possibly mediate between them, when favoring either one might ruin everything?

She looked at her traveling friends, but they could not advise her. They
had to let her make a mess of this on her own. Any one of them would
have been better qualified to do this. Sim would know, certainly. The
adults could make responsible guesses. Ilene was a sensible girl. Even
Nimbus knew the Demons and might have a notion what would work.

Only Fray was completely ignorant and inexperienced. Yet on her the dread decision fell.

She struggled to find a real solution, but no bulb flashed. She remained on her own. No Demon spoke; all were simply watching her, awaiting her nonsense.

Well, disaster it might be. But she would do what she had to do, the only way she knew how. Maybe it was the worst thing possible, but there was nothing else. She took a breath of air—in compacted form she had to do that—and nerved herself for doom. Or whatever.

"You said I have to make the decision. Well, I say you should compromise, even if you don't know how or don't like it. You should merge Moondania and Earth and share the unified world."

"The designated mortal has spoken," Xanth said.

"Share?" Earth asked querulously. "I do not know this word." Yet obviously he did, and hated it.

"It is a strange one," Gaia agreed with her exhilarating-summer-storm voice. But there was a hint of lightning in it.

"And get together yourselves," Fray continued doggedly. Or maybe it was catty; she wasn't sure. "Like boyfriend and girlfriend. So you don't mind sharing."

"Demons don't do that sort of thing," Earth said. The ground rumbled around him.

"But we can if we choose," Demon Xanth said. "I did. It can be rewarding on its own terms. What about that mortal girl who animated Demoness Fornax?"

"That's different."

Fray was amazed. Demon Xanth was helping her! Well, he must want to get this matter settled too, so there would be no further trouble at the border.

"She's never going to return your interest," Xanth said. "She has a mortal boyfriend. But Demoness Gaia could be everything you might desire. If she chose." He glanced meaningfully at her.

Gaia bared her teeth in defiance. Then she reconsidered. She had evidently thought of something. What could that be?

"Why should I ever want to get together with that cheating female thing?" Earth demanded. "What could she ever have for me? I am the heir apparent."

Demoness Gaia's cloud head turned human with lustrous features and hair. Her limbs became perfectly formed human arms and legs. She radiated beauty. "Like this?" her sheer-unadulterated-love-elixir voice asked.

Fray realized that the Demoness now considered it a challenge.

Demon Earth looked. He scowled. "That doesn't interest me."

Gaia's dress turned translucent, showing the scintillating outlines of well-mounted bra and panties. Fray was glad she was female, because otherwise she would have been in danger of freaking out. "No?" her essence-of-sex-appeal voice asked.

Earth's eyes began to heat. "No."

The underwear filled out more fully, quivering in key places. "No?" her passion-incarnate voice asked again.

"No." But his eyeballs were squeaking as their lubrication congealed. Fray saw the watching two men, the boy, and even the bird disappearing into freakout mode. Only Demon Xanth had the sense to conjure a very dark pair of spectacles to protect his eyes.

Wisps of steam rose from the hot items. All the pervasive power of nature animated them, and they could not be denied. "So you would rather not compromise, no?" her steamy-irresistible-force voice asked.

"No!" he said as his eyeballs baked.

"Then it seems we have agreed to the mortal's decision," Demon Xanth said. "The double negative cancels out. He says no but he means yes. You are the heir apparent, Gaia."

"I am," the rainbow-hued voice agreed. Gaia beckoned, and Earth went to her, overpowered. As he did so, there was a hidden but extremely powerful impact, as of two worlds colliding and merging. Moondania and Earth, Fray knew. The compromise had been achieved.

Gaia's cloud-head appeared before Fray. "How may I repay this favor?" her soft-as-night-dreams voice inquired.

Fray thought fast. "Put the Random Factor back the way he was, in his own body, and douse the curse. You don't need him any more."

"That is three favors," the chill-of-a-frozen-day voice said coldly. "To revert his talent, restore him to his own body, and abate the Factory curse. I proffer only one."

"Oops, I'm sorry." She was messing up. Evidently the soulless Demons kept very precise accounts. What single thing could she ask for that would really help?

Then she got a notion. It wasn't enough to light a bulb, but it would have to do. The curse oriented on the Factor's body when it did a transfer, so if he didn't transfer any more, maybe the curse would not apply. Maybe. That would cover two things in one.

The Demons waited silently. They had the patience of eons.

"Fix the Factor's talent. Undo your change."

The cloud faded. So did the Demons Gaia and Earth. Only the Demon Xanth remained.

Fray was left facing the other members of the party. "I think it's okay now," she said hesitantly. "I tried to fix it so the curse wouldn't matter."

"You succeeded," the Demon Xanth said. "The curse is now unable to orient, and will dissipate."

"But we're still in the wrong bodies," the Factor said.

"I'm sorry," Fray said unhappily. "I just couldn't figure out how to do it all." She tried to stifle a tear, which was this compacted body's version of rain, but it leaked out anyway.

The Demon Xanth was staring at her. Had she done something else wrong?

Nimbus turned to the Demon. "Daddy, don't let her be sad. Tears make me nervous. She doesn't want anything for herself."

"Son, you owe your existence to a selfless tear. It makes me think of your mother." The Demon glanced again at Fray, then at Hugo and the Factor. Then he faded out.

Hugo looked surprised. "I'm back in my own body!"

"So am I!" the Factor said. "But there's something else I need to ver-ify." He turned to Debra. "Where's your bra?"

She brought it out and handed it to him. He took it, and did not suffer any consequence. The curse was gone. The wings of his hat fluttered as he flew up to kiss her face.

"I can hardly wait to wrap things up here and get back to my own body too," Debra said. "Bra and all."

"Let's all get home," Wira said, glancing fondly at Hugo. They were old folk, but Fray realized that wasn't slowing them down much.

They organized for flight. Wira mounted Debra, with Nimbus next, and Fray last as they were all lightened. The party took off.

"You're okay," Nimbus said as she put her arms around him from behind to hold him in place.

"Thank you."

"For a girl."

"Thank you," she repeated, understanding his inability to be fully serious. That would surely change in the next decade or so. So she was a cloud and he was the son of the Demon Xanth; stranger relationships had happened.

"That was real smart, showing Daddy that tear. He had to do what you wanted, then. Mommy saved him when she shed a tear for him."

There didn't seem to be much point in confessing that she had had no such smart design in mind. "Thank you."

"Air apparent," he said. "That sort of matches heir apparent, doesn't it?"

"They do seem to mesh," she said. "Air and heir."

"Heir and air. Hair!"

"Hair," she agreed, smiling tolerantly. They had a vaguely definite future understanding.

As they rose high into the sky, something was odd. After a generous moment Fray realized what it was: she could see the gradual curvature of the world below them. It was in the shape of a peninsula with a chasm halfway down it. The seeming overlay with the world of Earth or Mundania was gone. Now the only connection would be via the moons of Ida. There would be no more Waves of invasion. That was fine with her.

Soon she would be home, and happily floating over the landscape in her natural cloud form. She was after all a creature of the air. Apparent or not.

Author's Note

This is the thirty-first Xanth novel in the series, or the fourth in the second magic trilogy of three cubed = twenty-seven novels. It may be awhile before we see a complete trilogy of magic trilogies. Meanwhile the individual novels can be read in any order, though they are chronological; each is its own story.

I am getting older. I'm into my seventies now, and slowing somewhat. I learned of the deaths of two of my longtime correspondents during the writing of this novel, and there may be others. Also, I had spot surgery on my right cheek to remove a suspicious patch of skin. It turned out to be pre-squamous cell carcinoma. That is, working its way toward one of the less dangerous forms of skin cancer. The dangerous form is melanoma, which my daughter had at this time; they think they got it all clear and she's okay. I also postponed surgery for the crushed disk that leaves me with a chronic backache, because I couldn't afford to be out of commission at this time.

Why? Because my wife's health is more precarious than mine. Early in the year 2005 she weakened until she could no longer walk or even stand. I had to heave her into and out of the wheelchair, and she practically lived in that wheelchair for months. It seemed that between the two of us we had some kind of medical appointment just about every day. One doctor after another checked her, not finding the problem. Then at last they made a diagnosis: chronic inflammatory demyelinating polyneuropathy, CIDP for short. It is a rare illness vaguely similar to multiple sclerosis or Lou Gehrig's disease, where the protective sheathing around the nerves—the myelin—gets eroded so that the nerves can't function. Think of an electronic gadget whose wires are stripped of insulation: it will short out and not work. Likewise the living body. Fortunately there is a treatment, an expensive four-hour IV infusion. After five days of that she turned the corner, and her arms and legs started responding again, little by little. At this writing—the end of OctOgre 2005—she is back on her feet and gaining strength, no longer needing a wheelchair, walker, or cane. But I don't let her go out alone, just in case. At our age, falls can be devastating.

Meanwhile I had taken over the meals, housework, shopping, and such. My wife was recovering, but we could not be sure how far that would go, or whether there would be a relapse. I needed to be able to do whatever needed to be done, and to heave the wheelchair into the car if we needed it. That's why I postponed my disk surgery. I also started writing this novel a month early, because I could not be sure how much time I would have for writing, and there was a deadline. As it happened, my wife continued to do better, so I had more writing time than expected, and completed the novel early. I still go shopping with her, just in case, and make most meals and wash the dishes, but things are looking up. There are more challenges ahead for each of us, some quite serious, but at present we're all right.

In this period—actually just before I started writing the novel—we bought a Toyota Prius hybrid car. We do what we can for the environment, and an efficient car helps. We needed to be sure it could carry a folded wheelchair, just in case, and that it was comfortable for my wife, and it is. It gets about forty-five miles to the gallon and seems alive. The motor stops when you wait at a stoplight, not wasting power. It indicates the mileage you are getting as you drive, so you know when you're driving inefficiently. You keep the key in your pocket, and it checks and won't run unless it frisks you and locates it. It's my kind of car. There's only one letter difference between Piers and Prius.

My wife's condition also changed my appearance. At first I lost weight, because I was doing more on the same diet. So we bought six-packs of that canned nourishment that I call glop for short. Then I started putting on weight, and had to cut back. I remain lean by preference, keeping my weight steady, and I exercise seriously; all it takes is discipline. We used to exchange haircuts; I haven't been to a barbershop in decades. But her illness prevented her from cutting my hair, so I grew it longer, and now I wear a ponytail. So my hair is receding in front and on top where I need it, and growing bushily on sides and back where I don't. A problem of age: male pattern baldness. Sometimes I wonder whether it was a mistake to pass seventy. Because I'm not apt at doing my hair behind my head where I can't see it, I use a small red or blue alligator-style hair clip of the type little girls have. I now notice ponytails on women, and actually there are some on men too. I complimented one woman on hers, and she said I had a prettier clip. My hair is like my imagination, bursting out all over, with a natural curl that refuses to be tamed. I never knew this until I grew it long.

We also had weather. There are those who refuse to believe in global warming, but here in Florida we are much aware of it, because it increases the force of our seasonal storms. Hurricane Katrina crossed south Florida with minimal effort, then revved up horrendously to take out New Orleans. That was followed by Hurricane Rita, which plowed into Texas. Later Hurricane Wilma formed as the most intense storm ever in this region, and crossed south Florida the other way, taking out electric power for six million people. But we here in central Florida were on the periphery of all three storms and suffered little damage. We were lucky—this year.

This novel, as you may have noticed, starts out as a murder mystery. But in Xanth it's hard to play anything straight for long, and by the end the mystery is something else. I hope you enjoyed it anyway. There are about a hundred and forty reader suggestions here. In some cases when I didn't have a name for a passing character I borrowed the name of the one who suggested the character or talent. Those readers may be surprised (and not necessarily pleased) to discover that, and I make no promises about doing it again. In general, I used up the ideas I had before OctOgre 2005; more kept coming in as I wrote the novel, and I couldn't keep up with them. Some ideas related to characters who aren't in the novel, so had to wait for a later novel. The unmentionable truth is that it would be easier for me to write these novels entirely on my own without reader suggestions, as I do with non-Xanth novels. But readers do think of things I don't, so I hope their participation enhances the story. Some of the suggestions have private histories I don't review here; there is more going on than the story. Some ideas that could have been major became minor, and some minor ones became major; some don't develop the way the suggester may have intended. Things don't always go the way I expect.

One other thing: I write a novel, a copyeditor goes over it, I proofread the galleys—and some errors still sneak through. My theory is that they grow on the page after the proofreading. There was one bad one in *Currant Events,* where the pun-guessing score was wrong. Countless readers called my attention to it. So I had somehow to explain it, as I do in this novel. These things happen.

Now for the voluminous credits:

Write a Xanth novel in the style of a horror novel—only I decided to make it a murder mystery instead—Henry Wyckoff; farm-assist plants producing many magic pills—Jon Bartlett; glove (mitt) puns, talent of summoning animals, comitea, mortalitea, Heisen-berg, amitea, battea, curfew, curtail, ab-cent, bucking, cent-inel, quies-cent, reminis-cent, omnis-cent, ex-cent-ric, magnifi-cent—Timothy Bruening; Earl the pearl—Lesli Audleman; Katydid/Katydidn't—Nicole Graham; Wira makes a quest to gain her sight—Jim Hull; Debra—Bob Kawaguchi; talent of freezing things in place—Stephanie Kay Fetterly; talent of knowing when to begin an action—Bev in Bellingham; talent of cooling or heating water—Timur I. Leng; fee-line, bo-vine—David Kaplan; medi-ogre—Linda H.; punda—Yaniv Pessach; dine-o-mite, twins summon and banish demons, e-racers—Greg Bischoping; spinal chord—Jesse Gordon; outstanding in his field, hydraponics, beauty mark—Lizzy Wilford; Bernie—Liz; bombshell—Michael Bissey; stop light—John A. Tolle; pathologist—Bill Seeley; Theresa—Gary Poole; Aurora Sky—Rebekah Joyce Vidal; giggles, river dancers—Thomas Pfarrer; illixir—Kevin Jett; Opti and Pesi Mystic—Lizzy Wilford; Psyche, with talent of role reversal, Moondania—Jon Bartlett; lan-tern—Stephen Dole; Breanna's son, with talent of making darkness—Gabe Pesek; pleasant/unpleasantrees—Jorge; family from Mundania, humoris bone—Vicki Gleason; Mike's girlfriend—Jaime Rocha; DeCrypt, who decodes things—Martinha Braam; mediocritree—Michelle Smith; ogre rated, zombie tree, plumpkin pie—R. J. Craigs; Random Factor's talent, Hypotho-sea—Jyllian; ground beef—Max Xiong; ogres curdle hair—Kris Kobb; bee guile—James

Willison; key board—Dawn Lisowski; wild card, Q-card—Lu Gifford; bumpkin pie—Lois Poison; pot plant—Jimmy E. Coats; Mystery Cat—Felicia M. Perez; pairing knife—Yaniv Pessach; sign language folk—Phil Giles; Petting Sue, being on the lamb—Robert Hawes; Gourd'n G'rd'n'r—Eric Herriman; Gnome Atter—Emma Snowden; white-winged snake—Era Scarecrow; Deniece and Denephew—Denise D.; Herb Sage—Leigh Killon-Purkey; paths to where needed—A. C. Sutton; Ilene, talent of making illusions real—Malcolm Shaw; air plain—Steven Barton; air drumming—William Bennett; medic air—Thom Lamb; Airon—Patty; tap water—Dassi Levin; waves waving—Russ White; Sim-ulation—John Surber; ants in rum, ruminants—Katrin; cowboy—Jonathon Hadley; cream tsoda—David Candler; hair clips—Kris Cobb; talent of not being able to finish what he starts—Curtis Terrill; Branch Faun gets his tree back—Sabrina Smith; Brusk/Becka's child—Ben Stallard; pigasus, hambrosia—Louis Steiner; wrong scoring in *Currant Events*—Michael Hawkins (first of a number who caught this); Sette family—Megan Ross; punnery—Heidi Hastie; potato ogre rotten (au gratin)—Keith J. Moseley; shade lipstick for ghosts—Amy Richards; horsefeathers—Louis Steiner; Fracto gets changed to human form—Misty Zaebst; maiden head—Brian J. Taylor; fresh err, err conditioner—Mark C. Purvis; closet door to imagination—Chris Walls; fatalitea—Albert J. Gallant; assorted Kings: Ass, Inn, Bar, Thin, Loo—John Edwards; de-ogrerant—Norm Mcleod; mirror writing—John Conrad, who really does write backward: it's his curse; dream dictionary—Ginger Kern; jinx—Harry Gilbert; talent of force field in air—Alison; talent of steering conversation—Carter; talent of not being able to say what a person will do—David M. Cary; cone-nundrum—Mindy Basilian; the nametaggers—Jacob Kott; Citronella—Krystin Dobbs; go to Ptero poles and back on other meridians to avoid changing ages—Kenneth Adams; flamma-bull—Bethany Henderson; Billy Jack, flip-flops—Billy Jack; Tell-A-Path—Kyle Chalmers; networking—Kris Kobb; talent: make a net that will stop wiggles—Ruby Suder; small-scale klutz, large-scale benefit—Tovi Spero; Besanii, who flatters folk—Bethany Henderson; Bill Fold—Amanda Penfold; invoking monster qualities, confusing monsters, talent of redirection—Troy Young; angel meets demon at love spring—Eric C. Daniel; angel marries Demon

Beauregard—Colleen Mercer; Gourd Moon—Christer S. Rowan; Obelisk—Eli Spiro; Xanth 2 as a World of Ida—Catty Philpot; Earth as one of Ida's moons, with Demon Gaia—Locke Berry; David Scalise— Nicole Hearnes.

And those who are interested may check my Web site at www.hipiers .com, where I have information on my novels, a listing of electronic publishing and services, and a feisty bimonthly blog-type column. Most of my interaction with my readers now occurs via that site; publishers don't forward snail-mail letters reliably.